Our Lives, Our Fortunes

Other Books by J. E. Fender

Easy Victories (Houghton Mifflin, 1973)
Under the pseudonym of James Trowbridge

The Private Revolution of Geoffrey Frost (UPNE, 2002),
Book 1 of the Frost Saga

Audacity, *Privateer out of Portsmouth* (UPNE, 2003),
Book 2 of the Frost Saga

Hardscrabble Books—Fiction of New England

Laurie Alberts, *Lost Daughters*

Laurie Alberts, *The Price of Land in Shelby*

Thomas Bailey Aldrich, *The Story of a Bad Boy*

Robert J. Begiebing, *The Adventures of Allegra Fullerton: Or, A Memoir of Startling and Amusing Episodes from Itinerant Life*

Robert J. Begiebing, *Rebecca Wentworth's Distraction*

Anne Bernays, *Professor Romeo*

Chris Bohjalian, *Water Witches*

Dona Brown, ed., *A Tourist's New England: Travel Fiction, 1820–1920*

Joseph Bruchac, *The Waters Between: A Novel of the Dawn Land*

Joseph A. Citro, *The Gore*

Joseph A. Citro, *Guardian Angels*

Joseph A. Citro, *Lake Monsters*

Joseph A. Citro, *Shadow Child*

Sean Connolly, *A Great Place to Die*

John R. Corrigan, *Snap Hook*

J. E. Fender, *The Private Revolution of Geoffrey Frost: Being an Account of the Life and Times of Geoffrey Frost, Mariner, of Portsmouth, in New Hampshire, as Faithfully Translated from the Ming Tsun Chronicles, and Diligently Compared with Other Contemporary Histories*

Audacity, *Privateer Out of Portsmouth*

Our Lives, Our Fortunes

Dorothy Canfield Fisher (Mark J. Madigan, ed.), *Seasoned Timber*

Dorothy Canfield Fisher, *Understood Betsy*

Joseph Freda, *Suburban Guerrillas*

Castle Freeman, Jr., *Judgment Hill*

Frank Gaspar, *Leaving Pico*

Robert Harnum, *Exile in the Kingdom*

Ernest Hebert, *The Dogs of March*

Ernest Hebert, *Live Free or Die*

Ernest Hebert, *The Old American*

Sarah Orne Jewett (Sarah Way Sherman, ed.), *The Country of the Pointed Firs and Other Stories*

Raymond Kennedy, *Ride a Cockhorse*

Raymond Kennedy, *The Romance of Eleanor Gray*

Lisa MacFarlane, ed., *This World Is Not Conclusion: Faith in Nineteenth-Century New England Fiction*

G. F. Michelsen, *Hard Bottom*

Anne Whitney Pierce, *Rain Line*

Kit Reed, *J. Eden*

Rowland E. Robinson (David Budbill, ed.), *Danvis Tales: Selected Stories*

Roxana Robinson, *Summer Light*

Rebecca Rule, *The Best Revenge: Short Stories*

Catharine Maria Sedgwick (Maria Karafilis, ed.), *The Linwoods: or, "Sixty Years Since" in America*

R. D. Skillings, *How Many Die*

R. D. Skillings, *Where the Time Goes*

Lynn Stegner, *Pipers at the Gates of Dawn: A Triptych*

Theodore Weesner, *Novemberfest*

W. D. Wetherell, *The Wisest Man in America*

Edith Wharton (Barbara A. White, ed.), *Wharton's New England: Seven Stories and* Ethan Frome

Thomas Williams, *The Hair of Harold Roux*

Suzi Wizowaty, *The Round Barn*

Our Lives, Our Fortunes

Continuing the Account of the *Life and Times* of Geoffrey Frost, Mariner, of Portsmouth, in New Hampshire, as *Faithfully Translated* from the Ming Tsun Chronicles, and *Diligently Compared* with Other Contemporary Histories

J. E. FENDER

University Press of New England
HANOVER AND LONDON

University Press of New England, 37 Lafayette St., Lebanon, NH 03766

Printed in the United States of America

5 4 3 2 1

Library of Congress Cataloging-in-Publication Data

Fender, J. E.

Our lives, our fortunes : continuing the account of the life and times of Geoffrey Frost, mariner, of Portsmouth, in New Hampshire, as faithfully translated from the Ming Tsun chronicles, and diligently compared with other contemporary histories / by J. E. Fender.

p. cm.—(Hardscrabble books.)

ISBN 1-58465-375-2 (alk. paper)

1. Frost, Geoffrey (Fictitious character)—Fiction. 2. United States—History—Revolution, 1775–1783—Fiction. 3. New Hampshire—History—Revolution, 1775–1783—Fiction. 4. Portsmouth (N.H.)—Fiction. 5. Privateering—Fiction. 6. Sailors—Fiction.

I. Title. II. Series.

PS3606.E53095 2004

813'.6—dc22 2003024055

Our Lives, Our Fortunes

I

IN THE FOUR EVENTFUL DAYS SINCE RETURNING HIS NEWLY NAMED PRIVATEER'S-MAN *AUDACITY*, EX-HM-SLOOP-O-WAR *JAGUAR*, TO HIS HOME PORT OF Portsmouth, New Hampshire, Geoffrey Frost's head had touched a pillow exactly twice, each time for less than one hour. A thoroughly exhausted Frost almost fell asleep during the brief crossing of the Piscataqua from his cousin John Langdon's dockyard on Rising Island to the wherry dock at the foot of Ceres Street. Gratefully, he welcomed the gaunt woods-cruiser Caleb Mansfield's strong right arm, ready to assist him out of the wherry. A captain other than Frost would have drawn great contentment from the fact that *Audacity* had completed a six-month-long cruise during which some eighteen thousand sea-miles had passed beneath her keel. Indeed, *Audacity*, despite an honorable and humanitarian detour almost to the bulge of West Africa to restore two crewmen lost overboard to Captain James Cook of HM *Discovery*, was arguably the most successful privateer a year and a half into the war being waged by a fragile coalition of thirteen colonies on the eastern seaboard of North America to wrest independence from the British Crown. But Frost was constantly nagged by the feeling that he could, he should, have accomplished *more*.

Having crossed in a cold November sleet, Frost flailed his arms vigorously against his torso to restore feeling to cold-stiffened fingers, then fumbled a shilling from a waistcoat pocket for his passage. How much was this shilling, coined by the old regime and representing the value of twelve British pence, worth in comparison to the new Continental dollars—which themselves vied with the state-issued currencies and indented state treasury bills of credit as lawful money?

Regardless of whatever ratio of exchange that jumped-up Continental Congress and the various states had decreed for various units of dubious paper currency against the hard money of an established regime, as a trader Frost had no doubt that the store of and innate metal value represented by the small silver coin issued by a sovereign against whom the United States of America was in rebellion would greatly exceed whatever rate the Congress and the states had so imperiously fixed. Frost had little faith in the abilities of governments to understand economic matters in times of crisis. Or, if governments in crisis by some accident of fortune possessed ministers who understood the intricacies of financial theories involving wealth creation and prudent preservation, their good advices would go largely unheeded by kings, princes, prime ministers and presidents.

The trade would, in due course, set the rate of exchange. Then would follow inflation, because there was no store of value in the paper currency, whether issued by the Continental Congress, New Hampshire, New York or Pennsylvania. And after inflation would follow the counterfeit, the bad driving out what little good would remain. In point of fact, a Tory sympathizer had already attempted the counterfeiting of the November 1775 New Hampshire treasury bills of credit.

A year before, an English shilling would have been an exuberant recompense for the five-minute pull from Rising Island. Frost pressed the silver coin into the wherryman's oar-callused and cold-chapped palm. The wherryman, who had been gawking at the large, rancid black bearskin in which Caleb was swathed, did not realize the value of the fare until he felt it in his hand. "I have no pence to give you back, Capt'n Frost . . ."

"Such a quick pull, boatman, especially on this dreich day, merits the tariff," Frost smiled.

"Thankee, soir, thankee," the wherryman cried, wheezing and sneezing and bobbing his head in unabashed delight. "Times be hard, and them prizes of yourn likely make the difference this winter in many folk starvin' or not."

"Yes," Frost said to himself grimly, "times indeed be hard." He thrust one foot tentatively toward the scarred and gouged float as another scream of sleet tortured the open wharf and rocked the wherry uncontrollably. He would have taken a tumble, a vicious one, save for Caleb's steadying arm. Wordlessly, Frost nodded his gratitude.

"How did ye find yere ma?" Caleb asked solicitously as Frost began picking his way through the pools of slush and up the short, utterly deserted Ceres Street to the ascent of Market Street. Frost tugged his hat and heavy woolen muffler tighter around his head and neck. He half-turned to get the wind to his back, and in the turn glimpsed an indistinct *Audacity* through a rent in the numbing curtain of sleet, mixed liberally with a cold, freezing rain, that danced across the sullen, overcast, wind-whipped, pewter- and bone-colored Piscataqua. Frost's *Audacity* was berthed just behind the completed and ready-for-sea *Raleigh* launched seven months earlier by John Langdon—ready for sea, that is, as soon as *Raleigh* had a proper complement of cannons and crew. His poor vessel, bearing all proper permissions and sureties of a privateer duly chartered by the Continental Congress and the state of New Hampshire, had been stripped of all her sails, and her yards were still all a-cockbill, as Frost had ordered upon his arrival to mourn all of the men who had died serving her during her just completed cruise. *Audacity*'s six-month cruise was regarded as singularly successful by virtually everyone in Portsmouth—a notion that Geoffrey Frost decidedly did not share.

"As vivacious as she has been anytime these ten years past, for she received this week visits from all three of the sons she bore," Frost answered shortly. Not in the least did Geoffrey Frost begrudge the time he had spent with the dear, gentle Thérèse Maria de Villette Frost. Indeed, Frost drew as much comfort as his mother did from their visits. But Frost did begrudge the cavalier manner in which his younger brother, Joseph, had so blithely gone off to join some obscure Continental Army brigadier general, a nutmegger from Connecticut named Arnold, in contesting the British passage up Lake Champlain.

Upon his return, Frost had quickly learned of all the Continental Army's reverses, including Arnold's mid-October defeat by Carleton. The course of the rebellion against George Three had taken many an ominous turn in the four months since Tommy Thompson, named prospective commanding officer of *Raleigh* by the Marine Committee of the Continental Congress, had so vaingloriously trumpeted American victories to Frost off the Isles of Shoals.

"Little good Carleton's victory will do the British this late in the campaign season," Frost consoled himself. But there was yet no word if Joseph and Juby still lived, or if their bones lay somewhere in the depths of the dark and somber faraway Lake. And Arnold's defeat was only the most recent failure of American arms that had occurred since Frost had brought in as prizes the two richly laden East Indiamen *Triton* and *Generous Friend* in July. But in Frost's single-minded view, the almost universal reverses suffered by the Continental Army were of no consequence compared to the uncertainty posed by lack of word of Joseph and Juby, his brother and his deeply revered Baba.

Frost took another reef in his boat cloak and huddled deeper into it as he quickened his pace over the slippery cobbles toward the lights that were barely visible from the State House through the descending darkness and sleet.

Caleb matched Frost pace for pace: "O'Buck, Lacey, Nason 'n' I did as ye bid us, we delivered the letters and solid British specie to all the widows of our men lost, mothers of them not married, and some daughters," he shouted above the furious hiss of the sleet.

Frost made no reply, but nodded his thanks again. By the Prophet and the Golden Buddha, he himself should have visited the families of men who had not returned as crew aboard

Audacity; he should have personally delivered the families his thanks for those who had walked through the wall between life and death for their ship and him. He held himself accountable for every death—each one a personal tragedy—aboard any ship he commanded. Just as he personally distributed the generous advances against prize monies Ming Tsun had calculated with quick, deft throws of his abacus and entered against the muster book of ship's crew.

He had visited Mother Anne Plaisted—he *had* to visit Mother Anne Plaisted—old and withered but every bit as proud and defiant as her noble, worthy son, Slocum, who had died preserving the life of a shipmate. She had refused to take the small leather purse filled with gold coins of large denomination, so he had gently kissed her on her wrinkled, furrowed and careworn forehead and left the purse on the woman's kitchen table, fitfully illuminated only by the flames from the kitchen hearth, no candles or dips at all. Mother Anne had valiantly held in her tears until Frost had closed the kitchen door behind him, but he had been pursued by her sobs of despair and anguish long after he had left the small cottage where she lived. Frost bitterly acknowledged himself quite the coward for not wanting to face any more widows and bereft mothers, for delegating the loathsome task, rightly his, to others. How was he to offset life and death against small round coins, even though they were struck from gold?

The door of the three-story State House at the corner of Market and Pleasant Streets was opened by Prosperous, John Langdon's slave and chief of the house. His broad, honest face showed his delight as he relieved Frost of his cloak, muffler and hat as Frost and Caleb entered the foyer. "Master John been waitin' mightily for this visit, Captain Frost." Prosperous eyed Caleb's bearskin dubiously as he took it. "Don't know if there has ever been such a garment in this State House before." He gawked at the splendid belt of white and black wampum beads in an intricate pattern that girded Caleb's new buckskins, even more so at Caleb's buckskin jerkin, elaborately fretted with beadwork in the Iroquois fashion. Frost found himself admiring the beautiful starbursts and rosettes of various colors that were expansively embroidered on the shoulders and front of the jerkin. Caleb had really tricked himself out for this visit to John Langdon, and Frost saw from the careful manner in which Caleb's multicolored black and white hair was combed and clubbed that the woods-cruiser had recently bathed.

"Waal, I ain't never been in this State House of yern," Caleb grumped, settling his elaborate knife sheath, trimmed with colored porcupine quills, more securely in his belt, " 'n' I wouldn't be here betimes if Colonel Langdon hadn't asked fer me personal. Leastwise he has it all to hisself since the Legislature be run to Exeter."

Prosperous leaned close to Frost as the servant draped the bearskin over his arm and whispered earnestly, "Darius got the money to buy my freedom, Captain Frost, but now don't be the time for you to be asking Master John to let me go."

Frost arched an eyebrow; Darius was Prosperous' son, whose freedom Frost had purchased and whose life had been saved by Slocum Plaisted. "I had intended to take up that subject with my cousin as the first order of business, Prosperous."

"Now don't be the time," Prosperous repeated in a lower, more urgent whisper.

"Very well," Frost said, perplexed, for Darius had asked him to broach the subject of his father's purchase from John Langdon at the earliest opportunity. "I trust you shall inform me when the time be accomplished." Prosperous did not reply, but his demeanor showed his relief as he led Frost and Caleb up the hallway to John Langdon's office.

"Master John's got some gentlemens with him; one be your cousin, Tobias, 'n' the other be the Judge." Prosperous paused and rolled his eyes. "But I'm instructed to bring you directly you appear." He pulled open the doors and bowed Frost into the office. John Langdon was warming his backside before the burning logs cracking behind the screen in the fireplace and turned as soon as he heard the doors open.

"Geoffrey! Finally you deign to visit me!" John Langdon

cried out in a voice of genuine satisfaction. "I am on tenterhooks to learn every detail of your voyage! How came you to fall in with those four richly laden victuallers berthed at your company wharf on Christian Shore?

"But first, have you not heard the intelligence? And real intelligence it is, since it shows tellingly how desperate the British government is to conceal the daring of a raid against their homeland! My word, Geoffrey! You have smote the boldest, the most brilliant blow done this age! A London newspaper scarce a month old arrived this morning by express from Boston. It attributes the destruction of the collier fleet at Tynemouth to the phenomenon of something termed 'spontaneous combustion.' Or perhaps it was 'sympathetic explosion.' I confess it is the first time such terms have struck my ear."

"I wager that paper don't say nothin' about what caused the fires 'n' them coal mines back o' the town," Caleb Mansfield growled, "nor was mention made o' ships run a-shoal 'cause channel markers 'n' ranges wus in untoward places."

"Goodman Mansfield!" John Langdon exclaimed. "I begged your attendance immediately I learned you as a joyful presence had been accompanying my cousin! You never received proper recognition for the assistance you and some other 'Indians' provided to me in relieving the magazine of Fort William and Mary of its gunpowder and small arms that mid-December night two years past. I wanted to confirm with my own eyes that you are a reformed man."

"We knowed this war be comin' once Mister George, the so-called king of the Britishers, put the embargo on munitions and arms to our shores. So we needed to git ready," Caleb mumbled, evidently displeased at being the center of attention. "Waal, the success of thet little skirmish be much like findin' a turtle on a fence post; neither happened thar by theirselves."

"Reformed man be damned, be doubly damned by a godly Christ sitting in ultimate and sublime judgment on all us sinners condemned." A man dressed in a well-turned black tunic, who had been stirring up the fire, now let the iron poker fall contemptuously against the bricks of the fireplace with a furious clang. "He's an unreconstructed rogue of unconstrained rascality what owes penal servitude for his crimes, though there'll be no salvation for him!"

"Judge Clagett," Frost retorted in as civil a tone as he could muster, recognizing the tall, stoop-shouldered man with a perpetual frown, "as acerbic, profane and rude as ever you were . . . and as misinformed and devoid of facts."

"Salutations to you, Captain Frost, and glad you should be that you were never hailed into my courtroom, unlike your rascal of a companion, who has been there on at least one occasion." Judge Wyseman Clagett, spittle forming at the corners of his lips, his mouth twitching in synchronization with the animated twitching of the great tufts of hair that formed his eyebrows, glared malevolently, first at Frost, then at Caleb Mansfield.

"Now Wyseman," John Langdon said placatingly, "the office of New Hampshire Attorney General requires a certain decorum that rightly abhors profanity and rudeness. You place me under the disagreeable necessity of asking you to wait upon me tomorrow morning at half nine to continue our discussion of the enlargement of the Court of Admiralty. My cousin and Goodman Mansfield are guests in this State House."

"I admit to gross embarrassment in the presence of idlers, adulters and murderers, John Langdon," Wyseman Clagett fairly shouted, showing a mouthful of broken, tobacco-stained teeth, "and their true desserts time will discover." He fixed Frost with a malignant, piercing black eye. "And you, Captain Frost, should have brought all the piratical crew of *Zeus' Chariot* back to Portsmouth for proper justice in my court, rather than the forty-one souls you delivered up. They was men wanted throughout all our new States. The leaders of that sad band would of certainty have repented their crimes as they stood trembling in my courtroom."

Frost smiled thinly. "On the contrary, Mister Clagett," he said, deliberately omitting the man's customary title, "remorse lay not in their bosoms, and they assiduously blamed not themselves for their sins, though they trembled abundantly at the approaching horrors of their certain dying. I brought justice to the pirates' leaders. Betimes, the Devil wanted them more."

Wyseman Clagett drew himself erect to his not inconsiderable height and made his way toward the doors of Langdon's office, where a wide-eyed Prosperous stood rooted in shock. Clagett paused at Langdon's desk long enough to help himself to a generous pinch of snuff from the large porcelain snuffbox perched on the corner. Frost frowned; the "snuffbox" was actually a *Chine de commande* tea canister decorated with an exquisite multicolored caterpillar on a black cherry tree in full flower. The caterpillar appeared lifelike enough to edge off the leaf and onto his cousin's desk. Frost had brought the tea canister back from his second voyage to China in command of *Salmon*, and he most heartily disapproved of its being used as a snuffbox.

"Pleased if ye would remember me to yere Miss Lettice," Caleb drawled as Clagett passed.

Clagett scattered the pinch of snuff all over the papers on John Langdon's desk and spun on his heel so fast that his cheap, ill-fitting wig twisted on his head, hanging perilously over one ear like an errant teapot cozy. He advanced toward Caleb, a fist raised. "You damned, insolent rogue . . ."

John Langdon stepped quickly in front of Clagett and seized the man by the arm. "Prosperous! Please fetch Judge Clagett's cloak and hat. He may wait in the loge while his carriage is summoned." Then the pair was through the doors, Clagett in loud protest, and Prosperous immediately closed them.

"Extremely apologetic for the Judge's tirade, exceedingly uncalled for in all respects," said the third man in the room. Tobias Lear, a cousin to both Frost and John Langdon, rose hurriedly from a large worktable heaped with a mass of ships' draughts. "I was completely bereft of speech by his outburst. Neither John nor I had any idea he bore either of you such magnitude of malice." Lear was of medium age and height and had a ruddy complexion; his spectacles were anchored so perilously low on his nose that they were in clear danger of falling off. He was dressed in clean, purposeful workman's clothing, his long breeches and heavy woolen stockings thrust into his roughly cobbled shoes. He walked quickly around the table to shake Frost's hand warmly, then extended a callused hand, stained with tar, to Caleb.

"Hello Tobias. You know my friend Caleb Mansfield by sight, perhaps, but certainly by reputation. I fathom the irascible Clagett, like so many others, regards me as the murderer of my brother, a calumny I much regret but cannot defend. Like so many of the Puritan ilk, he believes that decrying evil equates to doing good—pernicious thought! I know not, however, what loathing he holds for Caleb."

Caleb coughed as delicately as he could. "Waal, his wife once spoke to me 'n a voice of great kindness, atter I pulled her out the path o' spirited teams two rakes were flogging 'n a race down Church Street. Collect the lady even laid a proper gloved hand on my greasy buckskins. Next I knew Judge Clagett hailed me into this court o' his'n on charges of mishandlin' a woman, er somethin' similar. I weren't overly fond of his brand of justice, and when the bailiff wus hustlin' me off to gaol, somehow his jaw got busted, 'n' I never got to see the inside o' the judge's fine gaol. Keepin' myself scarce in these parts wus why I signed on with ye fer thet merry cruize to Bahama."

"It has been said of Wyseman Clagett that when congratulated upon his marrying a fortune in the person of young Lettice Mitchel, he retorted that he had not married a fortune, but a daughter of a fortune. Or as he chose to term it, a Miss-Fortune," Tobias Lear said.

Frost advanced to the fireplace, which threw out a prodigious amount of heat, and held out his hands gratefully.

"Waal, I pity the poor woman," Caleb said. "The only time I laid eyes on her she had the look of a fawn piteously frighted by a wolf." He leaned over the screen to spit into the fire.

"Cousin Geoffrey," Tobias Lear said, "I have been industriously applying myself to the draughts of your fine *Audacity*, ex-*Jaguar*. Capital lines she possesses! Exceptional lines indeed! Certainly the finest ever to come under my inspection. Truly an inspired creation of the French naval architect Derrez. The French design vessels so much better than the British! And the French build them ever so much better, even the British admit. Sadly, the French are so mired in self-denigration at their inabilities to prevail over the British in even the most minor of naval engagements that they have never learned to fight their superior designs properly.

"Master Shipwright Hackett and I have lofted her lines to construct the privateer *Portsmouth* now a-building, in which Cousin John owns a major share—I fear Judge Clagett likewise has some share—and Cousin John wishes Marcus Whipple to command her. We intend to lay the keel of a brig—perhaps a small frigate—following *Audacity*'s lines, though with Shipwright Hackett's sagacious modifications, since we imagine she'll be a brig right enough. We'll begin work at Cousin John's dockyard as soon as the weather will allow, January most likely. She shall be taken into the Continental Navy as the *Hampshire*, and John's special friend Captain Roche is to have her."

"John shall have to arrange a captain other than Marcus for his privateer," Frost snapped, scowling. "Marcus has paid great coin by his personal mutilation for the privilege of playing with his twins at his own hearth." Then he softened. "I am overjoyed, Tobias, that you have discovered a supply of that most desired article in giving life to a vessel, well-seasoned timbers. A brig's sail plan as you propose would be unwieldy, but a three-masted sloop, not a light frigate, mind, so built following the lines of my sweet *Audacity*, will be a formidable vessel indeed."

Lear paused. "We have no such laudable article, Cousin Geoffrey. The last such article among our stores was applied to your vessel upon your demand this April and May last. The need of the Congress to put warships upon the sea in the shortest time compels the use of any article of timber, seasoned or not, coming immediately to hand."

"Then the dry rot that comes from the green, unseasoned wood will render the vessel an endangerment to her crew inside three years, and unfit to keep the sea within five," Frost said quietly.

Tobias Lear shrugged morosely. "Aye, having some familiarity with the carpenter's craft, I know that to be true, but you know as well as I, it has always been our custom to build from green wood."

"This building with green wood is why our shipbuilding trade, despite shipwrights the equal of any in Britain or the Continent, is regarded poorly."

"Yes, Cousin Geoffrey," Tobias Lear answered, "but mark you, the British have long commissioned many a fine merchantman off the stocks of our goodly shipwrights. They have depleted their own forests long betimes, and fine seasoned timber is far harder to come by in England than such article is in New Hampshire. I doubt not that a full one third of the trade between the Caribbean and England is carried in bottoms built on these shores. And the masts, you cannot forget the masts . . . such stout and sturdy masts are not to be found anywhere else in the world, or our naval stores."

"Aye," Frost answered grimly, thinking back to his encounter with HM *Jaguar*. "Lacking access to our mast ponds will mean that many a British warship laid up in ordinary will remain so for lack of proper timber. But tell me, Cousin, why are you so all a-fire to build privateers? Ain't we better off building warships such as the *Raleigh*, and this *Hampshire*, as you've just named her, for the Continental Navy? You confiscate much good timber and usurp much skilled labor for privateers that could be going toward a proper Continental Navy. And why does this Continental Congress, which John prates on about, permit the various state navies?"

"You ken, no doubt, that John is both Continental and Navy Agent, Geoffrey, and there is much money to be made in this privateering line, it is true," Tobias Lear said in a voice so low that Frost scarcely heard it.

"Then it is a plaguey contretemps!" Frost said hotly.

"Who has need of shipbuilding at all when you fetch in such marvelously rich prizes, Cousin," John Langdon said chidingly but cheerfully as he reentered his office. "My faith, but I have fair rhapsodies when I reflect on the manifests of those victuallers! Bolts and bolts of best duck, cordage, uniforms, shoes, tentage, field packs, cartridge boxes, infantrymen's belts, artillery tubes and field carriages, harnesses, barrels and barrels of dried pease, casks of pickled pork and beef, pipes of wine and vinegar. Bless my soul, vinegar! And bags of sugar, rice, barrels and barrels of flour—and most glorious of all, barrels and barrels of gunpowder! Tons of powder, Geoffrey, the essence and lifeblood of revolution! Not to mention your taking of the Cadiz Packet with its cargo of sterling on merchants' accounts to the value of fifty thousand pounds, right from beneath the noses of the supercilious British Navy in the Bay of Biscay! But I forget my manners. Please seat yourselves, Geoffrey, and you, Goodman Mansfield. Prosperous, bring tea for Captain Frost. Goodman Mansfield, will you join my cousin Tobias and me in a bumper of port wine?"

"I'll be havin' what the Capt'n's havin'," Caleb said diffidently, sneaking a hopeful look at Frost.

"Well, Tobias, we shall have ourselves all the more enjoyment of this noble Portuguee port wine that Geoffrey dispatched to my table immediately he berthed his *Audacity* at my dockyard."

Frost sank down into a chair next to the delicate Deal table and loosened his stock, for John Langdon's office now seemed stifling hot. If he were not exceedingly careful, Frost would find himself falling asleep, as he had been awake fully these past thirty-six hours. Prosperous bustled in with a large silver tray bearing a teapot, two delicate cups, a decanter of tawny-colored wine and two long-stemmed goblets. Caleb uneasily sat in a chair on the other side of the Deal table, unsure if the light structure was capable of bearing his weight. As was to be expected of the Naval Agent for New Hampshire, his cousin was delighted with Frost's taking of the Cadiz Packet and her treasure. The affair quite sickened Frost. The Golden Buddha and the Sweet Infant! He morosely noted no distinction between his actions in boarding a defenseless British packet and relieving it of a handsome sum of hard money, and Gaunt Hutson's attempt to plunder the *Graciosa* nau. Except that Frost possessed several pieces of foolscap issued by the Legislature of New Hampshire and the Continental Congress that purported to legitimize his depredation. Frost was consumed by the mumchance of it all. Joss.

"Darius has instructed me in the proper way your tea is to be brewed, Capt'n Frost," Prosperous whispered gaily. "True, there be a slight trick to it, but I've learned it." He placed the pot and cups on the Deal table, then crossed to Langdon's massive desk and placed the decanter and goblets in front of Langdon.

Langdon poured port wine for Lear and himself, then raised his glass in a toast. "Geoffrey, why so droll! By my quick reckoning your share of all the prizes fetched in on your just-completed cruize shall easily exceed one hundred thousand pounds hard money!" Langdon sipped the port wine appreciatively, then patted his lips with a napkin.

Tobias Lear leaned forward eagerly. "Geoffrey, I know your proclivities toward the Portugee, having used their factors in the Macao, but think you we have sufficient cause to declare war against the Kingdom of Portugal? That kingdom's commerce is ripe for the plucking."

Frost took a sip of the tea and resisted making a wry face. Prosperous, regardless of his professions, still had not got the knack of making a proper pot of tea. "All the Kingdom of Portugal has done to slight us, Tobias, is shut its ports to us. The Portuguese are long bound to the British by treaties ancient and honourable. As allies nothing less could be expected of the Portuguese government. But mark! None of our vessels have been seized by the Portuguese. The nation is small, inoffensive, no longer peopled by robust seafarers, and the Portuguese neither mean nor can do us any harm. The trend of this conversation is to hold up Gaunt Hutson not as pirate but as paragon, had he but had the good sense and forethought to await a formal declaration of war against the Kingdom of Portugal."

Caleb carefully lifted the delicate Chinese porcelain cup and saucer in both hands to his lips, then set them down hurriedly. He spilled tea into his saucer and noisily blew across the liquid to cool it. "Don't see how ye can drink somethin' so hot, Capt'n. Somethin' this hot got to be saucered 'n' blowed proper before it be fit to drink."

The good manners of John Langdon and Tobias Lear caused them to avert their faces quickly to conceal their bemused astonishment from Caleb.

"John, how ironic it is!" Frost put down his cup quickly, seeking to remove Caleb from the center of attention. "I inducted farmers and brewers, glovers, millers and cooperers, and glaziers for a period of six months. There were of a vast certainty insufficient seamen with experience in this time of privateering madness! So I enlisted cobblers and clerks, silversmiths and milliners—indeed, took weavers directly from their looms—and fishermen. Farmers who heretofore had held only cow's udder, sickle and plough. They came aboard my vessel not knowing a halyard from a sheet from a line from a topping lift. Much less the terror of going aloft in a night howling with lightning to confront the demons resident in a tops'l a-flog in a gale. And they flinched like rabbits at the noise of cannons. But these fledgling mariners begin to understand their dependence upon their mates.

"Then, at the end of a six-months cruize, my precious vessel, the wondrous living thing she is, must come to your dockyard to be refreshed. Her sinews of tarred hemp must be rewove. Her limbs of masts and yards must be repaired, new booms shaved from seasoned timber. Her new skin of seasoned oak and pine and elm must be grafted to planks. Her raiment of sails must be replenished. Paints and pigments must add colour to her cheeks, a rouging more for preservation than to enhance her beauty.

"For months my officers or I gave the commands: 'Let go the lowlines! In topgallants! Up courses! Down jib and stays'ls!' Then at last we had trained our crew to dispense with such a plethora of orders, and needed only command 'shorten sail,' trusting the men knew their business and would go about it diligently. The crew achieved such a kinship with their cannons that they were able to discharge three fairly laid broadsides in just under five minutes, beginning with charged and shotted tubes, of course.

"Then I must cast this finely honed instrument—this great, grand weapon forged and sharpened over the past six months—back onto the beach because the cruize contracted is completed and I must pay off. And what were shortly before proper seamen in anyone's navy or merchant service now demand their ease, and their shares of prize monies!

"They are destined now to spend their time in indolence and sloth, and waste their sustenance in alehouses and brothels while my beloved vessel must submit both to the surgeons and the artificers—this most complex and complicated machine yet envisioned by the human mind and so lovingly fashioned by our hands!" Frost slumped in his chair and lapsed into silence, fatigue weighing heavily upon him. He had just delivered himself of far more words than he could ever recall uttering in so short a space.

"Sheer eloquence, Cousin!" John Langdon, joined enthusiastically by Tobias Lear, lifted his glass of port wine in salute.

"Gentlemens, please excuse th' askin'," Caleb interjected, "but I'm a-fire t' know this business o' prize monie, 'n' how it come to be. Mister Ming Tsun, now, he's advanced monie 'n quantity t' me—which I admit freely t' spendin' as freely. But how prize monie be calculated ain't somethin' a woods-cruizer like me rightly twigs."

John Langdon smiled. "Then far better we instruct you, Goodman Mansfield, than for you to receive your education in Judge Clagett's prize court. Prize monie and its division are as old as kingdoms. Kings have only come lately to the maintenance of standing navies—at ruinous costs to their treasuries and the discomfiture of their citizens! The pursuit of enemy vessels by other vessels documented with letters of marque and reprisal, or confirmed with privateers' commissions," Langdon smiled knowingly at Frost, "now my cousin Geoffrey considers such as looting, barely legalized. But the French named it aptly: *la guerre de course*—the war, or the hunt, of the chace."

"A blood sport, Goodman Mansfield, you may call it, though sanctioned by the Law of Nations," Tobias Lear broke in. "Faith, the rules are well known to any denizen of a port city in wartime. I allege, on my hope of salvation, that the citizens of our dear Portsmouth have calculated to the half-penny what Cousin Geoffrey's prizes will pay out."

"Goodman Mansfield," John Langdon said soothingly, "as the New Hampshire Agent for Prizes I assure you that my cousin's contract for prize monie division is exceedingly fair. The proceedings are *en rem* against the prize vessels. Half of the proceeds of the vessels taken as prizes and their cargoes, properly libeled and condemned and auctioned or otherwise lawfully dispatched, to the privateer vessel's owners. The other one-half to be divided among the officers and men enlisted for the cruize as per long-endorsed formula."

Frost coughed delicately: "Forget not, Cousins, that sometimes the prize court takes a wondrously long time to effect its intent. I learned immediately upon my arrival in Portsmouth that Judge Brackett's Maritime Court required over a year to apportion the cargo of the *Prince George*, so cunningly captured by Titus Salter and his matrosses in October last when her captain mistook Portsmouth for Boston and sailed in with a cargo of two thousand barrels of flour. When Judge Brackett's condemnation proceeds were finished, three-quarters of the cargo was awarded to the state. Titus was awarded only one-quarter of the cargo's value—and as anyone in Portsmouth will tell you, that be two hundred and twenty-five pounds, seventeen shillings and five pence—to be divided among seventy-one claimants." Frost smiled at his cousins: "Not down to the half-penny, but near enough."

"Yes, Geoffrey," John Langdon said hurriedly, "but appeal has been taken to the Continental Congress, and everyone is certain the division will turn out far more equitable."

"Goodman Mansfield," Tobias Lear said, "the Law Maritime governing division of prize monie for private men-o-war is far superior to that accruing to established naval forces. An entirely different set of rules obtains, so complicated that even Courts of Admiralty have difficulty cyphering them. If the prize taken is judged inferior to the naval vessel to whom she falls, then the government takes one half of the prize's value. Only if the prize is judged equal to or superior in force to the capturing naval vessel does the entire prize monie descend to the officers and crew."

"Yes," John Landgon chimed in, "as Tobias says, complicated formulae in the extreme! If there is a squadron commander in the offing, that person is entitled to five percent of the prize's value. The successful captor receives ten percent of the value, though if operating as an independent command, the squadron commander's five percent escheats to him. Ten percent is then shared out among the ship's lieutenants, sailing master, and captain of marines, if there is one. Another ten percent to be shared among the warranted officers, boatswain, carpenter, surgeon, and so forth. Seventeen and one-half percent to be shared out among the sailmaker, master-at-arms and so forth, and twelve and one-half percent to be divided among the remaining non-commissioned officers." Langdon glanced at Caleb in triumphant. "As you have already cyphered, only thirty-five percent remains to be divided among the vast remainder of seamen, boys in the crew, and marines."

Caleb raised his cup quickly in abject surrender. "I am regretful 'n th' extreme o' havin' raised th' question. 'Pears t' me thet Capt'n Frost be most fair 'n th' divyin' o' prize monie."

"But you must know of the bonds required to be posted by a private man-o-war, Goodman Mansfield," John Langdon said, now that he was hot on the subject.

"John, Tobias," Frost interjected, "I believe Caleb now is possessed of an absolute understanding of the arcane rules of prize division and requires no further education."

"Geoffrey," Tobias Lear said, leaning forward eagerly, "I

have gone aboard your properly called *Audacity* the day past. I expected her to be like all the vessels engaged in long-distance cruizing, holds fetid, berth deck malodorous to the extreme, miasmal vapors from the bilges. I had, I must admit, taken the precaution of a kerchief well sprinkled with oil of wintergreen to defend my nose. Yet your vessel was as sweet below decks as a newly constructed brig beginning its maiden voyage down to Jamaica."

Frost signaled Prosperous and asked if he could bring a pot of honey. Perhaps honey would make the tea palatable. "Once the crew understood the need for ship's cleanliness and hygiene of a personal nature, the men insisted upon it more than I. It is no great feat to instill pride in men once you have driven out fear, and they have pride in their vessel and trust in their mates." Caleb had finished his tea and Frost obligingly poured the woods-cruiser another cup. Perhaps Caleb would consume the entire pot and Frost would not have to drink any more. He reckoned that Caleb really thirsted for something stronger than tea but was reluctant to chance his wits or incur Frost's wrath by joining Langdon and Lear in a tipple.

John Langdon cleared his throat delicately. Frost was instantly on his guard. "Our forces have met with a series of reverses since last we met, Cousin," Langdon began cautiously.

"Or perhaps we have the wrong men leading our forces," Frost said quickly. "I know aught but what I have heard these four days since my *Audacity* was safely berthed at your dockyard. Half of what I've heard I give no credence, and I dismiss the half that remains as bawdy by men who would have done far less in similar situations. But it does seem curious to one so newly arrived that this Continental Congress of which you are so almighty enamoured could not have selected a better commander than this Virginia tobacco farmer, who has made a habit, nay, a virtue, out of retreat." Frost brightened when Prosperous returned with a pot of honey-in-the-comb. He spun a generous dollop into his cup and stirred vigorously before pushing the pot to Caleb.

"I have never known you to be critical of another, especially a man you have never met," Langdon said mildly.

"Your pardon I beg," Frost said, immediately contrite. "and humbly. Indeed, I readily confess I know not what vicissitudes His Excellency has encountered. This rebellion is afloat on uncharted waters. I am beside myself with worry over Joseph and our dear, dear Juby, gone off to the Lake on that scarum-harum scheme. Worry clouds my judgment." Frost busied himself stirring honey into his tea. "And I owe to a certain amount of despair when I was advised upon my arrival in Portsmouth that Commodore Esek Hopkins was censured by this Continental Congress of yours for his failing to press the engagement with the British light frigate *Glasgow* in the Sound of Long Island.

"To my certain knowledge no member of this Congress of yours was aboard any of the vessels in Hopkins' small squadron at the time. 'Tis true Hopkins' forces had great superiority of cannons, but Hopkins' commanders had no idea how to fight in concert—indeed, they had never done so, never having been given the incentive or opportunity to engage in concerted actions! They fought in pell-mell fashion, and the British commander was able to keep them at bay. It was unfair to the man, and petty of your Congress."

Frost sighed in frustration. "I must believe His Excellency is exerting his best efforts, better than a New Englander like Rhode Island's Nathanael Greene, or our own John Sullivan, the first New Hampshire soldier to be created a Continental general. I ken he coveted Washington's command—though not so covetous as the jealous John Hancock. But the times demand a paladin. Our rebellion could have ended in August when Howe was permitted to land on Long Island uncontested. Surely it would have ended had John Glover and his web-footed Marbleheaders not gotten His Excellency and what remnants of the Continental Army were not captured or deserted across to the New York shore."

"Geoffrey, there are those of us—among whom Tobias and I are ardently counted—who consider that George Washington is indeed a paladin. I love Hancock as a brother, but he never would have done, never would have done at all as a soldier, and certainly not that braggart Ward, with even less experience of the military affairs than Hancock. And I confess great sorrow, for this John Sullivan you have just named, a man I have long caressed . . . it pains me to speak of it . . . was taken prisoner in a skirmish on Long Island . . . some call it a great battle, but not I.

"Our Sullivan did not acknowledge the debt he owed our own Lord Sterling, who was resolutely leading New Jersey troops. Instead, he decamped in the face of the enemy, taking his Connecticut and Massachusetts soldiers with him. Most cowardly, and without even the good sense or integrity to warn Lord Sterling that he was leaving the American center undefended. Ultimately, this sorry excuse of a major general was flushed from a cornfield where he sought to secret himself, and taken craven prisoner . . . hiding in a cornfield, mind! This on top of Sullivan's dismal performance in Canada, when he relieved the dying John Thomas, so stout in the evacuation of Boston under His Excellency.

"This John Sullivan, once New Hampshire's pride, ordered an attack on the small village of Trois Rivières . . . only to run up against Gentleman Johnny Burgoyne, who set Sullivan aflame with the desire to forsake Canadian soil forever. After that debacle some forty Colonial Militia officers, once they had extricated themselves from swamps and cesspools where they had sought refuge from Burgoyne's Indian levies, sought to tender their commissions."

"Hold hard, thar, Yere Honour!" Caleb said hotly. "Ye'll recall, doubtless, thet John Sullivan wus with us at Will and Mary's fort, 'n' the takin' of thet powder ye're so all-fired proud of. He wusn't shy thet December night, not one whit."

John Langdon colored. "Right you are, Goodman Mansfield; a despairing intemperance seizes me when I think how we newly coined states are governed by no central plan. Indeed, we are guided by no central mind, no central hand calmly laid on the tiller of our political and military strategies with an all-knowing, predestined eye keenly aligned on a fixed constellation to find us safely in the harbor of tranquility." He paced to the fireplace and reflectively scrubbed his hands in its warmth. "I cannot berate John Sullivan, 'less I know how I should have treated in the same untoward calamities and grave distresses."

Langdon sighed and changed the subject. "As you have remarked, Geoffrey, George Three is throwing millions in sterling and tens of thousands of British soldiers and Hessian mercenaries into the battle against us. He desires to subjugate us anew, quickly and completely. This mid-month last no less than thirty-two thousand British and Hessian troops, their siege engines, field cannons, and all necessities to sustain them, were ashore on the Long Island, Manhattan, and the city of New York." Langdon turned his back to the fireplace and flipped up his coat tails, the better to warm his buttocks.

"Yet, upon reflection, time for such as I have occasionally at sea, Cousin," Frost said wryly, "it is true, is it not, that the purchase of mercenaries indicates a weakness, a disease, an acknowledgement that the British are not strong enough, have not sufficient men or pride in selves, to face our nascent states directly?" Frost sipped his tea, then spun more honey into the cup for the jolt of sweetening to stave off fatigue. "I must judge that George Three is of a most desperate cast and has gone to the well once too often when it comes to outfitting an army 'monst his subjects. Surely, such a weakness cannot endure against our arms.

"What requires this paladin from Virginia to dispossess us of the Brothers Howe and their combined army and navy?" Frost concluded querulously.

"Men, more men and arms, but presently His Excellency requires most of all food and gunpowder, for he has a dearth of both necessary articles. The enlistments of the soldiers still with him have expiry on the first of the New Year, and without some recompense for their sufferings, they most assuredly shall all set out for their hearths the first of January."

Frost nodded soberly. He knew all about the brevity of

enlistments. The crew of *Audacity* had signed for a six-months cruise—May through November. Now, safely ashore, with Frost's guaranteed advance against prize monies in hand, the majority of them could not be induced to take the sea again until their monies had been spent, or greed once again bestirred them. He had been fortunate indeed to quiet the grumbling of his crew by taking the Cadiz Packet. And then falling in with and taking as prizes the British victuallers south of Sable Island on the voyage to Portsmouth after going north around the British Isles.

"It would seem a simple matter to convey those necessary articles of food and gunpowder to His Excellency," Frost said critically. He had already gleaned an excellent idea of where this conversation was trending, for he knew his cousin John Langdon all too well. And he had already objectively considered and endorsed the plan he knew John Langdon would soon be proposing. Quite bleakly, if Geoffrey Frost ever hoped to return to the life of a trader, there was no alternative, and no one had vouchsafed him permission to stand aside.

"Easy enough," John Langdon agreed, pausing to refill Tobias Lear's glass, then his own, with the ruby-colored port wine. "If Washington's location were known with some exactitude. If the requisite provisions and gunpowder could be procured. And if the provisions and gunpowder could be gotten him."

"The latter will prove to be the most difficult," Frost said. "It is my intelligence that British Navy warships control the Sound of Long Island, as well as cruize the lower portion of the River Hudson with impenetrable blockade. Fortunate for me this diversion of Royal Navy ships, since no warlike vessels were available to harry my entry into the Ports of Piscataqua."

"Your understanding is correct," Langdon said, sadly.

"John," Frost said, attempting to draw out his cousin more quickly by abruptly changing the subject. "On my first day in dear Portsmouth, I was amazed to see, nay, mortified to see, a woman and her child of no more than eighteen months, both without shoes. Without shoes, John! In mid-November—I know not where she shelters, or whether she shelters at all . . ."

"I know that one," Langdon cried testily, "a professional beggar, an actress using the child as a property, as a real actress may use a fan. But knowing you, you gave her some money, and told her to repair to Parson Devon for more alms."

"Perish that thought, John. Parson Devon would only hector her as a harlot! No man has a harder heart toward the downtrodden than the professional man of the cloth! To him, Paradise is reserved for the pious and the propertied. Such as Parson Devon believe the nostrils of Saint Peter prickle at the aroma of honest perspiration. I believe the afterlife will prove more accommodating to the lowly born than the pompous, perfumed princes of pernicious, organized religion. The Protestant Book teaches that a good deed rendered to the lowest of the low is rendered likewise to the Master."

"I had forgot you were a student of the Holy Writ and sundry other religious tracts and theologies," Langdon said sardonically. Prosperous entered Langdon's office with a tray of small scones. Frost put two onto a plate, and after Prosperous had moved on to John Langdon and Tobias Lear, pushed the plate toward Caleb Mansfield, who seized the scones gratefully.

"As part of my studies of philosophy and theology in general," Frost replied evenly. "I gave the woman all the small coin I had and invited her to call at the Widow Crockett's, where she would find suitable employment upon application."

"And likewise had I forgotten your handsome investments in the Widow Crockett's inn," Langdon said tartly, "a kindred soul . . ."

"A place where a seaman can find a comfortable bed that neither rolls nor pitches, more restful by far than a hammock, as well as a warm tavern and generous food at a price the seaman can readily afford, a place where he need not worry that either his throat or his purse strings will be cut."

"A true Sir Gawain," Langdon taunted, "he who gives alms feeds three, the beggar, the godhead, and thee . . ."

Frost brought his left fist crashing down upon the Deal table. He had not thought the blow a hard one, had not intended such, surely, and was properly horrified when the immaculately polished top of the Deal table split cleanly, both halves, with the tea pot, cups and plate of scones falling to the floor. The sound of the pot's fall was muffled by the thick Chinese carpet, one that Frost had brought back on his last voyage to the Orient.

Frost was instantly apologetic: "I am so very sorry, John! I knew not the force my arm commanded, nor perhaps the depth of my anger. Be not dismayed. See! The break is a clean one. I have a prince of a carpenter who can mend and scarf the break so that no one can ever detect the harm."

John Langdon stooped to retrieve the split Deal table top, and regarded it with bemusement. "Cousin, I had scarce credited the tales related to me about the power of your sword arm. I engaged John Nason in conversation once, and when he spoke of the power of your sword arm in battle he spoke in terms of such awe I thought the man tetched. But I see he spoke without exaggeration."

"Cousin! We were speaking not of my prowess with a cutlass. In my arm reposes no special skill or cunning, just a force born of desperation permitting me to confound, thus far, the opponents fate has thrust into my path. My style of fighting with a cutlass is unorthodox to the extreme, and my opponents are perhaps discomfitted since I attack with the left arm, a sinister advantage they apprehend only too late. A proper swordsman would easily skewer me in the giblets, if given sufficient play to his arm. Fortunately, when attacking a mob, either a-ship or on land, there is no time for finesse, and much is gained in immediate rush of the enemy, thickly packed . . ."

Frost broke off. "We have veered on a new course, Cousin. I wish to return to our earlier tack, which is a query. This ambitious undertaking on which we are embarked, albeit myself far more reluctant than you—this undertaking that found voice in those fine, high-sounding words in that broadside Tommy Thompson gave me four months past—that so-called

Declaration of Independence: what purpose serves those mellifluous words of dignity, of the individual, prosperity and freedom, if they apply not to us all? If it is a truth that this Revolution is a tide that raises all boats, how can we abide to leave anyone—this beggar and her child included—behind?"

"Geoffrey," Tobias Lear said, deliberately ignoring Frost's allusions to the beggar and her child, "His Excellency General Washington is constantly being flushed out, and he moves nightly to keep from entrapment. He is unable to give battle due to a lack of munitions."

John Langdon twirled the goblet's stem between his palms. "The coffers of our infant State of New Hampshire are barren. As Continental Agent for New Hampshire I can attest that the Continental Congress has depleted its treasury, its credit and the patience of those financiers who have advanced money to our noble cause. More than one banking house has refused to honour bills of account presented for payment." Langdon stared directly at Geoffrey Frost. "The Continental Congress, knowing of the magnificent stores you harvested from the British, comes to you, Cousin, not as beggars but as supplicants."

And Frost confirmed the reason his cousin John Langdon had invited him to the State House. It was as he had anticipated. The Continental Congress was desperate, and it was bankrupt, in specie as well as new ideas. "Perhaps you may wish to summon the learned Wyseman Clagett, John, for his dissertation on the niceties of the Law of Admiralty. But I collect the prizes now crowding your dockyard are considered property of myself and my crew until knocked down by the auctioneer's hammer."

"With due allowance for the Court of Admiralty's commissions and percentages, Geoffrey," Langdon said, with just a hint of sarcasm coloring his voice.

"Then we may avoid Judge Clagett's Court of Admiralty entirely, gentlemen. I shall be happy to deliver all the powder and provisions suitable for an army's sustenance taken from *Audacity*'s prizes this cruize to the Continental Congress. That against a promissory note payable from the public purse five years to the day after a treaty of peace between our states and George Three's government is concluded." Frost smiled thinly, enjoying the incredulity reflected in the faces of John Langdon and Tobias Lear. "The payment must be in money of account. Whether correlating to the value of sterling or the Spanish milled dollar of eight pieces is not material, since their store is equivalent. I tell you now, I have no faith in any currency issued solely on the good faith and credit of the promissory of any state in North America."

Tobias spoke first, slightly in wonder. "You have no doubt how this rebellion of ours will end?"

"I doubt not that it will run through its time and end," Frost said. "I have a great interest in an outcome favorable to the increase of the liberties long cultivated in the world on our side of the Atlantic, so that I may resume my customary trade."

"A generous offer . . ." John Langdon began, ". . . as you deduce, the Congress' treasury is a sieve, unable to hold any funds, so great the demands upon it."

"Our rebellion may end with me dead, and our lands and peoples once again under British governance. In which case I collect nothing, for indeed a shroud has no pockets. You view the matter as clearly as I, Cousins?" Frost addressed them both: "If we are alive when this cursed war concludes, it will be because we have endured to our freedoms." And to himself Frost murmured: "In for a penny, in for a pound. Gracias a Dios, the Holy Trinity, the Great Buddha. Insh'allah."

"Geoffrey," Langdon said after a cautious sip of his port wine, "the sieve of a treasury—either of the Congress or New Hampshire—can advance you nothing as compensation to your crew for prize monies foregone."

"Of little moment," Frost said, shrugging. "I had set aside a store of silver for my next venture to the Orient. Silver, as you know, is the preferred medium of exchange with the merchants of China in Macao." Now that he had committed himself, Frost knew he would venture the entire way. He knew that was what his cousin had anticipated: if compelled by another to go one mile, Frost would go with John Langdon twain. "We shall have an accurate valuation of the powder and provisions—the other cargoes and the vessels themselves shall await condemnation and then sale to the highest bidder. I shall make available to the men who served *Audacity* so well in their efforts to give meaning to the words in Tommy Thompson's broadside their requisite prize monies in silver."

"As Congress' agent I can adjudge the value of the gunpowder, food stores, and military equipage," John Langdon said, picking up his leatherbound daybook and riffling through several pages. "I can tell you the remainder of the cargoes will command exceptional prices—as will the vessels, given the enthusiasm for privateering that burns within the breasts of our patriots. Your crew shall not begrudge their shares of the munitions and provisions purchased by the Continental Congress for our army's use."

"Purchased by me," Frost corrected. "And because of the gunpowder's destination, favor me by not mulcting the *Audacity*, prize vessels and their cargoes for the forts' powder tax." Frost paused for another sip of tea. "Now I've thought further on the matter, when you draw up the promissory note, include compounded interest at the rate of six percent per annum—being the same rate of interest I collect His Excellency General Washington is charging for expenses laid out from his purse. But I am a simple trader, not a military officer, as you ken, and this loan must needs bear similar interest. Also, Cousin, likewise value the bolts of duck and canvas, for I shall buy all so that *Audacity* may be bedecked in new raiment when we return to sea."

"I shan't quibble over the interest, Geoffrey, for it is fair enough in these unsettled times. I was hoping to purchase the sailcloth, since I have the *Portsmouth* privateer to outfit with a complete suit of sails, as well as the man-o-war *Hampshire*, soon to be laid down. Ah! Here is the entry! Gunpowder purchased by way of the Dutch in St. Eustatius was landed in Newburyport beginning of this month at twenty-five English guineas the ton."

Caleb Mansfield smacked his lips appreciatively as he drained another cup of tea and licked scone crumbs from his fingers. "Glad I be to hear the gentry discussin' the get of vittles to the men bearin' muskets agin the well-fed soljers of Mister General Howe. But His Excellency be somers thet way more'n a few leagues . . ." Caleb waved a hand vaguely westward, " 'n' we be camped here 'n the banks of Piscataqua, with gunpowder and pickled pork, 'n' flour right enough." Caleb fixed John Langdon and Tobias Lear with an accusatory eye. "Has the gentry figured out the get of vittles to the soljers been takin' a tuck to their belts rather than tuckin' into a three-legged pot of stew?"

"There you have us, Goodman Mansfield," Langdon confessed. "My kinsman Tobias and I were narrowly focused on winning Cousin Geoffrey's willing participation in our scheme to succor General Washington's forces that we had not pondered further on the means of its delivery."

"With all respect due the gentry," Caleb said reflectively, lifting the last scone he had rescued from the carpet and holding it aloft as a priest might elevate the host, "but this one bisket likely would give heart to a round dozen of General Washington's soljers, wus they to behold it." Caleb broke the scone in two and stuffed one portion into his mouth. "New York be a smart ways from the Piscataqua, a fact I ken be appreciated by all." Caleb slid the remaining half of the scone in his mouth and chewed slowly. " 'N' we be sittin' here mid-November, comfortable by this fireplace, with enlistments of Mister Washington's soljers out in fifty days or less." Caleb stared forlornly into his dainty cup.

Frost beckoned Prosperous nearer and whispered into his ear. Prosperous nodded and left John Langdon's office.

"You are far wiser than we, Goodman Mansfield," Tobias Lear said, "for you knew Cousin Geoffrey would agree quickly to our scheme, while our thoughts were solely devoted to winning him 'round. We have pondered little, as you so rightly deduce, on the method of delivering the powder and provisions to the troops of the Continental Army General Washington commands."

Prosperous bustled in with a bumper of clear liquid balanced on a beautifully lacquered Chinese tray. He proffered the beaker to Caleb. Caleb took it, sniffed appreciatively, then looked askance at Frost. Frost reluctantly nodded, and Caleb Mansfield gratefully took a mighty swallow of cane rum, neat.

"How many wagons, horses or oxen, drovers and mechanics have you organized to ferry powder and provisions to General Washington's needy men, Cousins?" Frost asked mildly.

Langdon and Lear looked at each other with chagrin. "Well, Geoffrey . . . we were proceeding one pace at a time . . . we have not concluded that wagons are the best way to freight warlike stores to General Washington . . . it may be that a fast vessel might reach the Delaware and the port of Philadelphia, and . . ."

"That is an exceedingly forlorn hope, Cousins!" Frost said more loudly than he had intended. "If what little intelligence has reached me is of any value . . . yes, I acknowledge that above some thirty thousand British soldiers and German mercenaries are now in the environs of southern New York . . ." Frost thought momentarily about Major Heros von Fendig. Surely that worthy had long since returned to British or German soil. "And the transports that conveyed those soldiers to our shores number in the hundreds . . . they infest our waters like herring gulls on a dead whale's carcass! They constitute a blockade that might prove porous . . . though I doubt it! Agree with me, please, that succor of General Washington by sea is both impracticable and improvident. Should any vessel freighting martial stores to His Excellency be intercepted by the British, then you would have lost all possibility of delivering the munitions and provisions you claim he so desperately needs—as well as the provisions themselves." Frost got to his feet and began pacing his cousin's office, unconsciously, as if he were on his own quarterdeck. "You have not taken the second step, logical as it must seem now to you. How many wagons think you are available for hire in the Ports of Piscataqua?"

Langdon and Lear exchanged another confused, uncomfortable glance. "Geoffrey, I doubt if there are available for hire, at any price, upwards of a dozen wagons capable of freighting heavy provisions in all the ports of Piscataqua," Langdon said.

Frost stopped his pacing long enough to seize a lead musket ball hammered into a pencil and a remnant of paper from Langdon's desk. He scribbled furiously for a moment. "From Ming Tsun's exacting cypher of the victualer prizes' manifests, we know they freighted one hundred tonnes of flour, fifteen tonnes of rice, and fifty tonnes of gunpowder among them. This entire tonnage is available for conveyance to Washington's troops. But have you any scope of the wagons necessary for such freight?"

Both Langdon and Lear stared at Frost dumbly, mouths agape. "Caleb," Frost snapped, "I am no wagoneer, but I collect you've had some small experience in freighting during the last war, because being a wagon-master for Braddock paid better than trapping. I do not believe a freight wagon can be laded with more than three tonnes of provisions."

"Waal," Caleb said, scratching his scraggly beard and taking another long pull at the bumper of cane rum, "the wagons made down in the Conastoga country of the Dutchies can bear the weight of four tonnes fer a short jog. But fer a long haul three brace of oxen can't be 'pected to pull more'n three tonnes, thet's sure."

"That's fifty-five wagons," Tobias Lear said, his voice far more high-pitched than was necessary, registering his dismay. "There not be a dozen wagons in all the Piscataqua region capable of such hauling." Lear had been packing a clay pipe with shredded tobacco. He paced over to the fireplace and took up a gleaming ember of snapping hardwood with a small coal tongs. Lear applied the glowing coal to the packed tobacco and sucked on the stem.

Lear remembered his manners in time. "If you will join me, Goodman Mansfield, I'll warrant you'll find a pipe somewhere in the clutter of Cousin John's desk."

After a quick glance at an unsmiling Frost, Caleb shook his head.

"And insufficient wood to fashion wagons on short order,"

John Langdon said plaintively. "The trees cut are awaiting the fall of snow so they can be hauled to the saw pits on Rising Island."

"Not be so fast, Mister Langdon," Caleb Mansfield said quickly. "Ye still have shipwrights at yere call, have ye not?"

"Aye, Goodman Mansfield," John Langdon began, "shipwrights I have . . ."

Caleb Mansfield shot Frost a glance of triumph. "But Capt'n Frost has goodly timber sufficient for wagon makin'."

"The bones of my dear *Salmon*!" Frost exulted. "She shall be honoured to have her timbers used so! John, your shipwrights shall begin building wagons tomorrow! We need nothing so well crafted as the Conestoga, a box atop axles and wheels only, a boat-wagon that can float, built with dispatch for one journey only."

John Langdon regarded Caleb for a long moment. "Faith, but you have posited an uncommonly robust idea, Goodman Mansfield."

Caleb shrugged modestly and took another pull at the beaker of cane rum. "Even a blind hog can find acorns now 'n' again," he said diffidently. "I can help Capt'n Frost with the findin' of drovers 'n' oxen, that is, if the Widow Crockett gives me leave." Caleb looked at Frost apologetically. "I've been livin' on the widow's generosity since we reached Portsmouth. Various times durin' the voyage back we played cards. Daniel O'Buck done cleaned me to the bone. I won a few pounds off him at High, Low, Knave and the Game, but he came back strong, he did, with solid rounds of Laugh and Lie Down. All my advances be weighin' now in his pockets."

"I should have warned you about Daniel O'Buck," Frost said, his face creasing in his caricature of a smile. "He is a person of fastidious honesty, but cards are enamoured of him and seemingly obey his will. Fret not, Caleb, Ming Tsun can provide another advance—against your word to forego games of chance with anyone."

"Until I played agin Daniel O'Buck," Caleb mumbled, "I alus thought Laugh and Lie Down wus truly a game o' chance,

’n’ favored the lucky, which, considerin’ I had kept my hair for such length, I figured I wus, but Daniel, he learned me better. Claimed he had read a book by some Dutchie arithmetick, somethin’ about calculations o’ hazards of the game, or sech like.”

“It is possible that Daniel has in some wise become acquainted with the Dutch mathematician Huygens, who published a treatise on gambling in the last century,” Frost mused. “The treatise was entitled *De Ratiociniis in Ludo Aleae*, and it incorporated many of the observations concerning probability analysis deduced by his contemporary, the French scientist and religious mystic Pascal, who doubtlessly you know as the originator of the famous wager.”

“I ain’t never heard of this fella Huygens, and I sure ain’t never heard of yere friend Mister Pascal,” Caleb said suspiciously. “What be the meaning of thet French or Latin, or whatever thet language ye just used?”

“It translates from Latin as *On Computations in the Game of Dice*,” Frost replied. “There are many facets to the theorems, but for your purposes it illustrates the absolute principle arithmetick that skill in the recollection of numbers is far better than the bare hunch of the gambler.”

“ ’N’ ye be tellin’ me . . .” Caleb said.

“Bear and retain in mind at all times the cards that already have ended their play, because you won’t see them again.”

“ ’N’ what about this wager of this Pascal fella,” Caleb said warily.

Frost looked around for John Langdon or Tobias Lear, but they were conferring over one of the draughts of *Audacity*. “Be assured that my cousins could answer far better than I, Caleb, but Pascal’s Wager goes to the question of whether God actually exists.”

“Yes . . .” Caleb said, “ ’n’?”

“Pascal postulated that reason alone is incapable of determining God’s existence. But Pascal reasoned that only two alternatives are possible. Either God exists, or God does not exist. The believer in God trusts that salvation and unity in

God lies at the end of the journey of life. However, should God not exist, nothing happens to the believer when life is extinguished."

"I ken," Caleb said quickly. "A nonbeliever balances on two alternatives. He don't believe in God, no sir. Supposin' God don't exist, the nonbeliever loses nothin' when he dies, 'cause ther be nothin'. But if the nonbeliever ain't twigged correct, and ther be a God, then the nonbeliever faces an eternity o' damnation on account of havin' disbelieved."

"There you have it, Caleb," Frost said with satisfaction. "You have posed the question: God is or God is not. In what manner should we ascribe?"

"Strikes me as . . . cynical," Caleb said, puffing with pride that he had thought of the word. "It shore do shrive all pleasure in playin' Laugh and Lie Down."

Frost laughed his short, unpleasant laugh, the only one he knew. "There was another famous student of the scientific study of gaming, Caleb, whose astute observations you may find enlightening: the celebrated Venetian Girolamo Cardano, a physician as well as an astrologer, and a gifted algebraist, which is how his treatise, *Liber De Ludo Aleae*, or *Handbook of Games of Chance*, came to my attention."

" 'N' what did this algates have to say about gamin' that ye mark him now?" Caleb said, more than a little petulantly.

"The simple maxim that the greatest advantage in gambling lies in not playing at all," Frost said, with another of his short, unpleasant laughs.

Frost heard horses and a carriage draw up in front of the State House. A moment later the entry doors opening from the street resounded to heavy blows. Prosperous, who had been serving more scones and port wine, scowled and set down his tray, marching away to determine the business of anyone with the temerity to disturb the labors of the Continental Agent, the honorable John Langdon, at this very late hour of the afternoon. Frost watched Prosperous' still, outraged back disappear into the hallway; doubtlessly the impudent caller would receive a suitable tongue-lashing and be sent packing.

Instead, moments later a flustered Prosperous appeared in the office and hurried to whisper directly into Langdon's ear. Frost's cousin rose to his feet with an alacrity that belied his bulk, glanced quickly at Frost, and hurried after Prosperous. Bemused, Frost crossed to the windows looking out onto Pleasant Street. He took care to remain in the lee of the heavy curtains and was startled beyond measure to see his father's covered landau on the street outside the State House. A moment later, John Langdon, swathed in a heavy cloak with Prosperous hurrying behind, trying to keep an umbrella over his master's head, hastened from the State House entry to the coach. The driver, the slave who had replaced Juby—Frost did not know the man's name—opened the door for Langdon to step inside, and Frost saw the dark shape of Marlborough Frost lean forward to converse urgently with John Langdon.

Yes, his father was sufficiently powerful to summon the Continental Agent to his carriage, Frost acknowledged. Marlborough Frost was perhaps the only man in New Hampshire who could do so. He looked steadily at the silhouette of his father in the sleet-dimmed November light of last day, wanting to reach across the gulf that separated him from his father. Their commercial transactions, carried out in writing, were studiously polite and punctiliously correct and accurate to the penny. Frost knew that his father would willingly die before he would permit his oldest son to be cheated of a pence. Frost was slowly bridging the gulf that Jonathan's death had created in the life of Thérèse Frost, though in her befuddled mental state his mother would never apprehend it. It was time, past time, to reach out to his father.

Impulsively, Frost strode as rapidly as he could toward the office doors, turned to the left down the hallway, and threw open the doors to the street. John Langdon, with Prosperous still ineffectually attempting to keep the umbrella over his master's head, was coming up the stoop. Behind master and servant, Marlborough Frost's new driver, rather inexpertly, Frost thought, was turning the matched team, Willow and Birch, around in the street. Geoffrey Frost had not been quick enough to seize the opportunity to attempt a mending of the breach with his father.

John Langdon looked bleakly at Frost as he moved past, throwing off the cloak to land on the ornate Chinese carpet on the hallway floor and sodden it with the cloak's wet. Prosperous dutifully scooped up the cloak, and Frost understood something else. He understood why Prosperous, now faced with the realization that his son had accumulated the money to purchase his freedom, hesitated. The slave was a-straddle a deeply perplexing dilemma. Slavery had been all Prosperous had ever known, and like any human, Prosperous yearned for his freedom. But what would freedom bring to a black man of his age? And Prosperous cared deeply for his master's family. The Langdons treated their slaves well. That did not make the curse of slavery any less opprobrious to Geoffrey Frost, but he understood the psyche. Prosperous, unlike his son, was afraid of the unknowns that freedom would bring.

As if divining his thoughts, Prosperous held up the sodden cloak John Langdon had dropped on the hallway floor, and quite ignoring his own soaking wet condition, sadly shook his head. "Now if I be gone from this place, Capt'n Frost, who there be to look after Master John and Mistress Elizabeth?"

Frost said nothing. Slavery was the greatest evil he eschewed, ever since . . . ever since. Yet, there were bonds other than chains, and slave and master were both accursed, condemned, and perhaps in the end, redeemed by something that approached love. The knowing was completely beyond him. He followed John Langdon back into the large office, where Langdon made directly for the fireplace. Langdon was shaking, and not from the cold or the wet. Finally, he turned and regarded Frost with infinite sorrow.

"Cousin, my good uncle just had word from Doctor Ezrah Green, who took a moment from his grisly duties of treating our wounded and sick at Crown Point to pen a line." Langdon looked Frost directly in the eye, and Frost was grateful that his cousin did not do anything maudlin such as attempt to put an arm around his shoulder. "Doctor Green confirms the death of

Juby, a most glorious death, defying the British on the Lake. He saw Joseph go overside the gondola on which he served when its powder exploded. But of Joseph's subsequent fate he knows nothing, absolutely nothing."

Tobias Lear uttered a loud, "Oh God, Geoffrey . . ." and started toward Frost, stopping when he saw Frost's defiant, smoldering eyes. And Geoffrey Frost acknowledged with fresh sadness, though not anger, that the chasm of despair between father and son was too wide, too vast to be bridged. Marlborough Frost, lying abed with the gout and the croup that Ming Tsun and Ishmael Hymsinger were jointly treating with their various and complementary healing arts, had bestirred himself, had come out on a dreich evening to provide his oldest son what scant information he had just acquired about his youngest son and the slave who had accompanied him from Portsmouth. But Marlborough Frost had deliberately chosen to provide that information through John Langdon, when he could have spoken to his oldest son directly. Not trusting himself to speak as he confronted the enormity of Juby's death and the wretched uncertainty of his brother's fate, Geoffrey Frost nodded his thanks to his cousins; motioning to Caleb, he turned to leave John Langdon's office.

II

WHEN HE SAILED *AUDACITY* INTO THE HARBOR OF THE ANCIENT AÇOREAN TOWN OF ANGRA DO HEROÍSMO, WITH ITS FADED, WHITEWASHED BUILDINGS roofed with weathered red tiles, in the first week of September 1776, Geoffrey Frost was vastly relieved to find the Portuguese nau *Nossa Senhora de Graciosa* already safely brought to the rendezvous by Struan Ferguson, his second in command. His confidence in Struan was boundless, but when last seen during the particularly savage early-season hurricane that had parted them the month before, Struan had been valiantly struggling to keep afloat the dismasted nau and its crew and passengers, just rescued from American pirates.

There also was the matter of fulfilling his promise to the Lady Cygnet, passenger aboard the *Graciosa*, to assist in the funeral rites for Signores Beretta and Garibaldi, the two Jewish musicians murdered by Gaunt Hutson, captain of the American pirate *Zeus' Chariot*. Now Frost and Ishmael Hymsinger, the half-Mi'kmaq shaman and mystic responsible for preserving the lives of Frost's brother-in-law and other American prisoners of war in the gaol of Louisbourg, somberly walked down the steep, winding cobbled street leading from the burying ground. Far below them in the harbor, a cable's length west of Porto de Pipas, the cat, ex-HM *Jaguar*, recently christened *Audacity* by two of her ship's gentlemen to the acclaim of her entire crew, sails neatly furled and sun awnings rigged, lay easy to her best bower and stream anchors. *Audacity* was snug in the roadstead under the rusted, toothless cannons of the Spanish-built Fortaleza de São João Baptista on the eastern flank of Monte Brasil, beneath the serene azure tarpaulin of the sky.

On the western flank of Monte Brasil, at Porto da Silveira, the yawl and pinnace belonging to HM sloop-o-war *Vulture*, mounting twenty 6-pounder cannons, were landing the first consignment of *Vulture*'s water casks. *Vulture* herself, flat, listless sails painted stark in the harsh sunlight of midday, was standing five cables off the southernmost point of Monte Brasil, to cover both roadsteads.

Frost, his eyes studiously averted from the British warship, was still bemused at the image of Lady Neville Maria de' Medici e Monteleone e Wyrley-Birch, the Lady Cygnet, fervently thanking him in Italian for providing the comfort of Hymsinger, whom she had never despaired would appear. "Who would have thought he knew the Jewish?"

Amber, the Lady Cygnet's servant, had awaited Frost on the quay at Porto Pipas as soon as he stepped ashore less than eighteen hours earlier. The former slave had quickly assured Frost that she had been granted full and unconditional manumission during the savage hurricane that followed their rescue. The two terrified and distraught women had clung desperately to each other in La Cygnet's cabin aboard the Portuguese nau for endless storm-tossed hours, drawing their only comfort and hope of salvation from each other's humanity and faith.

The Lady Cygnet required—no, humbly requested—the presence of Geoffrey Frost and Ishmael Hymsinger, the first to bargain with the Church fathers for permission to purchase a piece of ground for the interment of the hearts of Signores Beretta and Garibaldi, the second to consecrate the ground and pray their souls straight to heaven.

Lady Neville had meant to compliment Hymsinger for the sonorous liturgical chant he had intoned as the small casket containing the hearts preserved in best distilled spirits was lowered reverently into the earth in the corner of the burying ground that had been consecrated by the chant. Frost had translated Lady Neville's compliment for Hymsinger's benefit after Lady Neville and the two Catholic priests attending her were walking toward the carriage that had brought her small party to the cemetery. The cemetery's aged caretaker slowly advanced, and Frost watched the first shovelful of soft, moist dirt arc into the grave. He had earlier marked the casket as a plenteous rich reliquary of heavy silver studded with lapis lazuli, jasper and agates. He very much misdoubted that the valuable casket, so unlike the rough coffins or simple cloth shrouds in which the majority of Açorean dead were buried, would still be in the ground twelve hours hence.

Hymsinger had waited until he and Frost were walking away from the burying ground to make his answer. "The Jewish? Faith, Captain Frost, I know naught of the Jewish, though I glimpsed several books on the Hebrew religion in your library shipboard. I would fain learn the Jewish but I could." Hymsinger spread his arms and lifted his face skyward, his twin heavy braids of hair seemingly tilting his head upward by their weight.

"The Deity comprehends many tongues, and responds to them all equally," Frost said. "There is an unfortunate tendency in some ideologies that their claim to truth is exclusive, and the path to the Deity lies only through their religion scrupulously."

"I am but an insignificant servant of that greatest of Sachems. I was asked to perform a consecration of ground, and from my long association with the Abbé Le Loutre, I knew the good Catholic fathers would not have appreciated the Jewish—even had I known any. So I chanted a Mi'kmaq corn harvest song. I had painted a few Mi'kmaq symbols on a strip of canvas—properly heathenish in appearance to the papists. It was only through your gift of tongues that I was able to assure the worthy priests the hearts were those of pagans whose souls might yet be eligible for salvation be their hearts interred in Holy Soil. The Lady Cygnet, she seized upon those symbols to be the Jewish because she wanted them to be the Jewish."

Ishmael Hymsinger shook his head in incomprehension, his neatly plaited braids swaying heavily.

"It was quite easy to convince the priests that the souls of pagans are of much greater value than those of Jews," Frost said dryly. Thanks to his father, he could have chanted the proper oratorio, in the Jewish, had Hymsinger, far more a man of religion than Frost, not been available. The beautiful, distant, and haughty Cygnet had spoken to the priests only in Italian. Frost doubted the priests knew more Latin than that learned by rote and sufficient to recite the liturgy, but at least the priests, thanks to Frost's command of Portuguese, had understood Hymsinger's intentions. So Hymsinger's and his secret was safe. And regardless of the solemnity of the funereal ceremony, the souls of Signores Beretta and Garibaldi had long ascended to Heaven, or been consigned to Hell, according to their respective merits accumulated during life. Insh'allah. As the Great Buddha willed. Joseph and Mary and the Infant. Joss.

"In truth, though it saddens me to relate it."

"Best never to disabuse the Lady," Frost said. "And it becomes her that she is not infected with the prejudice of anti-Semitism."

"Not on my life," Hymsinger said quickly.

Frost concentrated on the scene in Porto Pipas. Workmen were swarming over the *Graciosa* nau berthed against the storm-worn quay of heavy stones fitted together ever so meticulously. Even at this great distance above the port Frost could discern among the diminutive figures Struan Ferguson, his second in command, and João Magalhães. The second officer of the *Graciosa* nau had succumbed to his wounds en route to Angra, so Magalhães had the command now. The two men were standing next to the sheers, where a gang of workers was struggling to step a stub of mainmast—the only halfway suitable stick of wood on the entire island of Terceira, Struan had assured Frost earlier that morning—for a replacement mast for the *Graciosa*. With a musket ball hammered into a pencil, and using the rough surface of a baulk of timber, Struan had sketched out the masts and spars plan he had devised to spread sufficient sail to take the *Graciosa* onward the thousand-odd sea miles to Lisbon. It was an unorthodox sail plan, no less unorthodox than the one Captain Richard Smith of HM *Lark* had devised to get his vessel underweigh after Frost had practically dismasted her in their brief but spirited engagement south of Nova Scotia little more than four months past.

Frost knew that whatever rig Struan devised would propel the nau. Miraculously, with the holes and gashes in the hull either plugged or fothered, the carpenter and his mates working watch-on-watch, and all hands pumping for their very lives, Struan had rigged enough canvas on the spars fished to the stump of a foremast—thanks also to a following wind from the southwest—to have made Angra. He had brought the nau to berth at Porto de Pipas two weeks before Frost had arrived and had been working to make the vessel ready for sea ever since. Struan Ferguson was doing the same superbly capable job of overseeing the nau's repairs as he had in overseeing the repairs to ex-HM *Jaguar* in John Langdon's dockyard on Rising Island in New Hampshire's Piscataqua River.

The clatter of hooves and ironbound wheels on the cobbles behind Frost and Hymsinger announced the imminent passage of the carriage bearing Lady Neville and the clergy. Frost and Hymsinger stepped quickly off the roadway into the shoulder-high hortênsias, their exuberant pom-pom sprays of flowers the color of amethyst as intense as La Cygnet's eyes. Frost reflexively tipped his much-abused tricorne, the only one he owned, which still bore the bullet hole through the crown that Ming Tsun, his servant and best friend in life, had not gotten around to mending. A rabbit started from underfoot, poised to dash across the cobbled road, hesitated, perhaps because of the clatter of approaching hooves, then bounded over the low stone fence and bolted across the field of short-cropped grass the color of emerald on the other side of the low fence. Frost heard the whistle of wind keening through pinions for no more than a second but recognized the sound and turned slightly skyward to see the stoop of the *açor*, the goshawk whose numbers had inspired Portuguese explorers to name these islands the Açores, a purplish blur, a javelin hurled earthward at an impossible velocity from the sky.

The *açor* struck the rabbit in mid-bounce, a blow of savage, shocking impact that carried clearly to Frost, and for the blink of an eye raptor and prey were one whirling, writhing tangle of brown and purple. Then the *açor* disengaged and pitched upward, its airspeed quickly bleeding off in the steep angle and gain of altitude, then winged over in a perfect chandelle that reversed the raptor's course and braked its descent with a beat or two. Wings flared in a graceful arc, feet and talons extended, it pounced upon the rabbit's carcass. The rabbit, head twisted at an awkward, impossible angle, alive scarce a dozen heartbeats earlier, was immediately and possessively covered by the *açor*. The bird regarded Frost with a sharp, knowing gleam of freedom, of triumph, and fanned its wings once, revealing the flash of cruciform white beneath its upper wing coverts.

The carriage swept by, pushing a slight bow wave of wind and the sour, not unpleasant smell of horse sweat. The priests nodded and smiled to Frost and Hymsinger; the Lady Cygnet, her face of classical beauty far purer than that of Nefertiti, regal Queen of Egypt, a soft blur behind a black mourning veil, reliving her pain in private, stared straight ahead. No, she turned her face at the last instant and stared momentarily to her right, but Frost could not tell whether she looked at him or at the goshawk.

Ten minutes later, his thighs and calves greatly protesting their unaccustomed exertion on land, and steeply pitched land at that, Frost, followed by Hymsinger, picked his way through the baulks of rough-sawn lumber stacked haphazardly on the quay. He reached Struan Ferguson, liberally covered with sawdust, just as the mainmast took its step on the nau's keelson and Struan called, his instructions translated into Portuguese by Magalhães, for the gang of workmen to slack the tackle falls and stand easy. Struan had been focused on his work and had not seen Frost's approach. Guiltily and hastily, he stubbed out the long, yellowish-brown Indonesian *kretek* cigar, blended of tobacco and cloves, that he had been smoking. "We shall have her ready for her ultimate voyage within the week, Geoffrey," Struan said cheerfully, "though I ken ye would prefer to make good five hundred leagues of westering this Tuesday week."

Frost did not reply directly, for he had shared his plan for *Audacity*'s return voyage to the Ports of Piscataqua only with Ming Tsun, and that but briefly.

Their route from the cemetery to the quay had taken Frost and Hymsinger past the imposing Palácio, which, until sixteen years earlier, had been the Colégio de Estudos, where priests of the Company of Jesus had dedicated themselves to faith and literacy. The Marquise de Pombal, Prime Minister for Don José I, had expelled the Jesuits from all Portuguese lands in 1760, and Frost recalled that young Magalhães was a kinsman of that powerful worthy. The Capitão-General of the Açores, who had his headquarters in the Palácio dos Capitães-Generais in Angra do Heroísmo, and the Commandant of the puny combined garrison of the Angra forts, had been polite but insistent when Frost had met with them earlier in the morning before walking to the cemetery. Their sovereign, Don José I, was an ally of the British Crown by long-standing treaty and mutual affection; and there was this embarrassing complication of a rebellion against George the Third's God-granted authorities and unquestioned dominations by ungrateful subjects in Britain's North American colonies. By his edict of 5 July 1776, José Primeiro had closed all Portuguese ports to rebel vessels.

And there was the additional, embarrassing complication of HM *Vulture*, en route to an unknown destination, having called at Angra to water only hours before. *Vulture*'s commanding officer, upon discovering the rebel privateer sheltering in the lee of Monte Brasil and citing the long-standing ties of formal treaty between the British and Portuguese crowns, had imperiously demanded that Frost and *Audacity* be delivered up to him immediately.

However, Capitão-General Moniz and Commandant Silva

were extremely attentive to and highly appreciative of the fact that Frost had taken *Audacity* to the rescue of a Portuguese-flagged merchant vessel when he had been under no obligation to do so. In addition to the salvation of the *Graciosa*'s crew and passengers, the nau's very valuable cargo included a store of gemstones and newly smelted Brazilian gold, most welcome, for the Portuguese king's depleted treasury.

The Capitão-General and the Commandant were graciously taking it upon themselves to grant *Audacity* and her crew the privilege of watering and provisioning in the city of Angra, until repairs to the *Graciosa* nau, under the supervision of Senhor Ferguson, had been made. They had no present intention of yielding to Captain Heflin Wolstenhulme's demands, and the three of them would converse again, and soon, but the Capitão-General and the Commandant understood that Frost's presence was required at the *cemitério*.

Struan brushed perspiration from his forehead with a sawdust-dampened forearm. "We hae been treated like royalty, Geoffrey," he said happily. "These people are truly wondrous hosts! Had I not the spur of knowin' ye and our cat were just below the horizon bearing here directly with every kerchief set, I well would have inclined to partake of the seductive lotus."

"I am informed this island is possessed of excellent sempstresses," Frost said to Magalhães, his tone one of statement rather than inquiry.

"*Sem dúvida*—without doubt," Magalhães responded. "Many of the great ladies of Portugal send here to have their garments stitched."

"I have employment for them," Frost said. He beckoned to Daniel O'Buck, who was tallying the empty water casks from *Audacity* being unladed on the quay. The giant black Newfoundland dog, George Three, that Whip Loring, gaoler of the American prisoners of war in Louisbourg, had attempted, but failed, to make as vicious as he, frolicked happily among the men unlading the casks.

Before Frost could speak to Daniel O'Buck, a great shout rang out: "Make way! Make a path there for a king's ship!"

Two sledges with iron runners piled high with water casks and pulled by sweating, staggering, swearing Royal Navy sailors heaved into view at the head of the quay. A squat, sun-blackened bosun's mate with an elaborate queue descending from beneath his round straw hat led the small procession. He plied an oar with great diligence to keep urchins at bay. A second bosun's mate with a starter rope dangling menacingly from his wrist brought up the rear. His eyes darted nervously from the sailors to the people crowding the quay. Nathaniel Dance detached himself from the *Audacity*'s men unshipping the mound of water casks from the launch and walked over to gawk at the spectacle of the *Vulture*'s men laboring to pull their vessel's water casks. He strayed a step too near the bosun's mate with the oar, and without warning the mate thrust the oar's blade viciously into Nathaniel's stomach.

"Teach ye to keep yere distance from true men off a king's ship," he spat as Nathaniel sprawled headfirst on the cobbles. Nathaniel stared up in bewilderment at the sneering bosun's mate, who spared him not a second glance and stalked away, oar clearing the path before *Vulture*'s watering crew. As any child of an age less than fourteen years would upon being so cruelly mistreated, Nathaniel Dance began to cry.

Then a snarling George leaped over a water cask and in two bounds was upon the bosun's mate, knocking him face downward to the cobbles. The bosun's mate's high, wailing scream of absolute terror was cut short as George seized the back of the man's neck in his powerful jaws.

"George! Halt!" Frost commanded. The great Newfoundland's jaws did not close, but neither did the jaws relax. The second bosun's mate trotted up, nervously twitching his starter rope, as if debating whether to strike George.

"You shall have completed the last of the three major mistakes in your life if you raise your arm," Frost said quickly. "The dog will bite through your mate's neck, and then be on you, tearing out your throat before you can deliver even one blow."

The man dropped his arm, and Frost strode over to pick up

the oar. He balanced the oar in both hands, then raised it aloft, held it for a long moment, and brought it through a short arc with all his strength behind it, the blade striking six inches from the bosun's mate's head. The oar shaft broke neatly in the middle. Frost kicked aside the broken oar blade. "The British Navy has issued defective oars to your vessel," he said mildly. "Better to learn of their defects ashore than in actual service at a time of need."

Frost clicked his tongue. "Give way slowly, George." George reluctantly opened his jaws, then seized the man's queue and backed away one step, rolling the bosun's mate onto his back. Frost stared down at the man in distaste. "You owe the lad an apology," Frost said.

"I don't owe nobody no apology," the bosun's mate said, his face heavily flushed, a cheek bruised from violent contact with a cobble. He attempted to scramble to his feet.

"Back away smartly, George," Frost commanded, and the dog responded, tumbling and pulling the man along the cobbles. "Faster, George," Frost urged, and the giant Newfoundland pulled even faster. All activity nearby had ceased and there was absolute silence on the quay. "Faster, George," Frost repeated.

The bosun's mate howled from the pain of his tormented hair. His hands fumbled above his head, attempting to grasp his queue. Frost struck the man's hands aside with the length of oar he held. "I apologize, I apologize," the man shouted, finally, through yelps of pain.

"Mister Dance, come here, if you please." Nathaniel dutifully walked over, still dabbling at his eyes with his kerchief, which had been advanced him by Frost. "Please help the gentleman to his feet," Frost said. "Cast off, George."

Nathaniel extended a hand. The bosun's mate sullenly ignored the outstretched hand and rolled to his feet on his own. He did not look at Nathaniel and made as if to walk toward the two sledges heaped with water casks. George growled, a low-pitched growl that grew in intensity as the dog stared unblinkingly at the man. The bosun's mate took a tentative half-step and George, still growling, crouched for a spring. "I apologize to ye, boy," the bosun's mate said quickly. "Acted hasty. Under strict orders to water quick as quick. Got a strict 'un for captain, sure." He glanced fearfully at the dog.

"Thank you, George," Frost said mildly, and George ceased growling, though his eyes remained fastened on the bosun's mate.

"Please carry on with your watering, Bosun," Frost invited.

The man walked hurriedly toward the two sledges and began shouting and cursing as he reached the watering party. The sailors picked up their tows, threw them over their shoulders, and leaned into the ropes. The sledges slowly began to move, sailors looking fearfully over their shoulders to see if the giant dog was following.

Frost strode over to Nathaniel and laid a calming hand on the youth's tense shoulder. "Mister O'Buck, detail whichever ship's gentleman you can the sooner find . . .," he glanced downward at Nathaniel, "and entrust him the task of seeing the water barrels properly filled. The water barrels must be well scoured with the finest sand, and the purity of the water determined before they are charged. It mayhap that the watering party of HM *Vulture*, appropriately named, could contest the fountain with us. In such case our people are to yield and patiently wait their turn to water, whatever the provocation, for there must be no violence between our respective crews on this land. On the launch's next return from our vessel, pray it begin fetching the bolts of cloth struck into our holds from *Zeus' Chariot*."

"Sir!" Nathaniel Dance said, wiping a sleeve across his nose to suppress a sniffle. "Thankee, and know ye now I shall never be made to cry by anyone in the British service."

"Well now, Mister Dance, between us two old files," Frost said affectionately, "it is never a shame when men with their full growth cry when the matter warrants. I have cried much betimes over mistakes made in my youth. Though silently, mind, or in the company of men likewise unafraid to cry, such as our incomparable Ming Tsun, or indeed, the fearsome

Mister Ferguson, though we go not about with our hearts pinned on our sleeves as a target for merriment or buffoons." He clapped the youth's shoulder awkwardly, but with true affection.

Frost dropped his hand and quickly turned to Struan Ferguson. "Struan, we shall have this island below the horizon this hour five days hence." He smiled at Ming Tsun, who hovered near with Frost's portable secretary. Ming Tsun rested the secretary on a handy baulk of wood, removed a square of paper from the recess beneath the hinged patten and wrote in ornate Portuguese calligraphy the brief message Frost dictated. Frost sanded the ink, folded the paper, sealed it with a wafer and his chop, and summoned a nearby barefooted urchin, one of many jousting for positions and clamoring to assist with the filling of the water casks for the few small coins they might earn. He handed the urchin the letter and an *escudo* coin with instructions to deliver the letter to the major-domo of the Capitão-General at the Palácio and await His Excellency's pleasure. Another *escudo* coin would be earned with the reply.

"It was most unfortunate this Britisher chose such an inauspicious time to touch here and tipple its water casks, Geoffrey . . ." Struan began, "bare hours after ye had entered this harbor."

"Joss. I shall return to our cat—to our *Audacity*—to refresh myself, then attend the Capitão-General to continue our conversations," Frost interrupted Struan Ferguson. Then to Daniel O'Buck: "Mister O'Buck, please make a place for Ming Tsun and me in the launch."

And again to Struan: "Five days you have, not one hour more, to complete this *Graciosa* for sea." Struan had begun the repairs to the nau; he could have the time to finish them.

"Five days shall be enough, Geoffrey, and I am overjoyed. This provides the time to attend the Lady Cygnet's operatic production. But Geoffrey," Struan said hesitantly, "this *Vulture . . .*"

Frost looked at Struan Ferguson and raised one eyebrow quizzically, again interrupting his second-in-command: "Pray, tell me, Struan, about this operatic production that sets you so a-fire."

Struan happily obliged. "To celebrate the *Graciosa*'s safe arrival at this harbor and to repay the generosity of the local peoples, La Cygnet is staging an opera with her troupe, one of the repertoire with which her company had been regaling the aristocracy of Brasil." Struan paused significantly. "Lady Cygnet, when she informed me some days ago of her plans to stage this opera, expressed the fervent desire that ye would arrive in time to be in attendance." Seeing Frost's scowl, Struan continued hurriedly. "It is an opera scored by some prodigy of a child whom the Lady Cygnet endearingly calls Amadé, and it is being presented to all the peoples of this island without charge of admission."

Frost had watched the urchin bearing his message to the Capitão-General out of sight as the child happily skipped away from the quay. He signed to Ming Tsun to accompany him and started toward the launch that Daniel O'Buck was just clearing of the last of the water casks. "Suffer the children to assist you, Daniel," Frost said quietly. "I mind these children likewise will seek to assist the British sloop in her watering. The wages we'll offer will be little enough for the work they'll perform."

"Geoffrey," Struan called after him, "it will be a prodigious spectacle, I assure you, it must be—with a title of *La Finta Semplice*."

Frost sourly translated the title: *The Pretended Simpleton*. He had a vague understanding of what opera was, had even attended several performances of *Kunqu* opera in Macao during one voyage when he was awaiting the Portuguese factors to assemble his cargo. But time was too precious for him to waste on something as frivolous as an opera staged by the imperious woman he had seen away a quarter of an hour before. Or was it?

"You must be aware, Struan," Frost said, somewhat unctuously, as he turned back to face his first officer, "that our goodly and sober American Congress has resolved to frown on such British macaronies and frivolities. Indeed, Congress enjoins us to take measures for the suppression of horse racing, cock fighting, gambling—and most particularly theatrical entertainments and routs. Such debaucheries are designed to promote dissipation, general depravity, and wholesale reduction of wholesome manners and principles. Indeed, our sainted Congress has held that any person holding an office under the United States so froward as to attend a theatrical, or even promote or encourage theatricals, shall be adjudged unworthy of holding such office. I can understand the dour and choleric puritans of New England being of such mind, but you wonder the fun-loving southerners did not dissent."

"Dismiss then now, Geoffrey, all yere thoughts of a political career," Struan said, equally unctuously, though quickly twigging the merriment in Frost's banter. "I am enlisting ye in the Lady Cygnet's theatrical, and I warrant ye shall have a rôle any man not afflicted with palsy or the weight of too many years upon his brow would deem close to the immortal."

Frost snorted in derision. "Mister Mate, I would fain your energies be directed toward readying this vessel for sea. I shall later share with you a marked aversion to returning directly to Portsmouth, and wish to explore another route perhaps more to your liking. However, if you are close to the Lady Cygnet at all, please request as a special favor her invitation of the *Vulture*'s commander and officers at this operatic performance." With that, Geoffrey Frost stepped into the launch, followed by a very wet George Three, who once solidly in the launch vigorously shook off the excess water, showering everyone in it. But no one complained, for all the crew loved the giant dog. They were lustily rowed out to *Audacity* by the launch's willing hands. Once away from the quay, Frost carefully explained to Ming Tsun, in sign language and low speech, all that he was expected to do.

III

THE SEPTEMBER DAY HAD BEEN EXTREMELY WARM FOR THE AÇORES, WIND-WASHED AS THE ISLANDS WERE, WITH THE SUN BURNING DOWN FROM the vault of a clear and cloudless sky, and the earth and its structures retained the heat until well after sunset. Backstage, behind the worn, salt-stained rumbowline canvas suspended from hastily assembled wooden latticework that served as the most makeshift of stage curtains and dressing room partitions, Frost sweltered in the trapped heat. For the fifth time in as many minutes he berated himself for having yielded, worn down by Struan Ferguson's exuberant insistence that he join the Lady Cygnet's operatic troupe's performance of *The Pretended Simpleton.* Frost had early on learned that there were only five "voices," as Cygnet called them—three women and two men—in the entire troupe to sing the seven rôles of the opera.

Frost's amused glance took in Struan Ferguson seated on a low stool behind the sailcloth partition that served as the men's dressing room. A large towel was draped over Struan's shoulders, and Darius Langdon was industriously sifting flour onto Struan's hair. Nathaniel Dance stood nearby, equally industriously brushing to raise the nap of an elaborate costume coat from the opera troupe's wardrobe that supposedly passed for the uniform of a sergeant in the Hungarian Army. Even more interesting to Frost was the fact that Struan had found the time to attend a rehearsal, though his task would merely be to move about the stage at certain moments and strike "elegant" poses while someone behind the stage actually sang the lines Struan was to mouth.

Frost peered from behind the stage curtains at the small temporary stage of some thirty feet's width, constructed, with the Capitão-General's enthusiastic approval, in the bullfighting ring on the hillside above the city. Struan had blithely assured him that Shakespeare's plays had been written for performance in the open air, so why not the opera of the child Amadé?

Frost knew that, of course, but wondered how Struan had come by his knowledge of Shakespeare, since Struan had long eschewed the slightest acquaintance with all things English. A Portuguese workman with a mallet and a mouthful of nails was just crawling from beneath the wooden staging, where he had been attending to the shorings. The workman paused to hammer a few nails into a cross-brace and an upright for good measure.

Frost fretted that he was not already two days at sea, but he had no choice but to be amenable to the Capitão-General's demands, couched in their flowery Portuguese as polite requests. Given Struan Ferguson's excellent supervision of repairs to the *Graciosa* nau, Frost was excused the duty of escorting *Graciosa* the thousand-odd sea miles to the approaches to the Rio Tejo and Lisboa. In any event, any obligation of escort had also been lifted by the unexpected arrival of HM *Vulture*, since it was foredestined that the American privateer and the British warship must fight each other. Capitão-General Moniz was adamant that the engagement would have to take place well offshore any of the islands of the Açores archipelago, and even if successful in besting Heflin Wolstenhulme and his *Vulture*, Frost would not be welcome to repair his inevitable battle damage in this territory of Portugal.

The Capitão-General's expression plainly conveyed his belief that Frost's vessel, though of similar size and weight of metal, would prove no match for the hardened professional crew of HM *Vulture*. It would be up to the vessels' commanders to arrange between them the timing of their departures from Angra and appointing of the ground for engagement. Lastly, evidently seeing it as the removal of an extreme embarrassment to the Portuguese king, Capitão-General Moniz, after exacting Frost's pledge that the American pirates would be tried in an American court, permitted Frost to depart with the remnants of the crew of *Zeus' Chariot*. Otherwise, the pirates would provide lengthy employment for the hangman and entertainment for the local populace even more interesting than the Lady Cygnet's opera.

Frost's promise to the Portuguese authorities meant that he would not be able to land the American pirates upon any neutral shore, as he had earlier promised the men to enlist their assistance in bringing the *Graciosa* through the hurricane. So the pitiful remnants of the crew Gaunt Hutson had recruited would go back to New Hampshire to stand trial for piracy there. Frost collected that the pirates would vastly prefer the uncertainties of criminal trials in the infant United States to the absolute certainties of the Portuguese hangman.

He had not yet told the pirates of their changed fates; better to permit them to contemplate the enormity of their sins until it was time to march them from their cells down to the quay to be embarked. Frost had not yet decided if he could trust the condemned American pirates enough to enlist them for the return voyage, or if he should clap them in chains straightaway. But Geoffrey Frost had seen all the men in shackles he cared to see, and of course there was this matter of HM *Vulture* to settle.

Like almost everyone in Angra—indeed, the entire island of Terceira—Capitão-General Moniz was quite intrigued by the Lady Cygnet and wanted to see La Cygnet's opera. The seats in the boxes on the other side of the bull ring were filling quickly with spectators of substance. The crude benches arranged in dense semicircular rows on the sable colored sand of the bull ring were filling with the common folk. There were several dozen hands from *Audacity*, mostly from Bosun Herbert Collingwood's watch, proudly if somewhat stiffly togged

out in their pantaloons and short jackets of heavy blue linen and blue and white striped shirts of a lighter linen.

The sewing of these quasi-uniforms for his entire crew had occupied every sempstress on the island for the past week. The infusion of hard coin at premium pay into the local economy had much endeared *Audacity* and her men to the merchants of Angra. Virtually all of *Audacity*'s men were accompanied by gaily dressed young women who looked as if they had been rented for the evening—which, Frost acknowledged, was indeed the case.

Under other circumstances Frost would have been hesitant to grant such liberal shore leave, but he could depend upon every man who had ciphered to the penny his share of prize money to be paid in Portsmouth being aboard *Audacity* when she weighed anchor. Prominent in the seats closest to the stage was carpenter's mate Quentin Fowle, with not one but two women, beauties the both of them. It was obvious that the carpenter's mate had not a thought to spare for his poor widowed mother back in Portsmouth.

Struan Ferguson, opulently rigged in his borrowed finery, strutted up to Frost and made a handsome leg and bow. "I trust ye still recognize yere first officer, I am a valet of Captain Fracasso only for this evening."

"I liked my first officer better with sawdust in his hair," Frost replied, attempting to repress his caricature of a grin. He had just caught sight of Master and Commander Heflin Wolstenhulme, Royal Navy, and a retinue of *Vulture*'s officers completely appropriating a loge, the next best to the loge already occupied by the Capitão-General and the Commandant of the harbor forts and their ladies. The group of officers was quite boisterous, and they were accompanied by an equal number of equally boisterous women rented for the evening. Frost scanned the audience for members of the *Vulture*'s crew, though he much doubted that the sloop's commander would have wanted his crew anywhere but aboard his vessel, ready to put to sea on the instant.

"Yes," Struan agreed, "the lads put more flour on me than

it would take Cook Barnes to bake a loaf." A streak of perspiration had already created a rivulet of damp flour on Struan's forehead.

Frost heard people stirring on the other side of the curtains; he peered out again to see two young boys with tapers lighting the candles in the footlights. The small orchestra of the opera troupe, each musician dressed in somber black and seated immediately in front of the stage, took this as the cue to begin tuning instruments. There appeared no more seats to be had, but late arrivals were still crowding into the spectators' boxes and along the circular inner wall of the bull ring.

There was a bustle and stir from the direction of the sailcloth draped to provide the tiny women's dressing room in the extreme rear of the backstage area. Two women, extravagantly dressed, elaborate powdered coiffures towering above their heads, exotic plumes sprouting from their hair, bright dresses of multicolored silk with numerous petticoats, held out sideways from their bodies below their thin bosoms by some interior devices with which Geoffrey Frost, entirely unaccustomed to women's fashions, was certainly not acquainted, bobbed around the backdrop of a garden painted and varnished on heavy canvas, cracked and crazed from much handling when seen up close. Frost was reminded of animated hand bells, the women's skirts the bells and their slim bosoms and heads, piled high with hair he suspected was not their own, the handles.

Behind the two women, walking in a stately, measured tread, came Neville Maria de' Medici e Montelone e Wryley-Birch, in equally elaborate costume, but her bosom was crossed with a broad black sash. She bore a fiddle case in her arms, and Frost reflected that she was truly as graceful as her stage name, a young swan.

"The woman in the red and white dress is Leocadia Montjoy. Her stage name is Cebôné," Struan whispered somewhat too loudly for Frost's liking. "She is a Creole with a divine voice who will be singin' the rôle of Giacinta. The woman, barely more than a girl, in the green and white dress is Priscilla

Thresher. She is too young yet for her voice to have steadied or to have acquired a stage name, but she sings a very creditable soprano as Ninetta."

Frost, his eyes fastened intently on Cygnet, did not even try to think of a proper retort. He knew, he absolutely knew, that with the exception of his mother, Thérèse, as he envisioned her in the full bloom of her youth and innocence, no more beautiful woman had ever walked the planet. "And what rôle does this woman sing?" he asked, with unaccustomed hoarseness in his voice.

"Rosina, the sister of Captain Fracasso; she is a baroness from some great empire on the Continent," Struan said learnedly. "A soprano also; all the rôles the young Amadé wrote for the women of this comedy are for the soprano voice. Most heavenly of voices, I assure ye. The ladies of the troupe are unanimous that La Cygnet is destined to be a great diva."

Frost, reflecting that Struan's perceptions were based upon one very hurried rehearsal, and that Struan's knowledge of opera was exceedingly superficial, nevertheless did not challenge his first officer's opinion but followed Cygnet with his beguiled eyes as she continued her stately walk to the center stage curtains. The two women preceding Cygnet drew aside the sailcloth curtains sufficiently for Cygnet to pass. As soon as she walked through the parted curtains, the small orchestra, which had ceased fidgeting and tuning, launched into a funereal air.

Frost, never having heard a European orchestra, immediately found the music discordant. The noisy murmurings of the audience quieted at the first strophe. Cygnet walked to the edge of the stage, went down on one knee, her dress standing our from her like some great, lovely water lily, and reverently handed the fiddle case to a musician who rose from his seat.

"That's Cavaletti, the concert master," Struan whispered. "He's taken over as the orchestra leader for the murdered Signore Beretta. Not nearly as good a fiddle, I ken, though the people of this island shan't know the difference."

Signore Cavaletti equally reverently removed the violin

from its case and held it aloft before the members of the orchestra, then returned the violin to its case and laid it on the stage immediately in front of the orchestra. Cygnet unclasped the black mourning sash she wore and handed it down to Signore Cavaletti, who folded it reverently atop the violin case. Cygnet rose to her feet and made a deep bow to the audience. Frost thought he had rarely seen such genuine pathos. The Lady Cygnet was presenting a far different, much more compassionate, face than the face she had initially presented to Frost when he rescued her from the would-be rapist and American pirate, Reedy Stalker, aboard the *Graciosa* nau.

"Well, I am on stage in the first scene, Geoffrey, and must ready myself," Struan Ferguson said, already walking toward his place with Ninetta and Giacinta, and a young man made up in a uniform even more garish that Struan's own in front of the painted backdrop of a garden. The violins of the small orchestra began to saw away in what was to Frost's ear nothing more than vigorous cacophony, and he remarked to himself with some amusement that Struan had not bothered to name the male singer. Frost sat down on a low three-legged stool given stability and balance by virtue of the fact that its three legs could accommodate a shortened leg admirably, next to the wooden tub recently filled with fresh water and the large sodden square of buff-colored nankeen cloth folded on another stool.

Frost shook his head ruefully, though he begrudged not the time, for Struan had always thought only of his ship and crew. Where had his first officer found the few hours to learn what little he knew about opera, and with such zest? He laughed inwardly as he regarded the water tub and heavy cloth. What was it Struan had said earlier? Frost would have a rôle "any man not afflicted with palsy would deem close to the immortal?"

His rôle was that of the wet blanket, a person scrupulously kept out of the audience's sight, whose only duty was to rush onto the stage and smother nascent flames if a performer's costume, perish the thought, caught fire from coming too close to a footlight's candle. An ignominious, insignificant rôle, and Frost ridiculed himself for being persuaded by Struan's earnestness to take it. But take it he had, and he knew very well the why of it. He pulled his kerchief from a pocket of his tunic, dampened it in the tub of tepid water, and mopped his brow.

The fiddles, and then the horns, were very loud and very discordant to Frost's ear, quite unlike the gentle flutes, muted bamboo pipes, clappers and drums, and soft voices of *Kunqu* opera. Frost was very far from being an expert or devotee of *Kunqu*, having attended only two operas in Macao, but he had appreciated the minimalism of the subdued orchestral accompaniment, balanced against the allusive, ornate singing. He was quite put off by the strident crescendos of the fiddles and the high voices of the women here—sopranos, he supposed, grated shrilly upon his nerves. To Frost the instruments and singing were as cacophonous as the dissonance of a pod of humpback whales that kept the old *Salmon* company for three days on one return voyage from China. "I fancy I understood the whales better than this trilling of Amadé."

Frost concentrated upon translating the Italian libretto, then focused upon how well Struan Ferguson mouthed the words that some man behind the painted backdrop was singing in a deep bass voice. The matching of mouth with aria and recitative was quite poor, but peering around the curtain into the audience, Frost could see that the spectators did not care, perhaps did not even notice. In any event, the young man singing Fracasso's rôle was doing a creditable job of covering Struan's exuberant errors. It was evident that Struan was enjoying himself hugely. At the end of the first scene there was even a brief aria that he mouthed through bravely enough before stomping off the stage.

"*Troppa briga a prender moglie, troppa briga in verità . . .*" Frost translated the words: "It's asking for trouble to take a wife, too much trouble, for sure . . ."

Frost kept track of the various scenes, awaiting the time that Cygnet would appear. There was a scenery change; rather, the curtains were drawn and another painted backdrop—this one of a room in a house—was pulled down and the previous backdrop rolled up while the heavily perspiring actors stood in their wilting clothes and fanned themselves.

Then the curtains parted to reveal Cygnet and the woman singing the rôle of Ninetta. By now Frost's ear had fairly attuned to the Italian words, and the words Cygnet sung in prosody were exceedingly poignant. "*Colla bocca, e non col core, tutti sanno innamorar*—Anyone can declare love with his lips, but not his heart; but let him who seeks constancy and love come and learn from me . . ." Frost smiled, for he was beginning to understand how the comedy was contrasting the stupidity and inanity of one faction of characters against the resourceful improvisation of the other faction. Cygnet's voice was lyrical and loud, though not overbearingly so. Above all, her singing voice was clarity itself. Even at the distance of thirty feet Frost saw the animation in her eyes, matching the color of the amethyst flowers of the *hortênsia*, and he knew Cygnet enjoyed singing and her rôle.

Frost smiled as he recalled the emphasis in *Kunqu* on elaborate, almost caricatured makeup, costume, and stylized, ritualistic, predictable and exaggerated movements. He reflected upon the irony that, while *Kunqu* opera featured strong female rôles, women did not play them. Indeed, the Chinese culture with which Frost was familiar considered a woman willing to parade herself on a stage as equivalent to a harlot. So in *Kunqu* opera female impersonators played the rôles of women.

Another male actor was on stage now, exchanging recitatives with the actor playing the rôle of Fracasso, and Frost recognized the voice as the backstage voice that had been singing Struan's rôle. As the actors strutted and pirouetted near him, Frost realized that the costumes were worn and shiny from much use; there were small, discrete patches and skillfully joined tears. But their voices were young, robust, and enthusiastic. Frost rose from his stool to peer through a rent in the sailcloth drapes. He doubted if anyone in the audience understood a word of what was being sung, certainly not the men from his crew, but the people in the audience were evidently twigging the substance of the comedy through the actors' pantomime, and their enjoyment was rapt and palpable. Frost surmised that no one on Terceira Island had ever experienced such a spectacle. And though the music was still strange and jarring to his ears, Frost was beginning to understand some of the word paintings in the music and the singing. At first he found that perplexing, but then he gave himself over to the increasing enjoyment of the singing voices and the music, as harsh as the unfamiliar instruments were to his ear.

Act One concluded; the actors on stage, who had been fanning themselves vigorously, retired to the dressing rooms to refresh themselves. Large candelabras scattered about the bullfighting ring and in the spectators' boxes were lighted, and the candles in the footlights were extinguished. The people in the audience moved about, some to visit the necessaries outside the ring, others to purchase meat pies, sausages, cups of wine and juices. Nathaniel Dance hoisted himself upon the stage near where Frost stood, flexing his arms and legs to expel the kinks and soreness from sitting long in one position. Darius Langdon handed up a towel-swathed bundle that Nathaniel unwrapped, producing a small teapot and a cup.

"Cook Barnes sent this to ye, Capt'n, thinkin' ye'd be needin' some refreshment by now."

"Thank you, Mister Dance," Frost said kindly, knowing that the lad had run all the way to the bull ring from the galley aboard *Audacity* to ensure that the tea would be hot enough for Frost's liking. "I have this entire butt of water for refreshment. Seek out the serving lady named Amber; the women of the troupe probably stand in greater need of refreshment than I do." Frost kept his eyes scanning the crowd, looking for Ming Tsun.

Young Nathaniel hurried away and returned scarce a minute later with the teapot and cup. "The tea all be drunk, Capt'n, and the ladies beg some water."

Frost frowned at the interruption, for he had been calculating how much time, given that the prevailing winds in

September would blow primarily from the northeast, it would take for *Audacity* to transit the Bay of Biscay if he stood twenty leagues offshore upon crossing the latitude of Cape Finisterre.

"Replenish the pot from this water butt, by all means, Mister Dance, and seek some other containers for water. Someone was remiss if water was not provided, for as you ken this business of singing is hot work." Frost retreated to his mental study, summoning all the facts he could recall about navigating the East Indiaman *Olney*, with its captain dead, senior officers either dead or near enough to death to be worthless to the ship, crew so ravaged by scurvy that fewer than twenty men were capable of dragging themselves aloft to handle sails during the Bay's crossing. How long ago? Fourteen years? And what were the chances of encountering another hurricane or tropical storm in late September?

He well remembered the squall that had blown up suddenly just as *Olney* rounded the Brittany peninsula, and the fact that his ship had not been driven onto the rocks of Île d'Ouessant was due entirely to Providence and not Frost's ship-handling skills. That same Providence had allowed a grateful Frost to bear *Olney* away westward for searoom.

Frost absorbed himself into that harrowing voyage fourteen years to the month before that had so vividly marked his transition from youth to manhood, recalling the wind directions, the sea states, the tides. He could expect a wearying beat to windward until *Audacity* was fair into the Channel . . .

"So, my dear sir, according to the dictates of the crafty old Portugee ruling these parts, we are left to our devices in setting the challenge." Startled, Frost looked down into the smirking face of the short, swarthy, bandy-legged Heflin Wolstenhulme, Master and Commander of HM *Vulture*, stock unloosed and weskit unbuttoned, standing at the margin of the stage, one hand clutching a brass-headed blackthorn walking cane, the other clutching a pewter mug. While Wolstenhulme stared up triumphantly at Frost, a slight Portuguese lad appeared at Wolstenhulme's side and unobtrusively refilled the pewter mug.

"My dear sir," Frost said, kneeling on the rough planks of the stage to bring his face more or less close to that of Heflin Wolstenhulme's, "it is my intention to sail on the morrow's high tide, which, I'm reliably informed, will occur in mid-morning."

Heflin Wolstenhulme threw back his head and laughed raucously. He waved one arm expansively. "As you can see, sir, British arms prevail here. I wish it lay within my power to offer terms, for you have a lovely sloop, lately taken by some treacherous rebel guile from the Royal Navy. Indeed, I do not look forward to knocking it into kindling. But it is that fact, I fear, that mitigates any show of compassion. I must have your submission first, and then we may debate the finer points of providing for the needs of prisoners of war."

"I assure you, sir," Frost said, feeling his anger rise but keeping it well in check, "I am well acquainted with the manner in which the British government provides for the needs of prisoners of war." He rose to his feet. "You may wish to return to your loge, sir. The second act commences."

Frost found himself face to face with a horrified Struan Ferguson. "Ye have told him yere sailin' plan even I dinna know," Struan said in wonderment and disbelief. Frost shrugged and looked toward the audience, where he glimpsed Ming Tsun in the company of João Magalhães and several Portuguese boys. Each boy carried a large flagon, and they were plying the *Vulture*'s officers liberally with the flagons' contents. Frost knew that given their arrogance as Englishmen and officers of the Royal Navy, neither Master and Commander Wolstenhulme nor any of his officers questioned the fact that wine was being provided to them gratis, while the other spectators were purchasing their own food and drink. He shrugged again.

Attendants, young boys, were relighting the candles in the footlights, and others were extinguishing the candelabras. Singers were rushing to their places—two people, Struan and the woman playing the rôle of a chambermaid. Frost barely repressed a laugh at Struan's appearance. His first officer had perspired so much that his flour-laced hair resembled nothing more than a lump of dough before Cook Barnes began kneading it with his one good hand and a large paddle threaded into the wooden cuff strapped to his left forearm rather than the cuff's usual hook. The young attendants were preparing to walk back the main curtains.

When the curtains parted to reveal a balcony painted on the backdrop, Struan Ferguson was on stage with the young woman singing the rôle of Ninetta. Who was Ninetta? Frost frowned: this comedy was exceedingly difficult to follow. What had been the name of the second *Kunqu* opera he had seen in Macao? Yes, he had it: *Dragon Trapping Net.* That plot had been no more outlandish than the plot of this *Pretended Simpleton.* As best as Frost had understood the *Kunqu* opera, and he had attended only at Ming Tsun's insistence, some magical net had existed that could capture and subdue dragons only as long as the possessor of the net was virtuous. There had to have been a lot more substance to the *Kunqu* opera than that, Frost had fathomed. And there undoubtedly was more substance to this *Pretended Simpleton*, but he much preferred to ponder upon the many unknowns and intricate variables he would encounter in crossing the Bay of Biscay.

Frost paid scant attention to the singers except to note that the heat was exceedingly wearing upon them. Twice during the second act he surreptitiously peered through a rent in the sailcloth curtain to gauge the mood of Captain Heflin Wolstenhulme. HM *Vulture*'s Master and Commander could certainly put away prodigious quantities of wine, as could his coterie of officers, for the industrious youths with their flagons were constantly in attendance.

By the end of the second act and the beginning of the third, Frost could discern that the copious alcohol was having some effect on the Royal Navy officers. A much larger kettle of tea and a variety of cups in proper saucers had appeared, courtesy of Cook Barnes and Nathaniel Dance, to revive the flagging singers. The women drank the beverage thirstily and gratefully, but the bass singing the rôle of Cassandro, whom from the libretto Frost had pegged as an exceedingly foolish character, jumped down from the stage and went in search of something stronger. He found a shower of wine poured down upon him from the loge occupied by the officers of HM *Vulture*. Gratefully he caught up a cup and fought his way through the crowd to regain the stage.

Frost was extremely grateful when the final scene of Act Three tediously arrived. He judged the audience, fatigued by the heat, was as grateful the opera was coming to a close. All seven actors, the four men and the three women, were on stage now, all singing lustily, except of course Struan Ferguson. But his lack of voice or knowledge of Italian did not in any manner diminish his enthusiasm for his rôle as the servant of a Hungarian Army officer incongruously displaced on garrison duty in northern Italy. However, Frost twigged that Struan Ferguson was likewise fiercely glad the performance was coming to an end.

The singers' voices reached a crescendo: "*É inutile adesso, di far più lamenti, già squeste del sesso son l' arti innocenti* . . . It's useless now to lament any further. The arts of innocence are those of the fair sex . . ." The two obviously fatigued youths who had been tugging the curtains opened and closed, equally glad that the performance was concluding, trotted the curtains closed, then opened them again to permit the performers to advance to the footlights to acknowledge the applause of an audience delighted by the performance—and also, perhaps, by its conclusion.

Frost was looking at the loge occupied by the officers from HM *Vulture* and was gratified beyond measure to see two of the junior officers, disheveled, blue coats and white weskits torn open and askew, jaws set in fierce concentration, tearing away from their seats, completely heedless of their uniform regalia or their dignity. He permitted himself a slight smile—only to have it torn away by the anguished shriek of a woman in mortal terror.

The woman singing the rôle of Ninetta, in making a deeply elaborate bow, had inadvertently flounced her dress too near a footlight, and the candle had fired the filmy muslin of her petticoats and then the silk and taffeta of her gown. In her terrified turning away from the footlights the woman's gown instantly fired the gossamer train of Cygnet's costume. The fabrics of the dresses were dry as tinder, and they flared like torches of fat New Hampshire pine-knots. Frost bolted off his stool, unfolding the heavy, water-sodden blanket of nankeen cloth as he ran and noticing with curious detachment that the bass singer had leaped off the stage and was futilely attempting to push a way through the confused throng.

The performers were running every which way on the stage. Frost tripped Ninetta with a foot as she tried to run past him, and threw the blanket atop the flakes of fire leaping from her skirt. "Struan," Frost shouted, knowing that the remaining male members of the opera troupe would be far less useful than tits on a boar hog, "extinguish this fire!" He left the blanket on Ninetta and pursued Cygnet, who had fallen off the stage, gotten to her feet, and was in the midst of spectators in the center of the bull ring. Horrified, they shrank away hurriedly before her, and Cygnet's panicked flight fanned the flames that had already consumed the greater portion of her costume. Then she stumbled against a bench, overturning one of the large candelabra and spilling its candles but permitting Frost to catch up to her. He threw her down onto the sand, his body stretching over hers and whipped furiously at the flaming cloth with both hands, blistering his palms.

Frost shrugged away the scalding pain, then cried out involuntarily as his own tunic smoldered and caught fire. A handful of sand scooped up from the ring smothered that nascent flame, but not before a tendril of fire seared his right cheek. With one arm he pressed Cygnet's body to his, so tightly he was fearful he might crush the life from her, while with the other hand he scooped up more sand to pile atop her wrecked garment. The last of the flames smoldered and went out, and Cygnet ceased struggling. Frost could feel her heart beating against his, and with a start and then acute embarrassment he became aware that Cygnet now wore no clothing above her waist.

"Back away, back away!" Frost heard Struan Ferguson crying, and then the water-soaked blanket fell over both Frost and Cygnet. Several of the spectators had picked up the candles that had not been extinguished by the fall from the candelabra and were pressing around them. Frost recognized Quentin Fowle among the onlookers.

"Fowle!" Frost shouted, "Trouble one of your lady friends for her shawl!" A shawl was quickly produced; Frost seized it and thrust the shawl into Cygnet's hand. "Madame . . . Cygnet . . . , please cover yourself with this shawl before the blanket is lifted." He scuttled from beneath the blanket and waited for a few seconds until Cygnet nodded, then pulled away the blanket and helped Cygnet sit up. Her clothing, what was left of it, was charred tatters, and her face, wearing a look of wonderment, was thoroughly smudged and blackened with soot.

Cygnet tightened the shawl around her shoulders as her maid, Amber, ran up, only to collapse in an anxious heap on the sand beside her. "Lady, Lady, are you unhurt?"

"Yes," Cygnet said slowly, looking up directly at Frost, "I am unhurt."

Frost started to get to his feet, and Struan's warning shout gave him the time he needed to reach up and catch the blackthorn walking cane, but not before it whistled down upon his right shoulder. He grimaced with the pain that arresting the cane caused his seared palm. He jerked the cane and Wolstenhulme, awkward and overbalanced, sprawled headfirst on the sand beside him. "You rebel bastard, you have killed me," Wolstenhulme said, his words so slurred Frost had difficulty understanding the Master and Commander of HM *Vulture*. The man's shoulders heaved as he puked, and Frost was aware of a foul and most disagreeable odor. The man had soiled his breeches. Wolstenhulme struck out with his arms, found Cygnet's ankle, fastened upon it and drunkenly attempted to pull himself across the sand toward the woman.

Cygnet, eyes dilated wildly and face flushed with incandescent fury and rage, kicked sand in Heflin Wolstenhulme's face as Frost stepped on the British officer's offending arm.

"*Rodomonte!*" Cygnet hissed, kicking the man in the elbow for good measure.

Frost pulled Cygnet erect. "Your mistress must be conducted to her lodgings straight away," he said to Amber. "Struan, please organize some conveyance for the Lady Cygnet and her maid, then shift from that mad costume into clothing more appropriate for a right seaman and prepare our *Audacity* for departure. Designate Quentin Fowle to pass the word to the crewmen here tonight to join our ship. I believe you know our sailing time." His eyes fell on Nathaniel Dance and Darius Langdon, who stood, mouths agape. "Gentlemen, you may summon a carriage for us, for we must be a-ship as fast as ever we can."

"*O que é isto?! O que se passa?! Porque foi que este homem te agrediu?*" A grim-faced Capitão-General Moniz was shouting as he and an aide strode toward the group around Frost, the spectators in the bull ring moving respectfully out of his way.

"You rebel bastard, you have killed me by trickery," Heflin Wolstenhulme gasped again, hoarsely. "It was in the drink."

"Capitão-General Moniz," Frost responded in Portuguese, "*Espero que tenha apreciado a exibicão. Penso ter sido uma verdadeira ópera, salvo pelo final completamente inesperado. Toda a populacão de Angra deveria aplaudir o grupo que ofereceu táo edificante espectáculo.*" He finished in English for Cygnet's benefit. "Faith, I am persuaded that neither Boiardo nor Ariosto could have fashioned such an ending."

The Capitão-General reached the group and stared down at Heflin Wolstenhulme. "*Este homem está embriagado! Além disso deu-lhe uma cacetada com a bengala quando estava de costas. É tão cobarde quanto bêbado!*" The Capitão-General remembered his manners and doffed his hat to bow, but it was toward La Cygnet's back as Amber hurried her away. "*Senhora . . .*"

"*Un grazie di cuore,*" Cygnet said over her shoulder, but not stopping, though she half-turned. Frost did not know if the words were meant for him or for the Capitão-General.

Moniz clapped his hat atop his wig. "*Em nome de sua*

magestade, apresento as minhas profundas desculpas, Senhor Frost. Em minha opinião os vossos navios podem guerrear-se, mas não era de esperar nem de prever que ele o atacasse de forma tão cobarde. Envergonha o seu país e o acordo de amizade que liga á séculos Portugal e a Inglaterra."

Frost shrugged as Ming Tsun bustled up with a flagon of olive oil and strips of muslin. Ming Tsun soaked oil onto a piece of cloth and gently bathed Frost's palms. The pain caused Frost to answer Moniz in English rather than Portuguese. "I intend to be away on the mid-morning tide, *senhor*, though I much doubt that Captain Wolstenhulme shall be in any position to direct his vessel."

"*De facto não o fará! Pelo seu imperdoável insulto a sua magestade, ficará confidado a uma cela da prisão pelo menos até dois dias após a vossa partida,*" Moniz said grimly.

Frost's face broke into his caricature of a smile. "Since I shall be taking the American pirates with me to be tried for their crimes committed at sea, mayhap you shall have a cell or two available."

"*Chama a Guarda Civil! Estes oficiais Britânicos . . .*" Moniz spoke the words with distaste, "*todos eles serão levados para a prisão de São João Baptista, e ficarão cativos até pagarem pela afronta ao nosso Rei.*" Moniz bowed to Frost, turned to walk away, but paused momentarily: "*Sim, foi um espectáculo extremamente interessante.*"

A *guarda civil* brought up the two junior officers from HM *Vulture* whom Frost had earlier seen fleeing toward the necessaries. They were clearly very uncomfortable, pale and wan and shifting uneasily in their disheveled, liquor-stained uniforms, breeches still unbuttoned. The other officers from *Vulture* were being escorted from the loge they had occupied.

"Gentlemen," Frost said formally, "your captain was observed to be suffering from extreme choler and remittent fever, unhealthy afflictions and easily communicable, for which a strong cathartic is the only specific. Your captain was purged, as were all who partook so liberally of the local wine, with calomel and jalap introduced. You also imbibed a mild camphorated tincture of opium. The purgation has been successful, you will agree, and all of you shall arise tomorrow greatly refreshed."

Frost favored the darkly threatening British officers with a brief smile and a slight bow. Ming Tsun had finished bandaging his blistered palms and had dabbed olive oil on his seared cheek. Frost heard a chaise draw up to the entrance to the bull ring and Darius' voice calling. It was time to be away, for there was much, much to be done to prepare *Audacity*'s departure. He momentarily gauged the time it would take to seek out the Lady Cygnet to say a more formal farewell—no, the lady would doubtlessly be indisposed. He thought briefly of telling HM *Vulture*'s officers that the white, virtually tasteless laxative powder of chloride of mercury, calomel, had also been introduced into all the water casks brought ashore to Angra for replenishing, but thought better of it. Doubtlessly the officers and crew of HM *Vulture* would discover that fact for themselves in due course.

IV

AFTER A REMARKABLY FAST RUN OF EIGHT DAYS OUT OF THE AÇORES, *AUDACITY* STOOD IN TOWARD THE ENGLISH COAST, MOVING SLOWLY westward, following the sun that had gone down in a murky, foggy overcast that somewhat surprisingly left the sky directly overhead brilliantly visible, ghosting in quietly from her sanctuary abroad in the heavily trafficked North Sea. She had the last two days masqueraded as a Royal Navy sloop-o-war awaiting her convoy of merchant shipping bringing naval stores from the Baltic, and had been virtually invisible. *Audacity* sailed out of a small but violent storm that had ceased some fifteen minutes ago but had regaled her crew with a vigorous display of the ethereal and wondrously beautiful Saint Elmo's fire, flickering and dancing from her mast tops to her bowsprit. Saint Elmo's fire eternally threatened to consume all the timber, cordage and sailcloth it touched, but eternally never did so.

Geoffrey Frost, a copy of the Royal Navy's coastal pilotage for the northeast coasts, Firth of Forth to the Humber River, beneath his arm, had his vessel laid on a very slight starboard tack into the breeze from landward. Two men were posted aloft in the foremast crosstrees with instructions to search with especial care for any indications of sandbanks just below the sea's surface, though they were still far from the shore. The light airs residual from the brief storm along the fifty-fifth parallel would see the *Audacity* fair into Tynemouth, toward whose lights, dimly visible in the light fog, *Audacity*'s gently heaving bowsprit now pointed directly. He could smell the land, and it was malodorous this approach into a river that was also a sewer, draining the ordure of thousands of people living cheek-to-jowl in squalor. Two leagues off the coast, the water was discolored with the suspension of brownish silt washed seaward by the recently ended storm, and awash with garbage. A ruined farmer's basket spilling potato and turnip peelings floated past, the contents raucously fought over by screaming gulls. A drowned cat, the tripes cast out by a slaughterhouse. And over all, the noxious odor of coal smoke that not even the abundant rains from the recent storm could scrub from the air. Mercifully, the polluted sea was soon left in *Audacity*'s wake, though the air still prickled the nostrils.

The coastal pilotage was part of the extensive inventory of charts and navigation instructions aboard ex-*Jaguar* bequeathed by the late Captain Hugh Stuart, for which Frost was exceedingly grateful. The shape of the land was becoming lost in the darkness, and to the west and south the lights of Sunderland at the mouth of the smaller River Wear began to materialize faintly. "The ancient Gauls anchored the eastern end of Hadrian's Wall at a fortified place known as Wallsend on the River Tyne," Frost said in a low, conversational tone to Struan Ferguson, who was standing beside him on his quarterdeck. Struan bore his targe on his right shoulder; his two Andrew Strachan all-metal pistols were thrust into a heavy leather belt; and his hands were crossed on the hilt of the heavy backsword, his father's legacy by way of his murdered, martyred sister. "From two hundred years prior to the birth of Christ, the Gauls patrolled the wall running all the way to the Firth of Solway in the west and emptying into the Irish Sea, defending their empire from the barbarians to the north." Frost regarded Struan archly. "Your untamed ancestors, belike."

Struan's face broke into a lupine grin. "It be twenty years after Culloden, Geoffrey, twenty years a-waitin' to avenge me da. It was inspiration most divine that directed ye here."

"The Divine takes no pride, indeed, has no hand in and assiduously avoids bloodletting, throwing up His hands in proper horror, Struan," Frost remonstrated mildly. "Inspiration had no hand in it, only the example of James Cook in his Whitby-built collier *Resolution*. With all George Three's warships not relegated to guard duty and stranded in harbor on their reefs of beef-bones a-fleet in the Western Atlantic on convoy duty, it was an easy deduction that no Royal Navy vessel of any consequence would hinder us here on England's northeast coast in her home waters."

Struan grunted something that Frost took to mean his ancestors were not barbarians and regarded Hadrian's Wall as keeping the envious hordes in the south from advancing too far into the Cheviot Hills and the Southern Uplands.

"We have no need to venture as far as Segedunum," Frost said quietly. An earlier ascent to the mainmast crosstrees with his best telescope, before the fog obscuring the water's surface had thickened, confirmed what the small coastal lugger, most likely trading in contraband spirits with some quiet, out-of-the-way port in the Low Countries, which they had spoken three leagues off Whitby, had averred: well over one hundred colliers filled to bursting with Wallsend household coal were holding in anchorages inside the estuary of the River Tyne.

"Serves them right," Struan snorted, "the locals, I mean. When the Gauls returned to their more moderate native climes of the Mediterranean, the locals invited Saxons and Angles from Germania and Denmark to protect them from my peace-loving Pict forebears. These invited mercenaries subjugated the locals, makin' them into fiefdoms, first called Bernica, then Northumbria." He snorted with disdain again. "A right lot of royalists they were, and are today. The Jacobites bypassed Newcastle, since 'twas well known Newcastle favored the Hanoverians. 'Twas said that Newcastle and all the area surrounding were 'for George,' and ever since these people have been known as Geordies. Now, twenty years after Culloden, the Geordies will have their turn under the sword."

"Enough, Struan!" Frost warned tersely. "Your party goes

ashore to destroy the mines' workings to the extent two hours will permit. Be not blinded as was Samson with such zeal to demolish the enemy's temple that you likewise perish. I shall see to the firing of as many colliers as that self-same two hours will encompass. The tide outflows at one hour past midnight. We must be back aboard and well away from all the cry and hue this venture will send up."

"Aye," Struan acknowledged, grudgingly. "I hae no stomach nor illusions for the slog to the safety of the Grampians so many leagues north, so never ye fear that I shall miss the tide. Though ye'll ken the ruckus we'll set up will be like that of yere self-same Samson when he caught the foxes and sent them with firebrands twisted in their tails into the Philistines' corn. It be sure to bring out every guard ship to our south than can spread the barest hank of canvas to meet us in the lower channel."

Frost said nothing, but he had absolutely no intention of bearing away south after his raid on the collieries and their transports, so vital to the wellbeing of England and her industries. "Mister Rawbone," he said to his master gunner, in a voice louder than he would use for normal conversation, for like all matrosses, Rawbone was mostly deaf from the tending of his iron charges, "once again you shall be left in charge of our vessel, our *Audacity*, with Bosun Collingwood as your indispensable aide. Since no one looks for us here, and since we are, to all intents and purposes, a British sloop-o-war, we can bear in until we are well fair into the mouth of the Tyne."

Frost glanced up at the red ensign drifting on a halyard behind the driver sail. He generally eschewed the use of false colors; in good conscience, he could hardly abide it. Yet the judicious use of the red ensign had almost fooled Captain Richard Smith and HM sloop-o-war *Lark*, and it had been crucial in his taking of the valuable Tortola Packet off Sable Island. And the ensign, displayed by what even the most unlearned observer on the north coast could twig as a Royal Navy sloop-o-war, meant that *Audacity* went unremarked.

Frost ran his eyes over the men picked for the expeditions

ashore and collier burning. With the exception of Caleb Mansfield's wood-cruisers, who would wear no garments except their homespun woolens and tanned skins, the men were rigged in their quasi-uniforms of blue linen pantaloons and jackets, the better to distinguish each other in the confusion that would ensue from their unexpected assault upon the coal pits and the collier fleet. But the quasi-uniforms would offer scant protection to any man unfortunate enough to be taken prisoner.

"The men are with you, Capt'n; most of 'em that is," Rawbone volunteered. "Some wish you had turned westward after taking the Cadiz Packet. No more'n a round dozen have said aught about this venture. Two that did had their ribs stove for their troubles."

"We shall course as far up the river as North Tyneside, where Mister Ferguson, accompanied by Daniel O'Buck, who avers a lifelong hankering to see this land of his ancestors, shall stroll ashore to visit the colliery pits," Frost said amiably. "The men under my command shall then provide a festive air to this late midsummer's night by imitating, as Mister Ferguson reminds us, the foxes of Samson."

"Be not taking the Scriptures so lightly," Rawbone said uneasily. "You'll recall, I'm sure, that Mister Samson was a judge, and judges of my experience be devoid complete of any smack of humor."

"Well said, Master Gunner. After you leave us ashore, fall down the river to the mouth and wait, sails aback, one red light above a green light hoisted from the foremast brace tackle pendants, as the signal to recover us. When respectively Mister Ferguson and I come within hail, a man in the bows will uncover a lamp with a red lens." Frost glanced again at the red ensign. "Mister Rawbone, our true disguise thus far has been our boldness, not so much the deceitful flag we've hoist. As soon as you turn downriver, please lower the flag of our enemy and raise our own rattlesnake flag. While we've yet spyed no British warship worthy of the name, this evening's festivities may occasion a fiscal's lugger on watch for smugglers to sally."

"Aye, our own rattlesnake aloft, that's a-sure. And I shall fire immediately into any vessel not displaying such signal as arranged," Rawbone vowed. "Do not misplace your flint and steel."

An hour later *Audacity* had hoisted out her two long boats—the second had been appropriated from HM *Vulture* in Angra Harbor the week previously, as Frost speculated he would have greater need for it than Captain Heflin Wolstenhulme. Boats towing, *Audacity* was abreast the north and south banks of the Tyne's mouth, riding easily on the inflowing tide, half a jibsail showing, fore topsail reefed to two points, as was the main topsail, with the fore topgallant fisted up atop its yard. Frost took the wheel from the quartermaster and gauged the obedience of the rudder. *Audacity* carried far more than steerage weigh and answered her helm with authority. They were well along on the broad river, and Frost had stopped counting the number of loaded colliers snug in their anchorages on both banks of the Tyne. North Tyneside seemed to be sheltering slightly more colliers, so he resolved to work that side of the river. No one from any of the indistinct and placidly anchored colliers challenged them. Men selected to follow Frost and Struan Ferguson formed lines at the heads and the lead-lined pissdales amidships to ease bowels and bladders before taking their places in the long boats.

"It is approximately here that I desire you to await us, Mister Rawbone," Frost said, just loud enough for Rawbone to hear. Ming Tsun had brought him a cup of honey-flavored tea and a hot bowl of rice and stewed fish flavored with a curry in which he could taste the cumin. Because *Audacity* was observing light discipline, it was now too dark for signing, so Frost spoke to Ming Tsun. "Bring the larboard boat alongside and lade it with the prepared torches, rumbowline canvas, and fire pots."

"Belike those pots carry the legendary Greek Fire," Rawbone said, somewhat fearfully.

"No one today knows how the legendary Greek Fire was compounded, Master Gunner, so secret and zealously guarded was its manufacture," Frost answered. "It was a concoction of incendiary materials by the Byzantine Greeks eleven centuries past. It could be confined in pots and thrown, or more deadly, discharged from tubes. Because it could not be extinguished by water, Mediterranean navies, particularly the Arabic, afforded the Greek vessels wide berth, especially so since an Arab fleet attacking Constantinople late in the seventh century was completely destroyed by the Fire's employment. I collect some Russians likewise fell afoul of Greek Fire a century or so later. And for additional centuries thereafter, all Mediterranean navies avoided the Byzantines, for they dared not risk their wooden hulls against so fearsome and unknown a weapon."

"But the Byzan . . . Byzantines never properly addressed cannons," Rawbone exclaimed.

"Precisely so, Master Gunner," Frost replied. "The Byzantine Greeks required vessels to engage closely so the Fire could be spread by tube or catapult. The advent of cannons gave the advantage to the Greeks' adversaries. The secret of the chemical died with those who had constrained science while the Greek navies went down in ruin."

Rawbone said in a tone of wonder: "Then has Mister Ming Tsun discovered anew this awful compound?"

"I think not," Frost said. "It is not some 'Chinese Fire' but ingredients Ming Tsun has collected from rummaging around in our stores, as well as some purchases made in Angra Town. Naphtha, brimstone, finely divided charcoal, turpentine, other compounds only Ming Tsun as alchemist knows. He has assembled ten pots' worth. It does not ignite spontaneously, and must be fired separately. But once the incendiary, it cannot be stopped."

"The Dear help the colliers," Rawbone said tremulously.

Frost did not reply but ate down his food, all but a morsel, which he left in the bowl for George Three to lick out appreciatively, though the large Newfoundland dog did "woof," shake his head and sneeze a time or two at the sauciness of the curry. A dozen half-barrels of gunpowder were being brought up from the magazine by barefooted men exercising great care in the small pools of light cast by carefully shielded lamps.

"Little enough to close all the pits," Struan Ferguson ventured as he supervised the carriage of the powder to the weather bulwarks where the starboard long boat was drawn up. "But I'll warrant we'll close several—sufficient to give the dreads to the Grand Allies of landowners who claim royal warrants datin' from Elizabeth's time to the coals." Struan peered closely at the ex-*Jaguar*, Tilman Gardner, standing at his elbow. "Ken ye still the road to the nearest mine shafts?"

"It be fifteen years since I was pressed out of Blyth on a market day when I wus mongerin' fish," Gardner replied, not shifting his gaze and standing resolutely. "But I mongered many a basket of herring and sole to the miners' wives hereabouts, and I misdoubt the roads be little changed."

Frost and Struan had briefly discussed earlier in the day the desirability of taking Gardner ashore as a guide. If the ex-*Jaguar* were to be believed, he had no family ties or affiliations that would draw him to the area. Gardner professed not to have seen the northeast coast in the fifteen years since he had been inducted by force into the King's service. He claimed to have learned years before that his wife had had him declared dead in the parish church and had remarried, something that greatly embittered him. And he had labored valiantly beside Frost as a helmsman in the desperate, relentless struggle with the hurricane. They had inclined to give Gardner their trust, and Frost always desired to make it easier for men under his command to do the right thing than anything else. But all the same Daniel O'Buck, who would be second to Struan, had been quietly told off to remain unobtrusively close to Tilman Gardner at all times while they were ashore. If there were the slightest sniff of treachery—but Gardner's services as a guide were needed for Struan's landing party to locate the nearest mines without delay.

"Mister Rawbone," Frost said as he drew out Jonathan's watch and held it close to the binnacle's shielded light, "in fifteen minutes we shall have the height of this tide, and Mister

Ferguson and I must be off to tend our respective affairs. Have a care as you fall down to the river's mouth to await us." He thrust the coastal pilotage into Rawbone's hands. "There are several sand banks about, and you may wish to have a lead going as the tide takes you back down the stream." The darkness amidst the fog was complete now, and several more carefully screened lanterns had appeared. In the sparse glare of one lantern he saw the three ship's gentlemen, Nathaniel Dance, Darius Langdon, and Hannibal Bowditch, their eyes wide and incredulous. Behind them George Three paced, sniffing pockets expectantly for edible delicacies.

"Ah, Gentlemen Sous-Officers! Mister Rawbone and Bosun Collingwood have need of your attentiveness. The pilotage in his hands hints at the finer points of navigating amidst shoals and bars, particularly so on an obscured night when we cannot expect Saint Elmo to provide sufficient illumination for regular navigation. Mister Rawbone anticipates your close attention to the printed page and the fathom line as an advisory, though of course his is the ultimate responsibility for our vessel's safe return to the Tyne's mouth."

Frost turned to the impassive Ming Tsun. A quick nod told him that their long boat was laden, and it was time to ship the chosen men. Frost grinned, though he was well aware the lads could not see it. "Mister Rawbone depends upon your sobriety and attentiveness, as well as that of George, so disappoint him not."

"Oh, no, sir!" the three youths chorused in unison. "You can depend upon it, sir!"

"Good," Frost said with satisfaction. "Mind George now, we can't have him paddling around in a British river looking for carboys to retrieve, can we?" A nod from Ming Tsun told Frost that his picked men were embarked in his long boat, and a glance across the quarterdeck in the fretful light of the shrouded lanterns showed that Struan Ferguson was following the last of the half-barrels of gunpowder overside into his long boat.

Frost handed his watch to Darius. "Mister Langdon, please

hold my brother's watch against my return. I dare not risque its wetting." He settled his cutlass in its shoulder carriage and thrust the brace of double-barreled John Bass turn-off-fire pistols Ming Tsun held out for him into his waist belt. Caleb Mansfield and half his mob of woods-cruisers were already seated in Frost's long boat; the other woods-cruisers were in Struan's long boat.

"Mister Rawbone, I shall appreciate a test of your cannons once you have determined the place for our rendezvous. You may wish to swing in toward the south bank of the Tyne and loose a broadside into the colliers rafted there to confound them." Followed by Ming Tsun, Frost climbed down into the long boat and made his way to the stern sheets, where Jack Lacey was seated as coxswain. The smell of turpentine-saturated rags wrapped around barrel staves for torches reminded Frost of the fragrant pine forests of his native New Hampshire.

Ming Tsun made a place for himself on the thwart in front of the stern sheets, the men already seated there giving way quickly to the fearsome halberd in his grip. "Out oars, but pull slowly so that Mister Ferguson will have the shore five minutes before we touch the first collier," Frost commanded in a low voice. The long boat pushed away from *Audacity*'s hull, and oars, heavily lubricated at their tholes pins with greasy slush from the galley, dipped quietly into the water and began the long boat's movement.

The foggy evening was extremely quiet and Frost strained his ears for any sound—the barking of dogs, the cry of a night watchman, the slap of a fish as it rolled in the water, the trill of a night bird, voices from one of the colliers. Nothing, except for the very faint, monotonous thrum of the oars, which he knew no one twenty feet away from the long boat could hear. Frost had heard the oars' thrum from Struan's long boat for several minutes, but now that faint noise was no longer audible.

Frost peered up at the night sky clearly visible through the tendrils of advection fog. Spread above him were the constellations of autumn: Pegasus, the Winged Horse; Cassiopeia, the Queen; Andromeda, the Princess, daughter of Cepheus. Nearby was the heroic Perseus in his own constellation, rescuer of Andromeda from the deadly rock where she had been offered as a sacrifice. In the west a brilliant Venus of gemlike quality, glimpsed earlier, had already set, but in the northeast Saturn should be rising. Frost went through the calculations. The northern hemisphere, unwillingly slipping into winter, had already grudgingly given up nigh on one and one half hours of cherished daylight to its brother in the southern hemisphere to augment its summer.

Yes! There was Saturn, plainly visible, a star the color of butter; a hard, cold, luxuriant diamond of brilliant light, standing prominently in the constellation of Gemini, the Twins. As Frost watched, entranced, a flurry of meteors streaked across the sky. What were they called? The name came to him: the Orionid Shower. Frost wanted to lose himself in the beauties of the night sky, as he had so often in the past, but he brought his gaze back to sea level and peered intently toward the northern shore through the fog: There! A light! He looked not directly at the tiny glimmer but toward a point some twenty degrees to the left of the light: the lantern of an anchor light marking a collier. "Steer toward that light," he murmured to Jack Lacey.

The light, when the long boat had covered another fifty yards, marked two colliers rafted together and hard by, less than twenty yards away, another raft of two colliers. "Lay me alongside the starboard side of that collier directly ahead," Frost said quietly. He nudged Caleb Mansfield, who was sitting just in front of him. "Pass the word: we shall board the nearer raft with half our complement. Oarsmen to remain at their stations and circle the raft to larboard." Then to Jack Lacey: "Cut the anchor hawses on the larboard raft, and let the tide take them down to the raft we've boarded. Await my signal to take us off."

The long boat touched the hull of the collier without a sound, and hands knuckled the long boat along the algae-slick hull until the starboard waist entry's steps and fenders. Frost was first up the entry steps, followed by Ming Tsun with a lantern he unshielded as soon as they were on the main deck proper. Frost waited until half the mob had boiled up from the long boat onto the main deck. "Two teams of axmen. Sever the larboard shrouds of the foremast and drop the foremast across the bows of the collier to larboard. Hack away the starboard shrouds of the mainmast and drop it across the raft to starboard. Caleb, your men know to shoot only if resistance is given. I would fain destroy these colliers without the loss of life, the Prophet willing. Ming Tsun, into the collier to larboard and give us a light from one fire pot. One pot only, for we find ourselves in an environment exceedingly wealthy in targets!"

Ming Tsun was away in a giant, soundless leap, first hurling his halberd ahead of him to strike, quivering, in the mainmast of the next collier rafted. Once aboard he pulled the halberd from the mast to slash down a tangle of tarred rigging to nestle at the base of the mainmast, then struck steel and flint onto tinder, which, on the instant properly a-spark, was touched to the short fuse of the fire pot. The pot sputtered momentarily, then burst into a spectacular umbrella of flames. Ming Tsun picked up a coil of rope and hurled it into the flames.

"What be a-foot here?" Frost turned to find an elderly man dressed only in his small clothes, barefoot, shapeless mouth bereft of his false teeth, sparse hair disarrayed in the wisps caused by sleep, rheumy eyes bulging, unbelieving, uncomprehending, just emerging from the companionway at the break of the waist.

"Ah, Uncle," Frost said, advancing in a mock bow, "I trust you learned long ago the art of swimming."

The elderly man instinctively ducked his head in the semblance of a bow, and Frost had the man's left foot, levering him upward and overboard. Frost waited until he heard the splash and splutter of the man's surfacing. "The nearer shore be off the stern," he shouted down conversationally. "It be a long stroke to South Tyneside if you take direction from the bows."

The despairing, water-choked cry "My livelihood!" floated up to Frost, but he had no choice but to ignore it. Instead, he marveled at how advanced the flames from the one fire pot were already. The flames around the mainmast had already reached the canvas of the reefed main course, and it exploded into a fearsome fireball that blossomed upward toward the main topsail loosely furled in its gaskets, and from there upward to the main topgallant, all sails blazing in conflagration within the half-minute.

A gust of tremendous heat blew past Frost, and for an awful moment the memory conjured up unbidden of the flames engulfing the Lady Cygnet's dress, and his desperate, despairing pursuit of catch up to her . . . "Ming Tsun! Ware!" Frost shouted. "Foremast coming down across you!" The crack of well-dried timber was welcome indeed, and Frost followed the foremast's quick trajectory as it lay over to trap and bridge the collier to larboard in its deadly embrace.

A rifle cracked, and Frost turned in time to see a naked figure dumped on the main deck. "Called on 'im to put down that dirk," Caleb Mansfield said sadly. "Didn't see no need to kill 'im, so I shot 'im through the arm." Caleb shook his head. "Didn't want to waste the bullet." Caleb motioned to two of his woods-cruisers. "Toss 'im overside, pull up a piece of thet gratin' so he'll have somethin' to float 'im." There was a tremendous crack and a splintering sound as the mainmast began to sag.

The naked man was hustled to the starboard bulwark by two woods-cruisers, while a hand from Frost's long boat pried up a grating and threw it overside. "God's pox be on you!" the man wailed.

"Stand clear!" Frost shouted as the naked man, wounded arm and flailing legs, was propelled overside. He saw the mast waver, then begin its majestic fall toward the two colliers rafted to starboard. He marveled at how rapidly the flames from the one fire pot were spreading. "Caleb, send up a shout for Jack Lacey. We need to get ourselves downriver!" Jack Lacey had evidently succeeded in severing the anchor hawses on the two colliers rafted upstream, for the raft was slowly drifting toward them, the mainmast that lay askew across the waists of the two colliers upriver buckling and groaning.

There! Frost spied the long boat in the fitful half-circle of light cast by the towering flames licking up the mainmast of the collier to which they were captive. "Mister Lacey! Inboard at once to bear us away!" He turned toward the other collier, anxiously seeking Ming Tsun, and was vastly relieved when he saw his friend swing himself nonchalantly onto the main deck of the collier on which Frost stood. "Into the long boat, all of you!" he shouted to his crew as the long boat bumped against the collier's hull. Frost counted the men as they fell into the long boat, then satisfied he had his complement, followed Ming Tsun into the stern sheets.

"Under the bows, Mister Lacey. Ming Tsun, sever the hawses as we pass. Mister Lacey, let us pass the next two rafts, severing the hawses as we do, then fall upon the raft following." A jet of orange-yellowish flame shot obscenely ahead of the long boat and Frost smelled the peculiar acrid odor of burning coal. The combined fires had already reached the hold of at least one of the four colliers behind them and had ignited its cargo.

There were shouts now, from the shore as well as the rafts of colliers—agitated voices, indistinct but shrill and sharply edged with terror. "The chickens 'er a-flutter in the coop, Capt'n, knowin' the fox be among 'em," Caleb Mansfield said, glee, an abandonment into the joy of combat of the closest kind, tingeing his voice.

"Chickens that mayhap have muskets and pistols embraced in their wings," Frost snapped crossly. "Our next boarding must be carried out quickly in the confusion. I know not when the vessels downriver may organize and offer resistance." The long boat was closing with the next victim swiftly, and somewhere nearby a musket boomed, but it was impossible to know if the musket had been aimed at the long boat.

The long boat struck the hull of the collier with such force that the long boat sheered away, but one of the woodscruisers, Singleton Quire, grasped the starboard main chains and wrestled the long boat to the waist entry. Quire hoisted himself aboard the collier by the chains and uttered a high-pitched shriek that ululated in tone and volume as he dropped onto the collier's deck.

"Abanaqui war song," Caleb Mansfield grunted to Frost as they scrambled up the entry steps. "Fair makes yere hackles lift yere cap of'n yere pate, it does!"

Frost saved the breath of a reply as he gained the deck and tripped a shadowy figure running aft. "Mercy, mercy!" the prostrate figure screamed. "Fend off the savages, for the Dear's sake!"

"How many men in your crew?" Frost demanded.

"Mercy, mercy!" the figure continued to wail.

Frost slapped the man harshly. "How many men in your crew?" he demanded again.

"Preserve me from the savages!"

"On the contrary, I shall give you over to the savages unless you answer my civil question," Frost said.

"Five of us," the man said tearfully.

"Call out to your mates that Indians from the new American states are aboard, and to save themselves your mates must go overside, do you ken?"

"Preserve me from the savages!" the man blubbered hysterically. Frost slapped the man until he stopped crying.

"Your salvation and that of your mates lies in the water overside." Frost dragged the man to his feet and pinned him against the starboard bulwark. "Call out to them!"

Two men from Frost's crew were hacking away enthusiastically with their broadaxes at the mainmast. A random chip hurtled back and struck the terrified man's forehead. That and the shaking Frost gave him channeled his terror anew. "Mates, mates, Davie, Scotty, Albert, Colin," he wailed, "if we're overside the savages won't hurt us!"

"Louder!" Frost demanded.

The man complied. "Good," Frost murmured, "now, overside with you."

"But I can't swim," the man wailed.

Ming Tsun, who had already set the fire pot ablaze on the collier rafted next over, heard the man's wail. He hefted a small barrel that had been rolling about the deck and threw it overside. "There's your salvation," Frost said, "cling to the barrel with both arms and kick with your feet. It will amaze how rapidly you can propel yourself toward the safety of the shore." He tipped the terrified man overside and turned to survey the devastation his men had wrought about the collier in less than one minute. The mainmast of the collier they were aboard was tottering as men hacked away at the standing rigging and the two axe men finished their work on the base of the mainmast. The fire pot on the collier next over already had ignited its mainmast as high as the cap.

"Ware the mast's fall," Frost called out sharply. Then: "All back to the long boat." Ensuring the head count was correct, Frost stepped down among his men. The fires from the colliers burning fiercely upstream cast a surreal, garish glow over the calm waters of the Tyne estuary. The fierce heat was actually creating a small windstorm that was dispelling the light fog. The tide was beginning to ebb and the upstream colliers, no longer tethered to their anchors, were beginning to move with the current. Frost felt another blast of heat as the foremast of the nearest collier, aflame from top to butt, toppled into the water scant yards away, the sudden quenching of flames throwing up a drizzle of steam and the reek of burnt tar. Without orders from Frost, Jack Lacey was maneuvering the long boat as rapidly as possible away from the colliers just fired.

"Gar! Looks like some o' the nobs er leavin' their ships!" Caleb shouted, pointing down river. The burning colliers behind the long boat illuminated the north bank of the Tyne a good cable's length, despite the fog. Indeed, tenders were frantically plying among the densely rafted colliers, taking off the even more frantic crews.

"Bear in toward that raft," Frost commanded, after the long boat had stroked some two hundred yards downstream from the last raft of colliers to be fired. He gestured toward two colliers from which a tender was pulling fiercely, all men aboard tugging at an oar. "Ming Tsun, please take one pot aboard the vessel and fire it. Singleton Quire, I'll thank you to accompany Ming Tsun to provide a guard. Caleb, two axe men aboard this collier to fell one mast only to keep the twain joined, and cut the anchor cables once the fire takes."

Every head in the long boat turned as one toward the sullen reverberation of an explosion somewhere to the west. Frost felt in his waistcoat pocket for his watch, then remembered that he had left the Bréquet with Darius. A fair approximation of the time elapsed since Struan Ferguson and he had rowed away in their respective long boats from *Audacity* was close on one hour. So Struan had found one coal mine shaft at least, and Frost could expect his team of sappers to return to their long boat more expeditiously than their route to the mine head. Two sea-miles downstream to the Tyne's mouth where *Audacity* waited. They should be aboard, to the vast relief of Master Gunner Rawbone, well before daybreak. In the meanwhile there were a myriad of colliers to destroy.

The fire-driven winds propelling the cloying, gagging smell of burning coal before them were indeed raising the fog. Ming Tsun had fired the pot and waited for the mainmast to quicken into flame before he and Singleton Quire scrambled into the long boat. A moment later, with the mainmast of the second collier in the raft commencing its rapid descent onto the collier just beginning to blossom into flames, the two axe men, wonderfully motivated to achieve the greatest speed, threw themselves into the long boat. Jack Lacey ordered the rowers away from the colliers as quickly as ever they could tug oars through water.

The night was alive with shouts and cries and the frantic plying of tenders among the colliers as anchor watches were taken off. The colliers burning behind the long boat cast grotesque shapes and shadows across the waters and the tendrils of fog. A glance upriver showed Frost that the colliers adrift from their anchors were being tugged into the center of the river by the slowly quickening current. That would not do.

"Mister Lacey, lay us alongside that raft yonder. Caleb, your woods-cruizers shall have to exchange their long rifles for oars, and you shall have the joy of learning the management of this long boat."

Frost felt the heated blast of wind whip past the long boat as one of the colliers dissolved, the majority of its burning timbers being thrown outward as the vessel disintegrated and its cargo of coal was released. "Mister Lacey, you shall have the larboard oarsmen, and I shall take the starboard men. We'll sunder the anchor cables of yonder vessels, drop sails and drive with more authority into the anchorages ahead." Just then Frost heard the thunderous clap of a cannon from the Tyne's mouth. Rawbone, the master matross, was announcing his arrival at the estuary. No, other percussions of cannons followed. A sea mile eastward in the darkness, where the towering flames of the burning colliers had not cast their awful illuminations, Frost saw the momentary, lurid flare of powder's burn reflect morosely iridescent off *Audacity*'s brailed up courses as Rawbone took something to the southward under fire, likely a collier whose crew had greater presence of mind than the others and had slipped their cable in an effort to use the outflooding tide to break away from the other vessels crowded into the anchorage. At this distance the burning fragments of wads scattered as ejecta when the cannons discharged twinkled momentarily like a thousand fireflies.

If that were the case, then the confusion and consternation among the massed colliers that had hitherto contentedly awaited their sailing orders would only increase. "Mister Lacey, you shall drive your collier along this shore. I fancy a diversion to the southern shore."

Another explosion rumbled in the distance. Frost suspected that Struan Ferguson was enjoying himself immensely. With a guilty tinge of remorse, Frost acknowledged that he was likewise enjoying this orgy of destruction. And so much remained to be done! Followed closely by Ming Tsun with two fire pots slung over his shoulder in a rectangle of sailcloth, Frost clambered aboard the collier he had chosen. The five hands that had followed Frost aboard went racing up the ratlines to throw off the gaskets on topsails and topgallants.

Jack Lacey raised his hat in salute as he gained the quarter-deck of the collier that was his quarry. "Good hunting!" he shouted. Frost did not reply, as he was taking the wheel and waiting for Ming Tsun to sunder the anchor cable. Another collier behind him burst in an inferno of flames and sparks, illuminating the Tyne from shore to shore in its terrible ruddy glow. Its hot maelstrom of fire-whipped wind filled the sails of the collier Frost was taking into the thicket of coal-filled vessels cowering along the Tyne's southern shore. As the heated, acrid wind, bearing with it the stench of quenched embers, nudged the heavily laden collier sluggishly toward mid-channel, Geoffrey Frost put all thought from mind.

He heard another tremendous clap of thunder behind him, and seconds later a massive rush of wind flew into the collier's filling topsails and bellied them into the shape of new mothers' breasts ready to give suck. The forecourse burst its gaskets and the sail dropped. An explosion caused by Struan destroying the mine heads? A coalition of doomed colliers exploding simultaneously? Frost searched desperately for the long boat now under Caleb Mansfield's erratic command. Caleb had as much experience husbanding a long boat as Frost had in husbanding a mob of woods-cruisers. Yes! There was the long boat, precariously tipped, but gamely, grimly rowed by Caleb's wood-cruisers, erratically pulling after the collier commandeered by Jack Lacey. So Jack Lacey could be taken off his collier by Caleb when he fired it.

Another great rush of wind came from astern, filling the forecourse instantly, overstressing the forecourse and its yard, splintering and bringing down the yard and a welter of blocks in a clattering, deadly hail. Ming Tsun and the men who had gone aloft! No, the five hands were still in the shrouds, two in the foremast and three in the mainmast, descending hurriedly. But Ming Tsun? Frost abandoned the wheel and ran to the collapsed forecourse yard and tangle of sailcloth and rigging. He shouted Ming Tsun's name repeatedly and tried to force his way into the confusion of rope and sailcloth. No joy. Frost darted to larboard, where the end of the splintered fore yard lay at an angle against the collier's bulwark, preserving it from lying flush on the deck and creating a space in the chaos of hemp and canvas into which he could crawl.

Frost clawed his way across the deck on his belly, pushing cordage aside, propelling himself deeper into the mesh toward the bow where he had last seen Ming Tsun. His groping hand encountered Ming Tsun's bow case, recognizing it instantly, and fishing about wildly Frost touched the silk of Ming Tsun's pantaloons. He pushed his questing hands through the thicket of ropes along Ming Tsun's body until they came up against the broken section of fore yard pressing Ming Tsun's chest against the deck. Frost tried to stand but was prevented by the webs and weight of cordage. He rolled over on his back, fumbled out his cutlass and savagely attacked the embrace of ropes, hacking an opening large enough to permit him to stand upright.

"To me! To me!" Frost roared to his crewmen as he got to his feet, hacking all the while at the clutching ropes. The first to his side was Quentin Fowle, carpenter's mate serving temporarily as a topman, and a good one at that, judging by the alacrity with which the fore topsail had been loosed. Frost grasped the underside of the heavy beam obscenely pinning Ming Tsun's chest and struggled to lift. "Fowle, as I raise the yard, draw Ming Tsun from beneath," he growled in a strangled voice.

"Capt'n, you kin't rise that weight by yourself!" Fowle exclaimed. Indeed, the portion of splintered yard pinioning Ming Tsun was one foot in diameter and at least eight feet in length.

"Do as you are bid!" Frost grunted, bending his knees and joining his hands beneath the yard, the splintered butt against his chest, and struggling to lift. How long had Ming Tsun been pinioned beneath the broken yard? How long had breath been choked off? A minute at least. Frost strained to lift the length of spar. The yard did not move. Perspiration popped out on his forehead and coursed down his cheeks. The muscles along his spine were afire with pain; Frost puffed out his cheeks to expel and then draw in a breath. The tendons in his lower legs were knots of agony. The spar lifted a fraction of an inch.

Another crewman, now two men, were beside Frost, wrestling with the yard, grasping it wherever they could, silently straining. Their desperate, combined strength pivoted the deadly spar another inch, then another. Quentin Fowle, aided by another mate, drew Ming Tsun by his legs from beneath the spar. Frost and the two men let go the spar and it struck the deck with a murderous thump.

Frost threw himself down and laid an ear to Ming Tsun's chest, hearing the fierce beat of the man's heart, though the chest did not rise in respiration. Frost recalled how Ming Tsun had revived a crewman who had fallen overside the *Salmon* and been fished, seemingly lifeless, from the cold Agulhas Current twenty-five leagues south of the Cape of Storms. With his right hand he pinched closed Ming Tsun's nostrils, tilted back the man's head, sealed his mouth against Ming Tsun's, and blew his own breath into Ming Tsun, while with his left hand he tentatively felt Ming Tsun's chest for collapsed or broken ribs. Frost sucked in great breaths of air that he expelled into Ming Tsun's lungs; and then Ming Tsun's chest expanded beneath Frost's left hand, and Ming Tsun rolled violently aside to retch in a convulsion of dry heaves.

Frost put an ear against Ming Tsun's back, listening for the rasp that might signal the puncture of a lung by a broken rib. Frost had prior experiences with broken ribs, but he heard only the sound of sweet respiration. By the Golden Buddha! Ming Tsun, Geoffrey Frost's best friend in life, lived! Frost staggered to his feet, lungs burning, and stared around the collier. The snap and lurch of the vessel told him that the helm required tending. He fought his way over the mass of cordage and shredded sail piled on the fore deck and tottered toward the quarterdeck. No more than two minutes had elapsed since he had quit the collier's wheel.

Hold! A boat starkly outlined against the flames thrown up from a mob of burning colliers on the north shore darted out, propelled rapidly by four oars a side. The boat was heading directly toward Caleb's long boat. A person in some sort of uniform stood up in the boat, unsteadily trying to aim a musket. "Caleb!" Frost shouted, "Behind you, danger . . . a boat behind you!" He put the helm hard over and the collier's bows turned, slug-like, to larboard.

The musket went off, and the musket shot, not Frost's shout, alerted Caleb to the danger behind him. Frost could see a dozen men, perhaps more, in some sort of uniform, most of them armed, crowded into the boat. He brought the rudder full over, then sprinted to the larboard bulwark, drawing one of his Bass pistols as he ran. The boat of armed men was drawing ahead of the collier; Frost raced for the collier's waist, almost tumbling into a dreamy-eyed Ming Tsun, who was calmly nocking an arrow on his bowstring. Frost steadied his left arm and let the pistol become an extension of him. The hammer came back, the sear held, and Frost looked directly into the boat that was now thirty yards in front of the collier. He fired as Ming Tsun opened his fist to release his arrow. Without waiting to see the effect of his first shot, Frost thumbed the slide to expose the other pan with its priming powder and recocked his pistol.

Several men in the boat turned toward the collier; muskets were pointed hastily in their direction. Frost selected a man just bringing his musket to cheek and carefully squeezed the trigger. The man yelped and dropped the musket. A rower sagged over his oar. The boat was thrown into confusion. Caleb and his woods-cruisers were firing now. The boat of armed men had lost all forward way, and the bows of the collier were slowly, inexorably, coasting down on the boat. The distance between the boat and the collier diminished. Several men on the larboard side attempted to get their oars going . . . too late. The collier's bows struck the boat amidships, not holing the boat but riding it over, spilling men, screaming, cursing men, into the fetid oily, coal-dust-covered waters of the Tyne.

Frost ran back to the helm and jerked the bows around to starboard, heading once again toward the south shore and the terrified colliers watching helplessly as doom bore down on them. But how would Frost, Ming Tsun and their abbreviated crew get off their collier once they fired and drove it into the anchorage of colliers rafted on the south shore of the Tyne's mouth? Por Dios, the Great One whose Name was Spoken in Awe would provide.

Frost put everything else out of mind and concentrated grimly upon inflicting the maximum damage he could upon the hapless fleet huddled in the mouth of the Tyne, to the great detriment of Great Britain and its economy. He felt an insatiable urge to lift his head toward the nascent quarter-moon visible here and there through rents in the fog and howl triumphantly like a wolf that had yet to surfeit itself with killing once inside the sheepfold. Afterwards, in the gratitude he felt for having Ming Tsun restored to life, he could not recall if he had really done so.

V

I T SEEMED TO GEOFFREY FROST THAT JOHN LANGDON'S DOCKYARD ON RISING ISLAND COULD ACCOMMODATE NOT ONE MORE ARTIFICER. TEN BOAT-wagons had already been rough finished and lay hull up on the frozen ground just above high water while caulkers wielding mallets and caulking irons judiciously forced spins of oakum into the plank seams under a lowering, pewter-colored, late November sky that threatened snow at any moment. A gang of stevedores was unlading a gundalow piled high with the last timbers brought over from the *Salmon*, that noble vessel, which had, in the space of three days, been reduced to a lonesome keel and little else. A team of oxen dragged a sledge of timbers to the saw-pits, where sawyers were trimming beams into widths suitable for planking the crude boat-wagons.

A black freedman dropped his shoulder to dump a heavy basket of fresh charcoal onto the bed of coals at the one outdoor forge large enough to make the iron hoops that would band the rear wagon wheels, each as tall as a man. Two blacksmiths plying long tongs lifted one hoop from the bed of coals, which was kept at white-hot heat by the vigorous pumping of large leather bellows by another freedman.

The blacksmiths dropped the circle of fiery, incandescent iron loosely over the assembled structure of the wooden wheel, laid out on a low granite platform with a slight depression in the stone that allowed the wheel to be held together in the dished shape that would give the wheel additional strength. Three wheelwrights with wheel rim pullers skillfully maneuvered the hot iron band over the felly rim, pulling and holding the band in place. Two young boys, faces begrimed with soot, stripped to the waist despite the cold and perspiring heavily, sluiced buckets of water onto the iron rim, quenching and shrinking the iron onto the wheel before the incandescent iron could scorch or burn the wood of the felloes. The wheelwrights and the youths were wreathed in scorching steam that set them coughing mightily.

Several carpenters were conjuring properly shaped spokes with deft strokes of their sharp draw knives out of square lengths of seasoned oak that the day before had been a massive rib in *Salmon*. Two other carpenters were just removing a wheel hub from the lathe turned by human muscle, upon which it had been shaped. They added the hub to a neat stack of raw hubs, which other carpenters with chisels were drawing to incise the mortises that would hold the butt ends of the spokes. At another forge smaller iron bands were being sweated onto wheel hubs already mortised for the spokes.

Another carpenter wielding an adze was rough-shaping a neck yoke for oxen from a piece of elm that Frost recognized as having been part of *Salmon*'s rudder. Frost was saddened as he walked among the stark bones of his beloved ship, but strangely comforted that *Salmon* was giving totally and without reservation everything she had to give—and willingly, not as a matter of surrendering to brute demand.

Frost glanced toward *Audacity*, forlornly nestled against the long wharf facing toward Portsmouth. The vast majority of ships' captains never loved their vessels, considering them implements only, hollow structures to move at their biddings and to be cursed when they would not. It had been vouchsafed to a few fortunate captains to love one vessel they had commanded, and he felt singularly blessed to love two vessels. No one could tell him that ships were inanimate objects devoid of emotions, for Geoffrey Frost knew that *Salmon* and *Audacity* loved him in return. He said a brief prayer to their spirits.

"Your place is with our *Audacity*," Frost said to the dour Struan Ferguson pacing beside him, speaking just loudly enough, with authority enough, to be heard over the din of shouted voices, beat of hammers, rip of saws. "As much as I need you with me on this strange voyage over land, Struan, our *Audacity* needs you far the more. With *Raleigh* not ready for sea, *Portsmouth* being built, and *Hampshire* soon to be started, competition for artificers in Cousin John's employ will be keen—and, I fear, far more concerned about receiving their inflated pay than delivering a decent day's work. I shall leave O'Buck, Rawbone, Lacey and Collingwood with you as superintendents to ease the burdens imposed by this refit."

"Duty such as ye impose affords no opportunity to square accounts with them murtherin' British bastards," Struan said bleakly, halting with Frost as Frost watched iron attach points being sweated onto a wagon's disselboom already shaped with heavy draw knife from a sturdy oak plank. Struan desisted, choosing not to remonstrate with his captain.

Frost picked up a handful of oak shavings and crumpled them, pleased with the solid dryness of the thin, clean wooden curls. The dear old *Salmon* had been a well-founded, well-tended ship, and she was willingly offering up her body for the spirit of rebellion. "I fear that even the snapping of George Three's neck beneath your thumbs would not assuage your loss of family and friends, Struan," Frost said quietly, kindly. "Remember that hate and revenge are acids corrosive of the phials attempting to contain them.

"There is suspect cordage to be examined and replaced, worn blocks good enough for others, but not for our vessel, to be sought out and replaced. Parrels for rehanging, balancing, and tightening. Sheets of copper below the waterline to be checked for security of attachment and scrubbed of all marine growth. Above all, new anchor rodes and freshly sewn sails of duck and canvas we fetched in. I intend to take our fair lady to sea as soon in the New Year as the danger of ice does not menace us—assuming of course that we can recruit sufficient hands from the bosom of sloth and indolence into which the majority have fled."

Frost had hoped to find a goodly number of his former crew working for wages, but except for Colossus Bennington, Cricket Dalrymple, and a few ex-*Jaguars* like Spider Urquhart without family in the Ports of Piscataqua, there were precious few men from *Audacity* working among the dockyard's artisans.

Thankfully, however, the total number of some thirty ex-*Jaguars* initially enlisted into the *Audacity* had been more than willing to sign on as his auxiliaries, his marines, for this strange landward expedition. They had lodged only one request, at once diffident, respectful, and imperious—that the diminutive, self-effacing Nathaniel Dance be their officer. Without exception, all the ex-*Jaguars* regarded the young Nathaniel as their own, a known, fixed quality, and incredibly plucky in the bargain, lots of bottom, so fortunate to be around despite his youth. Frost had agreed, though with a pang at the thought of one so young leading others into battle, most probably into death or mutilation . . . Joss, Jesus Christ and Mary, but he would need these marines. Nathaniel was even now, with the assistance of two of Caleb's woods-cruisers, Singleton Quire and Jack Daws, drilling the marines in musketry at the butts at the head of Rising Island, utilized by Caleb Mansfield the half-year before to whip them into some semblance of marksmen. Spider Urquhart had exhibited a degree of leadership, and Nathaniel had named the best topman serving aboard *Audacity* to act in the capacity of sergeant.

The marines were shooting off powder and lead at a fearsome rate, though Frost had it that marksmanship and rapidity of fire had become most credible. And old, querulous, profane Joshua Swaincott of Kittery, a one-eyed, one-legged veteran of the last French War, rowed himself over to Rising Island every morning to drill the marines enthusiastically in the proper employment of that malignant and murderously efficient weapon, the bayonet affixed to the muzzle of a musket. Frost collected stories about how much destruction Joshua had wrought with that instrument on the Plains of Abraham just under Quebec City, where both Wolfe and Montcalm had met their gallant, pre-ordained fates—and where Joshua had received his wounds. By the Holy Trinity, the bayonet and its cousin, the boarding pike, were effective enough, obscene enough, fearful enough, to loosen the bowels of anyone confronting their blunt points.

Twenty of Nathaniel's marines had been issued the short land pattern of 1768 Tower muskets seized from the magazine on Battery Island in Louisbourg Harbor. The other ten, the most dexterous of these auxiliaries, had been given the Ferguson rifles. The woods-cruisers who had fired them liked them well enough, but they were far more accustomed to rifles that accepted bullets from the muzzle, the way God intended rifles to be loaded, so they had given up the Ferguson rifles without grudge, even gladly. Darius had retrieved for Frost the Ferguson rifle he had consigned to his brother, Joseph, finding the rifle at his brother's lodgings in Marlborough Frost's townhouse in Portsmouth, where Frost did not venture. The rifle was still in the packet, unwrapped and unopened, exactly as Frost had dispatched it upon arriving with the East Indiamen prizes this July past.

In any event, Nathaniel Dance was all a-fire to obtain some distinctive uniforms for *Audacity*'s marines, of whom he was inordinately proud, and daily, it seemed, had been importuning the good ladies of Portsmouth to devise one or at the very least provide suggestions as to where proper cloth could be procured. The toils that had been discussed resulted in no more than salt-tanned buckskins of a tiresome brownish-gray color. No matter; some kind lady had come forth with the proposal for a handsome cockade in three colors, blue, white and red, and thirty such cockades had been fabricated. These cockades were worn proudly in the marines' tricornes.

Frost shrugged imperceptibly. The majority of the crew who had toiled mightily to learn the privateer's hard trade the past six months would come back when he advertised *Audacity* would be going to sea, of that he was sure. But in the meantime most of his former crew breached in North America preferred to stay close to a cheery hearth, quaff ale and mulled rum, and play with their children or brag of their exploits aboard *Audacity*—exploits that grew and were embellished in the retelling.

He looked into the cheerful face of Cricket Dalrymple, who was plying a spoke-shave with a dexterity Frost had not guessed the man possessed. Perhaps Dalrymple would be a good candidate for a carpenter's mate under Chips Brandon. The man had filled out remarkably since his rescue as a condemned prisoner from the schooner HM *Walrus* following her grounding and destruction on Sable Island this late May past.

"Thankee, Capt'n, fer the chance to earn more coin to set aside against the tavern I'll buy some day in this new land far away from the long reach of the British Navy," Dalrymple said. The vivid "R" brand of the run British sailor was no longer visible in the well-healed scar on his cheek, thanks to the medical skills of Israel Hymsinger, who had abraded the "R" with sharkskin while Ming Tsun had anesthetized the man with the healing needles. Dalrymple had remained conscious during the entire operation, to his amazement and the amazement of every man of *Audacity*'s crew, who had formed a gawking audience. "I ken it be yere money pays fer this all." Dalrymple paused in adding to the pile of oak shavings sprouting between his feet and swept an arm around the bustle in the dockyard.

"I need not your reminder of this cost," Frost said, though not testily. He smiled, "At least in this new country where you find yourself, Mister Dalrymple, men can file a petition for bankruptcy without risk of finding themselves cast into the debtors' prison." He regarded Dalrymple. "I wish more of your fellows were working on these boat-wagons."

Dalrymple shrugged, then touched up the edge of his spoke-shave with a sharpening stone and a judicious dollop of well-aimed spit. "Reckon a right bunch will come quick enough back to our vessel once the dollies euchre 'em out the last of their coin, er their women-folk drive 'em out the kitchen with broomsticks and curses and shoves aplenty." Cricket Dalrymple smiled slyly at Struan. "Now, Mister Ferguson, I ken he knows what it be like when the women-folk put the spurs in the soup. Time to go a-raidin' south below the border into England, it be!"

Frost was pleased that Dalrymple had used the collective possessive "our" when he spoke of the *Audacity.* "This labor over boat-wagons is of short duration, Dalrymple, finished within the week. Mister Ferguson is charged with readying our vessel," Frost emphasized the words "our vessel," "for departure immediately the ice permits. If you wish employment about the ship during her repair, make application directly to him."

"I be signin' with yere next cruize, Capt'n, that's a-sure." Dalrymple cocked a crafty eye at Frost, then tested the sharpness of his spoke-shave against a few sparse hairs on his forearm. "'N' happy I be to find employment readyin' yere *Audacity* for cruizin'. But tell me, Capt'n, yere next cruize not be goin' near the Isle of Anglesey, mayhap?"

"We shall cruize wherever British prizes are to be found, Dalrymple," Frost said. "Whether that cruize may take us near the Isle of Anglesey I truly cannot say."

"Yere fortune be waitin' there," Cricket Dalrymple said simply, and applied himself and the spoke-shave to the stave of wood he was shaping. Frost and Struan walked further into the din and bustle.

"I shall have our vessel," Struan Ferguson also stressed the two words, "herself ready for sea by Christmastime, and upon yere word sent after ye hae located this Washington chap I can hae a tranquil crew gathered smartly."

Frost nodded absently, Dalrymple's words already forgotten as he concentrated on the multitude of tasks that awaited his attention. The boat-wagons had to be towed over to his warehouse and mated onto their axles and wheels. Caleb Mansfield and his woods-cruisers were still resolutely scouring the countryside as far westward as Rumford, which really should now be called by the rightful name of Concord, and as far southward as Boston for oxen and draft horses. Frost had calculated that if each of the fifty-five boat-wagons needed a team of six draft animals, his expedition required a minimum of three hundred and fifty animals to provide for the inevitable losses of animals pulling up lame or sick. And in addition to the fifty-five boat-wagons to haul the gunpowder and food stores, he calculated another ten wagons to haul forage for the draft animals. He knew for a certainty there would be no forage available for the animals along the trek.

So the last fifteen or twenty boat-wagons he needed would have to be fashioned from what fragments of green wood he could wheedle from John Langdon and Tobias Lear. There was still the matter of providing or improvising sufficient harness and tack. And then there was the matter of fabricating sweeps, oars for the boat-wagons against the occasions the boat-wagons would have to be employed as ferries for river crossings. Oh yes, there had to be sufficient sweeps to propel the boat-wagons across rivers where there were no ferries.

Ming Tsun and Darius Langdon, who had laid aside his martial duties for the moment, were supervising the proper drying, resifting and stowing in clean, dry barrels of all of the captured flour that had been put up wet in obviously corrupt barrels by rapacious and venal contractors to the British Crown. The resifting got rid of the moist clumps of flour and the majority of the weevil infestations.

John Nason was likewise canvassing all the towns nearby for drovers—indeed, some dozen or so farmers who said they were drovers had already appeared and were camped near the warehouse with their families, where they, of course, expected Geoffrey Frost to feed and provide for them.

Cousin John Langdon had ordered away an unknown number of dispatch riders and messengers to gather intelligence concerning General Washington's whereabouts. Regardless of whether he had definite knowledge of Washington or not, Frost intended to sally as soon as Caleb Mansfield had mustered all the draft animals he could—certainly at a most hideous cost—and the boat-wagons were laden. In no event would he delay past the third of December. Washington was somewhere to the west, in New York, Pennsylvania or New

Jersey. West of the Hudson River was all anyone knew for certain. No matter, Frost would find His Excellency George Washington. After all, he had located Captain James Cook's *Resolution* off the Cape Verde Islands this September past and returned to Cook one royal passenger from the Society Islands and a royal marine name of Ledyard earlier swept off *Resolution* in a hurricane and drifted across *Audacity*'s bows courtesy of a hen coop.

Geoffrey Frost had much to accomplish, and very little time to see it all done. And this very evening his mother, the Lady Thérèse, was looking forward to his brother, Jonathan, just completing a voyage from China, dining with her at her cottage, *Bois de Jonathan*, or Jonathanwood, on the heights overlooking the Great Bay. Joss. Insh'allah. The Great Buddha, and Joseph, Mary, and Jesus. Like as not, later in the week the Lady Thérèse would hear that Joseph was back from the Lake and would desire him to dinner. And perhaps, just perhaps, before he sallied to find General Washington, his mother would hear of his arrival from some distant port and command his appearance. Joss. Frost grimly threw himself into the maelstrom of noise and smells of dried wood, shavings, tar, smoke, charcoal and sweat, and ordered work that bordered upon frenzy.

VI

THE PASTURAGE ACROSS THE ROAD FROM THE FROST TRADING COMPANY'S LONG WAREHOUSE ON CHRISTIAN SHORE WAS A QUAGMIRE OF MUD CHURNED UP BY the hooves of countless horses and oxen despite the steady swirl of snow that had accumulated close to half a foot on ground frozen in bitter cold. The forecourt was pure bedlam, as early morning was filled with shrill, boisterous yells, foul oaths, and crackings of whips by profane teamsters attempting to shackle beasts to the disselbooms of the crude conveyances heavily daubed with black tar that were half boat, half wagon. Women were hurriedly and haphazardly packing away kettles, soot-covered pots, iron grates, all the accoutrements of cookery in their assigned wagons. Several drovers were throwing tools, nails, iron bolts, linch pins, and short lengths of chain into the jockey boxes attached to the sides of the boat-wagons. Several children of families come from Portsmouth to gawk at the departure had detached themselves from their parents and were scurrying around excitedly, getting in everyone's way. A group of laughing ragamuffins was pursuing the squawking, terrified chickens that had not yet been appropriated into the hen coops of woven willow lashed atop the water barrels on the sides of the boat-wagons—or wherever else hen coops could be stored. Other laughing urchins were attempting to collect a sounder of pigs and deposit them into a wagon.

A frantic Mrs. Rutherford had appeared half an hour before to shepherd her white China geese, offspring of the pair Geoffrey Frost had brought back from China on his second voyage, to a tenuous safety in the barn behind the warehouse. Silas Rutherford, forthrightly and visibly armed with an ancient blunderbuss, though any close inspection would reveal the lack of a flint, and grim-faced, superannuated watchman Lamb Wilkes, self-importantly clutching a heavy cudgel, were patrolling around the warehouse to discourage any drover's thoughts of making off with any of the goods stored there.

Then Mrs. Rutherford had shooed her wide-eyed daughter inside the wing of the warehouse that was the superintendent's lodgings to preserve her from the lewd leerings and curses falling so liberally from the lips of every teamster as the reluctant oxen were maneuvered into their yokes and iron chains and leather traces. Now Mrs. Rutherford was hurriedly seeing to the belated packing of jams, pickles, potted meats and other delicacies from her larder into large panniers for Cook Barnes. Concerned that Cook Barnes should be permitted to rest from the incessant—and largely thankless—labors of keeping his ship's complement well fed, Frost has earlier inquired of his ship's cook if he would rather forego the rigors of this campaign by land after being at sea the greater part of the last ten months.

Cook Barnes had quickly dismissed the notion. "Ain't no gob to cook for, with the crew all dispersed spendin' their prize monies, most unwisely, I might confide. 'N' so far as keepin' Mister Ferguson in provender, reckon the Widda Crockett will see to him, right enough. Betimes, you've got them corduroy marines, and that bunch of wild uns follow Caleb Mansfield around, not to mention the young gentlemen. You've got Mister Ming Tsun to see after you, but nigh forty men, with the appetites o' twice their number, ain't got no one to see after them less'n old Barnes comes along." And then, with a shrewd wink, Cook Barnes confirmed to his captain what Frost already knew: Barnes would be quite chuffed if he were to miss out on a sharp fight or two.

Looking through the open door from the kitchen area of his quarters in the warehouse at the virtual anarchy prevailing in the forecourt, Geoffrey Frost knew that the accumulation of recalcitrant stock and ill-tempered drovers on this early Sunday morning, the first day of December, represented something far greater than a triumph of will in bringing everything together . . . in so far as things had actually come together.

His sister, Charity, and Marcus Whipple, her kindly, soft-spoken husband, whom Frost had rescued in May from the prisoner-of-war gaol in Louisbourg as partial offering in expiation of the guilt he bore for the death of Charity's twin brother, Jonathan, were taking their leave. Marcus clapped him heartily on the shoulder after shaking his hand, and took two halting steps toward the kitchen door, leaning heavily on his cane and walking with the awkward lift-and-limp of a man whose Achilles tendons had been severed. But walking all the same, and proudly, cheerfully.

Frost bent to take his sister's kisses on both cheeks, involuntarily inhaling the same clean, agreeable, utterly feminine scent that was his first recollection of their mother. He self-consciously kissed the top of his sister's hair, that lovely burnish the colors of carrot and pumpkin and maple leaves turning reddish-gold in the autumn. The exact same color as Jonathan's hair, and the reason he never had properly tanned beneath the sun at sea. He felt the firm squeeze of both of Charity's hands against the hand she held, and then she draped a folded flag over Frost's arm. "It is the Grand Union flag, dear Geoff, the same as is so proudly borne by His Excellency somewhere in the West. Maman, dear Elizabeth and I, with the invaluable assistance of Cinnamon, who somehow found the bunting, have stitched it . . . the four of us women wanted you to have a proper flag to identify yourself to His Excellency."

"Thank you, Pumpkin," Frost whispered so that only she could hear, using the child's name he had given her time immemorial ago, the only pet name he had ever given anyone. With a start that shook him to his soul he recalled another woman whose scent had been exactly the same . . . Frost recalled the smelling of it as he had pulled La Cygnet to her feet in the bull ring above Angra . . . the scent sharp and clear and clean, even above the burnt smell of her charred dress.

Charity's gaze traveled over Frost's shoulder at a patiently forbearing John Langdon. "John tells us that the rattlesnake flag flown with such pride over your vessels this better part of the year is really a naval flag, and thus not appropriate for display away from the sea." She grasped her brother's hand again for another brief squeeze and smiled as only Charity could smile, a smile that illuminated his soul. At Frost's nod, Ming Tsun draped Charity's fur-lined pelisse over her shoulders, and she turned away to take her husband's arm.

"Captain Frost, Captain Frost," the Reverend Claude Devon simpered, hastily downing his tea cup on the kitchen table and getting to his feet, fastidiously brushing away imaginary crumbs from his severely cut but well-tailored weskit with an elegant silk stock twined around his neck. The Reverend Devon had arrived uninvited and unheralded a few minutes before, and though the unexpected visit strained Frost's civility, his innate good manners prevailed. The Reverend had helped himself liberally to the raisin scones Ming Tsun had baked, consuming them all, together with the lightly tart and oh so wonderfully sweet clotted cream Mrs. Rutherford had provided.

Reverend Devon spread his arms cross-like, as if he had concluded the delivery of a lengthy sermon from his pulpit. "It is meet that we dispatch Captain Frost and the glorious mission of succor so well away properly with appeals to Our Heavenly Father to keep his feet affixed firmly upon the path of righteous on this pious day." The Reverend clasped his hands and bowed his head, then started to pipe in a pious, straining voice . . .

"Right you are, Reverend Devon," John Langdon said, clapping Devon firmly on the shoulder and abruptly stopping the parson's oration before it was fair launched. Langdon clapped the parson's shoulder again. "I agree, I agree most completely that devout prayers of the greatest sanctity . . .

ascending immediately to heaven to bestir Almighty God in protecting this assemblage of His piteous servants en route to succor General Washington should and shall arise. Indeed, I would fain address the drovers myself to exhort them to greater feats of patriotism.

"However," Langdon paused to thump Devon heartily on the shoulder yet a third time and wink conspiratorially at Frost, "my cousin is a-fire to be away, and has scorned the afford of time to pause the assemblage without, even for the most brief of messages. Therefore, I am persuaded we should set the solemn occasion for this Sabbath next, the eighth, two hours after the dawn. Then we shall congregate all the good people of the Ports of Piscataqua to raise their voices sublime and beseeching in North Church against your sermon of need for this convoy to achieve its end of putting might in the righteous fist of the Continental Army."

Langdon thumped the Reverend Devon again, so vigorously that the man's shoulders seemed driven down into his chest. Langdon produced a small snuffbox that he proffered to the parson with a flourish, though the parson declined. "Parson! I beg your indulgence at my lack of manners! I collect that you and your wife have occasion for great joy! I believe you may now, this fortnight past, be styled grandparents!"

"Exactly so," Parson Devon said, with greater severity and irritability than Frost, though inattentive, thought was warranted. "Our Hannah has indeed produced a set of twins for the edification of Missus Devon and myself, and not to say, obviously, of Hannah and her husband, Lancelot Duford, a student of theology at Harvard's University, which, as you know, is my matriculate. Thanks be to God that Hannah's confinement, though not the normal term, mind, has resulted in children of full term's appearance, complete with nine-months' fingernails."

"Yes," Langdon agreed instantly, "twins do that every time, assuredly! It is well known throughout the firmament that twins come due in but six months fully formed because of the greater weight the mother must bear. Anyone who says otherwise is an infamous liar, Parson! But come, my cousin desires to get underweigh, if we may parse the nautical term. Surely it would be more seemly to mark these honourable contributions to our cause of independence in an announced period of prayer and reflection, while calling God's benisons upon those accompanying Cousin Geoffrey in his unprecedented quest to aid our Continental Army?"

"I was desirous only of offering up a prayer for Captain Frost's safe journey," Parson Devon said, fiercely biting his upper lip until Frost was afraid the blood would run, "for I am as a-fire as any patriot to see the British devil cast out." Parson Devon fixed a disapproving eye on Frost, "And I want the prayers to ascend from a right pious Christian. I have it on the most scrupulous authority that Captain Frost has been heard, on multiple occasions, to call upon the heathen, outlandish idols of the barbarous religion of the Orient in conflict with the one true religion we avow."

"Next you shall have me doubly damned for a New Light adherent attentive solely to the sermons of the late Reverend Whitefield, safely buried these six years in Newburyport," Frost said shortly. "But I ken that whatever conflicts there are among religions arise only because we have failed to grasp the principles of our own religion," he continued quietly, "for they are all spokes leading to a central hub." Then: "John!" He cried, "I hope you have convinced Parson Devon the proper time for prayer is later, while I must live in the here and now, and the morning is far advanced. I beg the Almighty's pardon if I offend, but the more miles of the Dover to Boston Road that separate us come this day morrow, the better for our arms! Supplication on Sunday next for our success will see us fair launched, perhaps as far as Hartford! Expansive prayers raised several days hence by a volley of supplicants will speed us further along than extemporaneous, though well-meant, prayers this nonce."

John Langdon clasped Frost on the shoulder. "Well spoken, Cousin! And I have heard that Parson Devon's exemplary son-in-law, Lancelot Duford, is possessed of an extremely well-modulated tenor voice imminently suited to establishing communion with the Almighty. He and Parson may plan a service of inspiration that shall stand as an immutable witness to the struggles of those seeking to divest themselves of the tyrannical yoke of the British King. I fain believe the *Gazette* will report the services word for immemorial word."

"There you have it, Parson," Frost said, pretending delight. "Pray, delay your orison until it can be given sufficient tongue. The more tongue, the more spirit, the more attention paid by heaven above! Song!" he shouted out, "That's it, song! Few sinners are saved after the first twenty minutes of a sermon, no matter how well couched and sensibly reasoned to appeal both to spirit and intellect. But song! All sensations of time are lost when the soul is enthralled, held captive, ennobled with song!"

The rogue thought found expression before Frost could properly stifle it. "I am persuaded that my first officer, Mister Ferguson, is possessed of a most heavenly voice and desires naught to complete his life but to join your choir. Please address him at your leisure at the Langdon dockyard. Let him know that I would accord it a great favor, a great favor indeed, if he could join his voice with that of your son-in-law in smoothing the path we must traverse to locate the mysterious Washington and the army of our country."

Frost bowed the Reverend Claude Devon out of his kitchen with a flourish and saw him onto his palfrey with the greatest satisfaction. That Parson Devon would contact Struan there could be no doubt, and Frost would relish being present at the interview.

John Langdon strode over to the mounting block in the forecourt, where Prosperous stood holding the reins of a large, pale, gray-dun-colored mule, with its characteristic abbreviated tail, exquisite elongated ears lined with the softest fur, and dainty hooves. He took the reins and proffered them to Frost. "This molly-mule is Elizabeth's gift to you, Cousin," John Langdon insisted desperately, seeing Frost's look of absolute horror. "Damn it, Geoffrey, my wife wishes to gift you with the lady-mule that is her treasured possession. Elizabeth knows no better exercise than to ride this lovely creature along the foreshore of a morning. Mules are remarkable animals," Langdon continued. There was more than an edge of irritation on his voice. "Unlike horses, you cannot force mules to do things. You have to ask them, to consult them. Quite democratic, you'll doubtlessly agree. And their hard hooves do not require iron shoes. You yourself named the foal six years afore, though from whence came the name is something I can't fathom, that's a-sure."

"It would be unseemly for me to ride such a beautiful animal, seeing that those who accompany me shall be borne by shank's mare," Frost answered obstinately. He cast a despairing glance around the vast breaking encampment of draft horses, oxen, ribald teamsters and their trollops, and crudely thrown together boat-wagons, some with bonnets of rumbowline canvas stretched over willow bows, more than half without. Precious, irreplaceable cargoes of gunpowder and flour protected solely by a layer or two of worn-out canvas. Disbelieving, Frost saw Caleb Mansfield and half a dozen of his woods-cruisers busily levering the trains and tubes of two 12-pounder brass-barreled artillery pieces into a Conestoga wagon.

Truly, this assemblage had rapidly been eating Geoffrey Frost out of warehouse, purse and patience. His eyes smarted from the smoke of countless cook fires still tended by the various trollops and camp followers. With these tavern sweepings and bucolic, down-on-their-luck farmers, every man jack signed up for the thirty Spanish silver dollars bounty and found that Frost was paying he was expecting to succor His Excellency George Washington somewhere in the vicinity of Hudson's River? Any one of these drovers, motivated only by the hard money he was paying, might also be tempted to betray the wagon train to the British.

"Cousin, you are an exasperation in the extreme, debating with me in this cold and snow while dispatches reaching me three evenings past tell of the forts on the Hudson that our Continental Congress thought so impregnable that have been taken by the British and their German allies. Over three thousand Continental soldiers, the best of Washington's army, have been reduced to the status of prisoners—you know the fate of prisoners of the British well enough. Some prisoners unfortunate enough to be found clothed in winter uniforms destined for the British Army in Quebec—the uniforms taken out of the *Mellish* transport a month ago by Captain Jones of the Continental Navy, commanding the *Alfred*—were forcibly deprived of their raiment by their cruel captors."

John Langdon sighed wearily before continuing. "Lost also were dozens, perhaps hundreds, of cannons, irreplaceable cannons . . . when all I need to outfit my *Raleigh* are but thirty-two . . . captured, virtually all the Continental Army's tentage, bedding, entrenching tools, now in the triumphant possession of Howe's troops and his German minions."

"Aye, Cousin, I had the same report, not the same numbers, but close enough, from Caleb Mansfield, who has intelligence sources as reliable, if not more so, than your own 'monst his woods-cruizers." Frost tentatively stamped his feet to determine if he could still feel his toes. "And the greatest loss to General Washington be the thousands of militiamen from New York, Connecticut, Massachusetts and Rhode Island who have decamped without so much as a 'by-your-leave' and have lost heart in our cause."

"All the reason more why the provisions freighted in these boat-wagons are so precious. Those who tire of walking may easily hoist themselves aboard a wagon," John Langdon said testily. "You ken not that the pace of this circus of yours—for such it assuredly is, as you must admit—shall be one measured mile per hour throughout the day, assuming the happiest fortune. But you must be at many times in the forefront, and then again in the rear guard. Demands upon your time will come hard-pressed, just as demands have come against you while pacing your confined quarterdeck. But now your command extends over a far greater area. Think you can answer all your demands in time's necessity when you are likewise mounted on shank's mare?" John Langdon blew derisively through his nose, then added, "I lament exceedingly, Geoffrey, that no militia could be raised to accompany you as a protective force."

"So it would be thought," Frost said shortly. "Though it cannot be helped, and as you with me will gratefully acknowledge, in addition to Caleb's woods-cruizers we are augmented by a score and a half of ex-*Jaguars* willing to bear arms against their former countrymen, though they know their capture will mean their certain execution. I cannot think of a greater display of loyalty transferred to defeating our former oppressive master." Geoffrey Frost did not for a moment consider that perhaps the ex-*Jaguars* followed him and not some obscure notion of freedom or liberty.

"John, I cannot take Elizabeth's animal," Frost said with finality. "If I shall require a mount, I can procure one from the *remuda* recruited by Caleb Mansfield."

Langdon reached out to catch Darius Langdon's arm and pull Darius toward him. He wrapped the reins around Darius' arm. "Darius, watch over your errant master and preserve him from further foolishness, for my Elizabeth and I do ardently love your master and as ardently desire his return to our Portsmouth." He turned and stalked away without a backward glance, boots squishing noisily in the mud and manure muck, shoulders hunched beneath his cloak against the cold.

"I'm not your master, as you well know," Frost said testily, taking the reins from Darius Langdon. "I wanted not the refusal of this mule, because as you were completely untutored about how to conduct yourself upon the bosom of the sea when first you embarked in our *Audacity*, I likewise find myself unsuited for the quarterdeck of any four-legged animal." He regarded the mule balefully, staring directly into its eye, half-convinced that the mule was formulating a plan to nip off his arm or a leg.

Darius Langdon looked at Frost with his own calculating eye. "You gave this mule her name some years betimes, Captain. I know not from whence you drew the name, but whatever it means, Bwindi is a most beautiful name for such a lovely animal."

"Bwindi is a name given by some of the tribes inhabiting the lands south of the Island of Moçambique for a most noble animal that wears lyres on its head in place of horns," Frost said. "As it was explained to me when I sheltered in the Island of Moçambique, Bwindi means 'smoke,' and this animal could appear and disappear in the shuttering of an eye." Frost stepped back involuntarily as the mule started, but she was only reacting to George Three, who pranced up saucily, wagging plume of tail held high, and saluted the molly-mule with three short, joyous barks. Bwindi, settling quickly after her initial start, bent her regal neck to sniff and snuff at George.

"You ain't never sat astride a horse, nor mule," Darius said knowingly. "Ain't nothing to be a-feared of out of this 'un, Captain. That's why Mistress Elizabeth wants you to have this 'un so desperately. I was learned to ride so's I could accompany her, and it be astounding easy. Master John be right—"

"Mister Langdon," Frost said crossly, "we have exercised our gums in this regard before. You owe the title 'master' to no one." He glanced at the small saddle cinched atop the mule's barrel distastefully. "We may as well get on with it," he said, attempting to keep the resignation out of his voice. "Cousin John was right, of course. We are quitting the small but comforting compass of our vessel's deck and well-known, well-appreciated confines where we knew every cranny and could cross to any within the space of three minutes, for these boisterous animals . . . ," he indicated the oxen and draught horses, "and like some small gig afloat on this land that yet seems to rise up in tumultuous waves, I must yet maintain liaison with the myriad victuallers of contrary nature it is my lot given to command."

Darius kept his face serious as he drew the beautiful mule with the even more beautiful name, Bwindi, close to the mounting block. "Now, you step up onto this gig, Captain Frost—think of this mule as a gig to ferry you around your convoy, you being the sea-shepherd and all. You step up onto her, not down into her as you would a gig awaiting your pleasure at the waist entry." Once Frost was on the block, Darius helped him throw his right leg cautiously over the saddle, then transfer his weight onto the saddle, also ever so cautiously, until he was borne completely by the animal, whose patience he was too tense to acknowledge.

"Now," Darius said gently, after he had fumbled Frost's boots into the saddle's stirrups and handed up the reins. "These be like the tiller of your gig. When you wish your gig to go to starboard, you pull on this starboard rein. When you wish your gig to go to larboard, you pull on this larboard rein. It be totally different from the way you command your gig, when if you wish to turn toward starboard you must push the tiller to larboard."

Frost held the reins tentatively in his gloved hands. A violent swirl of snow surrounded him and threatened to tug away his tricorne; he was very cold, and felt very, very vulnerable sitting uneasily atop the molly mule. The churned, frozen ground seemed as far below him as the decks of his beloved *Audacity* viewed from the mainmast crosstrees. Frost could not remember a time he had ever felt so uncomfortable, so much in the midst of a situation he could not control. But of course, there had been that long ago painful, hateful time on the *Bride of Derry* . . . He fought off the attack of vertigo and swallowed back the bile rising in his throat.

"All right, Mister Langdon," Frost said testily, "I find that I am my own cox'n, but lacking my oarsmen, or a topsail breeze, how do I bestir this beast into movement?"

"With the most gentle of nudges against her ribs, Captain, sir." Darius caressed the mule's neck and tugged playfully at her wonderfully expressive ears. Bwindi tossed her head in appreciation, momentarily unsettling Frost. "She be not a British man-o-war, where the bosun and his mates employ their canes to start the men. Bwindi be like Mistress Elizabeth, gentle and dainty, willing to sew 'til midnight and beyond for a kind word."

Frost lifted the reins and nudged Bwindi's ribs experimentally with his boot heels. The mule tossed her head, bent into the bit and stepped out smartly, so smartly that Frost almost fell backwards. He compensated quickly, then overcompensated by shifting his weight too far forward. Bwindi stopped, unsure of her rider's intentions, and Frost found himself almost laid prostrate along the mule's neck. He bobbed erect and sawed on the reins, first one rein, then the other. Bwindi pranced, shifting her weight from one forehoof to the other, completely uncertain of what was being demanded of her. Frost had the presence of mind to tug on the starboard rein, and obligingly Bwindi turned to her right, where she was brought up short by the bulk of Caleb Mansfield.

"It pains me right smart to see ye abusin' such a noble animal," Caleb said sorrowfully. "I would fain borrow yere father's coach agin yere sure need, 'n' find ye a coachman, 'cept the road ahead be positive unsuitable fer coaches. Ye must learn to sit this rig if ye have any thoughts of commandin' this rabble.

"Now, there's a man who kin sit a horse admirable," Caleb continued, nodding toward Ming Tsun, who now approached, mounted like a centaur in a high Chinese saddle cinched to a deep-chested, dapple-gray, mean-looking gelded plough horse. Frost had no idea where Ming Tsun had gotten the Chinese saddle, or the elaborate bow-case strapped behind it. Brought from China, obviously, but as far as Frost had known, Ming Tsun's worldly possessions, aside from his halberd and bow, fitted quite comfortably inside a battered sea chest he had come by secondhand. There were many things about his best friend in life that Geoffrey Frost had yet to fathom—would most likely never fathom.

"How much time does it take these people to organize themselves?" Frost fretted. He brought Jonathan's watch from his wainscot pocket. By K'ung the Master, the time was approaching seven thirty! The sullen morning had been a-making for a good thirty minutes!

"Drovers be peculiar people, now, Capt'n. Particularly these drovers, since they ken how bad ye need 'em. 'N' it ain't like they's got the investment of wagon 'n' stock. These people be 'long strict for th' wages ye pay." Caleb sucked a tooth reflectively, Gideon, its locks wrapped with a strip of oiled deerskin, cradled carefully in the crook of his arm. "Wouldn't surprise me none if some of 'em don't demand more wages when we be half-along to wherever yere friend General Washington be keepin'."

"I'd admire to see that time come, if it comes, Caleb," Frost flashed grimly, "when we are at least half-along to wherever it is that we shall accost General Washington and our Continental Army. Those who may demand wages greater than those contracted shall answer for their impertinence."

"Waal, why don't ye and Mister Langdon here trot up ahead of this 'ere column and satisfy yereself that all the wagons be headin' general down the Boston Post Road. I've got our woods-cruizers suitable mounted and actin' as rovin' picquets, more to keep these drovers on course . . ." Caleb smiled. "How be thet, Capt'n? Ye got me usin' them seagoin' words."

"Just so, Caleb. It is meet that Darius and I give the drovers a look at us. They shall all have their surfeit ere long." Frost glanced sharply at Darius. "Where is your mount keeping?"

Darius raced around the corner of the Frost warehouse and returned a moment later astride a stout mouse-colored hinny of indeterminate age. He untied a tarpaulin jacket from behind the saddle and struggled into it as he stopped beside Frost. "It be a hinny I used to ride when I would accompany Missus," he explained. "Seeing as how my father did not wish me to purchase his freedom, as yet, I inquired of Master . . . Mister John if I might purchase this palfrey I knew. I'm obliged that Mister John sold her to me." Darius beamed. "Missus named her long betimes, name of Ariadne."

"Daughter of Minos, who defied her father to gift a man with the treasure of salvation, who later deserted her," Frost grunted. "An instructive for all women. Let us well away keep from Minotaurs and Labyrinths." He tentatively tickled Bwindi's ribs with his heels and was rewarded with a very willing, very eager forward gait, with George Three barking merrily alongside, a companion jolly boat to his gig. Frost found the motion jarring to his spine and was on the moment of pulling back on the reins when Darius cantered by, moving as easily aboard his Ariadne as kiss my hand. And here was Caleb coming up, mounted bareback on a solid gray cob with a dished face and small ears, one of which had been notched.

"Ain't nothin' to it, Capt'n," Caleb said triumphantly. "Bein' astride an animal again reminds me of standing in the front of yere vessel, that part just a-hind the bowsprit, and ridin' through the sea. Bend yere knees with the movement of the ship, but let yereself settle down onto the saddle. Besides," Caleb cast a knowing eye at Frost's mule, "a mule's one hull smarter then a horse. Missus Langdon, now she must cherish ye right smart to give up so fine an animal . . ."

But Caleb was talking to himself; Frost had spied the first onset of trouble, and he was nudging Bwindi with his heels toward where two boat-wagons had already cast a wheel each, and the drover of a third had in some wise managed to break the disselboom of his wagon and was looking stupidly at the oxen who stood pawing through the snow to the frozen ground beneath in vain search of some grass to eat.

Frost scowled as he drew up to the sullen teamsters, who were not even bothering to break out jacks or send someone for spare wheels. One teamster had dismounted from the huge Conestoga wheelhorse he had been riding, hooked his thumbs in his torn and dirty waistcoat pockets, and began calmly blowing smoke from a stogy. Frost reached down and jerked the vile-smelling, thick, rough twist of rum-soaked leaf that was the drovers' favored form of tobacco from the surprised man's mouth and threw it into a snowbank. "No smoking except close around a warming fire at night," he said harshly. "You may fancy that blowing yourself to hell along with a wagon loaded with gunpowder is all well and good, but our army has a better use for it."

Frost knew an overwhelming desire to snatch up a whip from the nearest drover's hand and lay about him with a will . . . but he was ashore now, and such would not do, absolutely would not do. Or would it? He was the forlorn, frustrated commander of some sixty-five wagons loaded to the gunwales with gunpowder, flour, hard biscuit, pease, beans, rice, salt, sugar, corn meal, several barrels of musket flints, and sundry other cargo of indeterminate nature. The entire cargo was cosseted and cushioned and padded with some five thousand blankets originally intended for the British Army in North America. And he had absolutely no idea where the Commander-in-Chief of the Continental Army was, or when he might find His Excellency George Washington.

VII

FIVE DAYS WEST OF BOSTON, ON THE RUTTED TURNPIKE PAVED WITH SHEETS OF ICE THAT LED TO HARTFORD, FROST FACED A SURLY, MUTINOUS CREW OF drovers, as he knew he must. He was heartily sick of deliberately ignored equipment failures, disobedience to his orders, stock that had mysteriously sickened, his own deprivation of sleep. He had literally gone past his tether when he came upon a drover deliberately abusing—grossly mistreating, actually—an ox with a goad. Frost, all patience thoroughly exhausted, threw himself off his mule and into the tightly knit pack of drovers standing around laughing and delighting in the ox's piteously bawled plaints at the indignities committed upon his nether parts.

Indeed, Frost actually enjoyed—no, he exulted in—thrashing the drover who had mistreated the ox. He could not deny that he derived immense momentary satisfaction from the beating he administered. Fleetingly, Frost found himself wishing that he had retained a flogging tool, a nine-tailed cat, so that a proper flogging could be administered across the bare backs of these malevolent, slovenly miscreants.

With great satisfaction Frost propelled the bloodied drover with the toe of his boot into the mob of sullen drovers formed in a semicircle around the scene of the thrashing. Frost spat on his skinned knuckles and rubbed them. "All of you! Back to your wagons! You!" he directed toward the drover who had mistreated the ox, "Give me your name at once."

"Felton." The drover spat out the single word along with a blackened, rotted tooth, the corners of his small mouth tugging down craftily and almost hidden in his black beard streaked with a band of white, reminding Frost of a skunk's pelt. He apparently regarded Frost as a necessary evil and thus beneath his contempt. His hat had been knocked off, and a furrow of blood was traced across his bald pate, which was as startlingly and unexpectedly white as a dead fish's belly.

"Brother Felton," Frost said, his breath coming in gasps from his exertions, "the instant I find you abusing these animals of mine in your charge—they belong not to you, ken—you shall be stripped to bare skin, lashed to a tree, and left for the crows." George Three, who had raced up to investigate the reason for the altercation, positioned himself immediately in front of Felton and barked furiously.

Felton's piggish eyes glowered, but the drover wisely held his tongue, and Frost knew the next dawn would see a half dozen, and more, drovers missing from the morning's enumeration. Frost stalked back to his mule, heart racing furiously, and easily swung himself into the saddle and clicked his tongue. He and Bwindi had readily formed a companionable bond, and the intelligent molly-mule responded as readily, seemingly knowing his mind, as did his wondrous *Audacity*. He sought out Caleb Mansfield, who was riding ponderously slow on his plug at the head of the column of boat-wagons.

"Caleb," Frost said softly, as he caught up to the woods-cruiser and his dainty Bwindi matched Caleb's horse's relaxed walk, "you've remarked, no doubt, that we are singularly fortunate to have journeyed thus far without encountering any hostile Indians."

Caleb regarded Frost quizzically. "Be ye feelin' puny, Capt'n? I ken yere bow's been strung pert tight, but thar be no Indians of war-like intent frequentin' these environs, I'll warrant. Grudge Indians thar be, certain. Don't blame 'em, considerin' how they been mistreated and murdered off by folk ain't anxious to share the bounty of this 'ere land."

"On the contrary, Caleb," Frost said with the slight lift of lips that was his caricature of a grin, "I have it on absolute authority that two months past, when Carleton swept down the Lake, he was accompanied, afloat and ashore, by a host of auxiliaries composed of several tribes of the Six Nations. Given the poor loot . . . ," Frost almost said "prizes" . . . "to come their way, I'm given to understand the Mohawk, Cuyahoga, Seneca and Onondaga have broken with Carleton and are even now marauding in areas where the men and muskets have been drawn away."

Caleb scratched his beard reflectively. "Now that I think on it, the Lake be only three days march north o' here. I know the Seneca well, wintered with 'em one year. They be much displeased at the coup they counted, scalps and prisoners taken. Won't surprise me none if a couple hundred er so lookin' out on us while we gab." Caleb sawed the head of his mildly protesting plug around. "Calls fer some advance picquets, I'll warrant."

"Scouts out, verily," Frost agreed.

"Waal, guess ye'd best see to yere primin', Capt'n," Caleb drawled as he nudged his plug into a half-hearted canter and drew away, then turned in his saddle, "Be sure ye fire high, mind. I'll say it agin, Capt'n, keep yere fire high."

The whoops and war cries came with a few ragged shots in mid-afternoon, as the temperature fell rapidly and snowflakes swirled and drizzled out of an overcast sky the color of a tarnished pewter shoe buckle. Frost was riding with Darius at his side a few yards or so behind the lead boat-wagon. Hannibal Bowditch was walking beside the boat-wagon, while Nathaniel Dance perched happily, swinging his feet in accompaniment to a tune only he could hear, on the left wagon board.

"Mister Langdon," Frost commanded, "instruct the lead wagon to tack sharply to larboard into that meadow alongside, the rest following the lead. Gallop halfway down this piteous column and instruct whichever wagon you choose to pick up the pace and tack to larboard and join with the other wagons in a cordon, or whatever we can contrive for an enclosure."

"Have we need of a fortress, Captain?" Darius asked breathlessly, eyes widely staring.

"Such as these poor hulls can provide, Mister Langdon, and quickly now! Further, alert Ishmael Hymsinger in his lazarette-wagon to the very real possibility that he shall be tending casualties in the half-hour." Frost felt for the grip of a Bass pistol and drew it from his belt. He tucked into Bwindi with his heels, and the molly-mule, mildly protesting, broke into a canter. Frost turned away from the meadow on the left and urging Bwindi from a canter into a run, heading up the slight rise toward the line of trees some three hundred yards away to the right.

Caleb Mansfield, holding the reins of another horse in his mouth, was riding, hell bent for leather, out of the line of trees. He was lashing his plug into a lather, his head bent low, while in tow on the horse behind him one of his woods-cruisers slumped backwards, alarmingly so, over the crupper of his horse, right hand clasped to his left bicep, from which protruded an arrow's shaft. Half a dozen or so men wrapped in gaudy trade blankets, ululating madly, came out of the treeline and fired a ragged volley at the two riders.

"Form a defense, form a defense," Frost shouted, as he urged Bwindi into a faster run. He passed Caleb Mansfield and brought his molly-mule up short. He took hurried aim with his Bass pistol and fired, noting with satisfaction that one of the gaudy figures pitched forward, struggled to rise, then got to his feet in apparent agony, and limped away, helped by another. Frost discharged the second barrel of his pistol, then turned Bwindi toward the bewildered ellipse of wagons slowly forming in the meadow.

Frost had no hope of catching up to the pelting Caleb Mansfield, so he calmly reined Bwindi, turned her toward the treeline, drew the second Bass pistol, thumbed back the cock, and fired. He was answered by two musket shots, the balls of which passed harmlessly twenty feet overhead. No, the shots came from long rifles, not muskets. He urged Bwindi into the noisy confusion of drovers, drovers' families, and the ex-*Jaguars* who comprised his marine guard and who were attempting to form a defensive line under the urging of Nathaniel Dance as he strode to and fro, brandishing his dirk.

"Belay a line outside the wagons, Mister Dance," Frost shouted as he galloped past. "Shelter your men inside the barricade formed by the wagons!" He glanced up in alarm as Bwindi galloped toward a wagon from which the oxen were being uncoupled. He watched Bwindi's ears attentively and saw that the molly-mule lay them flat back. Frost felt the mule gather her forelegs beneath her, then felt the raw power in her hindquarters as she skillfully leaped and soared over the disselboom. Frost whirled and discharged the last barrel toward the figures at the tree line. Their ululating cries came down to the people caught in the ellipse.

A frantic drover raced past, goad thrown down, arms pumping, legs lifted high. Frost recognized the bloody furrow on the pale, bald pate. "Teamster Felton!" he shouted, stopping the man instantly with the lash of his voice. "Marshall the wagons containing gunpowder into the middle of the ellipse. Surround the powder wagons with the wagons containing food barrels. Gather men to remove the flour and rice barrels from the wagons and form them into barricades at the disselbooms. Likely the Indians are forming for a descent upon us!"

"But I be a-frighted, Capt'n," Felton said, his voice little more than a miserable croak. "I be a-frighted true, and not able to grub up a hill of beans."

"All the more reason to find employment for hand and mind, Teamster Felton," Frost chided. "Come, I've marked you as a competent drover, and you surely know the wagons freighting powder. Ensure they are inside and protected by the food wagons. If the Indians can fire just one wagonload of powder we shall all be opportuning heaven this day!"

"Aside there!" Caleb Mansfield barked, kicking his plug through a mob of drovers frozen in paralysis. "Ishmael Hymsinger! Yere knives should already be sharp, 'cause we have a man sore wounded by an arrow buried deep." Frost noted with satisfaction that Felton had gotten hand enough on his fear to do his bidding, and then he saw that the woods-cruiser laid back along his horse's crupper was Tobin Tuttle, a recent addition to Caleb's *coureuse des bois* from beyond the notches.

Caleb threw himself off his plug and dragged Tobin Tuttle unceremoniously from his horse, the shaft of the arrow in Tuttle's shoulder protruding from between the fingers of Caleb's callused hand. He hustled Tuttle into the lazarette-wagon, where an exceedingly grave-faced Ishmael Hymsinger waited. He dropped a canvas curtain and pulled up the wagon's tailboard with all the solemn finality of a drawbridge's lifting up from across a moat.

But the Indians did not descend upon the slovenly defensive ellipse. Instead, they drew away reluctantly, with many a taunt, threatening yelps, and exaggerated, obscene gestures. Caleb Mansfield vaulted out of the lazarette-wagon and held up an arrow shaft snapped off just behind the head. "Onondaga it be," Caleb said, pointing to the fletching with a bloody forefinger, "and we seen hundreds, hundreds of 'em to eastard. Can't be sure, but looked like there war some women 'n' children took as prisoners. I've got two o' my woods-cruizers out still, countin' 'em bloody heathen to the last bowstring 'n' musket. Who's with me fer venturin' agin them Onondaga 'n' rescuin' them women 'n' children they've took prisoner?" Caleb Mansfield looked eagerly around the circle of blanched, ashen-faced drovers and their families. "Come on, them prisoners might be yere kith 'n' kin! Who shall venture out with me?" Caleb eagerly searched each blanched face in turn. "You, George Perkins from Ipswich, you, Thomas Runyon from the Falls of the Hampton River, you, Carl McCoy from one o' the Berwicks, I can't ken which one . . . ain't ye men eager to engage these Onondaga and acquit yere kinsmen plucked from their peaceful hearths?"

"We took Captain Frost's money and his word that these here supplies had to get to General Washington," one of the drovers in the mob spoke up forcibly, almost sanctimoniously. "We be given our sacred word."

"Yere sacred word when women 'n' children be took off to Canada 'n' slavery?" Caleb said incredulously. "Yere sacred word be damned, then!"

Frost slid wearily off his molly-mule. "Caleb," he said mildly, "how many Onondaga did you spy actually?"

"Multitudes, Capt'n, and not jest them Onondaga, but most like Mohawk and Seneca, 'n' dare I say it? A couple o' lobster-red uniforms. Carleton's men directin' the Indians back to Canada." Caleb Mansfield whipped the arrow shaft above his head. "Come on, who be with me fer the recovery o' those who might be our own kin?"

"Caleb," Frost said placatingly, taking the arrow shaft from Caleb's hand and rotating it reflectively between his palms to gauge how true the shaft would fly. "You say these Indians effectively seal us off from communications to the eastward?"

"Effectively so, Capt'n Frost," Caleb bellowed. "They bar us effectively from Portsmouth, from Boston, from all eastard liaisons. Appears they sit astride all the roads we took from Portsmouth."

"Drovers," Frost said soberly, "the prisoners of the cruel Onondaga cry out to us for succor." He paused to survey the men and their women assembled in front of him. Before he could speak further, all heads turned to the sounds of frantic, galloping hoofbeats, striking against the frozen ground like drum rolls. Cox Pridham's lathered great plough horse leaped the disselboom with all the aplomb of a seasoned hunter, then reined to a halt six feet from Geoffrey Frost.

"Care for that horse before he founders," Frost commanded sharply to two lookers-on who appeared from their rustic garb to have some acquaintance with the care of livestock. "Now, Pridham, share with us, if you will, the intelligence that drove you here at the extraordinary expense of your mount."

Pridham slipped from the saddle and stroked his horse's muzzle fondly. The horse blew a great gout of foam from its nostrils and rolled its bloodshot eyes wildly. Frost found the shrunken, withered winter apple in a pocket of his greatcoat that he had been saving for his Bwindi and held out the apple to Pridham's mount. The horse crunched it gratefully.

One of the rustics had laid hold of the horse's reins. "Walk the horse gently for a good five minutes to settle him," Frost warned. "Then rub him with sacks of tow. Allow him all the forage he wishes, but water only sparingly. Do you ken?"

The rustic nodded dumbly. "Be away on your business," Frost said abruptly.

"Dinna ken ye knew so much about the husbandry of horses," Caleb Mansfield said appreciatively.

"Horses, oxen, men, all God's creatures have similar needs when in distress, Caleb," Frost said shortly. Then to Cox Pridham: "Your intelligence, and quickly, then you must rest."

"Over a dozen towns to the eastard set to the torch—ain't nothing but ashes now," Pridham stammered. "Whole legions of militia slaughtered. Women 'n' children forced to watch their menfolks' brains dashed out with war clubs. Then gathered in great levies to be driven a-foot to the Canada . . ."

"Here, man, ye be a-thirst with the reportin' of such horrors," Caleb said, having sent Hannibal Bowditch scuttling off in search of liquor. Hannibal now pitched up with a handsome wicker-covered demijohn. It reminded Frost strongly of the carboy that had been set astream from *Audacity* to take a line to the dismasted Portuguese nau commanded by Struan Ferguson during the height of the hurricane that by all rights should have claimed them both. Pridham lifted the heavy demijohn to his lips and gulped gratefully.

Frost knocked the demijohn aside irritably and was rewarded for his trouble by the stunned looks of a host of thirsty men, who watched the rum gurgle out the demijohn with horror and exchanged stares of alarm. "Your intelligence," Frost said grimly.

"Woeful, woeful indeed, Captain Frost," Pridham began.

One of the drovers cleared his throat reluctantly. By the Great Buddha, it was Felton speaking unctuously! "Captain

Frost, sir, no matter how poignantly from their hearts the cries of our poor afflicted resonate for succor, our obligations lie with the men under the command of General Washington. We must carry on westward, and, though it pains me—indeed, all of us—extremely to say it, we cannot spare the diversion of men to pursue the Onondaga and their captives, and leave these wagons undefended."

What ho, by Jesus, Joseph and Mary, but this Felton was an orator! Indeed, judging by the preciseness of his words, of no small merit. Felton was as unctuous as Parson Devon, and as sincere.

"It pains me to hear you speak so," Frost snapped. "Mayhap you have kin even now being borne off to an enduring captivity . . . in times as uncertain as the Second Indian War of the last century, or even Philip's War exactly one hundred years ago."

Ishmael Hymsinger threw aside the canvas curtain than enclosed the stern of his boat-wagon *cum* lazarette-wagon. He let down the tailboard and wearily descended, his timorous step that of a man thrice his age. "Tobin Tuttle shall live, I have excavated the head of the arrow." He held aloft a bloody arrowhead forged from crude iron. "From my time with the Mi'kmaq, I know the head to be bloated with a poison, but it has been counter-acted."

"And be it counter-acted?" one of the drovers demanded. "By God, all this be happenin' too much! My poor brain cannot take all in! These be black times where Satan runs a lengthy trap-line."

"Thet not be all yere brain fails to take in," Caleb Mansfield said darkly. "Some things better be left without the knowin', but Ishmael the Healer says true, the poison be indeed countered . . . and ye ken how, ye pea-brained drover?" Caleb had judiciously recovered the demijohn before it emptied and had taken several healthy swallows of its contents.

"Waal, now that you've gotten us to the query, how indeed be poison on arrows be countered, Mister . . . Mister Woods-Cruizer?" the drover asked cautiously.

"Piss, man, piss," Caleb said, smacking his lips as he reluctantly put down the demijohn, contents spilling liberally upon his once new but now much besmeared buckskins; he noted Frost's look of disapproval and reluctantly drove the corncob plug into the neck with the palm of a hand. "A good wackin' piss direct into the wound. Next best thing to the lickin' o' a dog's tongue, though like as not, ye'd be in no lights to get a dog to lick any wound ye'd incur. Barrin' thet, a good clean piss is the best way to cleanse a wound."

"Why stand here talking about wounds and dogs licking 'em when we've got God knows how many Indians intent on separating us from our hair and hauling off our kin to Canada?" This from one of the anonymous drovers tightly gathered. No, the speaker was Felton.

"Waal, ol' hawg, you ain't got nothing to worry about in that respect," someone in the anonymous crowd hooted. "You needn't fear getting your hair lifted being you ain't got none."

"Enough!" Frost shouted. "Brother Felton twigs onto an uncomfortable, yes, a truth beyond the palatable." He glared fiercely around at the drovers, who stirred uneasily under his direct, accusatory gaze. "Let's out the truth. There are those among you considering abandoning your duty. You've advanced half your wages, with the balance being paid after delivery of these goods to the Continental Army and return to our dear Portsmouth. You have thought it a better deal with less hazard to slip away with half your wages in your pocket firm than continue on as agreed, upon your sworn word as agreed—do not deny it." Frost flung his right arm eastward in what he hoped was a sufficiently dramatic flourish. Thankfully, at least Struan Ferguson was not here to offer his critique of Frost's acting.

"Well enough! Anyone who wants to quit our company may do so now, and I shall write out a draft payable at my father's bank for the full sum of wages contracted."

"Aye," Caleb said, "and no loss ye'll be, thet's God's truth. 'N' the Capt'n's father will pay yere wages, a-sure . . . assumin' ye can get through the Indians the British have loosed upon our peaceful settlements." Caleb paused significantly, hefted the demijohn, and shook it, pleased with the sound it gave forth. "Now, if there be among ye those fit to go ahead with their duty, as the Capt'n calls it, waal, I reckon he won't begrudge the passin' around of this tipple." He shot the demijohn at Felton, who caught and held it protectively, but glanced fearfully at Frost.

"That demijohn you may finish, but not more, else you risk going to your maker with liquor on your breath. Those reconciled to their duty . . . back to your wagons, for we can make another two hours' progress before we pause for the night. Caleb, scouts ahead, and picquets behind, withdrawing at our pace. Underweigh now, and sight our next encampment. I must see how Goodman Tuttle fares."

The demijohn went rapidly around, torn from Felton's hands despite his futile attempt to swig more than one healthy swallow. Hannibal picked up the demijohn the drovers cast aside once empty. Frost watched the drovers back to their teams while Caleb threw his scouts forward. The boat-wagons ponderously got underweigh.

Frost clambered into the lazarette-wagon as it lurched forward. Tobin Tuttle, bare to the waist, was sitting up, drinking a cup of exceedingly cold coffee liberally laced with rum as Ishmael Hymsinger wrapped a bandage around the man's arm. Hymsinger picked up the freshly killed squirrel laying atop a barrel and squeezed several drops of blood onto the bandage, then made one more wrap before tying it off.

"Barked him right proper laying on a beech tree limb at fifty yards with the first shot of the fusillade we laid down. Fetched him along for supper, I did, though Ishmael here thought of a good use for this here squirrel before he goes in the stew pot." Tuttle winked as he drank off the cup of bitter coffee. "Be hell itself to pay, Capt'n, if those pilgrims ever twig to the fact that arrer came outa Mister Ming Tsun's quiver."

VIII

GEOFFREY FROST WAS IMMEDIATELY AWAKE AT MING TSUN'S LIGHT TOUCH ON HIS SHOULDER. HE REMEMBERED, JUST IN TIME, THAT HE WAS SLEEPING underneath the lazarette-wagon and did not sit upright, instead rolling out of his blankets into the intense cold and pulling himself stiffly, tired muscles protesting, to his feet by the spokes of the nearest wheel. George Three crawled out from where he had been sleeping beside Frost, shook himself vigorously, then licked Frost's face. Caleb Mansfield and two of his woods-cruisers, Row Gaffney and Singleton Quire, were crouched by the isolated fire, the only one ablaze in the encampment, blankets draped around their shoulders. Cook Barnes was busying himself, though quietly, with his pots and skillets, and then he thrust at the woods-cruisers cups of something hot that sent curdles of steam into the frigid air.

"Ain't seed it so cold for a long time," Singleton Quire said in a low voice, tilting his copper mug to his bearded lips. "Once we got on this side of the river we had to pick our way through the fishes that had crawled out on the bank and were buildin' their own fires to get warm." Around their solitary fire the population of the entire encampment, except for the picquets on duty, slept with many a snore and snuffle.

Frost pulled one of his blankets from atop the canvas mattress stuffed with dried corn shucks and sat down on a three-legged milking stool near the fire. Ming Tsun lifted a pot from coals raked out of the fire, poured liquid from the pot into a copper mug he got from Cook Barnes, and placed the mug into Frost's hands. The fire threw off just enough light for Frost to read Ming Tsun's signing that there was no more honey. Frost cocked an eyebrow toward Caleb Mansfield and waited for him to speak.

"Ain't no ferry 'tall at Springfield, 'n' there be a hull bunch of Tories hidin' theirselves in a town on the west bank awaitin' fer us to cross, unsuspectin' like, so they can fall upon us." Caleb was plainly exhausted, and his eyelids sagged wearily.

Frost smiled his thanks at Ming Tsun, who had placed the iron pot back on the coals. Cook Barnes was tending something in a large spider of a frying pan on the other side of the fire. "What of the ferry, and how do you cypher those congregated on the farther bank are Tories? What is their number, and how do you buttress your opinion these Tories, if that be what they be, do intend us harm, and how?"

"Ferry be burnt near as we could tell, no way o' knowin' by Tories or people call theirselfs fightin' with us. As fer the Tories, waal, Row Gaffney 'n' I practically introduced ourselves. We got as close to the gentry in charge as yere bed of repose yonder. We wus close again' their window—unseen, mind—whilst they wus gabbin'." Caleb fixed Frost with a long stare. "Where ye wus snorin' fair to wake the dead in all the graveyards within ten mile o' Springfield, we wus hoverin' all about the village they had put to the torch. Agawam its name was."

Frost ignored the jibe. He knew for a certainty that he had never snored in his life. "I hear tell that snoring is a sign of a clear conscience, Caleb," he retorted. "Continue with your report, and perhaps Ming Tsun can locate a small measure of rum to cut the bitterness in that awful coffee you are drinking." Frost was grateful for the mug of tea sending warmth through his chilled body, though he surely missed the flavoring of honey.

"Near as Row Gaffney and I can figure, those buckos be from down 'round New Haven, close on a hundret, we cypher, all on horses, with five, six wagons o' provisions, just awaitin' to greet whatever travelers happen to want to get across the Connecticut hereabouts."

"And you are certain they be Tories?" Frost demanded.

Caleb shrugged ruefully. "The gentry what seemed to be in charge ken who we be 'n' all, 'n' has certain designs on us. No coverin' up them wagons o' ours so people kin't see 'em, that's a-sure. Hull countryside knows who we be 'n' what we be totin'. They didn't have the right count o' wagons, but 'twas close enough. Said they wus goin' to reduce us to possession, if I recollect the words proper."

"They wus braggin' how they put a town just to the south of here to the torch three days a-fore," Row Gaffney said in a flat, cold voice. "Ain't sayin' nobody who calls themselves patriots like Mister Langdon or Mister Lear back in Portsmouth ain't never fired a Tory's house deliberate-like, but these folks were jokin' 'bout it, 'bout killin' men what had throwed down their firelocks. Makin' sport o' it," he finished in disgust.

Frost sighed wearily. "Two days ago, when Ming Tsun and I paused to buy eggs from a farmer, he warned us about a Tory from down New Haven way by the name of Rousseau. Said this Rousseau was meaner than a wolverine." Ming Tsun thrust a pewter bowl and a pewter spoon toward Frost. Frost set the copper mug of tea in the embers of the fire to keep the tea warm and tucked into the contents of the bowl. It was squash and apple soup, a thick, rich puree made according to the legendary recipe of Mrs. Rutherford. Exquisitely delicious, and truly welcome. "I take it a wolverine is some sort of animal that may be familiar to you, Caleb."

Caleb unwrapped a paper waxed with tallow taken from his possibles bag. Cook Barnes overturned the skillet above a platter and a large pone of cornbread dropped onto the platter. Barnes divided the steaming pone into six pieces, using his hook as a knife, then handed the platter to Caleb, Row Gaffney and Singleton Quire, then Ming Tsun, then Frost.

From its sheath on the strap of his possibles bag, Caleb

drew the small knife he used to cut mattress ticking to size as patches for rifle balls and began dividing the object he had unwrapped. "Ain't nothin' to share out but this piece of beaver tail. Ain't had time fer no huntin', Capt'n been movin' us along so. Had to dig through two feet o' beaver lodge to get this 'un, and he wus right poor." Caleb peered hopefully at Frost. "Might be time to butcher one o' 'em beef cows been lookin' puny and peaked, so we's could have some real meat."

"Those beeves are destined for the Continental Army, Caleb," Frost said, though not unkindly.

Caleb took a sip of coffee, almost choked, made a wry face, and looked dubiously into the cup. "Faith, there be such a quality of ox hair in this coffee thet one must assume it be a treasured condiment. But the better condiment be a fair measure o' rum." Caleb handed around the pieces of beaver tail. "Ain't even see a deer, nor a moose," Caleb said. "This country be more than middlin' bare." Frost declined the offer, so Caleb tendered the piece of meat to the great Newfoundland dog, who took his share with great dignity, then flopped down contentedly at Frost's feet. "Sure appreciate the hoe cake, Cook Barnes, it do go right well with beaver tail 'n' this coffee, particular with the flavorin' Mister Ming Tsun is passin' around." Caleb chewed a piece of cornbread reflectively while Ming Tsun tipped a pleasantly gurgling demijohn into Caleb's mug of coffee. "Now, if we wus to have a wolverine jump in 'monst us right now, which be the same animal as the French call a *carcajou*, we wouldn't be sharin' no pone o' hoe cake, ner drinkin' coffee, cause the wolverine would take it all for hisself. What he couldn't eat or tote away, he'd foul so we couldn't have the enjoyment of it."

Caleb swallowed the piece of cornbread and washed it down with a huge swig of rum-laced coffee. He wiped his mouth with the back of his hand. "Had a wolverine tear up my camp once. Weren't no call to what he done. Chewed 'n' fouled all the furs so they had no value fer trade, nor much else, now thinkin' on it. Killed a little panther-cat that had somehow took up with me, just to see 'er die. Ripped 'er belly open to spill 'er guts, but didn't kill 'er right out. Fouled every scrap of food that it couldn't get down its gullet, even gnawed the babiche o' my spare racquets so they warn't no good. Wiped me out total. Wolverines be like that by nature."

"Not a high recommendation for one of God's creatures," Frost said shortly, spooning the last of the squash and apple soup into his mouth, regretting immensely that there was no more.

"Don't reckon God took much pleasure in seein' what the wolverine made o' himself, ner people like yere Piscataqua pilot, Mister Stalker, ner a hull sight of other people I could name made of theirselves, after God created 'em. Can't rightly blame God fer the way people nor wolverines turn out." Caleb closed his eyes and took a long pull at his mug.

"The gentry called one o' 'em Rousseau," Row Gaffney said quietly. "Called him 'Colonel Rousseau.' This Rousseau's got a runnin' mate name o' Boyd, both bad 'uns judgin' from the heap sight o' widders and orphans they've created here 'bouts."

Frost sighed and gave the pewter bowl to George to lick, a task the dog performed happily and noisily. "Is there a place we can cross the Connecticut in our boat-wagons without encountering this so-called 'Colonel' Rousseau and his henchman cut from the same cloth?"

"Not like," Caleb said shortly. "Ye ken there be spies on both shores, 'n' this Rousseau's got mounts fer all his men. 'Pears to me belike that game ye, with help from Nathaniel, and Mister Ming Tsun and Mister Ferguson be playin' all the time. Move one o' them little ivory doodads and someone moves a piece of his'n that gives ye pause. 'Cept our wagons be slow, and this Rousseau fella and Boyd, they kin move a hull bunch faster than us. Wait fer us to cross the Connecticut, then fall upon us betimes."

"I am sure you have thought much on the starting charge for those two brass 12-pounders you brought along to gift General Washington, Caleb." Frost stood up and began pacing, hands clasped behind his back, the distance of the fire's illumination, a distance amazingly similar to the length of *Audacity*'s quarterdeck. He thought fleetingly of his ship and the men he had left to accomplish her overhaul and refit. Roderick Rawbone had wanted to accompany him, but Frost would not hear of it. Rawbone's place was with the ship, more so to keep John Langdon or anyone else from levying against *Audacity*'s temporarily inactive cannons for other commissions. And between him and Struan Ferguson was divided the heavy responsibility of keeping the Kendall chronometer properly wound. Caleb had proved his worth as a matross serving a long 9-pounder mounted as a makeshift stern chaser aboard the dear old *Salmon* during its relentless pursuit by HM *Jaguar*. He glanced briefly at the surround of boat-wagons, most of them hastily constructed from *Salmon*'s timbers. What little wood that had been left of the *Salmon* had been cut and stacked outside Mrs. Rutherford's kitchen to stoke her fireplace. The iron fittings had gone to the forge to be smelted into new iron. It was comforting to Frost to have parts of the *Salmon* close by.

"Made up some startin' charges, same as done with a rifle new-bought from the gunsmith," Caleb said with satisfaction. "Set one o' 'em twelve-pound balls, with the rust scaled off, square in the middle o' a piece of canvas 'n' trickled powder over 'er 'til she wus plum covered, but stopped there and measured the powder in a birch bark scoop 'til we got 'er exact. Made up twelve charges, all could be cut from a petticoat one of the drover's women left over a bush, convenient like, seein' we had no proper cartridge flannel."

Frost pulled Jonathan's watch from his pocket, pressed the spring lever to open its cover and held the face toward the fire. Lacking ten minutes of midnight. "Should do for iron ball or langrage, either one. I would be greatly favored if you would select a capable person to see to the mounting of the tubes on their carriages, Caleb. I think your twelve charges should be ample. I am sure you have them collected in some sort of shot and powder locker easily transported. Two lockers would be admirable. Row Gaffney, please oblige me by waking the ship's gentlemen asleep in the lazarette-wagon and inviting them to join our conversation. Singleton Quire, direct the unlading of the four wagons with the least forage remaining and start them on their way to a point a good two miles above the town of Springfield. We shall need a place with a gentle bank down to the river. You shall presently be joined by our marines. Insure sweeps go with the wagons. And a pot of slush sufficient to lubricate the thole pins."

Frost permitted himself a half-grin, although no one in the company around the fire could see it: "Please be solicitous of the fish huddled around their fires, whose efforts to remain warm you so eloquently described these moments past." He increased the intensity of his pacing. "Caleb, you and Row Gaffney hasten back to the village where these Tory friends of yours are encamped. I presume you still have access to whatever conveyance bore you to and from the west shore. Please rendezvous with me on the western shore two miles above the ferry landing one hour before sunrise. I have every confidence you shall be able to tell me the number of picquets watching the ferry landing."

He heard the awkward scrambling from the lazarette-wagon where the three ship's gentlemen berthed with Surgeon's Mate Ishmael Hymsinger. "There you are, Mister Dance," he said to the sleep-tousled youngster, blinking and rubbing his eyes as he stumbled across the frozen ground toward the fire. "Please be so good as to rouse your complement of marines, quietly now. Each man to have twenty cartridges in his cartridge pouch, except the riflemen, who shall carry double that. Issue rations to be eaten on the march." He held the watch so Nathaniel Dance could see the time. With his constant immersion in pedagogy, ashore as well as at sea, Nathaniel had easily picked up the knack of telling time. "You and your thirty marines are to be underweigh by midnight. Singleton Quire will guide your march, and I shall locate you presently with further orders."

Equally sleepy-eyed, Darius Langdon and Hannibal Bowditch, stuffing nightshirts into heavy woolen breeches, were scrambling down from the lazarette-wagon to be met by George Three, eager to play with his mates. "Belay your antics, George," Frost commanded, though not sternly, as he regarded the two youths.

"Misters Langdon and Bowditch, to you devolves the process of rousing this sleeping encampment and seeing that everything is properly stowed and underweigh toward the ferry landing at Springfield town exactly one hour before the sun's rising." He paused to take in the youths' bewildered stares. "Come, gentlemen, think well over the orders you shall issue. Be not daunted by the task, though I assure you that getting this concatenation of ill-starred, quarrelsome landsmen underweigh is enough to try the patience of a saint more forbearing than Job, so much so that preparing our *Audacity* to weigh anchor is small apples indeed." Frost paused, turning over in his mind what insurances he had yet to pursue. Yes, one item. "Please to have Ishmael Hymsinger sent over to the western side as soon as you fetch the Connecticut. With all his medical apparatus."

He did not pause to consider that he was leaving the exceedingly complex organization of two hundred and fifty people, most of them surly and recalcitrant, and the marshalling of three hundred and sixty-two oxen for a timely departure to two youths who were still several years away from their first proper shave. He had given them their orders, and because Geoffrey Frost accepted without doubt that his orders would be faithfully discharged, he strode away toward the roped-off areas that constituted the paddocks for the horses and mules. He knew that Ming Tsun was already there, saddling Frost's molly-mule and his own horse. He snatched up the copper mug of insipid tea from the coals where he had left it and found the tea satisfyingly hot, at least.

IX

THE PULL ACROSS THE CONNECTICUT WAS NOT AT ALL TO FROST'S LIKING, BUT HE WAS GRATEFUL FOR THE OPPORTUNITY TO SEE HOW THE boat-wagons, jacked-up and their wheels removed, would take to the water, even though it was night. The river crossings thus far had been accomplished by bridge or ferry, thankfully, and except for one boat-wagon launched at Langdon's dockyard and laden to determine how much weight the boat-wagon could reasonably accommodate, Frost had found no occasion to observe the trim of these crude vessels. The boat-wagons were then skidded down the embankment to take the water, flailing first through a heavy skim of ice and causing far more noise and commotion than Frost wished. He would quickly see on this, the broadest river the boat-wagons had yet crossed, how they would handle laden and under sweeps.

But the boat-wagons got underweigh with a minimum of fuss, the loading of Nathaniel Dance with his thirty marines, the eleven woods-cruisers, Frost's and Ming Tsun's mule and horse, the two twelve-pounder artillery pieces and the horses to pull them, all accomplished without showing any light. The ex-*Jaguars* now employed as marines were apportioned among the four boat-wagons to man the sweeps, tholes well greased with slush to muffle their noise, that were propelling the clumsy vessels—slowly—across the Connecticut. Not that the efforts to keep the sweeps as silent as possible made any difference, given all the noise associated with jacking up the wagon bodies, wrenching off the wheels, pushing the wagon bodies down to the Connecticut, breaking through the ice along the shore, and then loading the cannons and men.

It was hard rowing, and Frost feared that he had miscalculated the weight he could safely stow in each boat-wagon. Each boat-wagon rode perilously low in the water, and they were notoriously crank and exceedingly difficult to steer. The rowers had to row standing up, because placing boards across the wagon bodies to be used as thwarts would have taken up far too much space. But the boat-wagons were afloat, and they were crossing the Connecticut, no matter how tortuously. Bitterly cold water seeping in through the edges of the tailboards, hastily plugged with tow and leather, swilled in the bottom of the boat-wagon, lending an additional sense of urgency to a swift passage.

Bwindi, standing quietly behind Frost in the bow of the lead boat-wagon, tickled the hair at the back of his neck beneath his short queue with her warm breath as Frost peered intently at the far bank. He tugged the woolen muffler anchoring his tricorne and tucked it tighter under his chin, grateful for its warmth. It was a muffler their mother had knitted for Jonathan to take on his first voyage to the Orient with his older brother.

A small prick of light glimmered for two seconds, no more. He doubted if anyone in the boat-wagons except himself and Ming Tsun had seen it. He bent slightly to whisper to the rower nearest him. "Pass the word to the cox'n to bear two points to larboard." The boat-wagon had no rudder, but one of the marines was maneuvering a sweep as a steering oar. Frost did not stare at the point where the light had sparked, but moved his eyes all along the dark bank, and listened for all he was worth.

The unwieldy boat-wagon was in midstream now. Something large and dirty white appeared from upstream. "Ware ice," Frost cautioned. A small floe passed astern of the boat-wagon. A larger floe struck the stern a glancing blow, rocking the boat-wagon slightly. Ming Tsun's horse startled, but anticipating a whinny Ming Tsun instantly clamped the horse's muzzle between his gloved hands. The glimmer of light came again, this time a little closer to the shoreline, Frost judged. The boat-wagon was carrying directly toward the point where the light had appeared. The boat-wagon was less than fifty yards from the western bank, then twenty-five yards. The blunt bow of the clumsy vessel broke into the skim of ice, then the oars' blades struck the ice on the down-sweep, and though breaking through, they again caused far more noise than Frost wished. The light flared into a steady beacon as Caleb Mansfield held a lanthorn shielded by his bearskin overcoat to guide the boat-wagon ashore.

"Shore glad yere Tory friends have clear consciences, since they be all snorin' mightily, lucky so," Caleb said dismissively as he assisted a cold-stiffened Frost over the side of the boat-wagon. "Otherwise, they'd have heard all yere commotion in crossin' and would be layin' into ye proper."

"Please help trundle the field pieces out of the boat-wagons, Caleb," Frost said. "The tailboard seams leaked abominably since our efforts at caulking lacked proper oakum—we had tow and leather only—and were greatly abbreviated. I charge you with all care of the field pieces, seeing you know them best. We must be underweigh for this village of Agawam without pause. Row Gaffney shall be our guide while you harness the horses to the carriages." Frost quickly counted the shadowy figures moving awkwardly, stiffly cold-sodden, about the shore. Ten woods-cruisers, and thirty marines led by Nathaniel Dance. His heart ached for the lad, so young to be thrown into yet another dangerous, or so dangerous, engagement Frost would much rather avoid, though he acknowledged Nathaniel's abilities and confidence in the men he led, and their confidence in him. With Ming Tsun, Caleb, Singleton Quire and Row Gaffney, his small force numbered forty-four; forty-five including Frost.

Caleb Mansfield snorted derisively. "Row will lead ye direct to the Tories, never ye fear, 'n' I be behind ye matchin' yere every pace fer pace. I got a personal interest in these cannons, 'cause I admire somethin' bigger 'n' Gideon, no matter they ain't be nowise so accurate. I don't expects them Tories expect we be havin' cannon with us. I ain't changed my mind 'bout their numbers, right on a hundret. Probably thinkin' o' gettin' out of their warm blankets by now, but not really wantin' to step out onto cold boards."

"We shall need those cannons, Caleb, to compensate for our small number. Load with langrage and get a linstock alight."

"This business of carryin' 'round a hank of slow match ain't all that pert an idea," Caleb said, his voice distorted as he tried to talk around the bulky woolen glove he had tugged off one hand with his teeth, the better to buckle the stiff leather of a horse's headstall. "I been cypherin' how to rig a flintlock to a cannon."

"Slow match in a linstock will serve for the next hour," Frost said as he swung himself onto Bwindi's back. Ming Tsun handed up his Ferguson rifle and a pouch of cartridges, and Frost laid the rifle across his saddle. Confident in the sure-footedness of his molly-mule, Frost chirruped her ahead slowly, mulling how he would carry out the attack on the Tories in the village they had mutilated.

"Row Gaffney," he said in a low voice as he sensed, more than saw, that he was abreast of the woods-cruiser, "how many Tory picquets have the ferry landing under observation?"

"Aye, I wus planning to take us 'round them," Gaffney answered gruffly.

"You have been on your feet many an hour, and have slept little out of the last twenty-four hours; here, we shall change places, you in the saddle." Frost reined in his molly-mule, but Gaffney laid a restraining hand on Bwindi's neck.

"Never you mind, Capt'n, ol' Row ain't nowhere's near bottom, 'n' if I wus to change places with you, I'd likely nod off prompt."

"All right, please describe the village as we shall approach it, coming as we are from the north."

"Small holdings and dwellings on the approach into town, mostly put to the torch by the Tories, a commons, church, painted white o' course, on the south side, where all the pews be busted up for their fires. A lot o' Tories sleeping there. One man appointed as watchman, though likely he be laid his head on the table. Two floor dwelling to the right of the church made o' stone, dressed fine. That's where this Mister Colonel Rousseau and Mister Boyd be taking their ease. They sleeps upstairs, but they's been taking their meals in the parlor, which be why Caleb and I could listen to their scheming. No picquets around the house, but four, we counted, riding slowly around the town. Bushes the women like to have in their gardens growing right up to the windows, which, because of the heavy fires they had burning in both fireplaces, wus partially open." Gaffney laid a cautionary hand on Frost's boot: "Road branches here, Capt'n, left toward the ferry landing, and right around toward the town."

"And picquets at the ferry?" Frost queried sharply. He had not yet gotten a satisfactory answer from the loquacious Gaffney.

"Two we counted," Row Gaffney said quickly, realizing his error. Then added: "Two be all."

"How situated are the roads?"

"North and south, 'n' east and west. All meetin' at the commons."

Frost stopped Bwindi with a chirp. "Ming Tsun," he said quietly, "Singleton Quire." The two men marshaled on him. "Singleton Quire, lead Ming Tsun to the picquets at the ferry. Before the present hour is past they must join their ancestors. Ming Tsun shall see to it."

Ming Tsun was off his horse in an instant, his halberd in hand.

"Mister Dance, onto Ming Tsun's horse, if you please."

"Me, sir?" Nathaniel said, aghast. "I ain't never been aboard no horse afore. And I should be walkin' with my men."

"Then 'tis time to learn so you can astound your fellow sous-officers with your accomplishment," Frost said as Ming

Tsun boosted Nathaniel onto his saddle. "Mister Langdon sits a horse exceedingly well, though Mister Bowditch, like yourself, has never so much as been astride a horse. Think how envious he shall be. The horse is a pleasant beast. You may clutch the saddlebow if you wish, the reins loosely in one hand. The horse will not run away with you."

Frost nudged Bwindi into a walk with his boot heels. "The town lies how far, Row Gaffney?"

"Three mile, Capt'n."

"Then pass the word to pick up the pace. We must be there by the time the roosters celebrate their summoning of the dawn."

"Aye, I'll pass the word," Row Gaffney said soberly, " 'n' lead the pace, sure, though much doubts there be as to whether any chickens there 'bouts escaped the Tory stewpot."

Frost gave Bwindi her head to follow the swift-pacing Row Gaffney and thought how he would give battle to the Tories who had sacked and occupied the village of Agawam. It was a distasteful, dangerous task, putting his men at risks Frost would much rather avoid. But once his boat-wagons and their precious cargoes were across the Connecticut, the Tories could fall upon him at any time and place of their choosing. So Geoffrey Frost would fall on the Tories first. With but half the Tories' force. Joss. And the Blessed Trinity. Insh'allah.

The sky to eastward had lightened just enough so that from his saddle Frost could see the frozen ground and barely perceive the ruts cut by iron-shod wheels. His nostrils flared at the stench of stale woodsmoke that hung in the air. He urged Bwindi ahead and laid a cautionary hand on Row Gaffney's shoulder. He slid stiffly off the molly-mule and waited for the men to gather around him. "Picquets out, Caleb," he commanded tersely, "lest we find ourselves surprised by those we hope to surprise." He knew that Ming Tsun was a minute, no more, away. "Ming Tsun will require his horse, Mister Dance," Frost said, helping the youngster dismount, then issuing orders swiftly.

"Row Gaffney, I collect you can fire off a cannon and see to its reloading almost as quick as Caleb Mansfield. You are to take one cannon and guide Mister Dance and fifteen of his marines to the southerly road. Mister Dance, block the southerly road and permit no Tories to pass. Row Gaffney will provide your artillery support. Detail two marines to swab out and load under Row Gaffney's direction. You shall have fifteen minutes to achieve your position. One half of your marines remain at my disposition. I shall pass my orders through Urquhart." Frost allowed himself a fleeting smile. The seamen serving as marines had already shown their touchiness about receiving orders from anyone but their own officer or sergeant.

"Caleb Mansfield shall detail what men he deems proper to locate and remove the picquets. Upon signaling the picquets have been removed, my command shall advance in skirmish order, supported by Caleb Mansfield's cannon. Hostilities shall commence immediately the Tories cypher our intent." Frost snapped open the cover of Jonathan's Bréquet and held the watch close to his face. Not yet enough light to see the hands, but he judged the time was lacking fifteen minutes of seven. "Likely the Tories will be rising about now, calling for their breakfasts and reports of the picquets at the ferry landing, so away with you."

"Already sent Jack Daws 'n' Cox Pridham to search out them westerly picquets. Mister Ming Tsun 'n' Singleton Quire be comin' along now. They kin search out them's be easterly."

Indeed, Frost sensed Ming Tsun and Singleton Quire moving rapidly into the group congregated around him. Both men wore soft leather Indian moccasins stuffed with wool against the cold, so the frozen earth gave off no sound of their passage over it. "Mister Ming Tsun 'n' his sword on a stick sent 'em two back at the ferry to whatever reward the Almighty has fer Tories," Singleton Quire said quickly, as he absorbed Caleb's new orders to ferret out additional picquets. Silence soon replaced the tramp of boots and the brittle ring of iron-shod wheels and horses' hooves on the frozen ground, as Nathaniel Dance marched his marines away at a swift pace. Ming Tsun mounted his horse and helped Singleton Quire up behind.

"Urquhart," Frost commanded quietly, leaning from his molly-mule, "tell off two men to act as rammer and loader for Caleb Mansfield. We shall advance slowly along this road, as quietly as possible. As soon as you judge it light enough, pause your men to refresh their priming." The two horses pulling the 12-pounder field piece were coaxed to begin their efforts.

"Caleb," Frost still held the Bréquet in his gloved hand, "please blow on that slow match enough to illuminate my watch." He snapped the cover closed with satisfaction and nudged Bwindi into a slow pace. His reckoning of the time had been correct within two minutes. The smell of stale smoke grew stronger as his small band advanced toward Agawam. There was almost sufficient diffused light for the men to see to their priming powder. One hundred yards further Urquhart signaled the marines to halt. Urquhart went from man to man, watching as the pans were opened, the powder spilled out, and fresh priming powder carefully poured. Caleb did the same with Gideon, as did Frost, grimly concentrating on the new priming in the pan of the Ferguson rifle in an effort to quiet the eel of fear that was fiercely writhing in his bowels.

"Town's just 'round that turn, just a spit from what's left of th' house whar coals still be a-glowin' from them ashes," Caleb said, throwing out a hand grimly. "Got about two long rifle shots to th' town, 'bout two o' 'em cables yere alus talkin' about."

Frost slipped out of Bwindi's saddle and, clutching his Ferguson rifle, moved quietly beside Urquhart. "How do you intend to order your men?" he said quietly, conversationally.

Urquhart stiffened to attention. "Soon as we round that corner, throw out the men abreast—skirmish line believe it be called. Intervals of ten feet between men, except the five muskets in the center be like shoulder-to-shoulder to masque the cannon." Urquhart swallowed nervously: "Don't mean to think above my station, Capt'n, but maybe we kin keep them Tories from knowin' we's got this cannon by keepin' men in front of it." He glanced apologetically, timorously at Frost, waiting for a response, then continued: "Men told off to assist

Mister Caleb in loading, and trundlin' the cannon forward. Marines with rifles on points either side. Expect Mister Caleb's men to cover and warn of any attempt to cut 'round our flanks. We's to press along and drive 'em, the Tories, onto Mister Dance."

Frost nodded, pleased at Urquhart's ready grasp of tactics. "Excellent disposition, Urquhart. I particularly approve your desire to keep secret our cannon as long as possible." He winked at Urquhart. "Let us pray yonder Tories likewise be not hiding a cannon from us. May I suggest your riflemen be permitted to go to ground if we are opposed by a significant force and engage any Tory force with independent fire. We shall depend much upon the cannon and your riflemen to disrupt any charge."

"I'll pass our riflemen that word, Capt'n, and I'll be in front of the men, where my place is. Please to remain behind our muskets. We's apt to find ourselves in a hot corner the nonce."

Frost mounted his molly-mule, balanced the Ferguson rifle across his saddle and drew his small telescope from a tail pocket of his tunic. The marines hastened forward in the gathering dawn, and at the turning of the road Caleb unhitched the horses and he and his two pressed matrosses began trundling the cannon, muzzle first, down the frozen road. At the road's turning Frost swept the few buildings still unburned in the village of Agawam with his glass. He glimpsed movement at the edge of the telescope's field and saw a saddled but riderless horse trot hurriedly toward the southward. The easterly side of the village: Ming Tsun at work with his archery tackle. The telescope swept over a body dangling at the end of a rope suspended from a tree limb . . . he focused the telescope elsewhere, with an appeal to the Golden Buddha, and nudged Bwindi forward, wondering how the gentle molly-mule gifted him by Elizabeth Langdon would react to the deafening, unnerving racket of musketry and cannon fire and the harsh sizzle of bullets like angry hornets around them.

The marines had made the road's turning and were dispersed in good order, Urquhart walking doggedly in front, musket with bayonet already fixed in hand and carried like a hunter close on the track of game. He glanced frequently over both shoulders to gauge how the marines were dressing on him. "Easy now, lads," Frost heard Urquhart say quietly, confidently, "keep them muskets at shoulder arms until we's got to halt up and give fire. Riflemen, nobody fires without I order. Muskets, keep in front o' the cannon to screen it. I'll tell you when to move aside."

Frost paused momentarily to sweep the village with his telescope again and saw the door to the church swing open and a man step out, yawning and flexing his arms. The man leisurely unbuttoned his breeches, stepped to the side of the church and urinated. When he turned around he saw the thin line of skirmishers, Frost mounted on his mule behind them, gawked, shouted something unintelligible, then ran into the church. Frost estimated the distance to the church at three hundred and fifty yards. A moment later a rabble of men spilled from the church to stand and gawk at the line of silent men, purposefully advancing on them. Then someone in the mob yelled, and another, and most of the mob vanished into the church. Frost moved the telescope's arc to the large stone house seventy-five yards to the right of the church. People appeared in the yard in front of the house, pointing and gesticulating at the deliberately ominous and foreboding oncoming line, a very thin line, of men.

One of the men at the house, hastily pulling on a natty burgundy-colored tunic, dashed over to the church as men boiled out of the white building, hefting muskets and swords hastily picked up, milling around until the man from the large stone house cursed, kicked and cuffed the men into some semblance of a rank and file. Somehow the man formed the mob into a blunt disorderly column perhaps ten men across, firearms held every way askew, and drove them into a shambling advance forward on the lightly snow-dusted road to meet Frost's oncoming line.

Caleb Mansfield turned a purpled face streaming with perspiration toward Frost. "Sez I, we let 'em git within a hundret yards, then stop this cannon wherever it be 'n' wait on 'em to git as close as they want." He swiped at his glistening forehead with a buckskin sleeve already dampened dark. Caleb had long betimes shed his bearskin overcoat and had lashed it to the cannon's carriage, Gideon cradled within it. Two marines, their muskets slung over their shoulders, strained along with Caleb to keep the artillery piece moving forward over the heavy ruts frozen solid in the road. Two other marines with slung muskets stumbled heavily along after them with the shot and cartridge chest suspended between them, setting the slow pace for the marines in the skirmish line.

Another two minutes and the oncoming Tories had coalesced into a loose column of fifteen or so men abreast, perhaps sixty men in all. They were beginning to heft their muskets with greater confidence, since the Tories could see they easily outnumbered the oncoming line by at least three to one. Several of the Tories even pointed and laughed derisively. Burgundy coat was racing first across the front of the column, then down the side of the column, screaming and gesticulating with his drawn sword. Burgundy coat was the one to watch.

"Ask Mister Urquhart if he'd mind to pause," Caleb panted. "I's got to get this tormented slow match set fer its job."

Urquhart heard Caleb's plea and ordered "Marines halt! Ground muskets!"

Caleb pulled the coil of slow match he had wound through the belt of wampum encircling his waist and lustily blew on the smoldering end. "Drop 'er, boys," he ordered, and the two marines ceased pushing and unslung their muskets, grounding the butts as had their mates.

Frost placed the telescope in his coattail pocket and brought Bwindi to a halt with a soft tug on the reins. The march of the men approaching them slowed measurably, though they advanced. The man in the burgundy-colored coat dashed around the perimeters of the column, his screams and curses more strident. Frost sat his molly-mule and waited, feeling exceedingly vulnerable. He put his right hand on the familiar, worn handle of his cutlass and drew it an inch from its sheath to ensure it would draw free when needed. The marines in the center of the skirmish line still screened the artillery piece with their bodies shoulder-to-shoulder.

Burgundy coat shouted something in a high-pitched voice that Frost could not understand, and the column of Tories broke into a fast walk. Two, no, three men on the fringes of the column dropped out to aim muskets at the marine skirmish line. Frost saw first the small cloud-puffs of smoke from the combustion of the priming charges, then the heavy grayish-white smoke blossoming from muzzles pointed directly at him from a distance of one hundred yards. Bwindi pranced nervously but calmed once Frost tugged her head down with the reins and whispered to her. Something hissed by his ear, faintly fanning his cheek with a ripple of air.

Other Tories were firing their muskets, but taking poor aim. Yet Frost was not so much concerned with the mob in front of him as with the men he saw emerging now from other buildings around the commons of the ruined village of Agawam. He put them out of mind. The short line of marines held steady, implacable, muskets still at shoulder arms, though the men with the Ferguson rifles held their rifles at port arms. At a distance of eighty yards the column of Tories broke into a shouting and jeering, ragged, disorganized mob, running, bearing directly on the thin, thin line of Frost's skirmishers.

"They be close 'nough, Johnny Urquhart," Caleb Mansfield cried.

"*Jaguars*—marines in the center, left and right pivot step! Marines! Present arms! Level pieces . . ." Urquhart got no further in his orders as the marines masking the cannon stepped away briskly. Caleb ordered a small correction in the lie of the cannon, then stepped to the side of the carriage and stabbed the slow match down on the touchhole.

The front ranks of Tories stopped abruptly, frozen in horror as they saw the cannon uncover, the rear ranks caroming into the front ranks. The priming power in the touchhole fizzled out, but Caleb brought the smoldering slow match down on the touchhole again. The artillery piece crashed and bucked, wheels rising from the frozen ruts, recoiling backward a good yard and striking sparks from rocks caught in the frozen earth. The langrage ravaged the Tory column, scything men into moaning, screaming, bloodied shocks as easily as a farmer plying his long blade in a field of wheat. But altogether too many men were left standing for Frost's liking. Or for John Urquhart's liking, for that matter.

"*Jaguars*! Level muskets! Cock muskets! Take aim! Fire!" Ten marines discharged their muskets into the writhing mass of men. "Bayonets!" Urquhart shouted. "Engage forward on the double! Riflemen! Independent fire!" Urquhart paused to aim his musket, fired into the crowd of Tories, and then sprinted forward, followed by his savage, bloodthirsty men.

"No ye don't," Caleb Mansfield shouted, seizing by the collar one marine detailed to assist him in reloading the cannon, "help me load this 'ere cannon, then ye can get all the scrappin' 'n' killin' ye want!"

Frost slung the Ferguson rifle over his shoulder, the awkward distribution of weight making him feel off balance, then drew his cutlass and startled Bwindi into a gallop with a loud yell. On either side of him the five marines armed with Ferguson rifles had gone to ground and were firing deliberately. "You fight as you train," Frost told himself fiercely. He had settled upon burgundy coat, who had been tumbled to the ground in the concussion of the cannon's fire, but who had regained his feet and was attempting to marshal the Tories who were milling aimlessly and confusedly. Burgundy coat sensed by the clatter of hooves rather than saw Frost bearing down on him and whipped a pistol from his belt, firing point-blank at the mule looming over him.

Bwindi neighed shrilly, stumbled and fell, pitching Frost forward in a heap, though he kicked his feet free of the stirrups and managed to hold on to his cutlass, taking the ground heavily. The Ferguson rifle fell away when Frost struck the ground, and he was thankful for that as he scrambled to his feet and hastily parried the sword thrust burgundy coat swung at him. Frost stumbled momentarily before he found his footing and beat back another vicious attack with a quick parry and his own immediate riposte, which locked cutlass to sword for a brief instant. Frost anticipated the bent knee kicking toward his groin and chopped his cutlass downward with all the strength he could direct into his left hand.

He felt his blade biting deep into burgundy coat's leg and heard the man's agonized scream as Frost wrested his cutlass out of the living flesh. He brought the point of the blade through a savage, backhanded, flashing arc that cut into burgundy coat's neck. Burgundy coat's shriek ended abruptly in a spill of blood that stained the dirty linen of his shirt and shockingly, but curiously, was absorbed into the burgundy coat without changing its color. Frost kicked burgundy coat's body away, scooped up his Ferguson rifle, cocked it and without any remorse whatsoever shot through the head at a distance of ten yards one of two Tories who were closely engaging a marine with muskets wielded as clubs.

The cannon boomed again, and more of the Tory mob was down. The marines were engaged in a frenzy of stabbing with their bayonets at any Tory they encountered. The riflemen, at least, were keeping up a steady and accurate fire at individual targets. Men, Frost corrected himself. Men, not targets. The Tory mob was shrinking inside itself, men throwing aside their muskets and raising their hands. Frost raced into the mob, striking aside one marine's bayonet aimed at the chest of a Tory on his knees, hands upheld in supplication. Frost slapped the marine sharply. "Back to the cannon," he rasped harshly. "Get it reloaded and move it forward . . ."

"Behind ye, sohr!" the marine shouted, and Frost hunched over, turning, drawing and cocking a Bass pistol from his belt, then shooting the self-same Tory who had ostensibly just surrendered, then had caught up a musket and begun to cock and aim it at Frost.

"Should have let me finish 'm, sohr," the marine remonstrated.

"Caleb Mansfield needs you more," Frost shouted. "Mind the second mob, and get the cannon forward!"

Now where was Urquhart when he needed him? There he was, deep into the mêlée of now dispirited Tories, plying his bayonet with great dexterity and laughing. "Urquhart! Mind the second mob coming! Get your riflemen concentrated on them!"

"Grand music, ain't it, Capt'n!" Urquhart shouted, grinning at Frost as muskets and rifles popped all around them.

"Grand organs indeed," Frost shouted back, "but funeral music 'less you mind! Your muskets to help Caleb Mansfield lay the cannon. Riflemen to engage individual men in the mêlée gathering!"

Frost looked around for Bwindi and saw that she had regained her feet and was standing, bewildered, reins dangling, saddle askew, a shallow furrow of red marking a bullet's path across her neck. Frost grabbed up the reins, pulled himself into the saddle, then spared a moment to lean forward and rub the mule's ears.

The Tories from the first mob still on their feet disengaged and were falling back on the reinforcements coming toward them, but men in the second group were dropping to the accurate fire of the marines with Ferguson rifles, and the momentum of the second group was faltering. Three marines were helping Caleb muscle the twelve-pounder cannon forward. The cannon moved briskly with four men pushing, forcefully enough to roll over the bodies of the Tories sprawled grotesquely in the bloody snow. The Tory reinforcements were perhaps one hundred yards away, coming slowly now that they could see the cannon moving to meet them. A Tory pitched forward, but Frost had heard no rifle shot. Another Tory fell, and this time Frost saw the arrow's swift flight.

Caleb judged the distance to be right, swerved the cannon to aim it and ordered the tailpiece grounded. The Tory reinforcements halted as abruptly as the cannon had grounded, and men began breaking away from the group. Caleb stabbed the slow match onto the touchhole and the cannon coughed its third deadly charge, mowing a wide swath through the second group. The reinforcements who had not been touched by the malignant hail broke, turned and began running toward the village, away from the shock and carnage of the killing ground.

Caleb was beside Frost, left hand clutching Gideon while he clapped on to the left stirrup leather Frost kicked free. Frost nudged Bwindi into a fast trot, leaning to his right to offset Caleb's weight. "Press them closely!" he shouted. "Drive them on! They must be given no time to regroup!" A fleeing Tory fell heavily, and in the periphery of his vision Frost saw Ming Tsun and Singleton Quire, Quire now mounted on a horse of his own, galloping across a field with brittle clumps of wheat stubble standing up randomly out of the snow. Ming Tsun and Quire were *chasseurs* harrying the Tories now fleeing in a panic, the first of them now scrambling across the commons. Ming Tsun thundered up behind one lagging behind and struck with his wicked halberd. The man went down instantly, his life's blood staining the snow onto which he fell. Frost watched as Ming Tsun rode down another Tory, reflecting momentarily and sadly upon the unfortunate circumstances that had taught this most mild-mannered and serious of scholars the craft of efficient killing.

Frost galloped past Urquhart, who had marshaled his marines with muskets in line, keeping them together and quick-marching them while reloading on the trot. The five riflemen were sprinting ahead, pausing to select targets, aim and fire, then hastening on, likewise reloading on the run. Caleb kept his grip on the stirrup leather, bounding in long strides beside Frost, pulled along by the mule. Frost was approaching the commons; he reined Bwindi slightly to the left to avoid riding over a wounded Tory with a shattered leg who was desperately trying to pull himself off the road. The survivors of the two mobs so recently shattered by cannon fire encountered a dozen or so stragglers just emerging from the church and the stone house. A few muskets were fired off in Frost's general direction, then were thrown down as the Tory stragglers joined their fellows in flight, in full rout now, fleeing southward ever as fast as they could.

Four men on horseback galloped from a stable behind the stone house less than two hundred yards away. They were bent forward over their horses' necks, heads down, spurring them desperately as they disappeared behind the church. The men were in sight again seconds later, horses' hooves throwing back great clods of snow and ice, desperately riding south on the road leading out of Agawam. The horsemen rapidly overtook the mêlée of Tories fleeing on foot, and Frost galloped after the mob, Bwindi running easily, smoothly carrying Frost's weight and that of Caleb Mansfield clinging alongside.

A slight turning in the road, and there were the figures of Nathaniel Dance and his contingent of marines, tiny and black in the distance, though they were no more than five hundred yards away, spread across and blocking the road south. The mêlée of Tories pressed on, though not in a compact body. When the first of the Tories was seventy-five yards away from the blockade, Frost saw the bloom of smoke spout from the cannon's muzzle and watched men picked up by invisible hands and tumbled onto the newly blooded ground like broken dolls by the sheet of langrage. The marines were obscured by the roil of dirty smoke that erupted from the massed fire of their muskets. More Tories went down. The four horsemen had turned and were charging back. "Hold hard," Caleb said mildly. Frost reined Bwindi to a walk, and Caleb stepped away, watching the four horsemen pelting toward them.

"Th' gent thar on th' gray, now if he had a feather up his arse 'n' I had th' horse, we'd both be tickled," he muttered, difficult to understand because of the bullets he held in his mouth. Seeing Frost and Caleb halted with no one near them in the road, the four horsemen, sabers in hand, rode toward them grimly. Caleb raised Gideon, sighted along his rifle's barrel, kept his rifle moving, and fired. The man on the gray horse fell from his saddle; his right foot caught in the stirrup, and he was dragged by the thoroughly frightened, desperate horse. Caleb rotated Gideon's barrels and took aim at another horseman, who had closed to within seventy-five yards. Gideon barked, and the saddle emptied; the horse raced past Frost and Caleb.

The two remaining horsemen hauled their horses' heads cruelly round and spurred southward. Caleb grasped the stirrup leather again as Frost started Bwindi after them. The two mounted Tories punished their horses desperately to wring more speed from them. The marines stood their ground, but they had fired their muskets and rifles. The two horsemen were racing toward the center of the marines' line, toward the now useless cannon by which the diminutive Nathaniel Dance stood resolutely, holding out the cannon's rammer like a lance. Two marines flanked him, one on either side, their muskets with bayonets thrust as resolutely forward. Twenty or so unarmed Tories on foot were being flogged on the blocking marines by the two men on horseback.

The marines were being forced back by the sheer numbers of Tories pressing against them, for the Tories seemed to be more terrified of the two horsemen flogging them forward than of the marines. A breach was opening, and the two horsemen were forcing their horses through the grappling, struggling bodies toward it. Nathaniel Dance stepped into the breach with the cannon rammer and swung it at the head of the near horse. The horse screamed and reared; Nathaniel struck again with the rammer, as hard as he could, turning the horse. The rider struggled to regain control of his horse as the second rider pushed his way into the breach, his sword raised.

"No!" Frost shouted. "No! Oh God, NO!" A British square of infantry could stand against a cavalry attack, but not two men and one boy. The Tory would ride them down.

Caleb released his grip on the stirrup leather. Bwindi stopped and Frost raised the Ferguson rifle to his shoulder. Too late he realized that the rifle was unloaded. He dropped the rifle and dug the heels of his boots into Bwindi's ribs, starting her into an immediate gallop, but Frost knew it was late, too late . . .

Behind Frost, Caleb Mansfield poured powder down one of Gideon's barrels directly from the horn, then spat a bullet into the muzzle, slapping the rifle's butt downward sharply against the ground to settle the charge in a desperate field load. There was no time for the finer-grained priming powder, so Caleb spilled powder from the horn into the pan, slapped the frizzen closed and cocked the hammer as Gideon came obediently to his shoulder. The sword in the horseman's hand started its downward slash.

Frost saw the horseman's head snap back, then the man pitch forward from the saddle, before he heard the rifle's crack. By the Golden Buddha and the Holy Infant! In some wise Caleb had reloaded his rifle in time to save Nathaniel's life! But he still urged Bwindi into the mêlée of bodies, laying about him with his cutlass in a fury. The one man remaining on his horse dropped the reins and raised his hands in surrender. The marines pushed back with desperate vigor, and the Tories on foot slowly quieted, raising their hands after the example of the remaining horseman.

Slowly the anger and the blood lust flowed out of Frost. "Well done, Mister Dance! Henceforth you are appointed an ensign of marines, with pay commensurate for this commission." Then he commanded, loudly, for all to hear: "Mister Dance! These Tories are prisoners of your marines. Search them all carefully for anything that could be used as a weapon. Then march them to confinement in the church. Those unwounded shall search out, under guard, the Tory wounded, and assist as bearers. I don't suppose these fellows have anyone who might answer as a surgeon, so the wounded must await Ishmael Hymsinger's crossing this side. I shall have more orders for you presently." Frost looked down at Nathaniel Dance and kept his face stern, though he desperately wanted to smile at the youth.

"Told ye I'd never let a Britisher a-fright me again, Capt'n sir," Nathaniel piped happily. "These Tories be Britishers, and I be not a-frighted o' them at all."

"I can see that, Mister Dance," Frost said gravely. "Please be about your work. Take that fellow's horse. You've already had one riding lesson thus far today."

"Now see here," the solitary horseman began to protest, but Frost cut him short.

"Off that horse instantly, and you may at least retain your

shoes. If you force me to remove you, you dismount to bare feet." The man dismounted resentfully, and a marine boosted Nathaniel into the vacated saddle.

The Tories were sorted out by the marines, now augmented by the contingent that Urquhart had brought up, muskets and riflemen, and Nathaniel got them moving toward the ruined village of Agawam. Ming Tsun was at Frost's side now, signing to him that miraculously, not one of the men who had crossed the Connecticut with him had suffered injury or wound. Caleb Mansfield strode over to look at the man he had shot in the instant before he could kill Nathaniel Dance and force his way through the marine blockers to the safety of southward flight.

"Looks like I shot meself a wolverine," Caleb said. "This be Rousseau, Colonel Rousseau, he called hisself. Pity I killed 'im instant. Potted 'im in the head when I wus aimin' at his body." He shrugged. "Wus lucky to hit 'im at all with thet hasty load, but it all come together." Caleb looked up at a very haggard and tired Geoffrey Frost, then took Frost's cutlass and bent to wipe the blood from the blade with a piece of the Tory Rousseau's coat. "'N' I be thinkin' ye killed that other bad 'un, Boyd, a while back."

Frost said nothing as he slid the cutlass into its carriage, but turned Bwindi, telling her he was sorry to have used her so, and began riding slowly toward the village, following the dejected, defeated Tories. He tried not to dwell upon the silent, stiffening heaps that just minutes before had been living men, now strewn along the road amidst the windrows of bloody, bloody snow.

X

FROST, MING TSUN, SINGLETON QUIRE AND CALEB MANSFIELD DISMOUNTED BEFORE THE FRONT STOOP OF THE FINE-DRESSED STONE DWELLING fronting on the commons of the ruined village of Agawam. Caleb was inordinately pleased with himself, for he had caught up the gray horse, a fine, tall animal, a gelding, and he was equally pleased with the animal's fine saddle. "I've in mind another horse to join with my old plug t' make a true pair fer haulin' one o' 'em 12-pounder cannons," he said happily.

Frost, however, was in an extremely black mood. He had seen two more hanged bodies, villagers summarily executed by the Tories for sport, and the taint of smoldering timbers, burned shingles and roof beams was rank in his nostrils. "Singleton Quire, please to inform Mister Dance that once he has collected the Tory wounded into the church, all able-bodied Tories are to be set to work digging graves. Under close guard, of course, with orders to shoot any Tory attempting to run. The burying ground is the other side of the church. The ground be as hard as a Tory's heart, frozen as it is, but we must have these poor murdered inhabitants of Agawam village consecrated into the earth before our train comes up. I would take it as a great favor if you and your fellow woods-cruizers would gather in the murdered ones, gruesome task though that represents. I regret mightily we shan't have time to encoffin these innocents, though I doubt much if the Deity will object to winding sheets rather than inch-thick wood, lovingly planed and fitted close."

"The dead Tories," Singleton Quire began, "we kin gather 'em up . . ."

"One grave for all," Frost snapped, "though it may also be in the consecrated ground. Perhaps they, too, may be permitted to expiate and express remorse for their sins upon resurrection, for sinners and saints alike must face the judgment of resurrection." He passed a hand before his eyes. He was vastly experienced with expiation. How many men had he ordered buried thus far in this year of grace 1776, either in holy soil or cleansing, all-embracing water? Portsmouth, the joint crews of *Salmon* and *Jaguar*; the Gulf of Maine for Hugh Stuart; the cemetery at Louisbourg; the canvas-shrouded bodies of Slocum Plaisted and his mates somewhere in the North Atlantic; the hearts of the two Italian musicians in the cemetery above Angra on Terceira Island . . . Frost acknowledged wearily that he was deep into the mortuary business, and with all his soul he wanted to be shut of it. Inside the house he heard a clock chime eight o'clock. Insh'allah! Had all this desperate killing occurred in under one hour?

"Imagine 'em Tories wus 'bout to sit down to a fine breakfast," Caleb said brightly. "Ifen so, we would be coves t' let the breakfast go t' waste. Tories be mostly stomachs, I hear tell."

"Yes," Frost agreed, "you ate a piece of cornbread near midnight, and I judge that was the only sustenance in your belly the last two days. Perhaps the Tories may have been preparing a rasher of herring, perhaps some potatoes fried with onions, perhaps fresh bread, and even some tea. Dare we think of eggs?"

"I wus thinkin' on ham, fried, baked 'er boiled, mayhap corn porridge thick enough t' hold the spoon up straight, soused royal with syrup o' th' maple," Caleb volunteered. "Wouldn't turn down them small fishes, even."

"I believe my task be one best suited to 'n empty belly," Singleton Quire said. "I'll lead the animals 'round to the stable, ease their girths, halter them if there be forage, and water them." He looked at Frost: "Where should I collect the bodies of the people died from this village?"

"The parlor of this house," Frost said simply, "though the dead shall have to forgo any wake other than such winding sheets as we may find here." He slowly, with infinite tiredness, followed Ming Tsun into the stone house. A hallway, with the large, well-furnished parlor or keeping room off to the left, led straight to the kitchen, and the three of them were strongly drawn down the hallway by the tantalizing smells of food. Curiously, his physical hunger was so great Frost was not in the least put off by the thought of dining on food prepared for men dead within the half-hour. Caleb pushed open the door to the kitchen. The long kitchen table was set with delicate plates and bowls, utensils of actual silver, water glasses of French crystal, and dainty cups and saucers. Frost idly picked up a spoon and was not surprised to see Paul Revere's mark as silversmith. With a sniff of disapproval he noted the stench of stale pipe tobacco smoke in the kitchen.

Ming Tsun leaned his halberd against the wall near the fireplace and began lifting the lids of pots suspended from irons or placed on trivets near the coals. Caleb joined him for the inspection. "Stew, most likely venison, judgin' from th' smell, carrots, 'n' peas, 'n' little onions, turnips. But here's fresh bread, 'n' looks like butter fresh-churned, and lookee, my prayers be answered, corn mush! With a pitcher o' milk, only time I see th' need fer milk, 'n' syrup from th' maple! 'N' look, here be a basket o' eggs! Now, if thar just be a pot o' coffee sommers . . ."

Frost and Ming Tsun both heard the faint sound as Caleb happily busied himself around the pots and kettles. Caleb heard the sound also but kept up his spate of talk. The kris Ming Tsun always wore strapped to his left arm appeared as if by magician's conjure out of the sleeve of his tunic, and Frost withdrew a Bass pistol from his belt. Caleb kept up his patter and continued to lift the lids of pots and kettles noisily. "Ye won't be disappointed, Capt'n, here be a kettle o' water just past th' boil, 'n' here be a small casket containin' tea leaves . . .

’n’ Lordie, here be a kettle o’ coffee, from th’ touch o’ th’ kettle th’ brew be hotter ’n’ th’ hinges o’ hell . . .” Caleb make a great clatter with the lids and the fire irons, but he quietly picked up Gideon and placed a cautious thumb on the cock. He nodded at a door, leading without doubt to a pantry, ten feet to the right of the fireplace as the most likely source of the sound that had commanded their immediate attention.

Ming Tsun crept soundlessly to the door and placed his hand on the handle. Caleb raised his rifle, barrels thrust forward, butt just beneath his elbow, ready to bring to shoulder and fire on the instant. Frost nodded and Ming Tsun threw open the door, his kris poised, cobra-like.

The man was shielding the woman, who greeted the door’s sudden, unexpected opening with a small, repressed cry. They were both shrank back against the boxes, sacks and small barrels and bottles in the pantry. It was difficult to see in the dim interior, which had no window, but the man shielded the woman as best he could and looked out at the interlopers with terror and, at the same time, something very akin to dignity.

Frost held his pistol level for a long moment, but he knew instinctively that the man and the woman, who was wrapped in a gray woolen shawl, were innocuous and incapable of dealing harm to anyone. He let the cock of the Bass pistol go forward and returned it to his belt. “Who are you?” he asked. “Please tell me who you are.”

“And who art thou?” the man retorted, very tremulously, his voice almost breaking.

“A fair question,” Frost said. “My name is Frost. I am a mariner and a trader, but recently my colleagues and I have settled a bit of unpleasantness with some people who were bent on relieving us of our wares, indeed, our lives even. You most likely be acquainted with them, seeing that you are in the kitchen where these people were due to indulge in a fair breakfast.”

“Thou art not party of the violent men just fled, then? For that we give thee thanks. My name be Simon, this dear woman be Salome. We art of the Brethren.”

“Ah,” Frost said, “mayhap you cooked this meal. There

appears to be again more food than people to appreciate it. My colleagues and I hope we may induce you to quit your closet. You have my word that we intend you no harm."

The man came out cautiously, disbelieving but perhaps appreciating that he really had no choice. His face was greatly disfigured by the scars of smallpox, though he wore a broad, placid expression of good humor and trust. Frost bowed and held out his right hand. "This is my best friend in life, Ming Tsun, a great scholar and humanist who has ventured all this way from his homeland in the faraway country of China, and who, like me, is far more comfortable surrounded by books than implements of war. Please do not be disturbed by his countenance, it was not altered with his acquiescence. He has survived the greatest of misfortunes thrust upon him, as perhaps you and the lady have, seeing that you are alive and so many of the inhabitants hereabouts are . . . otherwise."

Ming Tsun had unobtrusively returned the kris to its sheath strapped to his left forearm; he advanced and bowed deeply.

"And this is Caleb Mansfield," Frost said, nodding toward Caleb as he shook Simon's hand. "I know not how to calculate his value. He likes it not to be known, nay, he will dispute it, but he possesses a gentle, Christian soul. I rely on the word of Caleb Mansfield to the same extent I would that of an angel who deigned to assume human form."

"Thy words could be taken in some quarters as blasphemous, Mister Frost," Simon said in a low voice with a slight tinge of disapproval, "but I perceive in these men a kindness that affords us heart. Do you vouchsafe that those men who fled so precipitously shall not, indeed, return for their breakfast?" Simon looked expectantly at Frost.

"I believe I may earnestly vouchsafe the men who were preparing to breakfast around this table thirty minutes before are in no wise likely to partake of the bounty here displayed," Frost said dryly.

Simon turned back to the pantry and called tremulously. "Salome, I bid thee please come forth. These men truly bode us no harm. I believe they shall assist us upon our way."

The woman hesitantly left the suspect sanctuary of the pantry. She moved with extreme care, and it was immediately evident to Frost that she was well advanced in pregnancy. The woman made a dignified, though given her condition, somewhat awkward curtsey. Frost returned the curtsey with a deep bow, then immediately fetched a chair. "Madame, we desire you please take a seat. If you have, as I suspect, prepared this breakfast, you must permit us to serve you."

"Those men . . . they will not return?" the woman said incredulously, echoing Simon's earlier question.

Frost bowed. "Madame, my colleagues and I assure you in absolute truth they will not return."

The woman did not take the chair but knelt awkwardly and prayed silently for a time. When she lifted her head, she said simply, "They were to murther us." She unwrapped her gray wool shawl to show a simple white blouse deeply stained with blood on the right side. "One slashed me with a long, cruel knife and uttered most lurid epithets, regretting that he could not tarry longer . . ." The woman named Salome began to sob, softly.

Frost was immediately attentive, though painfully aware of his awkward, woeful inadequacies around women. "Madame, you and your husband must retire to inspect and dress your wound. We possess a wondrous surgeon's mate, but it will be hours yet before we may expect him."

"But I am not Simon's wife," Salome said.

"I am her brother-in-law," Simon said, quickly. "My brother, her husband, Jesse, is dead of the smallpox this week past, though blessed be his memory. It was our sad, sad duty to bury Jesse in New Haven, then we continued northward in the company of some farmers taking apples and cheeses and pigs and young calves to market in Springfield. We fetched this Agawam three days before, and because Salome was . . . unwell, we were generously permitted by the owners of this dwelling to shelter in their barn. The farmers went on to Springfield, and the next day those . . . men came." Simon half-smiled and passed a hand across his face. "As thee may observe, I am well salted against that wretched sickness."

"The cut is nothing, sir, and weeps no longer," Salome said, her tears ending. "I shall tend it myself, presently, with lint. Now thee must take nourishment." She was a plain-featured woman with dark brown hair pulled back in a demure bun, but her face was radiant. Salome fairly glowed with a confident inner beauty.

The clash and clatter of pot and kettle lids intensified as Ming Tsun and Caleb hastily busied themselves with the cooking implements suspended in the fireplace.

"Your child, Madame," Frost said awkwardly.

Salome's radiant smile intensified, and with Frost and Simon's assistance, she got unsteadily to her feet. "The womb be not touched, never fear. But I may not be seated afore thee," the woman demurred, "it would not be seemly."

"But I insist you shall be seated first," Frost said, holding the chair for the woman.

"Then I thank thee," the woman said simply. "I tell thee truly, until thee intervened, I knew this was destined to be the last day of life for the three of us in this world—Simon, my child yet to be born and me, seeing that those men needed us no longer to cook for them."

"'Tis true," the man named Simon added soberly, near tears himself. "I heard some of them talk . . . about Salome . . ."

Caleb Mansfield noisily plopped large ladles of corn mush onto two delicate plates and set them before Simon and Salome. "Waal, since th' lady nowise needs any wound dressin' immediate, now, here, we've got vittles' stick t' yere ribs, what's fer sure. 'N' Mister Ming Tsun, he's goin' at 'em eggs in a skillet . . . ain't gonna be like he has access t' all th' condiments he keeps aboard ship, but mayhap he be findin' more 'n' pepper 'n' salt hereabouts. 'N' here," Caleb bustled over with brimming plates of stew, setting them upon the table, miraculously without spilling a drop of gravy upon the tablecloth.

"We thank thee," Salome said simply, "but before we partake of the Lord's bounty, we are very much obliged to return thanks." She held out her hands, one of which was taken by Simon, and the other by Frost. Frost beckoned Ming Tsun and Caleb Mansfield to join them, and Frost found himself, somewhat incongruously, clasping Caleb's hardened, callused right hand.

Salome said a simple, direct return of thanks, which only fleetingly touched upon deliverance, but emphasized grace, and was long on thankfulness—and forgiveness. "Thee may partake now of the Lord's bounty," Salome said quietly.

Ming Tsun placed a cup of tea at Frost's elbow and signed that he had not found any honey, but would Frost at least assay tea sweetened with syrup of the maple? Frost did so, shuddered and grimaced horribly, and Ming Tsun hurriedly withdrew the cup and replaced it with another, unsweetened. Frost appreciated this cup much more. He appreciated also the mug of cold buttermilk that Ming Tsun drew from an urn in the pantry. A plate of stew and a bowl of corn mush followed. Frost concentrated on the mush and then, miracle of miracles, on the plate of delicious cod soaked free of its preserving salt and well boiled that Ming Tsun placed before him.

"Thee shall see us upon the road to the Ohio Country," Salome said quietly, as she spooned corn mush diluted with milk into her mouth. "For that Simon and I be grateful eternally."

Frost's inborn dignity kept him from squirming in his seat, but he withdrew Jonathan's Bréquet from his waistcoat pocket and examined its face carefully. So strange that scarce an hour before he had launched an attack upon so many men who were now dead, and he was enjoying, yes, enjoying immensely the breakfast prepared for them.

"I am afraid we travel not near so far as the Ohio Country, Madame," Frost said, appreciating his tea, "and hopefully you will not take my comments in the wrong vein. But it is apparent that you should spare yourself all strenuous travel and be confined here to await the delivery of your child."

Salome dabbed at her lips with her napkin and pushed aside her plate of corn mush, mostly untouched. "My brother-in-law and I be destined for the Ohio Country, sir, and thy timely intervention with the men who had vowed to commit us to the Lord's judgment before light fails today is a message of sure passage vouchsafed by the Father who surrounds and beloves us."

Frost averted his face and rolled his eyes, sorry indeed that he had acceded to Caleb's jocular offer to dine upon a breakfast intended for Tories. By all rights he should be at the ferry landing from Springfield, attending to the crossing of the first of his boat-wagons. But the delightfully stewed, mildly astringent and oh so delectable cod and the hot tea and cold buttermilk were wondrously restorative, and he grudgingly acknowledged his famine. He chewed the codfish with full enjoyment and thought how best to extricate himself from his present quandary. Ming Tsun, even more inscrutable than usual, pointedly offered no help as he replenished Frost's tea.

"Ye must have family here 'bouts?" Caleb said conversationally, though busily spooning corn mush, ham, fried eggs and venison stew into his mouth. "Er how come ye find yereselves 'n this Tory-blighted village?" Caleb slurped noisily from a great copper tankard of hot coffee.

"My brother and Salome were just come from Plymouth to Newport in Rhode Island Plantation," Simon explained patiently, slowly picking at his bowl of stew. "I was come from Philadelphia, where I resided for some years, to join them in Newport. Together we were seeking to make our way to a settlement of Brethren newly founded in the Ohio Country. But all was turmoil in the town of Newport since British General Clinton had just reduced it on the sixth, instant, and Jesse, Salome and I were summarily ordered out of Newport, where we had hoped to accomplish her confinement." Simon placed his hands on the tablecloth, and Frost saw that the hands were those of a craftsman, hands shaped to some tools. "We seek a place of tranquility, away from this tumult of death and destruction."

"The Plymouth on the southwestern coast of England, you mean," Frost interrupted, "not the town of the same name in Massachusetts."

"Aye," Simon said, "I should have been more specific; thee please exercise patience with me."

Rapid footsteps sounded in the hallway, and Singleton Quire hurried down the passage. He stopped in mid-step and swept off his cap when he saw Salome. "I knew not a lady was here, Capt'n," he said quickly. "We are bringin' the villagers into the parlor."

"Have you discovered anyone alive?" Frost asked sharply.

Singleton Quire mutely shook his head.

"Very well, Singleton. Please do your best to prepare the dead of this village for burial. I must hasten to the ferry landing and see to the crossing of our boat-wagons."

"Thee shall permit us to help with cleansing the bodies of the dead and preparing them for burial," Simon said. "God would wish it so."

"Jesus, Joseph and the Sainted Mary, spare me another parson," Frost said to himself, but then aloud: "Your assistance will be greatly appreciated. Perhaps you know this house and what bedding is available for winding cloths." He drank down the last of his tea. "Singleton Quire, please pause a moment to avail yourself of the repast here provided. Caleb, please remain . . ."

"Capt'n, Singleton Quire's got th' gist of what's needs doin' here. Ye, me, and Mister Ming Tsun got t' hasten down t' th' landin' and see our train crosses pert smart." Caleb drank off the last of his coffee and slapped down the mug. "Ain't nothin' here he and Mister Dance kin't find the range."

"Mind the saddle girths," Singleton Quire said, "I loosened them."

Frost elected to leave the house of fine-dressed stone by the back door. He could not bear to see the frozen bodies of the villagers Caleb's woods-cruisers were soberly and with great compassion and tenderness bringing into the parlor.

XI

THE CROSSING OF THE CONNECTICUT CONSUMED AN INORDINATE AMOUNT OF TIME THAT FROST COULD ILL AFFORD, THOUGH HE CONCEALED HIS impatience as he waited on a slight rise one hundred yards from the shallows of the ferry landing. He and Ming Tsun sat on a driftwood log cast up by a long-ago flood while Frost consulted Jonathan's watch and the map that John Langdon had provided. He sighed as he watched the boat-wagons, bereft of their wheels, splashing their haphazard way across the water with their clumsy sweeps inexpertly pulled by drovers who had never laid hand on oar betimes. He was extremely dismayed to learn that the boat-wagons could safely convey no more than half the load he had earlier calculated. So once unladed on the western bank, most of the boat-wagons had to be rowed back to the eastern bank to take on more cargo.

For a moment he regretted that he had ordered Struan Ferguson to remain with *Audacity* to oversee her refit: Struan would have sorted out the drovers in an instant, and kept them cracking. But Hannibal Bowditch was darting about, seemingly in a dozen places at once, chivying, ordering, chiding, offering encouragement and a kind word, and doing a most creditable job of organizing the multiple crossings. Frost was greatly pleased that the lad was learning how to command, so he chose not to intervene and watched the crossings through his small telescope. Beside him, Ming Tsun kept meticulous account of the boat-wagon crossings, and enumerated their cargoes deposited on the western bank. At this rate the Connecticut's crossing would take the better part of the day.

A small team of drovers was jacking up the hulls of a few boat-wagons and refitting wheels. Three herd boys were sorely pressed to keep the congregate of beeves oxen confined in a field, where hay had been thrown down for them.

"It is so much more efficient at sea," Frost signed to Ming Tsun. "Aboard our *Audacity* the slacker would be taken aside and reminded of his duties by his mates, perhaps with a punch or two to reinforce the lesson."

Ming Tsun signed in return, "These drovers here are bent upon making a great show, but doing as little work as possible."

"Evident as you see," Frost signed in resignation. "But I must allow them their gross mistakes in hopes the better men among the drovers may profit and be shamed thereby. And our Hannibal, though facing a task that would make a Trojan cringe, is engaged everywhere." He returned to his scan of the boat-wagons and the eastern bank of the Connecticut through his small telescope. A mud-bespattered and obviously fatigued figure drooping over a tired horse appeared in the telescope's ellipse at the edge of the post road.

"Caleb," Frost said tersely, causing a brief, reluctant movement in the noisome black bear pelt that served Caleb Mansfield as cloak and blanket. "Mayhap we have an express rider with dispatches from John Langdon just now catching up to us on the eastern bank. I would take it as a signal favor if you cross over and escort the dispatch rider to this side."

Caleb Mansfield reluctantly unrolled himself from the bearskin, belched and farted, and got slowly to his feet, scratching fiercely at his armpits and yawning. "I wus dreamin' o' th' Widow Crockett, 'n' ye had t' go 'n' wake me," he said grumpily.

"It was a mercy I did so, Caleb," Frost said. "Perhaps sparing of our lives. You were snoring to drown out thunder, noise enough to draw every Tory or British Regular within one hundred miles to investigate the cause of an incipient terramoto."

"Hear him! Hear him!" Caleb said mockingly. "I have it on th' authority o' no less than th' Widow Crockett that I've never so much as mouth-breathed times I been with her, so I thankee to secure this business o' snorin'." Caleb harrumphed and blew his nose noisily between thumb and forefinger. "It be good teeth what prevents snorin'," Caleb said as he bared his own exceptionally good teeth, though much yellowed.

"Confirmed then that neither of us snores," Frost bantered, for he loved Caleb mightily. "Please select one of your woods-cruizers to explore to the westward and establish an anchorage for the night sufficient to accommodate safely our dispirited little fleet." Frost kept his telescope focused intently on the tired horse and rider just coming into view on the far shore. "I have not seen it yet, but you have crossed the Connecticut thrice in some vessel buoyant enough to preserve your life. I bid you cross quickly to the eastern shore and fetch over the dispatch rider in a boat-wagon."

"Be worth yere life t' trust t' one o' 'em tar-covered coffins," Caleb said, drawing his belt knife and paring a fingernail. "We have a curragh made o' ox hide hidden tight in yonder copse o' willows. She be a stout boat, as easy t' hoist 'n yere shoulders as an Abanak canoe laid up o' bark o' th' birch tree. A mind o' her own, t' be sure, but far easier t' convince along a true course, 'n' much faster with paddles, than 'em boat-wagons."

"If that indeed be an express from John Langdon I would fain he be intercepted before questions can be asked by our drovers. I desire that he report a great infestation of warlike Indians unleashed by the British upon our defenseless towns and trending rapidly in this direction."

"I espy Cox Pridham yonder, so he 'n' I'll meander over t' th' other side o' th' river and gab with yonder rider before any o' our mob be glad o' th' excuse t' put aside their work on our account 'n' yarn with th' express. If thet indeed be th' case. I'll send Davis Cummings 'n' Stephen Duncan westward t' scout a likely camp fer tonight." Caleb sheathed his knife, threw the bearskin over the gray horse's croup, the animal shying at the smell, and tightened the saddle girth. Ming Tsun handed Gideon up to him after he had mounted.

"Bid Ishmael Hymsinger trend this way, Caleb. The lazarette-wagon has regained its wheels, and young Darius has become adept at yoking oxen to the disselboom." Indeed, in the ellipse of the small glass, Frost observed Darius as he finished attaching the yokes and harnesses with a professional flourish, then turned with a great will to assist Ishmael Hymsinger in loading the cargo of the lazarette-wagon.

"Ye ain't be sendin' Ishmael t' tend 'em Tories, be ye?" Caleb said accusatorily. "Certain they wouldn't be studyin' on tendin' ye, if they had got in 'monst us like foxes 'n th' chicken coop. A cold bayonet stuck in yere guts, th' sooner to riffle yere pockets." Caleb sighed, neck-reined the gray gelding, and nudged the horse with his heels. "Ishmael be trendin' this way soon's I speak him," he called over his shoulder.

Frost continued his careful study of the confusion of the boat-wagons' crossings. Here and there a drover managed more proficiently than most, and he marked the man. He reckoned that wherever George Washington was, in New York or New Jersey, Frost was at least better than half the way, but there were many rivers yet to cross, including the great Hudson. Crossing the Hudson would take some doing, so Frost studied the men loading, unloading, and rearranging the cargoes of various boat-wagons, looking for men with some initiative, which regrettably had been in very short supply. The men enlisted in this effort to convoy supplies to the Continental Army were like the animals they drove. So be it: Frost could lead from the front, and he could quite well prod and spur from the rear. He marked the performance of three men and committed them to memory.

A few minutes later the oxen drawing the lazarette-wagon labored up the slight rise, Ishmael Hymsinger walking alongside, Darius Langdon sitting on the wagon-board drawn out from the left side. "Our men suffered no casualties, thankfully, Ishmael," Frost said, walking toward the shaman. "I know not the gravity of wounds sustained by the Tories. We treated them harshly, as indeed the encounter demanded. Nathaniel shall have gathered all the casualties into the church to await your attendance."

Ishmael Hymsinger nodded sadly. "I fear the delay in attending the wounded may give rise to more cutting and sawing than I have endeavored before under the tutelage of good Doctor Ezrah Green. I have been reading prodigiously of the books he so generously provided . . . though I had hoped it would be long before I would need call upon the knowledge the books have imparted."

"The road southward leads straight to the village. I shall join you once I have spoken with a rider whom I hope has been dispatched by my cousin John, and our train has been started to its next encampment." Frost looked steadily at Ishmael Hymsinger and Darius Langdon for a moment. "You shall find in ruined Agawam a man and a woman; the woman is springing with child. I would appreciate your accommodating the woman in your wagon, because they be like us, nomads, and in nowise can we leave her or the man in a place peopled solely by the dead."

Frost left Hymsinger and Darius gaping at him as he walked resolutely toward the landing. Hannibal Bowditch was doing a wondrous job of forming order from hubbub, but there were several recalcitrants among the drovers who apparently did not wish to receive orders from a youth. Frost massaged the knuckles of both hands as he resolved how to deal with the drovers who were plainly slacking and daring Hannibal to do anything about it. How much easier it was to keep order aboard ships he commanded, where he had a first officer, division officers, bosuns and bosuns' mates to instruct men in their duties and correct them when they went wrong.

The first recalcitrant was dealt with easily; indeed, Frost was not troubled to address another. The man had permitted a barrel of flour to break open—yes, had actually stood by while it tipped out of his wagon, the barrel's staves giving way as the iron hoops flew off in a coruscation of bright sparks when the barrel struck the flint-hard ground, leaving small mounds of flour as the remnants of the barrel rolled away. The man guffawed loudly at the spectacle.

Had the man not laughed Frost likely would have done little more than glower at the man and order him to sift up what could be saved of the precious flour. But the man had laughed at this deliberate spoliation . . . Frost was on the man in an instant and kicked him savagely as he could in the groin. Then he hoisted the man by his lank, greasy hair and punched him with all his strength directly on his nose, feeling the bones break beneath his knuckles with the utmost satisfaction. Frost threw the man headfirst into a mound of flour. He placed a foot on the man's neck and kept the man's face ground remorselessly into the flour. The man was convulsing, one hand snaked out to grasp Frost's foot.

Frost nimbly stepped away and brought his boot heel down on the man's hand, grinding the hand into the frozen earth. The man squealed like a hog being slaughtered. Frost kicked the man in the side of the head to silence him, and grasped the man by the collar of his coat. He dragged him to the nearest tree and gestured to three nearby drovers, who were staring at him in horror.

"You three! There are ropes on your wagons! Fetch the ropes immediately if you value your own sorry lives!"

The three men obeyed with alacrity. "Bind him hand and foot! Tightly! Do you not see? That barrel of flour would have made bread enough to feed half a company of soldiers, who most like have not had a taste of bread this month past. And this fool willfully destroys it! Tighter! Bind him tighter, or by the Golden Buddha you shall be bound on the other side of this tree." Frost picked up a handful of flour and forced it into the man's mouth. "Enjoy your last meal in this life, for here you remain for eternity."

The man gagged on the flour and sagged to his knees to puke bile and bloodied flour. Frost heard a step behind him and whirled round, a Bass pistol in his left hand. Teamster Felton stopped three paces away, his hat held respectfully in his hands at chest level; his face went as white as his bald pate when Frost leveled the pistol directly at Felton's forehead. Felton's hands milled helplessly. "Capt'n Frost," Felton began, "you have punished this man for his crime . . . just as you punished me for my crime of abusing an ox. We both have been abundantly deserving of it."

Frost, his face a hard mask, held the pistol unwaveringly trained directly at Felton's forehead. Felton swallowed heavily and turned a sweating face to his right, where a grim Ming Tsun, arrow nocked on bowstring, sat his horse thirty yards away. He turned back to Frost and swallowed hard again. "His name be Burley, and he was cuttin' the fool to egg on the rest of us . . ."

"And you were abetting him," Frost snapped. "You were gaping at his antics, applauding him, while he was encouraging you to disregard the orders Mister Bowditch was giving for the benefit of all."

Felton half-turned, looking at his fellow drovers for assistance. Everyone had his eyes on the arrow nocked on Ming Tsun's bow. "Capt'n Frost, we be a long way from our homes in Massachusetts and New Hampshire. There be many of us who heartily wish we had never heard your name, nor accepted your cash money. But we be a long way from our homes . . ."

"I find it difficult to believe that a knave such as this . . ." Frost contemptuously indicated the drover named Burley, "has a home, and he most likely had only one married parent. And Dios help us all if he has spawn in his image. Christ himself would weep."

Felton waved his hands deprecatingly. "Capt'n Frost, we have followed you into this wilderness . . ."

"Rather unwilling followers you have made," Frost said. His voice was as cold as the wind that blew off the Connecticut, but he sensed how the conversation was trending. "And now you would find yourselves stranded in this wilderness." His lips pulled up slightly into his thin caricature of a smile. "Without a guide you are foredoomed to wander first in one direction, aimlessly, then in another."

Felton inclined his head: "You are our Moses," he said quietly. "We knew not the vexations to be encountered when—to our rue—we accepted your silver. You have led us most far from our accustomed roads and fields. We know not when next we might confront the British Army, Tories under arms, or more hostile Indians."

"You have tested me needlessly," Frost said, advancing with menace. "This jackanapes has paid a dear price, for I indeed intended to leave him lashed to this tree for all eternity—or until his body rotted—as an example to all who would wantonly waste sustenance sorely needed by men who willingly fight to tear us away from Great Britain's domination."

"There is mutual reliance," Felton said, hastily backing away, his face spotted with alarm. "Though you may wish it not so as much as us teamsters wish we'd never taken your enrollment money, you must have us to marshal these wagons wherever it is you be takin' them." Felton half-smirked: "I warrant you do not know where that place be."

"Mayhap not at the moment," Frost said truthfully enough, uncocking the Bass pistol and tucking it into his belt. "But ere long, surely. I am glad we understand each other, Felton. You shall fetch the forage wagons and follow along the track to the village one mile south. Observe there what those who lived among us are capable of doing when the restraint of civilization is removed. You shall take along your colleague, Burley, who saw sport in the spoliation of flour that otherwise would have fed many hungry men breached in our country. He will surely find instruction in the view. Betimes, I would not leave him here to give the crows and jays indigestion. There be a store of forage in a barn behind a stone house. The inhabitants of the village no longer have use for the excellent forage collected there, though our animals will benefit immensely from their forethought and husbandry, so you may gather it for our purposes."

"You be our Moses," Felton began.

"If indeed I be your Moses," Frost snapped, "I have but one commandment, and that be for you and your fellows to discharge your trade, and discharge it with industry. Felton, think you that your fellows can eke out a ration of pride in their accomplishments at having come all this perilous way? Can your fellows yet step with pride as they go forward to deliver these victuals to men bare short of starvation?"

"I do not believe in miracles, Capt'n Frost," Felton said, wonder in his voice. "Though to some it surely must seem so. Have you any estimation of how far you have brought us since Portsmouth?"

Frost did not answer but snatched Felton's hat from his hands and tossed it lightly into the air. Felton stepped forward to catch it, then shrank back, his face as pale as birch bark, as Ming Tsun's arrow transfixed the hat in mid-air, the arrow's shaft vibrating from the energy released so quickly as the arrow struck and embedded itself in the trunk of the huge maple tree between Frost and Felton. Frost pulled the arrow from the bark in a motion that appeared easy, though the arrow was buried almost to the barb, slipped the hat off the arrow and, smiling, tossed the hat to a wide-eyed and open-mouthed Felton.

"How did the Chinee do that?" Felton expostulated, his face turning sickly and pale as he poked a finger through one of the holes in his hat. "I n'ver saw him take aim."

"He had no need to aim. Tranquility," Frost said. "Ming Tsun possesses a state of mental calm that frees an inner force to guide the arrow true. That inner force bids the arrow to take its own course, though the arrow desires the target of its own accord." He smiled his caricature of a smile and turned away from the perplexed, and thoroughly frightened, drover.

XII

"LET THEM ADVANCE ANOTHER HALF-CABLE'S LENGTH, CALEB," FROST WHISPERED.

"SURE," CALEB GRUMBLED, "AS ifen I knew what one o' 'em durn cables ye're alus talkin' about is. I'm fer lettin' 'em come another hundret yards through th' boscage afore my boys cut loose." Caleb brought Gideon to cheek momentarily and sighted at one of the approaching red-coated British light infantry soldiers, some of whom were just coming into view in the snowy woods some two hundred yards away.

Frost grinned his wry semblance of a smile. "Let us settle upon that ruined chimney protruding through the snow at one hundred yards' distance." Frost nodded toward the charred, tumbled remains of a small building of indeterminate nature in the middle of the once-cleared field now gone to scrub, downslope from where he and Caleb Mansfield crouched behind a blown-down tree just below the hill's crest. The smallholding had sheltered a peaceable family earlier in the year, perhaps a "patriot" family, perhaps a "Tory" family. It was immaterial the smallholder's politics; some people of another political persuasion had fired the small farm. The smallholder's family had either been killed or driven away. "Immediately the sergeant in the middle of the mêlée strides past that chimney, your men may fire."

"Agreed we got th' distance," Caleb said softly, "now I be

off t' give each man his individual mark." Caleb winced as he said the word. "No, I be givin' each o' my men a life t' take. This be a hard thing, Capt'n; it fair turns my stomach 'n' tears loose my bowels, waitin' in ambush. Ain't like stridin' up to 'em Tories back at Agawam 'n' havin' it out, toe t' toe."

Frost gazed bleakly at the sly woods-cruiser Stephen Duncan, who was drawing the British detachment on, floundering in the snow, falling down, thrashing, then getting up to stagger onward, flitting behind one tree, then another. Shrewdly, Duncan never remained still long enough for a British infantryman to assay a musket shot. Frost scooped up a ball of snow in his wool-gloved hand and massaged the back of his neck. He had been dismayed the half hour earlier when Jack Daws had reported how he and Duncan had surprised what was undoubtedly a foraging party that had cut their track as the two woods-cruisers patrolled for stragglers from their train.

An engagement with British troops was absolutely the last thing Frost needed, as at first light he had begun sending the boat-wagons across Hudson's River on their own bottoms. But deal with the British troops he must, and at least it was a comfort that the entire half platoon had hallooed away after Stephen Duncan, and that Jack Daws had been able to break away and bring word of the unwanted and unexpected encounter. So Frost had gathered Caleb and all his woods-cruisers on the east side of Hudson's River and hastened to intercept the British. He admired the way that Stephen Duncan appeared to be floundering aimlessly in the knee-deep snow, but Frost had observed on more than one occasion that precipitant flight greatly encouraged pursuit, and the British light infantrymen were indeed being drawn like hounds on the scent of a fox.

"I like it no better than you, Caleb," Frost said slowly, "but this unfortunate chance encounter leaves us without alternative. It was the purest bad luck for all of us that this foraging party crossed our track, though likely enough off on a frolic of their own, since there is no officer with them. The first of our boat-wagons should just now be arriving at the western marge of Hudson's River. We are far from any recognized ferry and shall require some hours to ensure all are across. If this foraging party carries intelligence of our presence to their larger force, then we are discovered to our ultimate doom, and our freight with it."

"I knows my duty plain," Caleb said wearily. "My woods-cruizers do as well, but holdin' with duty, necessary as it be, makes th' swallowin' none th' more easy."

"It grieves me beyond endurance that we must purchase our crossing with the blood-coin of men with whom we have no quarrel save the will and direction of their king. What knaves we, striving to purchase our freedoms with the lives of those who only follow the orders of those who disburse their paltry shillings."

"Ifen I could parley with 'em, likely I could convince most of 'em to look the other way while we skittle," Caleb said hopefully. He met Frost's sorrowfully knowing eyes for a moment, then looked away. "Aye," Caleb sighed, "all it takes is one t' get back t' his larger company. Thankful we be that Stephen wus able t' draw 'em off and buy us time to get ahead o' 'em." Caleb gestured futilely at the redcoats floundering around in the deep snow on the hillside below them and began to back away from the blown-down log behind which he and Frost were concealed.

"Caleb," Frost said carefully, "the sergeant is mine, and mine alone. Make certain your woods-cruizers devote their aim to others in the mêlée, as you select. We must not waste two balls on the same man. As soon as the sergeant strides past the chimney we have marked, I shall fire. Your men must fire at my signal."

Caleb nodded, "There be twenty o' 'em all told, 'n' only ten o' us, though Jack's got Stephen's rifle." He backed away far enough until he could half-rise and scurry off to identify exactly what their targets would be to the woods-cruisers lying concealed in the dark woods, spread out, waiting in the rough shape of a fish hook below the crest of the rising ground. Frost laid his forehead against the cold bark of the fallen tree and breathed slowly and deeply in a vain effort to quiet his churning stomach. He tried to think about other things, anything other than the approaching British light infantry struggling through the snow in chase of Stephen Duncan. How he longed to be away from this place, these people, and aboard a well-found vessel rounding the Cape of Storms fair for the Moçambique Channel and the Orient beyond. But that lay in the future. How Geoffrey Frost hoped that lay in the future—the very near future!

Four days before, the express rider from John Langdon had brought news that the Continental Army—what was left of it after a series of improbable, virtually unbelievable debacles—was somewhere on the western bank of Hudson's River, perhaps in New York, perhaps in New Jersey. Or perhaps retreated to eastern Pennsylvania to protect the Continental Congress huddling cravenly in Philadelphia. The express rider brought word that all of the fords south of Dobb's Ferry were in British hands, though thankfully the Royal Navy's frigates on the river had been summoned back to New York because of the danger of ice. So Frost had ordered his train of boat-wagons southwestward from the Connecticut crossing, working and cajoling the drovers mercilessly from hours before morning until hours after the bleak sunset, bearing toward the Hudson Highlands, where the British patrols had not yet, hopefully, reached.

The drovers, camp followers and draft animals were bone weary and irritable, but they bent stubbornly, some even pridefully, to their duties as Frost exacted as much distance made good over the wretched roads, as much as seventeen, even eighteen miles between the time the oxen were yoked and they were outspanned. Truly remarkable distance!

In the four days since leaving Agawam, the nights had been cloudless, and the night skies had been illuminated by brilliant showers of meteors originating from the Gemini constellation directly overhead. Some of the meteors had left contrails of smoke long after their streaks of light had extinguished. The sheer numbers and brilliance of the meteors had the superstitious among the drovers and camp followers—which was the majority of them—muttering fearfully about portents, auguries and apocalypse. One old hag, counting less than three yellowed teeth in her entire head, shapeless inside garments reeking of stale smoke from countless cook fires and held together by soiled patches crudely sewn, foretold imminent earthquakes of unbelievable destruction. A day later she prophesied heavenly chariots driven by angels pelting across the skies, raining down balls of fire and brimstone to destroy the world.

Frost had annually observed these Geminid showers in the December skies, had privately anticipated and welcomed them, and had long betimes enjoyed their spectacle from the quarterdecks of various ships. He wished he had been prescient enough to announce the Geminid meteor showers in advance as a physical manifestation of God's will. But he was content to keep his own counsel, so long as the meteors inspired fear of a return eastward and kept the drovers and camp followers ever moving toward Hudson's River.

Keeping well below the tree's trunk, Frost elbowed his way through the snow leftward along the fallen log to a clump of mountain rhododendron at the base of the tree, where it had been uprooted and blown down by some storm within the past ten years. A small oak sapling with a few brown, shriveled leaves still clinging to its frail branches had tried to grow inside the rhododendron. He brought the Ferguson rifle to his left shoulder and rose to a half-kneeling position, pushing the barrel slowly through the screen of rhododendron branches, searching for the British sergeant. There he was, twenty yards short of the ruined chimney, making heavy going of it in the deep snow, pausing now and again to exhort his men to greater effort to bring the cursed fox of a rebel they were chasing to ground.

Frost carefully checked the priming powder in the pan, then soundlessly closed the frizzen. He left the rifle balanced on the fallen log, and on a small square of clean buckskin Frost laid out two additional cartridges. Then he carefully tucked the Ferguson rifle into his shoulder and as silently as possible brought the hammer to full cock. His eye sought out the front sight, focused on the red coat bisected with two white cross-belts, struggling through the now knee-deep snow, and took in a breath. He exhaled half of it, then brought the front sight into the notch of the rear sight and focused the front sight into the blur of the red coat. The front sight was sharp and distinct, and he perched it atop the intersection of the white cross-belts. Joss.

The infantry sergeant's face was buried in shadow when he strode past the chimney stones marking the one hundred yards that would define the killing ground. Frost kept the front sight centered on the cross-belts. Then, inexplicably, the sergeant dropped from sight in the instant that Frost caressed the trigger. He neither felt the recoil nor heard the shot, and the smoke from the discharge hung sullenly in the still, cold air like a reproach. Around him other rifles were cracking; Frost rolled away from his initial firing position as a ragged musket fire from the surprised British infantry detachment popped in desperate reaction, then concentrated on reloading the Ferguson rifle. What a wonder it was to be able to reload while lying behind the safety of the log!

Frost rotated the trigger guard to expose the cavity of the breech, then bit off the paper twist of the cartridge and pushed the ball into the cavity as far as it would go. Then, holding the rifle slightly muzzle-down, Frost let most of the powder run into the breech, then rotated the trigger guard back into position, raising the breech plug. He sprinkled the remainder of the powder as priming into the pan and elbowed his way through the trampled snow behind the blow-down to a position where the smoke was dissipating. By Frost's reckoning the reload had been accomplished in fifteen seconds.

The sergeant was nowhere to be seen, but red-coated bodies were everywhere crumpled in the snow. There was movement partially screened by a beech tree, a woods-cruiser's rifle cracked and a British infantryman who would never again see Yorkshire or Hampshire or the Midlands flopped backward into the snow without a sound. Another long rifle cracked.

"Quarter!" The voice thoroughly laced with fear wavered across the killing ground. "Quarter, for God's sake!"

Frost hesitated for a moment, then shouted: "New England men, cease fire! Britishers, all on your feet, no muskets!" He was answered by silence. "All right then, no quarter!"

"For God's sake, stand up, a-fore they fire again," a young, tremulous voice sobbed. A redcoat moved reluctantly from the questionable shelter of a tree, arms raised. Another rose slowly from the snow, where he lay partially hidden. A third redcoat rose shakily from behind the body of a mate he had used to shield himself.

"All of you on your feet!" Frost shouted. "There are more than three of you!"

"I . . . I think we be all," the young voice said, breaking, "God's me witness. Everyone else be dead inside this past minute."

"Stand where you are! Any treachery and you die," Frost called to the British soldiers. "New England men, remain as you are until I have surveyed the ground."

"Reckon thet be my chore," Caleb Mansfield retorted from somewhere down the gentle slope. "My cruizers 'n' I'll do th' lookin'." A woods-cruiser's cap—Caleb's, appeared above and behind a rhododendron bush.

Frost spied the movement from the snow beside the chimney stones out of the corner of his eye and frantically swept his Ferguson rifle toward the motion. "Caleb!" A musket boomed and the hat spun away. Immediately two long rifles cracked and blended as one with the report of the Ferguson rifle. A small flurry of bullets whipped the snow alongside the chimney stones. The British Army sergeant rose half out of the welter and pit of charred timbers and shingles into which he had fallen, staggered backward, and collapsed without a sound.

"Caleb!" Frost shouted frantically, throwing himself under the downed log and scrambling to his feet on the other side. "Caleb!"

"I be right," Caleb calmly answered, rotating Gideon's barrels as he stepped carefully from behind an oak tree adjacent to the rhododendron shrub. "I twigged we had ourselfs a possum when yonder sergeant went down sudden like, 'n' afore yore bullet could have reached 'im." Other woods-cruisers warily appeared out of the mixture of hardwood and evergreen trees ringing the slope. The three shocked infantrymen remained where they stood, hands raised above their shoulders.

Caleb used Gideon's ramrod to retrieve his cap and clapped it grimly on his snow-dappled mane of gray-streaked hair. Woods-cruisers were warily circling the three soldiers, long rifles trained unwaveringly on them, while other woods-cruisers carefully searched the tumbled figures to ensure their deaths. Frost followed in the trail Caleb broke through the crusted snow to the small depression into which the British sergeant had unexpectedly tumbled. "Stumbled into th' cellar-hole, he did, just as ye shot. Reckon ye got a bullet into 'im this time," Caleb said with satisfaction, gazing down at the gore clotted on the sergeant's tunic, "as did Cox Pridham and Paul Libby." He picked up the dead man's musket.

Frost turned away from the body and looked at the three infantrymen who had surrendered, thinking how much easier it would be if they likewise were dead. He did not need the worry of prisoners additional to the Tories he had brought along from the ruined town of Agawam since he could not release them. The light infantrymen were no more than boys whose faces had yet to feel a razor. "Caleb, I'll thank you to see to the gathering up of all muskets and munitions. I regret extremely there can be no thought of burying these corpses under present circumstances."

"Waal, we'll slip their boots off right quick," Caleb said, looking down into the cellar-hole. "His'n don't look worn hardly at all, 'n' we got a-plenty folks needin' 'em."

Frost turned and raged at the three terrified surviving soldiers. "You! Bring your fellows to cast into this cellar-hole so they may join your sergeant in death. Get them into the earth quickly! Cover the pit with timbers and shingles, tree branches and chimney stones enough, and perhaps the wolves will not discover them. There will be no prayers said over them, and their shades shall nip sharply and incessantly at your heels through all eternity to remind you of your sins."

He glared fiercely into the eyes of the nearest soldier, a youth with a badly cleft upper lip, with a look that seared the man's soul. "And I strictly enjoin you to eschew the treachery displayed by your sergeant, for misdoubt not, upon the slightest reason, you shall join him." By the Golden Buddha, but Frost had been subject to sufficient British perfidy and duplicity this year to sate him forever. The British major at Louisbourg, the captain of the East Indiaman *Sagittarius*—good riddance to those fellows! He stoppered the anger quickly, for anger was futile and allowing it rein would pose distraction he could ill afford. Frost smiled bleakly at the three soldiers. "Hasten!" he commanded, then turned and struggled through the knee-deep snow and over the hill to the tree where Bwindi, his molly-mule, and the horses of the woods-cruisers were tied.

XIII

THE CONFUSION AT THE HUDSON'S CROSSING WAS MODERATE, FROST OBSERVED, COMPARED TO SOME OF THE RIVER CROSSINGS ALREADY ENdured. Some of the drovers were at last developing a degree of pride in their work, he was glad to note, and were actively assisting other drovers, who, if they weren't taking the assistance kindly, were at least accepting the offering of it. Nathaniel Dance's marines were good watermen, now quite adept at propelling the awkward boat-wagons, and Hannibal Bowditch and Darius Langdon had developed aptitudes for directing the unlading and stowing of cargo. And Ming Tsun was a constant presence, reminding everyone that Frost was never far away. But how Frost longed for the focus and discipline found aboard his dear *Audacity*, and the trained officers and mates who were adept at training others to their duties.

Five boat-wagons only—three forage wagons, the lazarette-wagon, and the wagon in which the most seriously wounded of the Tory prisoners were being transported—were yet to cross when Frost rode his molly-mule down the track that led off the post road to the crossing just below the small village of Cold Spring. There had never been a ferry here, but the land sloped gently down to the sharply angled river, where there was a flat sand bar, now well frozen. The sand bar made getting the wheels off and the boat-wagons into the water as easy as such an operation ever could be.

There was some sort of low island between the two shores, a slough in which a raft of wild ducks and geese, the large gray and white geese with the black throat patch from Canada and the smaller white geese with speckling on their bellies, contentedly dabbled in places where the water had not yet iced over, perhaps due to their movements. It separated the island and this eastern bank of the Hudson. Frost took out his small telescope and surveyed the towering heights of the Hudson highlands on the western bank. A high promontory poked a blunt knuckle into the river at the sharp elbow. Frost could not be sure, but he thought he spied some old stone works high on the opposite shore, perhaps some fortifications attempted in the last war with the French. It would be sensible, the fortifying of this natural choke point on a waterway bearing commerce—or an invading force.

He had never seen it, knew it only by the talk of others, but this height of land had to be similar to the height on which Ticonderoga was situated at the constriction of Lake Champlain. The sudden thought of Fort Ticonderoga and its cannons, and the cannons brought overland at such great expense by Henry Knox, conjured up the image of Joseph . . . Joseph. Was his brother alive, or had he died in Arnold's futile campaign on the Lake these two months past? Frost massaged his temples and dismissed the image of his brother. But truly, a fortress situated on the height of that western point would command and block all traffic on the river.

The boat-wagons waiting to cross were under the sober protection of two marines with one twelve-pounder artillery piece, the other already ferried across and emplaced on the opposite shore, and the great Newfoundland dog, George Three, whom everyone was avoiding for the moment, seeing that he had recently roused out a skunk and was rank with the fragrance of that encounter. Salome, sheltering in the lee of a rectangle of rumbowline sailcloth stretched between two boat-wagons and warmed by several fires, was assisting Ishmael Hymsinger in tending the Tory wounded. Two teamsters fallen overboard from their wagons and plucked to safety by Darius Langdon were dancing animatedly around another blaze ten yards away. As Frost cantered up, the marines rendered awkward salutes, and Salome greeted Frost with a radiant smile.

"Please thee observe, Captain Frost! I know not how he did so, but Mister Hymsinger in some wise treated this man's wounded leg so that it turned not gangrenous!" Salome held up toward Frost a strip of linen just removed from a Tory seated against a wagon wheel to show only a slight stain of yellowish-white pus, then reached out with a short, crude paddle to stir a large three-legged pot in which other strips of linen were boiling.

At another fire nearby, Ishmael Hymsinger was burning bandages horribly soiled with blood, pus and body fluids. He smiled deprecatingly. "Cleanliness and restorative food and rest have far greater efficacy than the exceedingly slight skills the Almighty has gifted me." He looked incredulously at Frost. "Sir, I have assiduously been reading the medical texts so graciously left me by Surgeon Green. One describes a universal treatment for diseases and wounds, indeed, all types of afflictions, by opening a vein to draw away blood! I can scarce credit it! The body generates its own curative liquid, and it does not cypher to waste such precious fluid through deliberate exsanguination!"

Frost returned the small glass to his coat pocket and dismounted from Bwindi, who shied as George pranced toward them, tail happily wagging in welcome. The sharp skunk musk assaulted Frost's nostrils and eyes, causing them to water, but he returned the dog's affection by playing with him a moment. George sneezed mightily; doubtless Frost smelled as offensive to the Newfoundland dog, given that he had not had the opportunity to bathe since departing Portsmouth, nor had he shifted out of his clothes more than twice. Thankfully, somehow Ming Tsun managed to find the five minutes to shave him every other day.

"I share your sentiments on the virtues of our bodies' blood, Ishmael," Frost said, pulling off his gloves and stooping to hold his cold-numbed hands toward a fire's warmth. "I've never given up any of mine willingly, and I twig that good Doctor Green believes alike, since he never sought to treat anyone with lancet and cup while he shipped with us." He scanned the river and saw Nathaniel and Hannibal standing together in the bow of one boat-wagon. He had work for them. The major of the Massachusetts militia in Springfield had readily accepted the Tory prisoners, even the lightly wounded ones, that Frost had asked him to accept. But the major had refused to take the more seriously wounded Tories to be a public charge until some captive exchange could be worked out. So Frost had reluctantly and grudgingly brought the wounded Tories, who were unable to walk, with him. But now he saw a way to rid himself of them.

Hymsinger dipped boiling water from the large pot into a bowl half-filled with tepid water, then gently began washing the Tory's wounded leg. Salome discarded the bandage into the fire, and following Hymsinger's example likewise washed her hands. Frost looked longingly at the boiling water. Salome retrieved a book from beneath a pile of linen strips that had been washed, dried and folded for bandages. She moved nearer to a Tory crouched on a small barrel several feet back from a fire. The Tory's head was heavily swathed in bandages, his eyes completed covered. The book was in tatters, pages loosely attached, not really a book at all. Frost remarked upon it.

"Oh Captain Frost," Salome said, beaming, "this be a most remarkable book of poems on various subjects, religious and moral! It was writ by a Miss Phillis Wheatley from your Boston, and has been the sensation of England since Mr. Bell in Aldgate printed it three years gone. I cannot tell thee how much comfort I have derived from its words." Salome sighed: "It was the only item other than the clothes that dressed us that Jesse and I carried away from Newport, so turbulent was our leaving of that place."

"Given the book's value to you, Madame, how came it to such estate?" Frost asked. He yielded to temptation and used the crude paddle to winkle a strip of linen out of the boiling water. Self-consciously but eagerly he washed his dirty hands and forearms, then attacked his face and neck with vigor. He finished his toilet by using a corner of the cloth, dipped once again into the boiling water and wrapped around a forefinger, to scrub his teeth.

Salome cast down her eyes. "I had the book with me in the kitchen as I was preparing food for those . . . people in the village of Agawam. Some desired to light their pipes, so they tore pages as spills to convey flame from the hearth to their bowls." Salome brightened. "But the poems I love best were preserved." She reached out to touch the cheek of the Tory. "May I read to thee, please? I fain believe the words will comfort thee, until thy bandages be removed and thee sees again."

The Tory nodded slowly. Salome fluffed out her skirts, sat back on her heels, rested the fragments of book on her swelling stomach and began to read.

> 'Twas mercy brought me from my pagan land,
> Taught my benighted soul to understand that there's a God,
> That there's a Savior too; Once I redemption neither sought nor knew.
> Some view our sable race with scornful eye, "their colour is a diabolic dye."
> Remember Christians; Negroes black as Cain, May be refin'd,
> And join the angelic train.

"I know of this Miss Wheatley by repute," Frost said shortly, "though this is the first time I have heard her poetry. She wrote a lament commemorating the death of the evangelical, George Whitefield. I collect she also wrote a poem commemorating His Excellency George Washington's appointment as Commander-in-Chief of the Continental Army. I collect that General Washington thanked her tolerably well for such signal honour."

"Indeed," Salome said brightly. "I am glad thee be acquainted with the young lady, though as thee say, by reputation only. Can thee, then, explain the meaning of 'sable race'? I have puzzled upon it exceedingly these many months."

"The young woman is a Negro, as her rime implies, and had been a slave," Frost said harshly. "She was stolen from her native Senegalese as a babe. Somehow she became the property . . ." Frost drew out the word, "of a Boston family named Wheatley."

"She is a blackamoor then! Like the dear youth Darius who treasures thee so and is keen to become a man of medicine," Salome exclaimed. "There were several so amonst the crew of the vessel conveying Jesse and me from Plymouth. But Jesse and I remarked that as a tint of skin colouration solely, most likely due to the vicissitudes of weather and climate where they are born, just as we born in the northern climes are bleached to our colour by the wind, the rain, and the cold." Salome paused, then continued with some incredulity in her voice. "But thee, Captain Frost, used the term 'slave.' I am familiar with the meaning of the word, since slavery is often mentioned in the Bible's Old Testament, and the New Testament as well. I am all too aware of the tragic chattel sufferings of the Irish poor, but surely such barbarism as the claimed ownership of one human creature by another is not in currency anywhere in this world!"

Frost returned the strip of fabric used for his toilet to the pot of boiling water and looked with equal incredulity at the woman's plain but serenely tranquil face. Surely Salome was disingenuously jesting . . . but no, the woman was in complete earnest. Frost looked at Ishmael Hymsinger, himself once a slave, and saw the same stupefaction, yet tender sadness, also writ large on Hymsinger's honest and open face.

Frost crouched beside Salome on the cold hard sand, looked her directly in the eyes and explained grimly, "Dear lady, I know not in what remote English village you have dwelt, but it was indeed a most wondrously sheltered venue where protections against the world's intrusions abounded. But unfortunately there still exists in this debased world the self-same cruel, most accursed commerce in human misery first described so eloquently in Exodus. Miss Wheatley's brief rime speaks to the gruesome enslavement of large quantities of members of her 'sable race' with the active connivance of many other human beings, both black and white, to their vast profits, as an inexhaustible supply of sinew and muscle."

Salome dropped the pages of the book and raised a hand to stifle a cry. "Thee cannot mean it, Captain Frost! Our merciful God would never permit such inhumanity . . ."

"By whatever name God is known by the multitude of religions on this planet," Frost said, "God is scrupulously neutral, though the falsely pious frequently bray that God sanctions their traffic in human misery and pain. Indeed, Miss Wheatley innocently subscribes to one of the touted pieties that enslavement provides salvation for poor souls that otherwise would escheat to the Devil."

"I should rather be a pagan than be looked upon as the property of another!" Salome cried, and tears spilled from her eyes.

Frost rose to his feet, as always acutely uncomfortable in the presence of a woman's grief. "I beg forgiveness for my words having been the cause of your additional sorrows," he said lamely, and he turned quickly to Hymsinger before Salome could reply. "Ishmael, ready your patients for a brief journey. It shall not be a protracted one."

"Mister Dance, Mister Bowditch," he called, immensely relieved for the excuse to leave Salome to the newly discovered sorrow he had unwillingly thrust upon her, "a word with you whenever you may find it convenient to attend."

The youths scampered over with immediate dispatch at their summons, each bubbling with enthusiasm. "Captain, sir!" Hannibal gushed, "I have made a definitive calculation of our longitude, building upon lunar observations taken these last clear nights—was not the phenomenon of Geminid meteors most prodigious?—and Nathaniel, that is, Mister Dance, was assiduous in recording the sums. I confirm that the west shore of Hudson's River is aligned along the seventy-fourth meridian westerly from the prime at Greenwich."

"And I begin to comprehend, though dimly, for I am so unlearned, the unity of the mathematic . . ." Nathaniel began.

Frost cut them short. "Ensign Dance, scour this easterly bank and sequester all boats of any size and any draught discovered for a distance of five miles below and above this point. Dispatch your best sergeant of marines to do likewise on the western bank. You shall wish to send detachments south and north simultaneously. All boats collected are to be marshaled at the north end of the small island yonder, where they shall directly serve double duty as warmth for these prisoners and a signal beacon for their compatriots.

"Mister Bowditch, investigate the island for a suitable encampment to accommodate these Tory wounded. They shall be placed in the care of three private soldiers of the British light infantry to await the arrival of a large British Army force I anticipate shall arrive in these environs sometime during the night, though assuredly by the first hour of tomorrow's morning, attracted here by the beacon we shall kindle.

"Ishmael, prepare your patients for discharge into the care of their compatriots. We shall alight a blaze of boats to guide them hither."

Frost saw the drover named Felton disembarking from the boat-wagon. "Drover Felton, you are to take charge of the ferrying of these remaining wagons, less the wagon devoted to the transport of the Tory wounded, and see them immediately conveyed to the far shore. Mind, all to be accomplished within the hour." He was obscurely pleased by the look of alarm and shock that coursed over Felton's face. "Come, Drover Felton, you have exerted yourself diligently, and I applaud the initiative you have displayed. It shall not go unrewarded." Frost grinned his caricature of a smile at Felton, heartily glad that he had other matters demanding his attention to the exclusion of Salome's sorrows.

"Four days ago you wondered how far you and your fellows have been led from Portsmouth." He calculated quickly; the longitude of the State House in Portsmouth he had once definitively ascertained to be 71 degrees, 46 minutes west. If the western bank of Hudson's River lay along the 74th meridian—and upon Hannibal's report he reckoned it to be so—

then the degrees of arc subtended equaled some one hundred ninety-six. "Thanks to an accurate determination of our longitude by Mister Bowditch, we find ourselves some sixty-five and one-half leagues westerly from Portsmouth."

Felton apparently had difficulty comprehending the information. "I confess ignorance of the meaning of the term 'league,' Captain Frost," Felton stammered, "and sure, sixty-five leagues does not seem a great amount of distance for all the time we have traveled."

"It is not," Frost assured the drover. "In units of measure perhaps more understandable, we have traversed slightly over two hundred miles in a straight line from Portsmouth, though you'll doubtlessly agree the turnings and deviations of the road have increased that distance twice, easily."

XIV

"ENSIGN DANCE," FROST SAID QUIETLY, "YOU WILL OBLIGE ME EXTREMELY IF YOU FORM YOUR MARINES INTO A GUARD TO HONOUR THE COLOURS we shall parade as we greet the cohorts of our Continental Army."

"Guard of honour for our colours, right you are, sir." Nathaniel Dance marched away full of purpose, oblivious to the sullen hard flakes of snow spat randomly out of an overcast sky the color of tarnished pewter.

"Ensign Dance," Frost's voice arrested Nathaniel in midstride. "We likewise require two staffs, each ten feet in length, straight and smooth as the ramrod of Caleb Mansfield's Gideon rifle." Then to the other ship's gentlemen standing attentively nearby: "Mister Langdon, Mister Bowditch, have either of you any objections to bearing our colours into General Washington's encampment?"

"May it please you, sir," Darius said, his voice extremely grave, "but I wish overmuch to bear our rattlesnake flag."

"Exactly so, Mister Langdon. You shall provide signal honour to our rattlesnake flag. Hasten you both to rig our rattlesnake flag and the flag of Grand Union." Frost wheeled Bwindi, Ming Tsun closely following, and trotted back along his convoy of boat-wagons, his eye alighting on Felton, the drover, riding on the tailboard of his wagon, legs swinging and head lolling, glassy-eyed. Felton had, in one of the mysterious ways known only to drovers and sailors, gotten into some spirits, or, to be more accurate, had gotten some spirits into him.

"Toppin' mornin' it be, Capt'n Frost," Felton burbled happily. "Don't mind tellin' you there was times I never thought we'd be livin' to see this day."

"It is along past mid-day," Frost snapped, "no longer morning, and a drunkard such as you is in no condition to be droving."

"Capt'n Frost," Felton expostulated as only one sunken in drink can, "I not be doin' the drovin'. The oxen be doin' the drovin', 'n' I be long just for the ride."

Frost smiled. "Aye, Felton, you have performed your duty, I'll grant freely. And I have marked you pulled more than your share in the recent crossings."

"Makes a difference, Capt'n Frost," Felton slurred, "when someone takes an interest in seein' you through."

"Quite right, Felton, and do not forget that once we deliver our cargo to the Continental Army, we must win our way back to Portsmouth. I have in mind to appoint you head drover. You must cypher out how many boat-wagons we must retain to accommodate our numbers, enumerate the oxen, and estimate the forage to be borne—unless it be your wish to remain with General Washington and serve as a drover in our Continental Army."

Felton exploded into a fit of laughter and sneezing than almost toppled him from the tailboard. "I be a far piece from desirin' the military life, Capt'n, 'n' I've been told General Washington don't hold with pressin' men into the Continental service. So I reckon I'll see to the returnin' to Portsmouth . . ." He regarded Frost shrewdly, letting Frost know that he was not so diminished by drink that he had not grasped Frost's meaning. "The post as head drover you mentioned did not pass me without notice, Capt'n. 'N' I assume that post brings some increase 'n the argent."

"If your efforts merit additional silver, Felton, you shall have it undoubtedly, but you must not bury your talent in the ground and expect recompense upon our return to Portsmouth . . ."

Frost broke off at the sound of hooves pounding frozen ground and looked around to see Caleb Mansfield pelting toward him on the magnificent gray gelding he had obtained at Agawam. "We done found Washington sure enough," Caleb panted when he drew rein a few feet from Frost. "Less than two mile off in a private house." Caleb spat. "Can't say much for his picquets, though. Rode right up to 'em, 'n' had we been British we could have slit their throats 'n' rode on t' perform th' same on His Excellency. Guess we would likely have gotten some sort of reward from th' Howe brothers for th' doin', but them brothers would still demand I give up Gideon 'n' await their pleasure. So no throats be slit, though as I reflect upon it, a few slit throats among th' picquets would encourage th' rest something wondrous. I said as much t' one serjent, as I gave him an aviso to convey t' this General Washington o' his." Caleb grinned. "Gave th' serjent a thunderin' clap upside his head so's he wouldn't ferget th' lesson."

Frost wheeled around at the shout and saw a horde of horsemen galloping toward him. He whipped out his small glass and held it, steadying his molly-mule with a single soft word.

Nathaniel Dance called from the head of the column of boat-wagons, his high falsetto barely carrying back to Frost and Caleb. "Marines formed guard o' honour, Capt'n Frost, sir."

"Our route of return shall be keeping the west bank of the Delaware River we crossed this morning with such great turmoil, Felton. I doubt that you had resorted to the solace of rum at that time, since the first British skirmishers were pouring onto the eastern bank as the last of our boat-wagons pulled away, and you were as lusty on your oar as any four men. Cypher that into your calculations of forage and provender necessary to sustain our crew, for the route we've just accomplished is foreclosed by the entire British Army landed in New York, and our voyage homeward shall of necessity be circuitous."

Felton gave Frost a mock salute, and his response, though slurred, was intelligible enough that Frost marked the man's comprehension. "I don't mind tellin' you, Capt'n Frost, that when I saw them redcoats swarmin' like ants out o' a disturbed heap as we pulled midstream—a few o' 'em fired their muskets off—that I was so scared you could not have driven a twenty-pennyweight nail up my arse with a maul. Made a right believer out of me, that shootin' did, and many another patched the same. I'll cypher on it, 'n' have figures to recommend when next you inquire."

Frost nodded in dismissal and turned Bwindi toward the head of his column. He had already worked out the weights and amounts of provender and forage he would require to see his people back to Portsmouth by a route up the Delaware to a crossing above the Forks, then striking eastward to the point where he had crossed the Hudson. He would be interested to see what kind of computations Felton would provide, but Frost was immensely cheered that the man had come around to being an asset rather than a burden. He frowned. What to do with the man, Simon, and his extremely pregnant sister-in-law? He found himself passing the lazarette-wagon and spied Ishmael Hymsinger walking at the head of the yoke of oxen on the off side, the great Newfoundland dog frolicking alongside.

Frost leaned from his saddle to address Hymsinger in a low voice that would not carry to the lazarette-wagon. "How fares the Lady Salome?"

A smile fleeted across Ishmael Hymsinger's neatly bearded, anxious face, framed between his two massive braids of hair. "She is in excellent spirits, which I believe to be composed equally of the joy she relishes in the prospect of bringing a new life into this world, and a desire to conceal her dread at the ordeal often attendant at a birth—particularly when she has never birthed a child a-fore, and she herself is but a mere child." Ishmael stroked Bwindi's muzzle as he paced beside the molly-mule. "I know something of birthing among my Indian family, but women are always more knowledgeable of these matters than men, so I have vetted the women in our company, and have determined upon two who are sober and industrious, and above all, have a regard for cleanliness. When her birthing is imminent, the Lady Salome shall be attended by two midwifes."

"Are you confident in these women's abilities, and when might the Lady's labours commence?" Frost asked sharply.

"The timing of the event is known only to God, though doubtlessly the Lady's body admits to some prescience. As to the abilities of the midwifes, I confess no notion, though if the Lady Salome desires me to be in attendance, I shall make it so."

"I am content with your judgment, Ishmael," Frost said and nudged Bwindi into a trot, the Newfoundland dog detaching himself from Ishmael Hymsinger and following the molly-mule.

Nathaniel Dance had performed his duties with alacrity, and the flag of the Grand Union stitched together so lovingly by the Frost women was being bent to the second staff. The tattered and stained rattlesnake flag was already bent to its staff and was stiffly held by Darius Langdon. Frost regarded the rattlesnake flag solemnly. Darius reverently fingered the edge of the flag, from which a strip had been torn, and a large tear formed in his eye. Frost had ripped the piece of bunting from the rattlesnake flag during the desperate fight with the renegade American pirates of *Zeus' Chariot* in a futile attempt to stanch the flow of blood from the pike wound sustained by his bosun, Slocum Plaisted. Slocum Plaisted had willingly surrendered his life to preserve the life of Darius Langdon.

"Mister Langdon," Frost said, hoping he was succeeding in keeping the huskiness out of his voice, "this ensign shall be retired at the end of this commission. Its retirement shall be accompanied by solemn ceremony. I desire you to consult with the ladies of Portsmouth-town to stitch another, and I desire that you preserve this ensign eternally in your keeping."

He turned away quickly. "Mister Bowditch, Mister Langdon, flags aloft and begin the march. Ensign Dance, at the head of your marines, yourself five paces behind our flags. Carry on along this road."

The horde of horsemen pelting toward Frost's column was almost up to the column now. Nathaniel Dance called out an order, then another, in a voice that barely hinted at his youth. The marines shouldered their Ferguson rifles and assorted muskets with all the snap and precision of Royal Marines long drilled in the maneuver, and stepped out smartly. Frost moved to the right side of the marching marines, Caleb Mansfield and Ming Tsun accompanying him. Behind the marines the drovers picked up the step, and the majority of them—no! all of them, camp-followers too—squared their shoulders and walked with pride, heads erect. The horsemen slowed from a canter to a walk when they were fifty yards away from the head of the column.

Frost scanned their faces, recognizing no one. The flag of Grand Union and the rattlesnake flag were drawing abreast of the horsemen. "Gentlemen, please to salute the flags we bear," Frost called sharply to remind the men of their duty.

The horsemen raised their right hands to the brims of their tricornes, and their salutes were duly acknowledged by Nathaniel Dance as he passed abreast.

"Frost!" someone shouted. "That's Frost, that's Geoffrey Frost!" A horseman detached from the mob, cantered briefly, and stopped beside Frost. A hand was extended and Frost scanned the face above it, still without recognition, even as he pulled the glove from his right hand and grasped that of the horseman's. "John Sullivan, Geoffrey! We have met only briefly, and that only twice. The first a little more than two years ago, when you had just arrived in Portsmouth at the culmination of one of your Oriental voyages. And then a month later at the wedding ceremony joining my good friend Marcus Whipple with your singularly lovely and virtuous sister." John Sullivan pumped Frost's arm vigorously.

Frost recalled the man now. Marcus and Charity had graciously advanced the date of their wedding by one month so that Frost would not miss the winds favorable for departure on his last voyage to the Orient. But the John Sullivan he had met perfunctorily had been a prosperous Portsmouth merchant; no, a lawyer, somewhat of a dandy, he recalled, and tending toward fat and pompous. The fellow astride an emaciated horse appeared equally emaciated, gaunt and hollow-cheeked, eyes sunk almost to the point of invisibility, black and brooding. The man's uniform was threadbare and so rumpled that Frost imagined the man slept in it. He wore no cloak. This John Sullivan was a far cry from the John Sullivan who was disparaged by John Langdon earlier, until reminded of his better accomplishments by Caleb Mansfield.

"Of course," Frost said as genially as he could. "I recall you well. Compliments from Marcus and Charity, John Langdon, and all the gentlefolk of the town." Insh'allah! But if such a fop as John Sullivan had been reduced to such a tatterdemalion state of *dishabille*, how did he appear to the horsemen greeting him? Indeed, Frost had slept in his clothes whenever exhaustion overtook him, and his face had not felt a razor since leaving Hudson's River.

"When did you leave Portsmouth?" Sullivan asked eagerly, finally letting go of Frost's hand.

Frost checked his memory, fretful that it served so slowly. "Exactly three weeks ago."

"Mother of God!" Sullivan exclaimed, "But you have made an exceptional journey with this mass of wagons. They are wagons, aren't they? I confess never having seen such conveyances a-fore."

"Wagons they be right enough," Frost replied a bit testily. Yes, the like of these wagons had never been seen, and likely never would be seen again. But they had done their duty, not counting the innumerable broken wheels and disselbooms, frayed and repaired chains, and rewoven traces and ancillary harnesses. Tired oxen, and weary, footsore drovers. Geoffrey Frost felt very possessive of the boat-wagons he had designed and supervised in the construction.

"And they are all laded with food for our army, and powder for our arms? That is the rumor we have heard. Please tell me now if it is not true. Life would be impossible to bear if you disabuse us of what we have been told is conveyed in these argosies—these marvelous argosies of yours."

"Your intelligence is accurate. These argosies bring flour, rice, corn meal—and powder." Frost was pleased with the term *argosy* and wished he had thought of it.

"Prodigious amounts of powder?" Sullivan asked hopefully.

"I know not how you define prodigious, John Sullivan—I'm sorry, General Sullivan—but there is here some fifty tonne."

"Geoffrey, I fair swoon!" John Sullivan cried. Then, he leaned close to Frost and whispered conspiratorially, "Dare we hope that you have conveyed hence that indispensable item second only to gunpowder . . ."

"There are freighted somewhere aboard these argosies three great hogsheads of rum, General Sullivan," Frost said shortly, "though I cannot attest that somehow the Devil has not been able to reduce the strapping; for sure the Devil's spawn have attended and sorely tried me on this voyage."

John Sullivan leaned over to clasp Frost familiarly on the shoulder, a familiarity Geoffrey Frost thought entirely unwarranted. "Friend Geoffrey, you and your argosies are indeed paragons! I am away to General Washington directly! He shall, without doubt, wish to welcome you personally!" Sullivan spurred his emaciated steed with an enthusiasm that Frost found abhorrent. Nevertheless, the horse responded nobly.

Frost watched the horsemen pelt away with more than a tinge of exasperation, which he signed to Ming Tsun. "We have come all this perilous way to find the Continental Army is more interested in rum than powder and food."

"No," Ming Tsun corrected, "the man named Sullivan inquired as to the availability of rum only after he ascertained you brought powder." The brusqueness with which he then signed "You learned long ago you cannot hold others to your standards" told Frost that his dearest friend on earth was close to being cross with him.

Frost made the sign for "joss." Indeed, it was so, and nothing he could do would ever change it.

XV

THE THREATENING SNOW HELD OFF, SAVE FOR OCCASIONAL HARD DRIBBLES OF SLEET THAT STUNG WITH THE FORCE OF AN OPEN-HANDED SLAP ON cold-numbed faces, as Darius Langdon and Hannibal Bowditch marched the colors while the diminutive Nathaniel Dance called the step. His marines, for they were entirely Nathaniel's, Geoffrey Frost acknowledged, to a man devoted more to the youth than whatever cause he served, marched with an awesome precision that initially struck dumb the remnants of the Continental Army turning out to greet the convoy of argosies bringing their relief. Frost reflected that the term *argosy* was indeed appropriate, and also the fact that men served in units, and were loyal first to those units, which was why it was absolutely imperative that those units served the larger cause.

Frost focused intently and incredulously upon the individual men, scarce comprehending what he was seeing. Never had he seen such rabble, not even in the teeming Calicut. Their stench assaulted his nostrils, and every step of his molly-mule revealed an even more dispiriting vista of men without uniforms, without firearms, clasping fragments of blankets around hunger-thinned shoulders, urine-stained breeches, rags wrapped around their feet in place of shoes and sturdy boots. Blankets! Why had he not brought all ten thousand blankets instead of half that number? The Golden Buddha curse him for a dog! Five thousand blankets, though of typically mediocre British contractor quality, had been left in Portsmouth! How heaven sent it would be to have those additional five thousand blankets to distribute to these poor, dumb, starving soldiers!

Bwindi walked slowly, placing her hooves carefully, with all the regal dignity of her breed, and Frost dourly regarded the soldiers, peering keenly at them, judging their fitness for duty. He saw not a man he could rate a landsman, much less an able seaman aboard any vessel he would command, and he knew shame that upon this pitiful rabble the future of the nascent United States of America was completely and utterly dependent.

And then the scarecrows that were men in appearance only began cheering. And they kept cheering, and their hoarse voices rose in intensity and excitement as the argosies, axles groaning and oxen protesting mildly, passed the scraps of frayed canvas spread haphazardly over small hollows excavated with great effort in the frozen earth that were laughable, pitiful shelters to the soldiers' misery. Knots of shivering men, every thread they possessed tugged about their long-unwashed and extremely rank bodies, huddled by smoky fires in desperate efforts to absorb some feeble measure of warmth. And still they cheered and waved their dirty, bloody rag-wrapped hands. And Geoffrey Frost bowed his head and pulled his tricorne low so the soldiers of the Continental Army of the United States would not see his tears.

The cheering men crowded down to line both sides of the rutted ice road, held from crowding into the lane itself by split rail fences, and Frost's face took on the hardness of the ground over which Bwindi paced. He had regained his composure by the time his column reached the low two-story house of poplar logs hewn square and daubed with clay painted white, standing in a grove of tulip trees at the head of the lane branching off from the road along which the remnants of the Continental Army were encamped. Nathaniel Dance looked askance over his shoulder, and Frost nodded. Nathaniel ordered the marines to halt, the colors also; then, with a great clashing of rifles and slapping of fore-stocks, Nathaniel faced the marines toward the house and shouted them through "order arms" and "present arms" as several men emerged from the house and walked slowly across the porch.

Frost's attention was drawn to the tallest figure in the group. Frost was quite tall himself, but this man, dressed in white breeches and a simple blue tunic with epaulets of gilded wire, topped him by a good three inches. He judged the man was approximately twice his age. Frost stepped wearily from Bwindi's saddle and stood watching the tall man advance to the edge of the porch. At a whispered command from Nathaniel Dance, Darius Langdon and Hannibal Bowditch extended their flag staffs at thirty-degree angles toward the porch. The tall man walked slowly down the four steps from the porch to the frozen ground and stopped in front of the two flags. The man's right hand swept off his tricorne to reveal a carefully powdered wig, and he reached out with his left hand to lift the hem of the flag of Grand Union to his lips.

The hat was then clapped firmly atop the tall man's head, and he turned his gaze on Geoffrey Frost, Ming Tsun and Caleb Mansfield. The man's gray eyes scanned them, looking not at them but piercing through them. The man's presence was commanding, but at the same he was possessed of the egalitarian courtliness and manners of an Athenian noble, or what Frost's reading of Thucydides' admiring descriptions of Pericles had led Frost to conclude an Athenian noble would look like. And Frost knew he was in the presence of someone truly remarkable and extremely rare.

"Thank you, gentlemen," George Washington said gravely to Darius and Hannibal, "I am heartily glad to welcome your colours." His gaze returned to Frost: "Captain Frost, I am indeed most indebted to you for that excellent sea-terrapin you dispatched to Mrs. Washington and me. It was the centerpiece of the last dinner we enjoyed together in Cambridge." George Washington's gaze traveled to his right, carefully scrutinizing the boat-wagons that were bumping and squealing to halts as the wagons in front of them ran onto their fellows in front.

Washington's eyes fell on Frost again, and Frost felt as if his soul was being probed. "But the sustenance for our Continental Army you have fetched along surpasses wonderment, and I am hopelessly bereft of words of a nature appropriate to thank you." Washington advanced through the ranks of marines and extended his right hand, first stripping off his glove. Frost bowed, then met Washington's own clasp with one equally firm. He stared directly into Washington's eyes and momentarily glimpsed there all the miseries and woes of the world.

"Yes, Your Excellency, delivered by one of those rascally privateersmen you so abhor," Frost could not refrain from saying with all the tartness he could summon. For Washington was a southerner and Frost had heard that Washington had scant love for New Englanders.

"Yes," Washington replied simply, "so you are, but welcome in the extreme for all that." Then Washington's eyes widened as he took in Ming Tsun and Caleb Mansfield, and he said with great astonishment: "Why, I mistake not, but you be Goodman Mansfield . . ."

"Aye, Yere Excellency. The same as with Boone wus scouts to Braddock and gave him notice o' th' trap th' Frenchman de Beaujeu had set fer him on th' other side of th' Monongahela ford, though as ye ken Mister Braddock didn't want t' hear nothin' from a Continental that went agin th' grain o' his thinkin'." Caleb Mansfield peered equally intently into George Washington's eyes.

George Washington placed a hand on Caleb's shoulder. "You still have that double-barrel rifle, I see."

"Barrels been freshened twice, but same as shot those two Ottawas off ye whilst ye wus formin' a line of yere Virginia skirmishers t' forestall th' rout," Caleb said placidly. "Which, as ye collect, wus when th' first horse wus shot from under ye, and yere nose wus broke."

"Yes, and you set me upon another horse, and that was the last I saw of you, Goodman Mansfield. I had long given you up for dead, though I made diligent inquiries for you." George

Washington's hand slipped from Caleb's shoulder to clasp his hand.

"Ye knew my particular line o' work, Yere Excellency, and I had t' be about it," Caleb said quickly.

"Yes, quite so," Washington said, equally quickly. "So it must have been you who roused the sentries so!" He turned back to Frost. "Captain Frost, General Sullivan has given me some brief intelligence of the stores you have brought, but I fain would learn more from your own lips. If you have a manifest of stores, I hope you will be kind enough to share it with me over a cup of Arabica."

Frost turned to Ming Tsun, who presented the secretary and lifted the lid to withdraw the manifests wrapped in protective light canvas. He handed the packet to George Washington with a bow. "Your Excellency is very kind, but I must first see to my teamsters and their animals. If you could have someone designate a place where we might outspan our train I would be most grateful. Perhaps you may wish to provide the manifests to your Commissary-General, so that a general accounting may ensue." Frost heard the collective sharp intake of breath from the small group of men standing on the porch behind Washington and judged he was being more than a little impolite in declining Washington's invitation for coffee. He did not care. The people and animals under his care came first.

George Washington smiled; it was a sad smile, but it was a smile nevertheless. He bowed toward Frost. "Quite right, Captain Frost. I shall hold my invitation open. Please, present yourself to my aide-de-camp whenever it suits." Washington nodded in the direction of a youth of moderate height, attired in an artillery officer's uniform.

Frost bowed, and together with Ming Tsun and Caleb Mansfield he turned to leave. But Washington laid a restraining hand on Caleb's arm. "Goodman Mansfield, I would treasure the opportunity to have a word with you . . . in private."

George Washington ushered Caleb Mansfield ahead of him up the steps to the porch and then into the house, pausing only long enough to speak briefly to John Sullivan. Sullivan saluted and skipped down the steps with all the enthusiasm of a child. "Frost, I say, Frost, General Washington bids you establish yourself wherever you can find sufficient scope for your wagons. I'll spot you several locations." Sullivan leaned close to Frost and whispered, "You have, I'll wager my hope of salvation on judgment day, a small measure of rum close to hand in one of those argosies, and the other officers and I are fair desperate for a drop."

"Sure," Frost said harshly, "you need not choke on judgment day. I can gift your mess with some quantity of cane spirit. But first I require a pasture of at least five acres extent, near your commissary and galleys so the provender we've freighted can be the more easily transferred to your cooks."

Sullivan looked at Frost blankly. "Galleys and cooks? Why, man, we have none of those—kitchens, you mean? The men are their own cooks, appointing one of their own to draw rations they prepare over individual fires. Though in this hard time our commissariat is empty of all, save a few hundred weight of hard biscuit brought out from Philadelphia."

Frost was incredulous. "When last had your men a decent bate of food?"

"My own regiment? Perhaps a few of them have snapped up something in the way of foraging, but we last ate something of substance whilst in New Jersey. As to the rest of the army with us, I cannot say."

Frost put boot into stirrup and hoisted himself aboard Bwindi. By the Great Buddha of Gold and K'ung the Master, and all the major prophets, this was a sad way to care for men! He had work for Cook Barnes and the women of the train. He turned his molly-mule with a word.

"Frost!" John Sullivan moaned. "What about the rum?"

"After all the men collected here are decently fed, General Sullivan," Frost said, giving full vent to all the asperity he felt. "I have a fancy to that large field across this lane between the two tent cantonments. If you would be good enough to arrange a draught of men to bring wood for our cook fires, the sooner the cane spirit for your mess shall appear."

Frost collared Cook Barnes within two minutes of leaving John Sullivan, literally riding down the column of sixty wagons, calling out loudly for his cook to show a leg, and spied Barnes, hook upraised in astonishment at hearing himself thus paged, walking companionably beside Felton. Seeing Frost rapidly bearing down upon him, Barnes thrust the ceramic pottle of whatever liquor it was he had been sharing with Felton into his waistcoat. Frost brought Bwindi to a halt, took in the scene quickly, and snapped his fingers. Barnes grudgingly drew the pottle from his waistcoat and handed it up to Frost.

"Cook Barnes," Frost said quickly, as he upended the pottle and let the contents dribble onto the icy rutted path, disregarding the pained expressions Barnes and Felton wore. "You are to prepare a feed for the Continental Army of our United States, some five thousand hungry souls, or thereabouts, I judge. Very hungry souls, as you no doubt ken. All the women who have obligingly followed us hither shall be glad to assist you in the Herculean task you must accomplish ere sunset this day. Anyone not wishing to assist you shall be escorted to the Delaware River and bid to cross over to cook for the British and Germans. I am of a mind to send a dinner directly to General Washington, and I hope you may be able to persuade one of the dames to part with a hen no longer laying, and stew it properly for His Excellency's table."

"Teamster Felton," Frost said, looking directly at the drover, who appeared to him at this time to be absolutely as sober as a newly born babe. "I value your judgment on the state of cattle. Examine our stock and select the—" Frost sought for a number. How many beeves to feed five thousand men? An able-bodied seaman was entitled to two pounds of salt beef or pork a day, spread over two messes. A beef animal on the hoof might weigh seven hundred pounds. Subtract three hundred pounds for skin, blood and bones, but retaining the tripes, and the beef animal would render four hundred pounds. One beef animal would feed two hundred men, and he must feed a minimum of five thousand. No, it would never do to feed these starving men two pounds of beef each, they could easily consume that much, but their stomachs would reject so much meat. Frost conjured a number. "Select from among our animals twenty of those you deem the most succulent. Not the oldest, nor the most truculent, the beasts on their final legs. But the twenty beeves whose flesh you would wish to savor as you smoke a pipe by the hearth of your favorite tavern and watch your dinner turning on the spit."

Frost brusquely ordered some idlers gawking nearby to take down the rails of the fence bordering the lane—stacking the rails neatly nearby—and lead the wagons to the encampment site he would show them. He nudged the ever willing Bwindi into motion and shouted orders to the other teamsters and camp followers as he cantered down the line of wagons, starkly illuminated by the thin sunlight filtering through the pewter-colored sky. It had taken three hard weeks to instill a sense of pride and community into the people of his train, but now they obeyed his orders without hesitation, even with a fair degree of enthusiasm.

As he passed the lazarette-wagon, he looked the pregnant Salome full in the face, and she smiled happily. Her face bore all the joy and mystery of a woman about to birth, though apprehension, too, of the uncertainty of the times. Frost returned her smile and paused Bwindi to watch as the rail fence was quickly removed and the wagons began turning into the gap. He leaned forward and whispered to Bwindi, and she surged ahead with enthusiasm; the great Newfoundland dog George barked happily as he bounded alongside. Frost put Bwindi before a section of the split-rail fence that had not been taken down; the molly-mule pelted toward it happily and Frost gave Bwindi her head. She sailed over the obstruction easily, gracefully, despite Frost's weight and the snow's clutching, and a second behind her George Three cleared the wooden barrier but came down on a patch of ice, legs flying out from under him and tumbling the dog in the snow. George found his footing, shook himself, bemused, then barked excitedly.

Frost, marveling at the foolish deed he had just performed —yet in three weeks' time he had formed a strong bond with the molly-mule, enough so that he could put her to the jump—cantered quickly to the top of the slight eminence of the encampment he envisioned. Bwindi's hooves kicked up clods of snow and ice behind. He directed the approaching wagons toward the destinations he chose for them. The wagons began straggling by, and he issued orders for the establishment of a butchery, for the digging of latrines—never mind the frozen ground, latrines must be dug—did not the drovers have pick-axes? Had they not come all this way without a single case of camp fever, not even so much as stomach cramps, because common hygiene had been practiced? Orders for the feeding of the oxen and beeves; orders for the siting of the wagons, for the placement of the galley; rather a quick word to Cook Barnes to build his fires behind a line of wagons to break the wind. A quick word to Barnes, also, that the men were to be served and served well, but under no circumstances were they to be overfed. And then the grievous sight of the scarecrows that were the soldiers of the Continental Army of the Thirteen United States as they began trudging anxiously through the snow to positions where they could observe the preparations Frost was directing. Then, collectively, the soldiers, perhaps five thousand in number, circled and squatted down on their heels in the snow, drawing their ragged blankets around their thin, hunched shoulders, eyeing the preparations keenly, hungrily, but patiently and passively waiting, waiting.

Their patience was a physical blow to Frost, and he threw himself into the details of establishing an encampment with a frenzy of guilt that kept him from looking toward the starved, silent, expectant soldiers upon which the future of the United States inexorably depended.

XVI

THE YOUNG AIDE-DE-CAMP, WHO APPEARED TO BE SOMETHING OF A FOP AND WHO INTRODUCED HIMSELF TO FROST AS CAPTAIN ALEXANDER HAMilton of the New York Artillery, ushered Frost down a short hallway, where several clerks seated on folding campaign chairs around a harvest table mounded haphazardly with papers were scribbling furiously, into the keeping room that served George Washington as an office. Washington rose to his feet and came from behind the harvest table that was his desk, hand extended in welcome. The keeping room was illuminated by tallow dips as poorly as the hallway had been. Washington dismissed Hamilton with a word of thanks and bade Frost seat himself in one of the plank-bottomed chairs ranged in front of his desk. Washington walked over to the fireplace of rough-fired brick and stood for a moment, shoulders sagging, hands clasped behind his back, warming himself.

Frost was very, very tired, but at least he had been able to snatch five minutes in which Ming Tsun had barbered him, and he had been able to sponge himself hurriedly with hot water and soap. Salome had taken time from her duties ladling out rashers of food for the endless lines of exceedingly hungry soldiers to press his one good tai-pan's coat. Simon had likewise taken time from his pursuit of firewood to clean and black Frost's boots and brush the dust and mud from his tricorne.

So at least Geoffrey Frost felt himself presentable enough to meet George Washington formally.

"Our Continental Congress this time the year past decreed that a soldier enlisted in our cause shall have a daily ration . . ." Washington emphasized the words "shall have" "of one pound of beef or salt fish. Failing that flesh, three of four quarters of one pound of pork. Likewise, one pound of bread and one pint of milk. Also, one quart of beer or cyder. The Congress also specified rations weekly of pease, beans, vegetables, Indian meal and molasses for issue per company of one hundred men." Washington sighed as he walked slowly back to his desk. "I do not know when last my soldiers received any rations akin to those decreed by Congress, or in the quantities enumerated. We have been constantly destitute of virtually all articles necessary for the sustenance and health of our soldiers, and completely bereft of all articles for comfort and welfare."

Washington peered intently at Frost, and Frost felt his soul was being probed again. "And then your train appears. I received an express from John Langdon earlier this month advising you had set forth upon your journey, but no word thereafter. I fear subsequent expresses have been intercepted by the British. Our forces have been harried and moved about so much—not to say sadly diminished. And the route you would have to traverse was so beset with hostilities and difficulties of every kind that I had only the faintest of expectations you would win through." Washington squared his shoulders and sat more upright in his chair. "I had not given it hope—but you won through! And in the cold fields outside, our soldiers at least sleep now with full bellies. Extraordinary, Captain Frost. You wear no uniform, and while your dress is simple, bearing no badges or trappings of rank, you are imbued with the aura of command all the same. Care you to articulate how you succeeded in coming all that perilous way?"

Frost noticed that Washington's false teeth were ill-fitted and evidently pained him greatly, for he attempted to shift them inside his cheeks. Every now and again a word was pronounced with a slight lisp or whistle. But instead of diminishing Washington's stature, the lisp endeared the man vastly all the more to Frost. He recalled suddenly that he had stuttered much as a child, and the ceaseless efforts that had been necessary to overcome his stuttering.

"No," Frost said. "Any incidents encountered during the journey are insignificant compared to the vicissitudes you and the Continental Army have weathered. I am a creature of the sea, not of the land, and can only marvel at your fortitude. My trek has not been as arduous as that of Henry Knox exactly the year past, who freighted sixty tonnes of dead metal, a tonne of lead for bullets, and a barrel of gun flints to your aid in besieging Boston." He paused, and then with familial pride continued, "My younger brother was privileged to accompany Knox on that venture, and I believe acquitted himself without fault."

A tentative knock sounded at the door to the keeping room; Washington faced toward the door and said "Enter." Hamilton opened the door, then stood aside to permit a mulatto servant bearing a wooden tray to precede him into the room. Washington beamed. "There you are, William! Thank you for bringing my Arabica." He moved a sheaf of papers from the corner of the table serving as his desk. "Put the kettles just here." The mulatto servant placed a cup and saucer before Washington and then a cup and saucer for Frost at the edge of the table. The servant placed two pots, a sugar bowl and a small pitcher of milk in the cleared space. "Thank you, William. I believe we can see to the pouring ourselves," Washington said. Then to the aide: "Captain Hamilton, you may admit Colonel Reed when he arrives, but I wish to savor the company of Captain Frost without other interruption."

Alexander Hamilton bowed and closed the door as soon as the servant named William passed into the hallway. "I understand you prefer tea, Captain Frost, so that pot with the complete handle is for you. The pot with the broken handle contains my Arabica. I regret extremely that I can offer you no honey, and hope you may find sugar from Barbados an acceptable substitute, though I find that a pinch of salt picks up the taste marvelously."

Frost regarded George Washington through hooded eyes. "Caleb Mansfield has been remarkably free with information about me, Your Excellency," he said, shrewdly guessing that Washington's knowledge of his preference for tea could have come only from the woods-cruiser.

Washington did not reply but busied himself with the pouring of coffee, then stirring the barest pinch of salt into his cup. "Yes, Colonel Knox performed a most wondrous and daring feat, and then his maneuvers in front of the British convinced General Howe that our army was present in awesome numbers. But you, Captain Frost, have wrought an improbable miracle, and one so like that of the manna showering down upon the Israelites in their wanderings in the wilderness. Your argosies and their contents are truly heaven sent! I shall personally remain forever indebted to the supplies you have delivered, and for feeding my soldiers so generously and completely. I was just giving the order to issue rations from the stores you brought when I learned that the women of your train were preparing a most prodigious meal." Washington pushed the sugar bowl toward Frost, but Frost declined. He took a sip of tea, and good manners helped him repress a shudder. Why was it so difficult for people to accomplish the simple act of steeping dried tea leaves the appropriate length of time in boiling water? This tea was even worse than the vile brew thrust upon him by Prosperous.

"I would be interested in hearing first hand about your assault on the Tory forces occupying Agawam," Washington said as he sipped his coffee.

"Very little to be said," Frost opined. "Caleb provided their intentions and their location. Once he brought that intelligence under my observation, I resolved immediately to fall upon the Tories before they could form a more cogent threat."

"You determined upon a swift hit-and-run attack, such as I found to be a formidable tactic of the Indians when I campaigned in the Ohio Country during the war against the French," Washington said approvingly.

"No," Frost said. "The Chinese warrior-scholar Sun Tzu

penned the axiom that 'in war let your object be victory, not lengthy campaigns.' Amazingly, few people seem to realize that when you fail to address a problem directly and quickly, something external will impose a solution, perhaps not of your liking."

"Then you subscribe to the philosophy of the three S's," Washington said, arching his eyebrows over his coffee cup.

Frost smiled; this general was astute. He recalled his conversation with his cousins John Langdon and Tobias Lear a bare six weeks before and was heartily sorry he had ever referred to Washington as a "Virginia tobacco farmer." "Simplicity, security and surprise serve a trader well in peaceful negotiations. They serve sanguinely well when there is the possibility of a musket ball in your gut rather than the pecuniary prospect of mere Sycee money lost."

"It would seem that you and I agree on tactics perfected by the Indians, then, Captain Frost? A lightning strike against an unprepared or at least an unsuspecting enemy?"

"I admit to an abysmal lack of experience in the fighting of Indians, the first occupiers of this continent, Your Excellency," Frost confessed. "Nor do I wish to gain the experience. Yet, when beset by Malay pirates in their straits, it always seemed the best recourse to me to set immediately into their numbers and belabour them with every sinew. I've always fancied those who believe themselves impregnable in their positions are much attached to their ease, including their Arabica," Frost nodded in the direction of Washington's cup, "while those happy souls prepared to forego sleep and vittles for the winning of a greater cause can surely gain it."

"Well said, Captain of Privateers," Washington exclaimed. "Now, for my edification, please share with me how you were able to infiltrate into the very heart of the major coal trade in England. I understand the damages you caused were extraordinary. By the by, my paternal ancestors derived from the small town of Washington just west of Sunderland, and south of the Tyne. I have some familiarity with the names of towns in that area."

"The British collieries sustained losses to their mines and bulk shipping through something termed, according to my cousin John Langdon, learned from perusing explanations of the occurrence in their newspapers, 'spontaneous combustion.'" Frost said without further elaboration.

Washington hid a smile by lifting his cup of coffee. "Then you disclaim knowledge of the navigational buoys and range posts denoting safe channels into the River Tyne and nearby headlands that were destroyed or moved—by whoever it was that caused such devastation of a vital British industry?"

Frost shrugged. "A prudent mariner, Your Excellency, always must assure his vessel's position, even in well-charted waters. Storms and tides have been known to shift aids to navigation. But that is all they be—aids. And currents shift the locations and extents of sand bars in a rhythm known to no mariner, so constant alertness . . ." Frost was interrupted by a knock at the door.

"Enter," George Washington commanded. Hamilton, quite nattily turned out in the scarlet-trimmed black coat and high black boots of the New York Artillery, ushered in a florid-faced, stoutish man of indeterminate age, attired in a Continental Army uniform far more resplendent than the uniform worn by George Washington. "Colonel Joseph Reed," Washington said to Frost by way of introduction. "Colonel Reed is my adjutant general."

Reed advanced toward Washington without waiting for permission and without saluting. He held the bundle of manifests without its protective jacket of canvas for the cargoes Frost had with so many difficulties fetched from faraway Portsmouth. "These manifests overstate the actual tally as inventoried by our commissariat, General Washington," Reed said self-importantly. "Though a Chinee trader known for sharp dealing may have brought along barrels of sand for all I ken."

Frost stiffened in his chair and tightened his grip on the pewter spoon that had lain on the teacup's saucer so that the spoon bent double.

Washington put down his cup of coffee and pushed back his

chair, the legs scraping noisily on the wide pine boards of the keeping room's floor, a sound not unlike the truckle and complaining whine of gun carriages being run forward. "Adjutant Reed," Washington said sternly, "I misdoubt greatly if Captain Frost would have dared the perils of four-hundred-odd miles across country so greatly contested with a cargo of sand. Have you reason to believe in any fashion that Captain Frost is known for sharp dealing in his trade?"

Reed paled, stammered, and averted his eyes from Washington's stern glare. "A figure of speech only, sir. I have heard that this man trades with the Chinese, and since that trade is a monopoly of the British East India Company, he would have to be a sharp trader to be in that line at all."

Frost, sensing that Washington would handle the awkward matter to his satisfaction, bit back his angry retort and calmly straightened the spoon to its original shape.

"I lament exceedingly your unreasonable inferences, Colonel Reed. Those inferences are demeaning to the person proffering them, and utterly demeaning to their subject. And imminently specious, if the inferences are to Captain Frost. Indeed, he did not recognize the British strictures—indeed, most likely regarding them in the same vein as we viewed the Intolerable Acts, and traded extensively with the Chinese and the Portuguese, so I am reliably informed. Sharp traders do not remain in that line, perhaps not lasting a single voyage. Furthermore, Captain Frost performed a signal and extraordinary service for our cause these three months past when he destroyed a great number of British colliers, at great cost to the British economy, and a devastating blow to the British aura of their invulnerability in their home islands."

Washington was clearly angry. He held out a preemptory hand for the manifests, and Reed handed them over as if they had suddenly become as heated as a smoothing iron to the touch. Washington sat down at his desk and pulled the candlestick holding the tallow dips close. He glowered at the manifests in the poor light, made a moue of disgust, and rustled among the papers on the desk until he found a spectacles case.

Washington perched the steel-rimmed spectacles on his nose and hooked the temples over his ears. He peered at Frost, a mischievous grin playing about his lips. "Captain Frost, I pray you will respect an old man's vanity and mention to no one that I must, on occasion, resort to these prisms when the work is close and the light less than sufficient. I contrive not to wear these spectacles in public." Frost did not think that a man aged forty-four years, though some eighteen years his senior, was particularly old. He nodded his assurance that Washington's secret was safe with him, and Washington studied the manifests intently, one page at a time. Then he shuffled the papers together and looked expectantly at Joseph Reed.

Frost cleared his throat. "I believe the count is short ten barrels of dried pease, twenty bushels to the barrel; eleven barrels of flour, two-hundred weight each; and fifteen bags of rice, each of one hundred-weight, for an accurate reconciliation. The powder should reflect an exact total weight of fifty tonnes, if the barrels be weighed, not merely counted. Wait, I lie. There should also be a shortage of one small hogshead of cane spirit, forty gallon by volume."

"Exactly so," Washington said, surprise large in his voice, "but given the several thousand tonnes of foodstuffs and powder conveyed here, these are shortages of a fraction of one percent."

"The measures of pease and the rice lacking were given over to the people of my train who prepared food for your troops. As were ten barrels of flour. The eleventh barrel of flour fell upon hard ground through mischance and was spoiled."

"A negligible, extremely negligible percentage of spoliation, Captain Frost. Infinitesimal in comparison to the great weight you have so diligently conveyed hither. It is impossible to assign a value—especially the powder." Washington stopped abruptly and glowered at Reed. "I believe several large kettles of beef stew with dumplings, savored with pease, numerous loaves of flat bread, as well as at least two gallons of rum were consumed by my officers in their mess earlier this evening."

"Well, yes . . ." Reed stammered.

"Your officers did not ask for the meal—other than a request for rum," Frost said sardonically. "Your officers could not be seen watching the kettles and pots as the common soldiers, so the same fare as the common soldiers partook was consigned to their mess."

"I was most appreciative of the dinner of stewed chicken conveyed my way by your three young sous-officers," Washington said. "The three of them are lads of transcendent merit, and until the arrival of those warm baskets I twigged not how I might be fed this eve." Washington fixed his adjunct general with a stern gaze: "I misdoubt not that the kettles and pots dispatched to your mess have been scrapped to the last morsel, and the rum has been drunk straight down." Washington continued to glare at Joseph Reed.

"The other officers enjoyed a fine repast," Reed said, stiff with annoyance and exasperation, "but I was immersed in the inventory and missed the feeding. Had my orderly not kept back a plate for me, I would have gone without. And my brother officers spared me not a dram of rum."

"I am sure Captain Hamilton will be glad to share his pot of Arabica with you, Colonel," Washington said. Then to Frost: "The powder and foodstuffs, and the blankets, I must not forget the blankets, you have so diligently delivered to this army cannot be assigned a value. However, knowing the frugal New Hampshire Continental Agent as I do, I confidently expect that John Langdon has derived a price."

"John cyphered the value, no duties paid or assessable, landed at Portsmouth, as forty thousand sterling, on date of 1 December, when my goods train got underweigh." Frost looked directly at George Washington. "To which I have ascribed another ten thousand sterling as drayage costs, to inculcate the costs associated with building the boat-wagons, purchase of draught animals, and wages of the teamsters who willingly joined in the freighting." Frost spared himself a slight smile at his use of the word "willingly."

Washington frowned. "Fifty thousand sterling to have brought all these tonnes of supplies hence? Cost, insurance and freight? The sum is cheap, yet not even the inestimable John Langdon could have raised such a sum."

"I advanced the purchase price," Frost said quietly, "from my own accounts. You may have overlooked the final page of the manifests is a promissory note payable to me, or my heirs or assigns, six years after the signing of a treaty of peace between our United States and the British government, late belligerents, with interest to be computed as specified in the note. The promissory note requires acceptance by a signatory with the authority to bind the Continental Congress." Frost paused and stared hard at Joseph Reed. "All consistent with the practices of a sharp trader."

"Indeed," Washington said dryly. Frost watched the mythic figure that was the sole hope of the American Revolution unhook the spectacles and rub his temples wearily, knowing that Washington was attempting to massage away the torments of his grave responsibilities. But just as the effort had always failed him, he knew it would fail Washington. "An exceedingly fair price considering the invoiced sum is actually only cost and freight, since in no wise could insurance on this consignment be obtained, given the perils and uncertainty of its transport."

Frost smiled, but said nothing.

"I flatter myself that I am vested with the necessary authority to bind the public exchequer for military supplies," Washington said. He selected a quill from a holder on the desk and carefully opened the ink well. He dipped the quill's point into the ink and slowly, painstakingly, wrote: "Received of Geoff Frost, Esq. To the value of fifty thousand pounds sterling, money of account of Great Britain, for the supplies enumerated above for the needs of the Continental Army of the United States of America, presently in western Pennsylvania." He signed his name, Geo. Washington, and wrote beneath his signature, "General-in-Chief, Army of the United States of America."

"I am without sand, so we must wait for the ink to dry of itself. I ask Adjutant Reed to attest my signature, and insert the proper date." Washington held out the quill to Reed. Reed hastily wet the nub and scribbled his signature and the date. Washington held up the manifest page and blew gently on the ink to speed its drying. Then, putting the signature page on top of the manifests, he handed the bundle of papers to Reed. "Colonel Reed, please give these papers to the clerks without; no, please bid my aide Tench Tilghman, he has the fairest hand, to copy these documents into my day book. Two fair copies should suffice. The originals are to be returned to Captain Frost, else he shall have no way to claim reimbursement six years after this plague of a war is consummated in our favour—though only God knows when that fortunate day shall be."

Reed fairly snatched the manifests from Washington's hand and strode from the room quickly, though he was careful not to slam the door.

"Tell me," Washington said, "in what regard is your cousin, Woodbury Langdon, now held, seeing it has been rumoured that he is a Tory fled to England for safety."

The question took Frost completely by surprise. Without conscious thought he got to his feet and began pacing the planks of the keeping room, hands clasped behind him, as if he were on his own quarterdeck. "It be a sore point for his family, a very sore point," Frost said at length. "Woodbury's leaving without notice, especially aboard a British vessel that came into the Piscataqua under a flag of truce, certainly left his brother John with sails all a-back. The prattle has not abated, but I abjure gossip in all its forms." Frost thought of his meeting with a heartsick John Langdon the late spring past, when he had returned the prisoners of war taken from Louisbourg Fortress to Portsmouth.

"I stand not in his shoes and draw no inference that Woodbury is a traitor or a loyalist by his abrupt withdrawal to England. He does have extensive business interests there . . ." Frost left the sentence unfinished, because Woodbury Langdon had departed abruptly with the unsavory characters of Reedy Stalker, a Piscataqua River pilot, and St. Jean Lithgow, the lieutenant of HM sloop-o-war *Jaguar* who had attempted to kill Frost after her captain had surrendered his vessel.

Well, if George Washington could ask him a completely unexpected question, Frost had one of his own. He stopped his pacing for a moment: "Your Excellency, do you recall a British artillery officer by the name of Smith who was with you on the Monongahela?"

Washington kept any surprise he may have felt at the question as well masked as Frost had done at the mention of Woodbury Langdon's name. "Well, we all serve in our special ways," Washington said enigmatically, then: "There was a Royal Artillery major by the name of Smith, Absalom Smith, on General Braddock's staff. Major Smith was sorely wounded in both arms, and he was offered evacuation on the tumbrel used to remove General Braddock from the field. But he remained with the main body of retreating soldiers, entreating them to master their panic and be solicitous of their fellows who could not convey themselves off the killing ground." Washington rose to his feet and crossed to the rope bed along one wall, where some personal items were thrown in a heap. He drew a pistol from a saddlebag and returned with it to his desk, where he sat down and examined the pistol reflectively.

"I recall Major Smith as a consummate gentleman and officer who behaved with extreme gallantry in a horrific event from which no one emerged unscathed. General Braddock thought likewise, and before he died he gave me one of a brace of his pistols, this one." Washington held out the pistol to Frost. Frost took the brass-barreled flintlock pistol, noting its unusual flared cannon muzzle, and read the inscription on the escutcheon, E. B., which he interpreted to be the initials of Edward Braddock, and the maker's name, Gabbitas, on the brass lockplate. "General Braddock was deeply appreciative that Major Smith had put the welfare of men shattered in soul and body ahead of his own torments—other officers had not been so steadfast. He insisted that Major Smith accept the mate, though Major Smith demurred that he had merely performed his duty."

Frost handed the pistol back to Washington with reverence. "How come you to know of this officer?" Washington demanded.

"I have met his son, a naval officer in the British service," Frost said simply, in a manner than indicated he was reluctant to discuss the matter further. "The son is as much a credit to the father as the father is to the son. The son sorrows at having to fight Americans. Though he does his duty."

"Aye," Washington said soberly. "So it would be with the father, though I continue to caress him dearly."

Frost was startled to hear Washington use the phrase to describe his feelings for Major Absalom Smith. His son, Richard Smith, had used the exact phrase to describe his father's feelings for the twenty-three-year-old George Washington, who had organized the rear guard that protected Braddock's retreat and kept several thousand British soldiers and Continental Militia alive—men who otherwise would have fallen before the ambushing muskets and hatchets of the French and Indian force numbering only some eight hundred.

"Speaking of firearms, Captain Frost, I believe you have gathered up muskets from Tories in Agawam and a patrol of British infantry to the sum of one wagon load." Washington rose to his feet, drained his coffee cup and poured more from the pot. "I can offer the full faith and credit of our Continental Congress as surety for the arms' purchase from you."

Frost did not change his expression. "I find it much preferable to abstain from commenting about matters of which I know nothing, such as the full faith and credit of the Continental Congress, than to confirm my ignorance by declaiming vacuously. Since such of my people who desire have already possessed themselves of arms from those escheated, I had already determined to leave the remainder for the use of the army."

Washington nodded his pleasure, then rummaged among the personal items on the rope bed and seized upon a split willow basket with a sigh of satisfaction. "I have here some chestnuts, pecans and hickory nuts, Captain Frost. These nuts will provide a provident dessert to the prodigious meal the dames of your train so kindly conveyed by your young gentlemen." Washington placed the basket near the hearth. "I understand you have in some wise come into the possession of remarkable rifles?" Washington took the fire tongs and racked aside a pad of coals, onto which he spread a handful of nuts.

"Of a design by the cousin of my first officer, Scotsmen both. My Struan Ferguson has taken the rifles as the Devil's invention. My chief *courier-des-bois* much prefers his muzzle-loading double rifle. Yet, I have had occasion to use the rifle and have been awed by the simplicity of its principle. I acknowledge that this ominous arm lends itself not to serial production, and I incline to believe the rifle will not be well received by officers trained in the tactics of massed musketry on the battlefield."

"Such a rifle can wreak great mischief if General Howe were to perceive merit in its employment." Washington gazed thoughtfully into the flames.

"There will be no exemplars of his diabolic rifle in North America other than those we possess until Patrick Ferguson can have others fabricated and brought over. I have no idea as to their arrival, only that if Patrick Ferguson is as determined as his cousin, they will appear on these shores sooner rather than later." Frost resumed his pacing.

"For myself, I fancy a fowling piece," Washington said, "for I do heartily enjoy a bit of ducking, and hunting of the blew wing. In my former life as a surveyor of our backwoods, I frequently employed a fowler to keep my party in meat, otherwise we would have gone hungry to our blankets many a night. My agents in London in times past, Mister Robert Cary and Company, procured several fine fowlers for me. One was particularly rigged out for my stepson, Master Custis, fourteen years old at the time, to train him in the proper employment and enjoyment of arms. Three feet and two inches it was in the barrel, and silver mounted. I collect it shot exceedingly well." Washington chuckled with nostalgia, then swept up several chestnuts, jiggling them in his palms so as not to burn himself.

"But my fowlers are at Mount Vernon awaiting the happy day when hostilities are ended, and when I advise Mrs. Washington that I am 'going afield' she will ken I shall be frequenting a duck marsh and not a ground upon which to do battle with our country's enemies."

Washington held up half a handful of the roasted chestnuts to Frost as he paced by. "May I be so bold as to inquire of your intentions now that you have delivered to this army these many tonnes of food, blankets and powder—all barrels and bags filled with the stuffs warranted on your manifests, and not a grain of sand betimes," he said with a small laugh. "You are not a sharp trader, Captain Frost, by no means, but you are a shrewd trader."

Frost cracked open a chestnut and ate the kernel before replying. "I must rest my teamsters and animals, but no more than two days, for the going has been sore for men and beasts; then decide upon the number of wagons needful to convey my people back to Portsmouth. I have a vessel to fit out, and a crew to raise, to go a-privateering as soon as the ice is out in the Piscataqua." The chestnut was delicious, and he could not recall when last he had eaten one. "If your army wishes any draught animals remainder after I survey my needs I shan't mind a promissory note for their value, the same terms and conditions as exist in the note you earlier signed."

"The army would welcome the opportunity to obtain your remainder draught animals. I did remark approvingly upon their fettle when I observed your wagons earlier today. You brought your people and animals through in fine trim." Washington chuckled as he jiggled another handful of roasted chestnuts. "You should know that the Congress has on several occasions exhorted me to obtain supplies for the army by expropriating animals and food at the point of a bayonet, should the putative owners not accept Continental currency as payment for their goods. Happily, Mister Morris is not one who thinks along those lines, and I know that, like yourself, on many occasions he has advanced our cause from his own pocket. What will be your route of march, Captain Frost?"

"A singularly bankrupt policy of expediency, Your Excellency, and totally against all principles of liberty the Congress supposedly represents," Frost said pithily. "Keeping to the Pennsylvania side of the Delaware until I am above the Forks, then eastward. I intend to transit Hudson's River where I crossed earlier, below a massive knuckle on the western side."

"Yes," Washington said, "I know the place. West Point. It requires effective fortifications to block the British from advancing up the river to Albany."

Frost paused. "Before departing, I beg leave to circulate among your army and inquire if anyone was with the nutmegger Arnold on the Lake, and might give me intelligence of my brother."

Washington deftly slit open a chestnut with his thumb and tossed the meat into his mouth. "You have a brother who was with Arnold? I must tell you, that was a most heroic action. The United States shall always be grateful to those who delayed the English expedition up the Lake, then overland to the Hudson, in order to split off the New England states from those of the south."

Frost shrugged, a movement that went unnoticed in the dim light. "Yes, the same brother who moved the King's iron from Ticonderoga with Henry Knox. I have no familiarity with the British strategy—nay, any sense of strategy at all. But Caleb Mansfield has traded for furs over much in the country between Hudson's River and the Lake's origins. He allows there is some one hundred miles of heavy forests between the two waters, forests exceedingly difficult to penetrate on foot by a woods-cruizer able to live off the land, much more so when thousands of men must carve a road for themselves and their baggage wagons. Perhaps the wilderness and the winter would have defeated the British without there was any confrontation on the Lake."

"General Braddock, that honest and honorable brave soldier, who just prior to his death confided he would know better how to deal with his enemies at another time, was able to carve a road through the wilderness," Washington said, winkling out another kernel of chestnut meat. "Though he was over long in so doing. Since the British now invest the City of New York, they command much of the northern part of the country and have communications with their forces in Canada. So delaying physical linkage until the spring campaigns indeed does have a strategic overlay."

"Discussions . . . thoughts of strategy are alien to me, Your Excellency. I am a mariner and a trader. I can warrant only what you undoubtedly already ken, that trade gives birth to a mercantile class, and the mercantile class generates wealth. Wealth and the desire for its growth lead to consultative rule and diffused power, since arbitrary rule and power concentrated in the hands of but a favored few stifles any growth of the mercantile economy and dooms sound finance."

"What you say is absolute truth," Washington said approvingly. "Trade creates enterprise and sunders shibboleths and superstitions. Trade encourages liberties, and opinions openly debated."

"I confess to having thought long on such concepts while plying my trade—there is time, occasionally, at sea when one may capture a moment to reflect—but another has articulated far better than I . . ."

"You must mean the Scotsman Adam Smith," Washington said, a statement, not a query. "I read his *Theory of Moral Sentiments* soon after it was published—I believe I came into possession of a copy in the year sixty and applauded it immensely. I am apprised that Mister Smith has published a *magnum opus* of economic and political thought earlier this year. Regretfully, I have not had the opportunity to acquaint myself with Mister Smith's recent philosophies."

"The *magnum opus* to which you refer, Your Excellency, is entitled *An Inquiry Into the Nature and Causes of the Wealth of Nations.* This epic of economic common sense was published in March, and a copy, fortuitously, was in the possession of the captain of a victualer I fell in with and took as prize. Your army profits from the victuals taken out of her, but I profited more from the challenging ideas presented in the *Wealth of Nations.*"

Washington sighed, "If you can somehow contrive to get a copy of the Scotsman's book into my hands, Captain Frost, I shall be eternally grateful."

"I shall dispatch the copy from the prize once I have finished perusing it," Frost promised. "Though I cannot know when that might be, since it is a book that begs the rereading . . ." Frost was disgusted with himself; here he was indulging in discussions of economic theory when his every waking moment, now that he had fulfilled the obligation he had willingly assumed to convey the materiel of war to the Continental Army, was the welfare of his brother, or to discover his end. "I want only to learn my brother's fate. It is a particularly hard charge I bear for our mother."

"The Germans have garrisoned small towns on the New Jersey side of the Delaware," Washington said, changing the conversation unexpectedly, flinging the chestnut hulls into the fire. "The Germans are mercenaries purchased from their princelings for seven pounds sterling the head." His voice conveyed his bitterness.

"Actually seven pounds, four shillings, four pence per head, Your Excellency," Frost said, his pacing unabated.

"You are singularly well informed about German mercenaries, Captain Frost," Washington said quizzically.

"This past summer's cruize, my privateering vessel sank a victualer conveying some hundreds of Brunswickers to Halifax. The Germans who were saved out of her were packed aboard another victualer with but limited provisions and a strong suggestion that the wind was contrary for Halifax, but fair to convey the victualer back to England. Later, as I perused documents from other prize vessels, I noted an entry concerning the nominal cost of a mercenary to the British Crown."

"Was that the same event when you discovered the Ferguson rifles?" Washington leaned forward and extended his hands toward the fire. "Who would have thought it? George Three purchases soldiers bent to his will at substantially less specie than a guineaman at any of the markets from Boston to Savannah."

"I find any trade in human life distressful in the extreme, Your Excellency, colour of skin irrelevant."

"Spare me sermons, Captain Frost," Washington said quickly. "I acknowledge that I own slaves, though I wish with all my soul such an abominable institution had never found root on these shores. Slavery is a boil that requires a vigorous lancing before we shape a society and a government that shall be just, egalitarian and enduring. But not now, not now in these times." Washington scooped the last handful of nuts from the coals. "You may move freely among this army and question whom you will . . ."

"Is Knox here?" Frost asked eagerly. "I ken that Knox holds my brother in some regard, since as I mentioned earlier my brother was of some assistance to Knox in draying those tonnes of cannon from Ticonderoga that you used so tellingly to convince Howe it was in his best interests to quit Boston and repair to Halifax."

"Yes, Knox is here," Washington said carefully. "He commands my artillery—and I understand you have augmented our pitiful ordnance with the tubes of two 12-pounder field pieces. For those additions the army thanks you, though I believe my young aide thanks you more, since he is resolved to have them for his company of New York cannon men."

"I had not thought to return to Portsmouth with them, Your Excellency," Frost said dryly. "If that slip of a youth has men to employ them effectively, then the New Yorkers are welcome to them."

"And will you assay a return to Portsmouth without the company of Goodman Mansfield?" There was a steely edge in Washington's voice that Frost had not detected before.

Frost was momentarily at a loss for words. He commanded Caleb and his woods-cruisers, and yet he did not command them. Caleb was free to go and come as he saw fit, at entire liberty to do as he willed. But the thought of proceeding without Caleb Mansfield freighted Frost's soul with dread, as much so as the prospect of having to get along without Struan Ferguson. Geoffrey Frost was keenly aware that he exercised his will only through others. "I divined earlier, Your Excellency, with some amazement, that you and Caleb Mansfield enjoyed some prior relationship unique between you, and that he mayhap had been the *chefe des guides* for your General Braddock. Caleb Mansfield must, however, do whatever it is that Caleb Mansfield believes he must do. And I must do whatever I believe I must do. And that is to rest my men and animals and inquire among your army for intelligence of my brother. Then in two days' time begin the return trek to Portsmouth, where I must see to the care of my vessel."

"Goodman Mansfield, I am sure, desires a swift return to the comforts of Portsmouth as much as do you, Captain Frost. But I begged a boon of him, and he consented, I must say with all willingness and without reservation. The freedom to inquire of whom you wish within the army is yours unquestionably. I would detail Adjutant Reed to assist you, but he earlier today indicated his desire to resign from my service. He had asked for command of the cavalry, a position for which unfortunately he has no qualifications, and to which of course I cannot acquiesce. But you shall have the indefatigable Captain Hamilton to aid in your quest for Joseph . . ." Washington stopped abruptly. "Your brother's name is Joseph, I believe you related, or perhaps it was Goodman Mansfield who informed me."

"I thank you most heartily for the freedom of inquiry, and I mark Captain Hamilton as only slightly older than my brother—if my brother lives still. I shall value his assistance, and yours, in making him available. But two days shall suffice for the resting of my men and animals, and Caleb Mansfield or no, I must begin the journey to Portsmouth then." Frost was quite aware that he had not mentioned his brother's name.

"Quite so, Captain Frost, but do you think you can prevail upon your good cook and dames to prepare food for this army until your departure?"

"I shall inquire immediately of my cook and the women who followed us here. I cannot speak for the women, but my cook's, Barnes, second happiness is presiding over the preparation of large rashers of vittles served out to hungry men."

"His first happiness? Dare I inquire?" Washington asked.

"Cook Barnes relishes a good set-to. He has a hook in the stead of one hand which he brandishes famously, and he fights with all the strength and zeal of a cohort of Caesar's legionnaires, all the while keening like a banshee."

"I fear my own heart would quail at the prospect of a banshee with a hook for a hand. I beg, please exert your utmost to convince your man Barnes and your women that I would consider it a signal pleasure if they would deign to feed my soldiers for the next two days. The system long devised for armies on the land—which I appreciate is quite different from the method of feeding men shipboard—is to issue out uncooked rations to squads of men who prepare their own food around their individual cook fires. But my soldiers are currently too enfeebled for such exertions. I have ordered the issuance of the blankets freighted here in your 'argosies' as your fellow New Hampshireman Sullivan so aptly named your wagons. The soldiers of our sorely depleted Continental Army shall sleep with full bellies in some semblance of warmth tonight, Captain Frost. I wish my soldiers to rest and eat solid victuals such as they enjoyed this night, in order the more quickly to regain their strength." There was no hint of plea in Washington's tone, just a straightforward request for whatever assistance Frost might be able to render.

"If my people are able to draw prudently against the stores you have accepted, I have no doubt that my people will eagerly endeavour to bring the cheer of decent, hot food to your men during a time of the year that is generally considered festive."

"What?" Washington said absently, his thoughts seemingly elsewhere. "Oh, yes. Of course. Christmas, as marked by the calendar, is only three days away." He frowned wryly. "I had forgotten. Yes, your cooks may draught as they deem necessary on the foodstuffs you have brought all this long way. And two days hence, before you hie yourself away to Portsmouth, I would appreciate the pleasure of your dining with my officers and me. Let me have a word with young Captain Hamilton. He shall seek you out tomorrow morning and be at your complete disposal to conduct you where you will. I fear I must now attend to other matters, and must beg you to excuse me."

Frost and Washington bowed formally to each other, and Frost saw himself out the door from the keeping room into the hallway. He paused a moment to consult his watch in the fitful flare of light cast by the clerks' dips. He had conversed with George Washington for less than fifteen minutes, but Geoffrey Frost had never experienced a more memorable or intellectually stimulating fifteen minutes in his life.

XVII

FROST FOUND HIMSELF LIKING THE SHORT AND SLENDER ALEXANDER HAMILTON, WHO HAD IMPRESSED HIM INITIALLY AS A VAIN AND ARROGANT FOP. The young man was arrogant, he decided, or perhaps it was that Hamilton simply possessed a healthy confidence in himself that was at the same time modest and humble, an indication that he would not flinch to undertake the most arduous task, and complete assurance that he would master it. But Hamilton certainly did know how to dress and keep himself well, in a time when a confident appearance engendered confidence in the minds of others. The young man with the deep-set eyes, light brown hair and fair complexion, who early on told Frost his Caribbean blood had not thickened enough to withstand the northern winters, was well educated in political and economic theory. And Frost was impressed to learn that Hamilton had raised his own company of one hundred men to serve the few pieces of artillery left over from the French war that New York had been able to muster. However, Frost was quick to discern that Hamilton was currently possessed only of a cursory knowledge of artillery; nor had he selected for his company men who did, because there were none to be had. The American Army suffered woefully from a lack of skilled matrosses—artillery men—and engineers.

In any event, Hamilton was an assiduous guide, constantly at Frost's side, accompanying him as Frost rode Bwindi about the Continental Army encampment searching for Henry Knox. But Knox was nowhere to be found.

"In Philadelphia or Bristol," a Major of Continental Artillery who admitted to serving under Knox said, pointing vaguely southerly, attempting to conjure cannons where no cannons existed. No, the major opined, he had heard of some battle of small consequence on Lake Champlain but had no personal knowledge of any participants, particularly a young man by the name of Joseph Frost.

"General Knox may have gone with Colonel Reed," Hamilton said, perhaps thinking to be helpful. "General Washington dispatched Colonel Reed into Pennsylvania in hopes of mustering militia units."

In the early afternoon, after a frustrating day and in a steady, numbing fall of wet snow, though thankfully without any wind, Frost withdrew to his own encampment. Cook Barnes, definitely in his element and bursting with pleasure and pride, was presiding over the preparations of a second grand feed for the Continental Army encamped in Pennsylvania. Nathaniel's marines had rigged a patchwork of frayed rumbowline canvas as large open-sided tents to shelter the long line of cook fires and steaming kettles, pots and spiders.

Ishmael Hymsinger had appropriated a large piece of canvas —Frost recognized it as a much frayed middle staysail—and shaped the canvas over a crude latticework of willow branches into a Mi'kmaq sweat lodge some one hundred yards removed into a grove of birch trees from the teamsters' encampment. Hymsinger led Frost to the sweat lodge, where Ming Tsun relieved him of his stained, torn and foul-smelling clothes, and a bone-weary Frost crawled into the close, stifling, steam-fogged lodge where Nathaniel Dance, Darius Langdon and Hannibal Bowditch were already crowded. The lodge was unlighted except by the faint, dull, cherry-red glow of the heated rocks. In the faint light Frost could distinguish only vague shapes and recognized the lads only by their voices. They had been comparing notes as Frost entered, for they had, on their own initiative, spent the morning inquiring after Joseph throughout the Continental Army's scattered encampment.

Hannibal waited until Frost had fumbled his way to a sopping wet square of canvas spread over balsam fir boughs that served as a rough seat around the mound of heated, faintly incandescent rocks in the center of the lodge, then dipped a bough into the wooden bucket beside him and spattered water on the heated rocks in the manner of a priest regally employing an aspergillum. Hot, cloying steam hissed from the heated rocks and filled the lodge, concealing its occupants, starting copious flows of perspiration, burning deep into Frost's lungs and searing his nostrils so that it was painful to breathe.

"It was almost like the soldiers had orders not to say anything to us," Darius complained. "Those I spoke were pleasant enough, but I could not help considering some of them evasive in response."

"I think likewise," Hannibal agreed.

Frost did not heed the lads' conversation. He was beyond fatigue, despairing and disheartened over the lack of information about his brother, and he would have nodded off to sleep save for the hot steam searing his lungs and nasal passages. He reached for the gourd beside the bucket, filled it, and dribbled water onto his head. When the gourd was empty he ran his fingers through his hair, then massaged his heavily perspiring face with both hands, prodding and probing his temples and forehead vigorously, hoping to drive out and sweat away all his demons. The hot steam searching into the depths of his lungs gagged him, and he coughed uncontrollably for several moments. The spasm passed, and he relaxed backward until his torso sagged against the hot canvas. Fortunately, Ishmael Hymsinger had built the walls of the sweat lodge sturdily enough to bear the weight, and for a few very blessed moments, his snarling, hateful demons driven to the edge of memory, Geoffrey Frost knew absolutely nothing at all.

He was bought back to reality, reluctantly, when Ishmael Hymsinger crawled into the lodge with a basket of heated stones freshly raked from fires around the cooking kettles.

"Mustn't endure the sweats overly long, Captain," Ishmael said anxiously. "Please to dash out now and thrash around in the bank of snow, then inside again for no more than five minutes. Ming Tsun has fresh garments for you and will convey you away for a shave."

The three ship's gentlemen had already wiggled through the sweat lodge's narrow opening and were making much hubbub and merriment when Frost crawled out. He immediately received a wet snowball directly in the center of his forehead. Frost shook his head and was instantly alert, glaring at the three youths, bodies steaming in the cold air twenty feet from the lodge, George Three romping among them. " Who cast that ball?" he thundered fiercely.

"I did," Nathaniel Dance, shocked, said falteringly.

"No, sir, I did," Darius Langdon said in a breaking voice.

"No, Captain Frost, it was I who cast the ball," Hannibal Bowditch said, tremors of horror in his voice.

"Well, all of you! Prepare to repel boarders!" Frost roared, and furiously began pelting handfuls of snow at the ship's gentlemen as fast as he could. Realizing that their captain was not angry with them over their youthful indiscretion, Hannibal, Darius and Nathaniel, laughing delightedly, scooped up handfuls of snow and hurled the rough snowballs at Frost. The snowball fight was quite one-sided, and though George came over to his side, his bulk offering some protection, Frost was getting by far the worst of it. He slipped on an icy patch and fell backwards into a snowbank but instantly rolled to his knees, facing the three lads, who were gawking, hands holding snowballs, but no longer pelting him. Frost reached behind him for another handful of snow. Instead his groping hand touched leather. He swung round to look directly into high leather boots, well worn. Mouth agape, Frost's gaze traveled upward, past the worn once-white breeches, sword belt, salt-water-tarnished buttons on a worn blue tunic, a seaman's stained boat cloak, and atop a rumpled neck stock, a ruddy, lined face framed with reddish hair just touched with gray. He vaguely recognized the man.

The seamed face broke into a lopsided grin. "Hello, Frost. I'm John Glover, from Marblehead, come to pay my respects to the most successful privateer captain of this accursed war." A well-muffled Alexander Hamilton, shoulders of his cloak and gaudy artilleryman's shako sodden with snow, stood two paces behind Glover, fingers of one gloved hand held to his mouth in a valiant, vain attempt to mask his amusement.

Frost threw a handful of snow upward at Glover, then hurled a snowball at Hamilton so accurately that the ball dislodged Hamilton's gilt-trimmed shako. "*Audacities*, rally on me!" Frost shouted to the three lads. Darius, Hannibal and Nathaniel immediately and enthusiastically resumed throwing snowballs, with remarkable accuracy, and after a moment of open-mouthed confusion, and a feint at retreat, both Glover and Hamilton replied with an enthusiasm, though not the accuracy, to match Frost and the three ship's gentlemen.

After a furious thirty seconds' exchange of snowballs, Frost, heart racing, chest heaving, perspiring and steaming heavily, vastly amused by the incongruity of the situation, held up his hands. "Gentlemen! Have you no shame? Attacking innocent bathers in such fashion! Divest yourselves of your garments and join us in our bath, or pray have decency enough to suspend hostilities until we are suitably clothed." He drew himself together formally, with all the dignity he could muster in his naked state, before crawling into the sweat lodge, followed immediately by the ship's gentlemen, who, forgetting they were gentlemen, were all three fit to dissolve completely into laughter, though they dared not in their captain's presence.

When Frost, much refreshed, emerged from the sweat lodge a second time, Ming Tsun was waiting to drape him with a warmed blanket and led him to a small tent nearby, where razors were laid out on a rough split-log bench next to a pannikin of hot water and a soap cup. Frost gratefully thrust his feet into heavy felt slippers and gave himself over to the unutterable luxury of Ming Tsun's deft hands first trimming his hair, then shaving him. As the razor plied over his face, he recalled the youths' complaint that soldiers they had queried about Joseph had appeared evasive. That observation now correlated with his recollections of his frustrating interviews. But why, if anyone among the pitiful remnants left of the Continental Army actually knew anything of Joseph Frost, would he not divulge that information? It was perplexing in the extreme.

Very well, he would conduct further interviews. Failing to find Henry Knox, he would seek out John Glover, with whom just a few minutes prior Frost had exchanged a fusillade of snowballs. To be exact, Colonel John Glover of the 14th Massachusetts Infantry, or the 14th Continental Regiment, as it was variously known, or more commonly, Glover's Regiment, or even more appropriately and simply, Glover's Corps of Marblehead Mariners. Before the war began, Glover had owned ships sailing out of Marblehead and nearby Beverly. He had been prominent in Massachusetts politics and had, by dint of honest effort and much hard work, become a member of that state's codfish aristocracy. The soldiers of his regiment, virtually all trained seamen, had saved the Continental Army for Washington and the nascent United States by evacuating the army in a flotilla of small boats from the army's perilous and exposed positions on Long Island to New York in late August.

Frost's father, Marlborough, had factored several cargoes of Spanish wine, sugar and salt for Glover when Glover's vessels had been forced by contrary winds into Portsmouth. On another occasion Marcus Whipple had taken one of Glover's vessels northward bound out of the Caribbean under tow after the vessel had been dismasted in a squall and took her all the way to Beverly. Frost had spoken one of Glover's vessels off the Chesapeake during his last outbound voyage to the Orient, a small but comely two-masted schooner some sixty feet on the deck, he collected. The schooner had been named *Hannah* for Glover's wife, and Glover had given her over as the first vessel in the little flotilla of eight armed vessels commissioned by Washington to prey upon British shipping, bringing supplies to Howe's besieged forces in Boston. Frost had met

Glover on at least two occasions, and if Glover had never met Joseph, at least he would know who Joseph was.

But first, Frost reflected, as he dressed in clothes that were as worn as the garments he had taken off before entering the sweat lodge, but felt and wore so much better because they were clean, he had to identify the wagons and stock he would need for his people when they commenced their return journey to Portsmouth two days hence.

XVIII

THE TEAMSTERS AND THEIR WOMEN WERE EAGER TO BE AWAY, BUT NOW EACH DROVER WAS ANXIOUS TO POINT OUT THE SUPERIOR QUALITIES OF the boat-wagon and team of draft animals he had tended all the way from Portsmouth. Frost had told his people plainly that the journey back to Portsmouth would take less than half the time consumed in freighting the gun powder and food-stuffs to Washington, since only the minimum number of wagons necessary for their rapid conveyance would be taken. No drover wanted to have his wagon marked as unfit, or the draft animals placed in his charge deemed too poor to make the return trek.

Heavily muffled against the cold and snow-turning-to-sleet, Frost critically inspected each wagon in turn, accompanied by Ming Tsun and aided by Captain Alexander Hamilton, who had attached himself to Frost as tightly as a barnacle to a ship's hull. Hamilton had a good eye for axles and running gear. "Faith, Captain Frost, I had been given to understand that these argosies of yours were hastily built, to serve only long enough to search out our Continental Army." Hamilton fixed Frost with an impish grin: "I dare say you will agree with me that these argosies are somewhat crudely turned out," Hamilton emphasized the word "crudely," "but, God's truth, all the argosies I compass are sound, and capable of much useful service still." The teamsters following the three men and the frolicking Newfoundland dog hung on the artillery captain's every word.

"Captain Frost," he continued, "it may be presumptuous of me to suggest such, but would you concede the Continental Army the sale of the argosies you can no longer use? Our General Washington intends to rest the army over the coming winter, and our transport is sadly deficient, especially so given the supplies your people have so unselfishly conveyed to the army fighting for their independence." Hamilton winked covertly, and Frost thought the young fop was laying it on a bit thick, but a furtive glance at the knot of teamsters showed that virtually all the men were puffing with pride.

"I require but twenty of these 'argosies,' as you and General Sullivan have termed them, to convey my people back to Portsmouth. Since you have the ear of General Washington, I can compile an invoice reflective of the costs incurred in constructing these wagons, less depreciation, costs for harnesses and yokes, and other furniture, and the fair value of the draught animals." Frost threw another coil of woolen muffler around his face so that no one could spy his wolfish grin. "I believe the teamsters of the wagons selected for the army's service should remain with their draught animals." A covert glance showed that the knot of teamsters was hurriedly dispersing out of earshot and out of sight.

"Captain Hamilton, I had resolved to abandon the boat-wagons excessive to my needs in any event," Frost continued quietly. "If the Continental Army has a use for the surplus, so much the better, for I intended to break them for firewood. You should know that the majority of timbers fashioning these wagons are the bones of a ship most dear to me. The fact that these boat-wagons have so famously withstood the rigors imposed by near a month of incessant harsh usage speaks most highly of the smiths who crafted them, as well as the goodness of the timbers from a vessel that served me well and faithfully."

"I am fearful General Washington will only be able to execute a promissory note similar to the ones already given," Hamilton said lamely.

"That shan't be necessary; I was resolved to take as draught animals only the horses, for which there are enough for twenty-one teams. The oxen, mayhap, those animals that falter, may augment your commissary, though it pains me to give them over as provender, for they have been faithful to their task, extremely so."

"Then you have two span of horses to spare," Hamilton exclaimed. "You must sell them to me. I must have them for the two 12-pounder cannons you brought."

Frost smiled. "You possess a stylish uniform, a handsome one indeed, Captain Hamilton, yet I mark you as a scholar, with wealth accumulated in your brain, but not your purse."

Hamilton threw Frost a startled look. "Has your man a quill and a scrap of paper?" he threw another look at Ming Tsun.

"Ming Tsun always is possessed of pen, ink and paper, Captain Hamilton," Frost said. "Not a day passes but he records his observations meticulously."

Ming Tsun approached Frost and Hamilton and sought out the lee of a boat-wagon as partial shelter from the snow and sleet. He withdrew a pencil of hammered lead and a square of ivory-colored foolscap from the portable secretary and spread his cloak as additional shelter.

"What value do you assign to a span of horses, Captain Frost?" Hamilton asked, imperiously.

"Five hundred pounds for ten animals. You shall need four animals to team each artillery piece—the tubes and limbers for 12-pounders are decidely heavy—but you shall have need for the two spare animals, I assure you."

"Done!" Alexander Hamilton said, enthusiastically grasping the pencil and foolscap and gratefully sheltering in the lee of Ming Tsun's protective cloak. He wrote furiously for thirty seconds, then scribbled his signature with an elegant flourish. Hamilton thrust the foolscap out to Frost. "I promise to pay the bearer of this promissory note five hundred pounds, plus interest at six percentage simple, on the sixth anniversary of the treaty marking the sovereignty of the United States of America!" Hamilton laughed. "I left out all that codswallop about heirs and assigns. This is a simple bearer's note. Whoever possesses this note six years following the execution of a treaty of peace need only to present it to me for payment. From state funds, of course."

Frost took the note and the lead pencil. He hunched his shoulders and edged as gratefully into the lee of Ming Tsun's cloak as Hamilton had done. Frost annotated the bottom of the note: "Terms accepted for ten horses, selection as made by the seller to the buyer, this date." "You have a singular grasp of the trader's simple contract," he said, as he folded the sheet of foolscap and handed it to Ming Tsun for him to file away. "Trade is best when its terms are simple to comprehend and beneficial to both parties."

"Economics, sir, pure economics, and the study of the human avarice," Hamilton exclaimed. "Though I confess I fathom a complete lack of the avarice in you. Indeed, I see it not, though I have searched for it."

"You had no need to execute even this simple bearer's instrument," Frost said. "A shake of hands would signify as well. Indeed, should we both survive this war—a cypher to which neither of us, as the Deity surely knows, possesses the key—I should be quite happy for you to present yourself personally with hard state money in hand six years from the date a treaty of peace with our cousins is concluded." Frost smiled his lupine grin. "I assure you, Captain Hamilton, even though hostilities will cease, our cousins will prolong the peace negotiations excruciatingly in hopes of gaining advantage." His grin broadened. "It is a trick of the sophisticated trader, well known, looking not to a mutually beneficial pact but his own narrow advantage."

"And when hostilities cease, Captain Frost, though no prophet exists to foretell that happy day," Hamilton questioned formally, "where shall you stand?"

"Assuming I am standing on that happy day you mention, I shall depart on the next tide for the Orient, to resume my trade this war has so grievously interrupted." Frost glanced along the line of boat-wagons smartly drawn up for inspection, and took a small knuckle of chalk from his coat pocket. "I suggest we with this chalk mark the wagons destined for the service of the Continental Army with as large an A as we can manage on the larboard side. I shall immediately separate out my twenty wagons and marshal them separately."

"Larboard?" Hamilton said hesitantly.

"Meaning the left side," Frost said somewhat testily, for it defied all logic that anyone who had ever worked for a factor for shipping or a freight agent, positions Frost had heard Hamilton describe as having held as a youth in Nevis and St. Croix, was unacquainted with nautical terms.

"Certainly," Hamilton said quickly, his lower face assuming an apple-red color not necessarily caused by the cold. "I ken the term, though I have been so long out of trade the meaning momentarily evaded me. Now, Captain Frost, now that the matter of argosies and draught animals has been settled, how else stand you in need of assistance?"

"You may accommodate me a great boon. I seek a place where a woman mightily springing with child and near her full time may safely be delivered. The lady and her brother-in-law have professed an unalterable desire to join with others of their sect settled in the Ohio Country."

"Has the lady a husband?"

"Dead of the smallpox, and the woman and brother-in-law were spared death a few hours in order to prepare meals for the Tories who had invested the town of Agawam." Frost gestured toward the lazarette-wagon at the end of the line of wagons. "Her confinement is there, since more shelter offers than a tent. I owe a responsibility to see them upon their way, with a necessary pause, seeing they will not go with me to Portsmouth."

Hamilton screwed up his handsome face in thought for a moment. "I believe I conjure a solution that will benefit the woman. There is a small shed used as a sheep cote attached to the back of the house where General Washington presently makes his headquarters. I fancy it is tight against the snow, and warm enough inside. The shed can be swept out and hay spread on the floor inside as additional proof against this insidious cold. I twig where there is a good rope bed that can be installed easily. In addition, the shed has its own entrance, of course. The well is near by, and there is a convenience not far off." He nodded emphatically. "Yes, it is settled, but please say nothing of the woman to General Washington. Hearing of her condition, he would be moved to vacate his own bedroom to accommodate her there, and General Washington sleeps little enough as it is."

Frost nodded. "We must make it so. Please show this place to Ming Tsun, and obtain the bed. I shall dispatch people to perform the scullery, and as soon as the place is presentable, we shall convey the good woman thither, together with such midwives as my surgeon's mate has discovered, for the lady's time is undeniably nigh."

XIX

FROST HAD GIVEN HIS FINAL ORDERS TO THE TEAMSTERS TO READY THEMSELVES FOR DEPARTURE ONE HOUR PRIOR TO DAWN ON THE MORROW, and that meant wagons loaded and horses in their harnesses and traces. Those who had not completed their breakfasts could either abandon their food or eat it along the way. Any drover unable or unwilling to rouse himself in time to accommodate Frost's orders for movement would likely find service in the Continental Army. Now, in the late afternoon, under a lowering sky threatening to spit snow at any moment, Frost was circulating, as unobtrusively as possible, through the knots of soldiers eagerly devouring their second hot and wholesome meal in who knew how many days or weeks.

Cook Barnes had seen to it that there was plenty of freshly baked bread to accompany the succotash and hearty beef stew with carrots, potatoes, onions, pease, and whatever else Barnes had thrown into the large kettles and pots over which he reigned supreme. One of the camp followers had come forward to share the butter she had churned in a large crock thanks to the rocking motion of the boat-wagons. The woman had obviously intended to keep the butter for herself and her drover, but she had been moved by the plight of the soldiers to share it out. True, the allowance per man was slight, but the woman stood by her churn and spooned out a small dollop onto the steaming hunk of bread on the plate of each soldier, brushing aside tears as she did so.

Frost walked over to the table, where a round dozen of Nathaniel Dance's marines were ladling out rum and water into the assorted wooden, copper, pewter and ceramic mugs held out by the supplicating soldiers. He seized a ladle and tasted the mixture, swirling it briefly in his mouth before spitting it out. "Add more juice of the lime from the small barrel, Jenkins, and dispense it all, if you please," he ordered. He had brought the barrel of lime juice all the way from Portsmouth and knew the juice was about to sour, but judging by the bleeding gums of the soldiers marshalling for food, they required the scorbutic far more than his people did. "And a bit less rum in each tot, unless you wish to make each man drunk."

"Ain't that what these men want, Capt'n?" Jenkins replied with a wink, as he rolled a small barrel from beneath a trestle.

Frost turned and came up unexpectedly hard against the solid bulk of a man wearing a Continental Officer's tricorne, but with a mud and snow-daubed blanket draped over his shoulders so Frost could not see the man's epaulettes of rank. The man was thick-bodied and bordered upon the corpulent, and Frost estimated the man's weight at near on seventeen stone, sixty pounds more than Frost's weight. Frost beheld the first soldier who could in honesty be termed "well fed" that he had seen in Washington's forces. His glance took in the officer's left hand, which lacked two fingers.

The officer extended his right hand, and Frost found himself looking slightly down into the eyes of a person who was approximately his own age, though the man's youth seemed to have been extinguished and his slightly bulging eyes were faded and dull.

"Captain Frost," the officer said, "my name is Knox, and I have long anticipated meeting you."

"Likewise I have looked forward to meeting you, Colonel Henry Knox," Frost said joyfully, and took Knox's hand enthusiastically. "Joseph spoke of you as he spoke of God, and I hope that you bring word of my brother."

Knox hesitated significantly, though he continued to shake Frost's hand enthusiastically. "I bring greetings from General Washington, and he inquires if he might have the pleasure of your company."

"I have enjoyed General Washington's company the evening past, and no one would derive greater pleasure from his company than I, but I most earnestly beg, have you word of my brother?"

Knox ignored the question and turned away. "Come," he said. "The walk is short."

Frost, accompanied by George Three, hurried after Henry Knox, Artillery Master of the Continental Army, who was setting a brisk pace through the lines of soldiers standing patiently and holding the cups, dented plates, calabashes, or whatever served as their mess kits, hungry eyes fastened expectantly on the rough boards set atop trestles as they waited their turns at the food service. Ming Tsun, who with the three ship's gentlemen had been ladling food from the kettles into mess kits, caught up a napkin, filling it with rice cakes, and Frost's boat cloak and followed.

"Colonel Knox!" Frost said sharply as he drew abreast, "I know you to be a gentleman, and I beg you indulge me with whatever you know about Joseph."

Knox turned his ruddy face, now wearing a countenance of sorrow, toward Frost, but kept up his rapid pace. "Your brother is in hospital in Philadelphia. Ill with camp fever. Very ill. I went there to gauge whether he might be removed, but the one poor sexton attending the dozens of sick advised strongly against the attempt."

"I shall start out for Philadelphia immediately," Frost said, his heart pounding with fear and an exuberance he had not felt for many months. "Please tell where in Philadelphia I shall locate him."

"I'll send a man to show you," Knox said shortly, "when the time appoints. Presently, we are commanded into General Washington's presence." They were coming up on Washington's headquarters now, and Ming Tsun managed to throw

Frost's worn boat cloak over his shoulders. Two ragged sentries challenged them. "Colonel Knox and party," Knox shouted. "Give way, General Washington expects us."

Knox, Frost and Ming Tsun swept past the befuddled sentries attempting to salute and up the squared wooden logs serving as steps, onto the porch and through the main door into the hallway, where the same clerks were sitting in the same chairs, raising their eyebrows at Knox's intrusion. Knox pounded on the door to the keeping room and threw it open at the command to enter. Frost immediately noticed that the room was better lighted than the last time he had been with Washington. Captain Alexander Hamilton, seated directly in front of Washington's desk, was intently reading a broadside. Caleb Mansfield stood by the fireplace, in the act of plunging a hot poker into the tankard he held. The poker hissed as the tankard's contents were mulled. Frost smelled the warm aroma of spiced cider.

Knox saluted self-consciously. Washington smiled. "Give you joy, gentlemen. There are chairs about, or you may stand as you desire. Thank you, Colonel Knox, for bringing these broadsides to us." He held out toward Frost a broadside similar to the one Hamilton was reading so avidly. "Written by a most singular individual, attached to our forces as a volunteer, not enlisted as a soldier, though he helped make the withdrawal from Fort Lee more orderly than it otherwise would have been. The broadsides were run off a press in Philadelphia this morning, though I believe the author, Tom Paine, used a drumhead as his desk three days afore. Mister Paine is a printer, encouraged to our country by that greatest of all North American printers, Benjamin Franklin."

Frost took the proffered broadside but did not glance at it. "I am far more concerned about my brother, who Colonel Knox gives me to understand is languishing in a Philadelphia pest house."

"I am informed about your brother, Captain Frost," George Washington said tiredly. "Brigadier General Arnold acquainted me with his career on the Lake, and I understand your brother was a member of a detachment sent by Major General Gates to strengthen my army. I regret extremely that all of the men of the detachment came down with the camp fever and were taken to hospital in Philadelphia."

"Then you readily understand, sir," Frost said stiffly, "why I am away for Philadelphia as soon as I can throw saddle over my molly-mule—and I regret that you deigned not to share your knowledge of my brother's fate when I first broached the inquiry with you."

"Don't reproach His Excellency or yereself, Capt'n," Caleb Mansfield said, advancing from the fireplace, in front of which George Three had contentedly stretched himself like a great black rug. Caleb sniffed appreciatively. "Belike thet napkin conveys 'em rice cakes made by Mister Ming Tsun."

Ming Tsun held the napkin out to Caleb, who took a cake, then Ming Tsun spread the cloth open on Washington's desk. "May I?" Washington queried, but without waiting for a reply took one of the rice cakes and popped it into his mouth. "Delicious! Marvelously delicious!" he exclaimed. "My sainted mother employed a slave who could concoct such delicacies. I have not enjoyed a rice cake so delicious since Maude died in the year sixty-seven."

Caleb touched Frost's arm. "Capt'n," he said gently, "His Excellency didn't tell ye what he twigged about Joseph 'cause he weren't sure Joseph still lived. He sent Colonel Knox to ken fer sure."

"And where did His Excellency dispatch you, Caleb?" Frost said, trying to conceal his despair. Two days, two entire days that he could have spent with Joseph!

"I prevailed upon Goodman Mansfield, whose capabilities as a scout were long ago proven to me, to undertake some most hazardous designs," George Washington said, looking longingly at the pile of rice cakes on his desk, into which Colonel Henry Knox and Captain Alexander Hamilton had made substantial inroads.

Ming Tsun signed; it was difficult to capture every nuance of hand movement, but Frost caught the gist and lifted his eyebrow. "You asked Caleb to spy out the British forces encamped on the eastern shore of the Delaware."

"Waal, Capt'n, I volunteered 'cause His Excellency needed t' know fer sure he'd been passed th' right skinny by a chap common t' both camps." Caleb bit into another rice cake and washed it down with a draft from his tankard.

"Captain Frost," George Washington said, rubbing his forehead tiredly. Henry Knox claimed the next-to-last rice cake. Frost quickly picked up the last cake and threw it to George Three, who rose to his feet in one fluid motion, casually snapped the cake out of midair, then contentedly flopped down before the fire to chew it. "Captain Frost, I beg your forgiveness. I did not wish you to leave this encampment until Goodman Mansfield confirmed my prior intelligence. I have unashamedly prolonged your pain to learn of your brother, because . . . because if the intelligence be confirmed, as it has, I would supplicate of you . . ."

"And what boon in your favor could I possibly discharge, sir?" Frost said quickly, wishing to be away as fast as ever he could to Philadelphia.

"Not a boon of mine alone, Captain Frost, but for the country we are establishing," Washington said simply, lifting his head to stare directly at Frost. "I intend to fall upon Trenton across the Delaware, where a host of German mercenaries has taken up garrison. I believe I can successfully emulate your audacious example in resolutely attacking the Tories in Agawam. But for that I must beseech the aid of your argosies to convey my soldiers across the river. Colonel Glover has collected a wondrous armada of large Durham boats, but they are insufficient for all the infantry, horses and artillery that must pass over the Delaware if our forces are to have any chance of success. It may have been wrong of me, but I desired you kept here until Goodman Mansfield confirmed that the earlier intelligence could be relied upon, in hopes your seamen marines and argosies would augment Glover's web-footed mariners as our means of passage."

Frost grasped his hands behind his back and began to pace

fiercely the length of the keeping room. So! Washington had deceived him! Washington had known all along where his brother was confined. If Washington had shared out that information, Frost would now have had two days in his brother's presence. The camp fever was the ship's fever was the gaol's fever, and it was almost invariably fatal. Joseph might even now be dead, and Washington had deliberately delayed Frost's efforts to determine if his brother could be counted among the living, or had been given over for dead. Two days . . .

"Capt'n Frost," Caleb said diffidently, hesitantly, "ye know I'd gladly give up ten years o' my life so's yere mother could have one glimpse o' yere brother's face afore he departed this world. But General Washington, he don't have no choosin'. Me 'n' a few of the cruizers slipped 'cross th' river and spied out the Germans, easy enough it were. It galls me t' say it, but there be a bunch of Brunswickers from thet bunch ye done yere best to send back t' George Three. They broke their parole fer sure." Caleb fell into step beside Frost and thrust his face close to Frost's. "General Washington, now most o' his men's gonna skittle 'n seven days or less, when their enlistments be up. There ain't gonna be no Continental Army. Sanctity o' contract, er somethin' they call it. But there be a great chance for a victory kin give th' men heart, give heart to all th' former colonies." Caleb scratched his beard warily. "Kin't deny yere bein' riled, Capt'n, but there be no denyin' it war deliberate."

"Yes, Captain Frost, it was deliberate," George Washington said softly. "This country we are trying so mightily to birth has need of you."

Frost laid a hand affectionately upon Caleb's shoulder, stopped his pacing, and gazed candidly at Henry Knox. "Joseph was with you all the way to Ticonderoga and thence to Boston, so you entertain some view of his endurance. Truly, think you Joseph can weather this encounter with camp fever?"

Knox may have been unfamiliar with the nautical term, but he understood the question well enough. He threw off the blanket that served as his cloak and stood nearer the fire, delaying his answer. "Joseph Frost possesses endurance equal to that of the cannons we drayed so tediously from Ticonderoga," Knox said finally. He stared into the flames rather than look at Frost. "But even iron can rust. I can tell you honestly that Joseph still lived when I quit his side this noon. I know not if he lives at this moment."

Frost took a chair, the better to distract the fear and dismay writhing like a serpent within him. He glanced down at the broadside he still clasped, and as further distraction tried to read it. He got no further than the first line. Frost stared at George Washington. "Yes, General, these are truly times that try the souls of men. This chap, Paine, knows what of he writes.

"Would that the King of the English and his ministers could read these words. But they are like the inquisitors of the great Galileo; they dare not look through the telescope. Otherwise they would see that we immigrants to the easterly coast of this large continent, we English, Germans, Dutch, French, Swedes . . ." Frost paused, "and other immigrants fetched, distressed and against their will, from the continent of Africa . . . have grown into a nation. We developed independence and resourcefulness because of remoteness and lack of attention from our mother countries. Headstrong and rash, but we have reared ourselves independent of sovereign, and rankle when those liberties harvested from the soils of this New World at the pangs of our labour are threatened with curtailment."

Frost heard a door somewhere toward the back of the house slam, and heard voices raised in excitement, though muffled, the words indistinct through the thick wooden walls.

"You gleaned not those sentiments from such quick perusal of Mister Paine's tract, Captain Frost," Washington said quietly. "The right values are never easy or advantageous, and you have cultivated them assiduously. Your comparison to the Italian scientist is apt. While encamped in Cambridge awaiting the train of artillery of Colonel Knox—I knew not then that your brother accompanied him—my officers and I made the traditional toasts to the health of the British King. We kept up the façade that the Crown was being misadvised by his ministers, and that we would be reconciled through recognition of our status as co-equals, with our own representatives elected by ourselves to serve in the Parliament."

Washington pushed his chair back from the desk, got to his feet and began to pace the length of the keeping room, hands clasped behind his back. "But the tumultuous events of July past ripped away that comforting façade. Yes, we have evolved inevitably into a free people because of the benign neglect by the Crown that made us depend upon ourselves. The English King and his ministers dare not look through the telescope; the knowledge that the world as they wish it known is not the way the world is would be too devastating." Washington reached the end of the room and turned, head low on his bosom, though everyone in the room heard him distinctly. "So now we are engaged in this war to win that which should have been recognized as the true order, and acknowledged long since."

And Frost realized that the agonizing, frustrating problem of knowing his brother's fate, and whether any intervention he could offer would be timely, would have to wait. "I have already told Captain Hamilton that the boat-wagons excess to my needs would be given over to the service of the Continental Army, General Washington. My seamen marines shall augment Glover's Regiment of mariners as oarsmen, gladly so. You need not question that Caleb Mansfield's *coureuse des bois* will fail in their rôle of scouts. With your approval and Captain Hamilton's permission, I should like to attach myself and my seamen marines—once landed on the east bank of the Delaware—to his artillery company."

Alexander Hamilton jumped excitedly to his feet and thrust out his hand. "I should place myself under your command, sir, since I ken you have far larger experience with cannons shipboard than I have with cannons upon the land."

"I am content, sir, to serve as you require," Frost said, taking the young man's hand. And Washington, coming up to them, placed one hand atop theirs.

"Gentlemen, I have orders to write out, so I must beg you

retire. But all my officers . . ." Washington looked steadily at Frost, "among whom I count you, Captain Frost, shall congress in this room tomorrow forenoon when I shall describe my plan. Though it shall be a plan modeled on your own, a disciplined march at night to fall upon the enemy at first light. Speed, simplicity, surprise—and audacity. Though I confide to you in strictest confidence that winning a victory over the Hessians will only be as the result of a God-wrought miracle."

"On the contrary, sir," Frost said, the hands of the three men still joined, "we must not ask God to accomplish an endeavour that is rightly our task."

Conversation ceased abruptly, and every head turned toward the wall behind Washington's desk, ears straining to hear the sound again—the high, thin but lusty wail of a babe taking its first breath.

XX

FROST, ACCOMPANIED ONLY BY GEORGE THREE AND BWINDI, KEPT WELL BACK IN THE COPSE OF CEDARS JUST BELOW THE CREST OF THE SMALL HILL A BARE half-mile from the Pennsylvania bank of the Delaware River, holding some dozen yards to the left of the rutted road leading down to the ferry landing. In point of fact, he was concealed deep inside a cedar, both to partially escape from the harsh, cold rain lashing down from a mean-spirited sky the color of an oyster shell, and to steady his telescope across a bough. He swept his glass in slow oscillations along the New Jersey side of the river, indistinct in the steady rain, not really expecting to see human activity, but alert, as always, to the possibility that there might be such, and he would have to know it.

Bwindi wormed her way, lynx-like, into the shelter of the cedar and shook herself vigorously. Frost had just forewarning enough to throw a fold of his boat cloak over the telescope to keep the lenses clear of water. The molly-mule nudged Frost's shoulder, and he foraged in a pocket for the last carrot he had saved from the small supply of root vegetables Ming Tsun had somehow been able to find in the ravaged countryside. He eased the bit from her mouth, and Bwindi daintily lifted the carrot from Frost's gloved palm, blowing her warm breath on him as she did so. Frost scratched the mule's ears affectionately.

He had been much occupied since leaving Washington's headquarters the noon before, the twenty-fourth. He, Caleb and Brevet Ensign of Marines Nathaniel Dance had stood in the back of the keeping room, shoehorned against the wall by the press of generals and colonels, some looking like peacocks in their uniform finery, and others, like Knox and Glover, businesslike in their worn uniforms. It had not been a congress or a debate: Washington had introduced Frost as a "gentleman with some experience in the employment of cannons" who would be nominally attached to Knox's artillery corps but with the flexibility to operate independently as the situation warranted; then Washington succinctly issued his battle orders and the password for the assault: victory or death. Frost thought the password a touch dramatic, though appropriate for the desperate effort now unfolding. Frost made one final sweep of the opposite shore, then as movement caught the corner of his eye, he focused the glass upstream. A Durham boat, small in the distance, emerged from a spate of rain. He closed the glass, taking pleasure as he always did at the soft snick of well-machined, well-fitted brass ferules sliding smoothly and concentrically into a compact length. He left the protection of the cedars, Bwindi following without the need to catch up a rein, around the side of the hill and down to the hasty encampment beyond.

Soldiers, indifferently cloaked and muffled against the now freezing rain, were clotted in the open field at the base of the hill, huddled miserably and protectively around small fires that steamed and sputtered in the rain. A soldier, lips blue with cold, sopped streams of water from his face with a dirty coat sleeve. "This 'ere damnable rain be worse'n a cow pissin' on a flat rock," he announced to no one in particular and bent even closer over the fire, virtually disappearing into the wood smoke and steam rising from the sodden garments of his fellows.

Ming Tsun, Caleb Mansfield and Alexander Hamilton were sharing a fire with several Continental Army officers. Hamilton was speaking to John Glover as Frost joined the group. "The British General Howe despoils my adopted city of New York for his army's winter quarters," Hamilton said bitterly. "But the cantonments garrisoned by his German mercenaries are widely separated, and given our army's unenviable record of defeats and retreats since we were driven from Long Island, no British or German entertains the scintilla of a thought that we might attack them during their Christmas ease. I look forward to the coming engagement, and trust it will be sharp. I mind that General Washington told me of a letter he wrote his mother during the French war when he mentioned the charming sounds made by musket balls passing close."

Nearby, Nathaniel Dance, his shortened cutlass in its shoulder carriage no longer an incongruous appendage, was soberly inspecting his men, assuring himself as to the condition of their firearms, short swords or hatchets, and that their cartridge pouches held full allotments of ammunition. He was quietly informing each individual marine that his task would be to protect the matrosses who would be husbanding the cannons assigned to Captain Hamilton's field artillery. There was a brief stir as Cook Barnes hastened up, a short tarpaulin jacket barely concealing the heavy belt into which a brace of pistols was tucked. A well-worn cutlass, brass hilt partially wrapped with a strip of shark's skin, swung in a carriage over his right shoulder. Cook Barnes tossed Frost a cheerful salute with his hook.

"Fine day fer a fight, Capt'n, eh?" Cook Barnes reached out with his hook and tapped a marine on the shoulder. "Hey you, Spider, stay close to me when we get into the pitch-up. I need you to reload my pistols, ken?" The marine—Frost saw that he was Spider Urquhart—glanced nervously at the steel hook screwed into the round wooden block at the end of Cook Barnes' forearm and tried to sidle away. The steel hook flashed up to touch Urquhart's ear and the marine stopped. "Now, Spider," Cook Barnes said soothingly, "stay you close to me 'n' ram down powder 'n' ball when I be needin' 'em, 'n' I'll cook you a great puddin' duff scrumptious with raisins, all your own."

Nathaniel Dance grinned at both men. "I believe the promise of one of yere raisin puddin's all to himself would keep the Devil at heel to sponge and load for ye, Cook Barnes." Then he removed from an ammunition box the stiff leather collar studded with wicked spikes that George Three had been wearing when Frost first encountered the giant Newfoundland dog in Whip Loring's apartments in Fortress Louisbourg and soberly buckled it around the dog's neck.

Caleb coughed. "Waal now, them Brunswickers might be takin' their Christmas ease, Mister Hamilton, 'n' th' gin 'n' rum 'n' beer 'n' hard cyder be a-flowin' mighty free, but don't go expectin' to see th' Brunswickers all pie-eyed from drink when we get up t' 'em. Officers mayhap, but don't go thinkin' th' soldiers be. They got discipline, right enough, 'n' this ain't gonna be no game o' jump th' broom." He stooped to the fire and used a short length of dead birch limb to rake several yams from the coals. "'Course, fact be we got woods-cruizers 'n' teams o' two, one t' shoot 'n' one t' spot 'n' keep watch, on th' other bank. They be havin' theirselves a right high time a-pottin' Brunswickers 'n' keepin' 'em cooped up, 'n' not patrollin' as they rightly should." Caleb smiled wickedly. "'Course, a bit more snow, some heavy sleet, 'n' a ringtail snorter o' wind would a-sure make 'em appreciate th' warmth o' their barracks all th' more."

Frost held his amusement. He was quite sure that Alexander Hamilton's anticipation of battle had never been tempered in the reality of actual conflict. Caleb threw Frost a yam; he rubbed the ash from it, partially peeled it, and bit gratefully into the moistly succulent, deep orange flesh. The yam burned his mouth and he chewed quickly, hungrily, since he had last eaten two hours before dawn, a porridge of oatmeal seasoned with prunes. He fed the peel to Bwindi. "The first of your Durham boats hove into view from my vantage point on the hillside, Captain Glover, not five minutes ago." Frost deliberately used the nautical title rather than Glover's military rank.

John Glover smiled as he blew onto his rough and blistered hands. "I appreciate the intelligence, Captain Frost, as I appreciate the men and argosies you have detailed to assist our crossing. With your permission, I'll hurry them along to the ferry landing and get the wheels off the argosies."

Frost nodded and rummaged for a moment in the bag behind Bwindi's saddle. He located the remaining pair of wool mittens knitted for him by his mother and held them out to Glover. A surprised Glover nodded his gratitude, quickly pulled on the mittens and strode away.

Frost glanced around, contrasting the smart seamen marines, the ex-*Jaguars*, to the Continental soldiers who were beginning to shuffle, hunch-shouldered, to their marshalling points under the shrill commands of their sergeants. A splat of sleet growled from the pregnant sky. Frost thought of the woman, Salome. He had heard the cry of a babe being birthed, but what of the condition of the mother and child? He had been too busy with the embarkation preparations to think of them or Joseph. He was intensely grateful for that.

Hamilton walked over to the two 12-pounder artillery pieces Frost had brought all the way from Portsmouth and inspected the horses that were to pull the cannons once the assault force was landed on the New Jersey shore. Then he inspected the matrosses, and finally the cannons themselves and their ammunition limbers. Frost thought Hamilton had his inspection priorities slightly awry, but he kept his opinion to himself.

Returning to stand by Frost, Hamilton asked nervously: "Tell me in all candor, Captain Frost, what think you of General Washington's plan of attack?"

So! The young West Indian was nervous enough to be questioning the plan of his commanding general! Frost smiled his caricature of a smile, though hidden in his woolen muffler, it went unnoticed. "There are only two kinds of plans before hand, Captain Hamilton, those that may produce the results desired, and those with flaws readily discernible. You must judge for yourself the merits of General Washington's plans."

"I mean no disrespect to General Washington . . ." Hamilton said quickly, "but I confess a certain unease about my own abilities, never having been tested in such manner. I doubt not the General's plan but strain for some signal that my conduct may not be found wanting—in the hard time ahead."

"You cannot be more uncertain of your ability to surmount your own demons of private doubt than I in confronting the demons I entertain immediately," Frost replied. "But as Pericles constantly reminds us, courage is the knowledge of what is not to be feared. And there are entire constellations of things we know not to fear."

But just how viable was Washington's plan? Frost asked himself in the quietude of his soul. The plan of attack was simplicity itself. A division of Continental troops under Lieutenant Colonel John Cadwallader would cross at the Bristol Ferry and engage Hessian troops under the command of a Colonel von Donop deployed on the southern outskirts of Trenton town. A second division of Continental troops commanded by Brigadier General James Ewing would cross at Trenton Ferry and fast march to the bridge over the Assunpink Creek south of Trenton town, then take the bridge and stopper it against any British or Hessian troops retreating in that direction. Washington would cross to the New Jersey shore at McKonkey's Ferry with twenty-four hundred men, then divide into two corps for the nine-mile march southward to Trenton town to fall upon Hessians under the command of Colonel Rall. Thanks to the intelligence gleanings of Caleb's *coureuse des bois*, Washington was well acquainted with the names, numbers, regiments, and dispositions of his adversaries.

But Frost was concerned about communications, that is, the absence of communications, between Washington and Ewing's and Cadwallader's divisions. At the meeting in Washington's headquarters, he had heard no provision for messengers, runners or dispatch riders to shuttle between the three widely dispersed wings of the Continental Army. The three wings would indeed be operating independently of each other. Did that lack portend a fatal weakness? And there had been some vague mention that General Putnam would also be bringing along a force to form a fourth prong of the attack on the British garrison. How did all of this fit together strategically or tactically?

Frost drove his demons into the dungeon that confined them by the simple expedient of turning to other pressing matters, though all the same extremely glad that Ishmael Hymsinger, Hannibal Bowditch and Darius Langdon were riding up on their nags. Both Darius and Hannibal wore large, awkward haversacks over their short cloaks, and other haversacks were thrown over their horses' croups. Hymsinger's nag had an equal number of bags suspended from it, and Hymsinger wore a lugubrious expression as well as a haversack stitched from heavy sailcloth slung over his shoulder.

"Captain Frost, the lads and I bear here such surgical instruments, medicinals and lint as we believe may be efficacious for the dressing of minor wounds." Hymsinger's expression grew even more mournful. "The medical men attached to the Continental Army have advised me of their intentions not to cross with the army but to establish a hospital in a barn nearby where the grievously wounded are to be evacuated."

"Decent of the medical men to permit you the honor of crossing with the army and tending any man unfortunate or intemperate enough to interpose his body in the way of musket or cannon ball, or shard of exploding shell, while they bravely wait on this side of the Delaware," Frost said laconically. He smiled at Darius. "Mister Landgon, I have insight that you aspire to be a man of medicine."

Darius glanced up, startled. "Oh, no, sir, never in life could I aspire to such a lofty station, though Mister Hymsinger says that I have the touch. It be enough for me to have some small part in the alleviation of pain."

Frost grunted noncommittally, though with a plan forming at the back of his mind. He thrust that plan into the same cell occupied by the demons of fear. Time enough to think on the plan later. Would there be a later? Yes—if the Prophets and the Holy Trinity so willed. Insh'allah.

"Ishmael," Frost began, "we have all been sorely pressed for time, but can you share a word as to how the woman Salome progresses?"

"Alas, I was able to visit her but for a few minutes some

hours into her labour and waft the sacred smoke to ease her pains. I know only what you know, that her time was accomplished and an infant born."

"Please, sir," Darius said, looking up at Frost, "this place be filling up with soldiers and horses a-plenty, and our own boat-wagons. Can you name me this place?"

"Well, Mister Langdon," Frost said patiently, "we find ourselves presently in the midst of a large field, and though doubtlessly some farmer hereabouts has given this field a name, I know it not. But over yonder hill is the Delaware River, and we wind toward a crossing place called McKonkey's Ferry, in honor of a gentleman who saw the advantage of siting a ferry service in this place."

John Glover, walking at the head of a double company of his Fourteenth Continental Regiment, which was escorting half a dozen of the boat-wagons formerly belonging to Frost, passed by, displaying far more spirit than the harsh weather seemingly would permit. Glover tipped his hat to Frost. "We had best make our way to the crossing," Frost said to his men. He tightened Bwindi's girth, stepped easily into the saddle, and caught up the Ferguson rifle Ming Tsun extended to him. His small group pushed through the mob of soldiers marching hunch-shouldered beneath the lashing rain, over the crest of the small hill and down to the ferry landing where Durham boats were arriving from upstream in quantity.

"Waal, look at 'em nobs," Caleb said as they jogged up to the large plain between low hills that marked the western terminus of McKonkey's Ferry. Colonel of Continental Artillery Henry Knox, astride the wide-barreled, short-legged cob that Caleb had quickly forsaken once he caught up the spirited gray gelding for which a certain Tory no longer had any earthly need, was riding about ceaselessly at the water's edge, shouting orders to matrosses bustling in confusion about the hasty park of cannons drawn up near the landing. Nearby, a Continental officer of indeterminate rank and regiment, though kitted out in an elegant uniform of blue silk and white taffeta, all surmounted by a cloak of beaver skins, sat an equally elegant horse. He wound through the elaborate ritual of taking snuff sprinkled upon the top of a gloved hand, then inhaling it and sneezing decorously. The procedure was quite comical, as the officer had pulled his head deep inside his cloak, like a turtle into its carapace, to shelter his glove from the rain and wind.

Caleb shrugged and turned away from the spectacle. "Time I be takin' passage t' th' Jersey shore."

The elegant Continental officer fixed Frost with a disapproving eye as Frost and company drew up in the midst of Glover's Regiment. "Sir," the officer said, addressing Frost in the nasal tones of the most prestigious Philadelphia salons, "I cannot but observe there are a number of Africans in this body, the sight of which, to persons unaccustomed to such associations, has a most disagreeable, indeed, regrettable, effect." If any black man among the dozens enlisted in Glover's web-footed regiment, who were quite visible in the mob of tarpaulin-trousered, callused-handed seamen-turned-temporary-soldiers hastening the boat-wagons down to the river, heard the words of the anonymous officer, none paid any heed.

"Indeed, sir," Frost said, inclining his head ever so slightly but gravely in the officer's direction, "the incessant struggles for our freedom from the British crown segregates us all into the acknowledgement of our truest aspirations toward the ideal of liberty."

"Well spoken, sir!" the anonymous officer exclaimed. "Please take snuff with me, I would deem it a signal honor."

"I regret duty compels me to keep my nostrils clear for the scent of the enemy," Frost demurred, shuddering and inwardly wondering how anyone could find enjoyment in the inhalation of finely powdered noxious leaf of sun-dried tobacco. He pulled Bwindi out of the mob of soldiers and marveled as the men milled down to the ferry landing, obedient to the orders of their sergeants. They waited patiently, then filed silently into the Durham boats nosed against the slight embankment, held against the solid ground by men leaning heavily on eighteen-foot oars or iron-tipped setting poles.

He marked soldiers from regiments of New York, Massachusetts, New Jersey, his native New Hampshire, Pennsylvania, Maryland, Delaware, Virginia, and Connecticut. He was awed by the fact that men whose enlistments would expire in six days were willingly shouldering their muskets, obedient to Washington's orders. Yes, these soldiers were cheerful and determined. Frost scrutinized the face of each man as he passed. All were underfed, and a goodly number without proper shoes or boots, feet swathed instead in bulky rags, though every man had a blanket draped as a cloak over his shoulders and protecting the firelock of his musket.

The blankets were British quartermaster issue, of mediocre quality though extortionate cost, purchased from the midlands contractors, but not a Continental soldier would possess a blanket now had not Frost found blankets among prize cargo, paid for them himself, and brought them all the tortuous way from Portsmouth. Frost sighed; any one of the men filing slowly past him as he sat Bwindi could be the last unlamented, unmourned, unremembered soldier to die in the abortive pursuit of American freedoms and liberties.

And then General Washington himself, astride a magnificent dappled gray stallion measuring at least fifteen hands at the withers and accompanied only by Major Generals John Sullivan and Nathanael Green, drove into the mêlée. "Give you joy, Captain Frost," Washington said simply. "I could not help but observe there was some confusion at the embarkation, and came myself to the river to see if I might reinforce attention upon the obvious need for adherence to our plan for speed and surprise." Washington flicked rain from his forehead with a gloved hand. "How far do you judge yonder shore?"

"Not quite two cables, Your Excellency," Frost replied, though the question in Washington's eyes at the strangeness of the nautical term caused him to amend quickly: "Just a fathom or two past three hundred yards, Your Excellency. Not a tremendously great pull in these great Durham boats, which I see are well-built, with seasoned men at the oars, though the floes of ice are coming down with a greater intensity than I would wish and promise encounters that would delay our crossing."

"Yes, these Durham boats," Washington said with satisfaction. "An enterprising invention of the engineer, Robert Durham, who saw the need for boats large enough to freight cargo from the iron works north of here down to the city of Philadelphia." Washington fixed Frost with a keen stare. "Know you, Captain Frost, that Philadelphia is second only to London in population among the English-speaking world? Who would think it?" Washington lifted an eye toward Frost briefly but keenly. "I have been given to understand you recently enjoyed an illuminated view of the British colliery fleet at anchor in the mouth of the River Tyne but did not go ashore. Have you ever trod British soil, Captain Frost?" Washington had to bow his head to shelter his face from the storm's lash as much as possible beneath his tricorne.

"I sighted the British Isles on several occasions," Frost said bitterly. "By the tenor of your question you doubtlessly have heard that Caleb Mansfield and some companions engaged a brief promenade in the vicinity of Newcastle this September last. But I touched only briefly in the year sixty-six, when I was finally able to transship aboard a brig from Liverpool bound for Newport."

"Every officer and soldier of this Continental Army would have been heartened by the spectacle of the River Tyne glorious in pyrotechnics," Washington said dryly, "I most of all, though my antecedents hail originally from the small borough of Washington, immediately west of Sunderland."

Frost wondered mildly at Washington's repetition of something he had said earlier, then realized that Washington was anxious, and was disguising his anxiety as Frost had himself dealt with anxiety, by unknowing repetition.

"Here now, General Washington," John Glover said, appearing beside Washington in the gathering dark, "time to get you aboard yonder Durham boat. If you'll be so kind as to dismount, we'll secure your horse first, then you may embark." Glover took the horse's reins and looked around. "Private Russell, take the General's horse," but the man Glover sought was no where to be seen. "Russell," Glover repeated, in a sharper tone, then to Frost in chagrin: "Captain Frost, the man appointed to take charge of the General's horse is not to be found when needed. Have you a reliable man?"

Frost turned in his saddle: "Mister Hymsinger, Mister Langdon," he called toward the clutch of his men waiting patiently to clamber into a boat-wagon. Ishmael and Darius immediately detached themselves from the clutch and, followed closely by the giant Newfoundland dog, George Three, quickly made their way through the treacherous slush of rain and ice covering the rutted ground. They looked at Frost expectantly. "Please lead General Washington's horse aboard the Durham boat designated by Captain Glover to receive both horse and rider. Once aboard, I'm sure Captain Glover will find advantage in your pulling an oar."

Darius took the reins from Glover and gently stroked the horse's forehead, whispering to it, as Washington dismounted. "Faith," Washington said as George's vigorously wagging tail threw slush onto his cloak, "the animal is as large as a colt! No, I marked his size before, when he lay stretched before the fire." He peered intently at Darius in the rapidly failing light. "Know you the watchword, young man?"

"Yes, Your Excellency," Darius answered confidently. "Victory or death."

Washington grunted with satisfaction, clapped Darius on the shoulder, and followed as Darius and Ishmael led the way to the Durham boat to which John Glover pointed.

Henry Knox walked his plug of a horse to Frost. "I'm to be last over," he shouted. "Torches ain't much use in this rain, and we don't want to draw the attention of any British scouting parties. I fancy my voice is loud enough to be heard to mid-river." Knox grinned at Frost. "I am glad indeed to have found as my mount this paragon of *equus caballus* among the draught animals consigned for the cannons' drayage. Most fortunately, there is no great distance to the ground should I fall."

XXI

MORE THAN HALF OF THE CONTINENTAL SOLDIERS FERRIED ACROSS THE DELAWARE IN THE BOAT-WAGON WITH FROST BECAME VIOLENTLY SEASICK during the trip. The river was high, with a strong, piercing wind roiling, a strong current running, ice floes thick, and then the cold rain turned to sleet slugged about by the vicious wind. The sleet obscured what little visibility there was and formed ice on the oars and push poles. Once Frost reached the eastern shore, half a dozen cold-soaked soldiers followed Bwindi out of the boat-wagon and huddled against the molly-mule's flanks to absorb her warmth.

As soon as the soldiers were disembarked, Nathaniel Dance and his crew of marines pushed off for the unenviable return to the Pennsylvania shore. Caleb Mansfield materialized out of the sleet and darkness and led the way to a grove of oak trees. "Tobin Tuttle assures ain't no Britishers lurkin' hereabouts, so's these fellas kin make a fire."

Frost set the soldiers to scavenging wood as Caleb and Ming Tsun huddled close around a small pile of birch bark Caleb had collected and plied with steel and flint to kindle a fire. Within ten minutes half a dozen small fires were flickering fitfully among the oaks, with shivering Continental soldiers congregated around each fire. Frost and Ming Tsun carried brands down to the shore to act as beacons for the Durham boats and boat-wagons that crept so agonizingly across the turbulent

Delaware. Slowly, ever so slowly, the Continental Army on the New Jersey shore grew in size. And then a thoroughly chilled George Washington was clambering from a Durham boat before it was properly run up on the shore, wading the last few yards and beating off the ice that sheathed his cloak.

"This won't do," Washington said, catching sight of Frost. "This won't do at all, Captain Frost. The crossing goes too slow! Our forces must be marshaled on the outskirts of Trenton town by six of the morning." Washington sloshed up to the small fire, drew his watch from a waistcoat pocket, bent to the feeble flames and peered at the watch closely. He thrust it back into his pocket. "My timepiece has been stopped by the damp," Washington said in exasperation. "May I trouble you for the time, Captain Frost?"

Frost drew out Jonathan's Bréquet. "It is half two, General." He hesitated, then extended the watch to Washington. "Please accept the loan of my brother's watch until we return in triumph to the Pennsylvania shore."

Washington seized the watch appreciatively and snapped open the lid to confirm the time. "I shall guard your brother Joseph's fine timepiece most jealously, Captain Frost, and similarly pray that when you deliver it your brother he will be restored to health."

Frost did not tell Washington the Bréquet had belonged to the third son of Marlborough and Thérèse Frost. "As you noted in your passage, General Washington, the river is most tumultuous, and with so many vessels contending for place on its bosom, disaster lurks an oar's stroke away. John Glover's men realize that to push any harder will result in a capsize and the loss of all aboard, for no one could live in that water. Therefore, I pray you endeavour to bear the delay." Darius came up with Washington's horse, followed closely by Ishmael Hymsinger, who in addition to his medicinal bag was clutching a large piece of rumbowline canvas.

"Ah, Mister Hymsinger, please light along to the grove of oak trees above and rig that canvas as a windbreak where His Excellency may consult with his officers out of the constant lash of rain. Mister Langdon, you behaved prodigiously well rowing the General's barge, though such attention was only to be expected! Now you have charge of the General's horse—I beg you include my molly-mule also in your care." Frost took in the frisky antics of George, the great Newfoundland dog; it was exceedingly difficult not to, since the playful animal almost knocked him down with the vigorous motion of that great saber of a tail. "We all rejoice in seeing George togged out in his special collar, the one with all the nails. He must display total animus on the morrow." He turned to Washington: "I make so bold to suggest, General Washington, that you follow my surgeon's mates and retire to the relative shelter of the oaks half a cable—one hundred yards along the ferry road. My surgeon's mate will rig . . . ah, here is your *chef des scouts* with a horn lantern to light your way. You will undoubtedly be more comfortable . . ."

"And you shall not have me to delay your rôle as beach master, or interfere with the men and equipment being landed," Washington said perceptively. "Goodman Mansfield, I follow you gladly, for our commitment to your intelligence is total. Captain Frost, the beach is yours. I ask only that you send along all senior officers to our council fire whenever—and however—they may pitch up."

And with those words George Washington turned and walked up the rutted road, ankle deep, already, in icy slush, then veered off into the copse of trees, Ishmael Hymsinger and Darius Langdon running ahead, medicine bags bouncing, and the horse and mule trotting along companionably. "I'm glad to be shut of them," Frost told himself thankfully. "I know naught of the General's grand strategy, and better he plots it anon, but with Jesus, Joseph and Mary as my witnesses, I do assuredly ken the landing and proper dissemination of cargoes." Putting aside his sodden clothing, and with the unobtrusive assistance of Ming Tsun, Geoffrey Frost naturally assumed command of the beachhead at the eastern terminus of McKonkey's Ferry, separating out and sending their various ways the Continental troops being landed so haphazardly.

"Philadelphia Troop of Light Horse? Yes, you are seconded to Colonel Knox's Continental Artillery and State Batteries. Maryland Rifle Battalion Volunteers? Yes, you are with Brigadier Hugh Mercer's Brigade, who is under Major General Nathanael Greene's command. Please to form up over there with the First Maryland Regiment, Continental Infantry.

"Hello! I recognize you people of the Second Regiment, Continental Foot. You were earlier the Third New Hampshire Regiment, I collect, and why all the numbers and state affiliations were changed, only the Dear knows. But you are part of Brigadier General St. Clair's Brigade, and his forces are detailed to Major General Sullivan's Command. Don't worry, lads, you'll have a New Hampshire man leading, all you have to do is keep him in sight, and fire when he tells you to fire.

"First Regiment, New York Continental Infantry? Right, we can sort this out readily enough. You men are detailed to Colonel Sargent's Brigade. Please to muster over there with Colonel Ward's Regiment of Connecticut Continentals. You are all part of Colonel Sargent's Brigade, and you'll be mustering under Major General Sullivan's Command. Please to clear the ferry landing! Lively now! There are two more Durham boats in the offing, and they must have places to discharge!

"Captains Washington and Flahaven! You have reached us just in time! General Washington commands that each of you shall take forty men; you are to seek out and secure the Pennington and Lower River Roads outside of Trenton. You may wish a word with His Excellency before you take up the march. You shall find him in conference with other officers inside the oak grove just there. But please, content yourselves with a minute."

Frost walked the beachhead tirelessly, naming the units as they landed, directing them to their marshalling areas, designating the marshalling areas as he went along, dictating the names of the regiments and troops as they landed to Ming Tsun, ceaselessly in motion. At one point Frost sank down, tired beyond all caring, on a driftwood log and dully studied the list Ming Tsun had copied. Soldiers from New York, Massachusetts, New Jersey, New Hampshire, Pennsylvania, Maryland, Delaware, Virginia, Connecticut were all ashore now, and only a half-dozen Durham boats and his crude boat-wagons remained in the offing. As the last of the Durham boats ran into the bank, a faint gleam in the east told Frost, now temporarily without his brother's watch, that a new day was anxious to be birthed.

"Ahoy, Captain Frost! Is that you I espy? Is 'ahoy' the appropriate maritime word for recognizing a person? While the shelves of my shop on Boston's Cornhill Street certainly harbored books with nautical themes, I confess I was far more interested in texts on cannons and their employment." Henry Knox's voice boomed loud enough that it was likely heard all the way to Trenton, or so it seemed to Frost. Indeed, Frost fancied he had heard Knox's bellow a time or two all the way across the two cables' width of the Delaware. "Can you assist me to rise? I fear I am frozen to the bench of this wretched barge."

Frost, having long lost all feeling in his feet, did not hesitate to wade out to the mid-point of the Durham boat and assist Knox to his feet. "You shall retain a modest degree of comfort if you disembark over the bow of the boat, Colonel Knox, rather than step into this water." He was solicitous of the stout man who had befriended Joseph, and whose intellect he admired, though Frost found it hard to believe that he and Henry Knox were of an age.

Knox made his way slowly and carefully, in the manner of all persons carrying far more weight than they should, to the bow of the Durham boat. Still leaning on Frost's arm, Knox stepped ponderously, with a grunt of satisfaction, onto the frozen mud of the eastern shore of McKonkey's Ferry landing.

"There!" Knox said with some triumph, "I am the last across, and I bring the last of the artillery tubes. Where is General Washington? I am deucedly late, I know, but this storm has been an abomination, and potential disaster accompanied every stroke of the oar."

"Every man destined for McKonkey's Ferry has crossed

safely, Colonel," Frost said. "I cannot speak for those putting across at other ferries, but Glover's web-foots have brought off a miracle."

"Indeed," Knox harrumphed. "Good man, Glover, saved us at Long Island, he did! All his fellows, white and black alike, are most noble, as I took pains to impress upon that Philadelphia Militia buffoon who uttered those sanctimonious, unfeeling remarks by which he revealed his petty and prejudiced mind. I have discerned no reason to count them myself, but Glover advised there were over one hundred and fifty men of colour enlisted in his regiment—and the men of his command gladly accept any competent seaman, regardless of colour of visage." Knox looked around him. "Now, where is my horse? I really must have my horse."

"Glover and I are of like mind regarding merit as the only valid quality of measurement, and glad you share it," Frost said. "We'll catch up your horse presently, but I believe it better that both of us walk the few yards to General Washington's temporary bivouac in order to restore some semblance of warmth and tone to our muscles." The walk to Washington's fire brought searing pain to Frost's feet as feeling returned.

"There you are, Colonel Knox," Washington said with a touch of asperity as Knox came into the firelight. "We are a good two hours late and must take up the march immediately."

"Aye," Knox responded, "our sage, Mister Shakespeare, well knew of timeliness when he had Macbeth, villain though he may be, decry 'if it were done, when 'tis done, then 'twere well it were done quickly.' However, Captain Frost presents us the joyous news that all our force be safely across."

"And what of Ewing at the Trenton crossing, and Cadwallader at Bristol?" Washington demanded. He knew the answer from the silence that greeted his question. "We march immediately. Colonel Knox, limber your cannons as quickly as you can and follow with all dispatch. Now where is Goodman Mansfield?"

Darius brought up Bwindi and Washington's horse. "Girth be tightened, General, sir," Darius said.

"And you found some way to wipe him down," Washington said with gratitude.

"Yes, sir," Darius replied, "Captain Frost keeps a sponge in his saddle pocket for that exact purpose."

Caleb Mansfield rode his gray horse into the firelight. "Road be clear all the way t' the Bear Tavern, General. Fact is, a few o' yere sojers got thar already 'n' seein' how th' owner be fled, they helped theirselves t' such strong drink as could be found."

"Rum on an empty stomach makes for a poor breakfast, Goodman Mansfield," Washington said trenchantly. "We should be encircling Trenton town just now. Instead, it is passing four of the clock this morning of the twenty-sixth day of December, and we are nine miles north of the town. Please lead the way."

Henry Knox elbowed Frost in the ribs and whispered, "There were buckets of rum being passed among the men on the far shore to dull the edge of their hunger. Methinks if given the chose, most men would prefer the warm-bellied comfort wrought by a stiff tot of rum to allay the cold and gripe against Mister Paine's wondrous fine missive, such as was read complete to the soldiers yesterday morning." Knox turned and stumped away on clumsy feet to see to limbering his artillery.

Frost stiffly climbed into Bwindi's saddle, looked to his right, where he knew Ming Tsun would be, took the Ferguson rifle, and slung it awkwardly over his shoulder. Ming Tsun no longer wore the placid aspect of a gentle scholar accomplished in the healing art, and his ravaged face was beginning to nod in time with the tempo, if ever so slightly for the nonce, to the wild rhythm of impending battle. Frost chirruped to Bwindi, and he and Ming Tsun cantered after George Washington.

The combined wings of Greene's and Sullivan's corps made the two miles to the Bear Tavern in thirty minutes. The sleet and wind, out of the north, was at least now at their backs, but it was very dark in the trampled yard in front of the tavern when Washington paused to consult a map. Caleb Mansfield ducked inside the tavern and returned with a stable lantern that cast a fine glow. "Ah, the indispensable Goodman Mansfield," Washington said with pleasure, "in all and every way anticipating my needs." Washington held one corner of the map while Major General Nathanael Greene held the other, and Major General John Sullivan held the lantern over the map.

"Right," Washington said, rolling the map into a tube with a snap of finality, and looking around sharply, able to discern in the darkness some of the dim shapes of men who had dropped to the ground. "General Greene, rouse your corps and take Pennington Road as rapidly as ever you can. Command of the corps vests in you, though I must perforce accompany you. General Sullivan, your route of march is southward along the River Road. Captain Frost, although I earlier asked you to accompany Glover's men in General Sullivan's corps, would you and your colleagues serve by communicating between these two forces I intend to pincer the British and Germans, so I am acquainted with General Sullivan's advance?" Washington smiled wryly in the wan light of the stable lantern. "I neglected to provide for messengers to acquaint me with the progress of my officers Ewing and Cadwallader, and I am paying the anxieties of such lack of forethought. It shall not happen again."

"Certainly, General Washington," Frost replied formally. "My colleagues and I shall be happy to provide liaison between the two wings." Indeed, Frost thought, he, Ming Tsun, Caleb and such woods-cruisers as were nearby and mounted were unencumbered with any great weight of kit, and they could all move quickly.

"A report by some hand every thirty minutes . . . I am sorry, I have your watch," Washington said, and fumbled beneath his cloak.

"I need it not, sir," Frost said, speaking just loudly enough to be heard above the wind. "A mariner can gauge the passage of time quite handily, even without a glimpse at the stars. You shall have a report promptly on the thirtieth minute." He laid the left rein along Bwindi's neck, and she immediately turned to her right and broke into a brisk walk.

A number of the officers on horseback had used the brief pause to bind rags over their horses' hooves, as had some of the matrosses riding the draught horses pulling the cannons. Some of the matrosses were also wrapping rags around the wheel rims of the carriages. Bwindi's small hooves were exceptionally quiet, and in any event Frost did not want his molly-mule's surefootedness to be compromised. Frost did not believe the rags would last long against the sharp ruts and craters of the ice-covered road, but those who took the time to wrap hooves and wheel rims with rags evidently thought the effort would do some good. At least their minds were diverted, to some degree, from thoughts of the coming engagement.

Frost and Ming Tsun joined Sullivan's corps. Caleb was nowhere to be seen, nor had Frost expected Caleb to remain with him. Caleb had too many secretive affairs to be about. Some fifteen minutes into the march by Frost's calculations, and just as there was a hint of light in the east, a slight lessening of the darkness, he turned Bwindi around and rode back to a dim path along the northern bank of a frozen brook striking eastward that he had marked. A soldier was collapsed face-down in a snow bank immediately by the ice- and snow-choked trace. The soldier still clutched his musket.

Frost dismounted and rolled the man over onto his back. The soldier looked up with a sickly smile, his face clearly marked with the pinch of the ground itch. "I be sorry, sir," the soldier said, taking Frost to be a Continental officer. "My legs, they just plumb give out on me."

Frost looked at the man's legs. His dirty, once white pantaloons were shredded, and from the mass of rags swaddling his feet, several bloodied and grotesquely swollen, translucent toes with ragged, broken nails protruded. Frost gathered up the man, marveling at his lightness, feeling the man's bones easily through the thin, worn fabric of his tunic and blanket. He swung the man into Bwindi's saddle; the man's legs were too short for the stirrups, but Frost knew he would have a Devil of a time shortening the leathers, so he curtly commanded: "Hold on to the saddle."

"My musket! I mustn't leave my musket, sir!"

Frost pulled the heavy musket from the snow, noting briefly that it was a Tower musket of the short land pattern of 1768. He wondered if perhaps it was one of the muskets he had taken from the magazine on Battery Island at the entrance to Louisbourg Harbor half a year ago, before thrusting it into the soldier's hand as the soldier slumped forward. Frost took Bwindi's reins and started eastward along the trace as rapidly as he could push through the ice crusted on top of the snow. The snow was little more than ankle deep in the trace, but Frost would break through the crust of ice every other step or so, and he found the going heavy. Ming Tsun passed him and rode slowly ahead, his horse breaking trail so Frost would have an easier time of it.

Caleb Mansfield, looking anxiously for Frost's report to Washington, rode up the trace from the east and held a map close in front of Frost's eyes as he walked. In a few terse words spoken hoarsely as he kept the pace, grateful for the dim light of sunrise filtering through the forest, Frost confirmed the position of the lead elements of Sullivan's corps. Caleb cantered away to take the report to Washington.

Frost looked up at the soldier: the man's hands firmly gripped the saddle, but his head was hunched and lowered against the breast of his tunic. Frost, feeling the chill piercing to his bones, broke into a faster gait, a half-shuffling gait, and lowered his head into the sleet that the wind from the north blew through the trees. As he had so many times in his life when he faced the stupefying, mind-numbing dullness of hard physical labor, Frost retreated into a mantra that he kept repeating in his mind. The mantras always came to him unbidden, they just formed, and he concentrated on their repetition in order to block from mind the physical pain and weariness his body was enduring.

The particular mantra his mind had suggested just now to ease his burden was a pleasing one, and with a sharp intake of labored breath, Frost recognized he had been repeating, over and over, a sprightly tune from Mozart's opera *The Pretended*

Simpleton. The words flowed easily through his mind, first in Italian as he had heard them sung by Rosina, then in English as he laboriously thought through their translation.

Nel mio cor ho già deciso, ma il mio cor nessun lo sa: In my heart I've already decided, but no one knows my heart. The Lady Cygnet . . . Neville . . . where was she now? The last words she had spoken in his presence came to mind, and the palms of his hands tingled afresh, remembering the pain of having beaten out the flames devouring her costume. Or perhaps the feeling came only from the bitterness of the constant cold that searched out and demanded the last scrap of warmth sheltering in his hands. Cygnet, Cygnet . . . Frost shook his head fiercely. To think further of the Lady Neville Maria de' Medici e Monteleone e Wyrley-Birch at this time was nothing more than a precursor to madness. Frost savagely shook his head several times and succeeded in chasing the mental images of Cygnet and the opera performance in the bull ring above the ancient town of Angra in the Açores out of mind.

Frost stumbled out of the trace onto a Pennington Road made slippery by the churn of so many hooves, iron-bound wheels and feet. He saw blood, quickly congealed, on spikes of iced mud that bore imprints of human feet as he turned south and crossed the culvert over the creek. Ming Tsun touched Frost's shoulder to gain Frost's attention, and when he had it, gestured, then signed: "The man's spirit has departed from his body, Tai-pan."

Frost stopped, and obediently Bwindi halted also. Frost looked up, eyes blinking involuntarily against the lash of sleet. Yes, the soldier was dead, probably had been for some minutes, though Frost could see the man's eyes were wide-open and fixed straight ahead, his lips slightly parted, revealing rotted teeth, and sleet catching and not melting on his crushed hat. There was just a wisp of fine hair on his upper lip, for the soldier was just a boy, far too young to have begun shaving. Now he never would.

Frost walked stiffly around to Bwindi's right side as he led her just off the road so the soldiers of the First Maryland Regiment of Continental Infantry, attached to Brigadier General Hugh Mercer's Brigade, could continue their trudge past without interruption. Ming Tsun was beside him, helping, and they gently removed the boy's surprisingly light body from the molly-mule. Frost had the body in his arms now—he could bear the weight easily. He cradled the boy long enough to close the boy's eyes, and reached up to stop two soldiers shuffling past, heads down, shoulders hunched against the beat of sleet. "This boy—this soldier, do you know his name, his regiment?"

The soldiers glanced briefly at the boy's face, shook their heads mutely and trudged on. Frost stopped the next knot of soldiers filing past and repeated the question. One soldier peered intently at the boy, then shrugged: "Looks a bit like Mattie Paxton's boy from Baltimore, but I collect Mattie's boy come down with the pox 'n' died two months past, or mayhap he got hisself killed at Brooklyn Heights. All the same he be filling a grave somewhere."

Another soldier peered eagerly at the boy's musket. "Don't reckon I got no way o' knowin' him, but he don't need thet musket no more, 'n' my musket's broke its frizzen spring." The soldier unwrapped the dirty rag swaddling his musket's lock and thrust out his musket for Frost's inspection.

Frost nodded to Ming Tsun, who exchanged the muskets without expression. The soldier coughed pointedly, "My old piece don't have no bayonet."

"Of course," Frost said, and Ming Tsun removed the bayonet on its frog from the boy's cartridge belt. "The bayonet likely will prove useful later in the morning."

There was a stir and bustle from the men ahead; men were moving to one side of the road, giving way to someone riding against the tide of soldiers marching southward. George Washington reined his great hunter to a stop three paces away as Frost knelt and laid the boy's corpse gently on the frozen, sleet-streaked snow at the base of a large birch tree. He wrapped the sodden blanket around the boy's legs to cover his bloody feet, then unfastened his heavy boat cloak and wrapped the body in the cloak.

"No one can give me a name for this boy!" Frost shouted up at Washington, his voice almost breaking, tears that had somehow started already freezing on his cheeks. "Tell me, General Washington, how do you recruit soldiers such as these?" His look around took in the files of Continental soldiers stumbling past in loose knots. "Men marching on frozen stumps, without food, enlistments ending in a week, but marching on until the dreich cold steals their lives."

Heedless of the hiss of sleet and wind, Washington lifted his tricorne and bowed his bare head in respect for a long moment, then fixed Frost with the saddest expression Frost had ever in his life seen on a human face. "As you and all you brought were recruited, Captain Frost," Washington said with infinite sadness. "And it is of these recruits that great things are expected."

"We must leave him now, Tai-pan," Ming Tsun signed.

"Yes," Frost signed in reply, "but we shall return to give him proper burial."

XXII

FROST FLOGGED HIMSELF UNMERCIFULLY, MING TSUN UNCOMPLAINING, ALWAYS FOLLOWING, TO MAINTAIN TIMELY COMMUNICATIONS BETWEEN the two wings of the continental army marching south toward Trenton along the Pennington and River Roads. Frost spared his molly-mule as much as possible, walking fiercely, no, half-running, through the forest between the two roads. No mantra surged through his brain now, and he was glad of the oblivion that blocked out all thoughts of the Lady Cygnet and the Continental soldier some miles back now who had frozen to death, and quite happily so, in the service of his nascent country. By the Great Golden Buddha, and the Holy Trinity, and the Countenance of the Prophet, but the physical exhaustion was welcome, even exhilarating, because there was no need for thought, or thinking—just doing. Just moving his legs as quickly as ever he could in order to move—and warm—his body.

Frost was brought up short, roughly, by Caleb Mansfield and Tobin Tuttle. In point of fact, Caleb, Tobin and Ming Tsun were actually restraining him. Frost pressed mightily against their restraints, because the simple, sheer physical test of muscle against muscle, strength against strength, exorcised the final remnants of illusive, jumbled, disturbing thoughts rooted in the past from his mind, and he was entirely freed to concentrate solely upon the present. He threw back his head and laughed, acknowledging his friends' concern.

"Trenton town be thar," Caleb whispered quietly, flinging a hand to southward, "half a mile past thet sign post. Few Britishers, just some light-horse, pity's sake, but more German hirelin's ye can shake a stick at." Caleb nodded to Tobin Tuttle. "Tobin's got th' odds, which is we already passed t' General Washington, so's we's got no more spyin' to do."

Frost was firmly rooted in the here and now; he realized that his party was on the Pennington Road, ahead of Major General Nathanael Greene's corps. Pennington Road and River Road were converging, so the first elements of Sullivan's corps had to be less than half a mile away to the right. He could smell the woodsmoke from the fires cooking breakfast in Trenton. "The odds, if you please, Tobin."

"Three German regiments, Capt'n Frost, little over a thousand 'n' a half men, commanded by von Lossberg, von Knyphausen. Knyphausen claims to be a general, though Rall, a colonel, seems to be 'n overall command. Rall's headquarters be in the house owned by Stacy Potts, though can't tell if he be Tory, or just unfortunate to have his house coveted by the Germans. Can't miss the Germans, Lossberg's, they be wearing the same scarlet as the British; Knyphausen's men be tricked out in black, 'n' Rall's men be wearing dark blue. There wus supposed to be another regiment in Trenton town, Colonel von Donop's troops. But some Jersey militia under the command of some colonel named Griffin drew his regiment off to the south." Tobin Tuttle made a wry face: "Allus be far better dressed then our'n. 'N' there be a draft of Brunswickers saved off that Indiaman you sunk spread through the three regiments."

Caleb Mansfield had been busy drawing the charge in Frost's Ferguson rifle. Actually, he had simply rotated the trigger guard of the rifle to expose the breech, and with the rifle turned upside down and at an acute angle he drove the ball and powder out with a ramrod. He swabbed the barrel vigorously for several moments, and before ramming home a fresh charge he snapped the cock several times to judge the amount of sparks the flint shaved off the steel battery of the frizzen.

Caleb grunted with satisfaction at the fine shower of sparks that sprayed into the pan. "Hold close enough, 'n' ye more likely 'n not kin pot yereself a German. With proper luck, it'll be one o' 'em Brunswickers thet went agin thar parole."

"And if General Ewing has been able to secure the crossing at Trenton's Ferry, he can block German reinforcements hastening from the south to augment the three regiments we face in Trenton," Frost said with an edge to his voice. "Perhaps I'll be lucky enough to find Major von Fendig in my sights." He had no real hope that Ewing, or Cadwallader for that matter, had been able to get across the Delaware. Nor did he have any time to dwell upon the acts or omissions of Ewing, Cadwallader or von Fendig.

"Waal, ye be set now to do fer 'im," Caleb agreed, reloading with a cartridge he had taken from Frost's pouch, then loosely wrapping a wide strip of tanned deerskin, impregnated with sperm whale oil, around the lock.

"Capt'n Frost, sir," Nathaniel Dance piped, tugging on Frost's stirrup to gain his attention. "My marines be employed in close defense of the artillery, but ain't we got a banner to hold aloft as we move southard?"

"Why, Ensign Dance," Frost said with some surprise, "I harken that somewhere in our baggage, given over to the care of Mister Langdon and Mister Hymsinger, we have our rattlesnake flag, somewhat tattered from its long service, 'tis true, and the flag of Grand Union sewn by the indomitable ladies of Portsmouth, yea, the fearsome ladies of Portsmouth. But cypher me this, Ensign Dance, think ye we can spare the men to hoist our banners?"

"I can hoist one banner, Capt'n Frost," Nathaniel Dance said excitedly, "my preference bein', as ye know, the rattlesnake flag, and an even dozen of ex-*Jaguars* will give the last eyetooth they possess to hoist the banner of Grand Union."

"Very well, Ensign Dance, make it so. Light along to find Mister Langdon. Please to locate our banners. But caution you, we have not the luxury of bearing aloft our banners at a time when every man shall be required to stand to the enemy's fire."

"We shall fold the banners in our bosom," Nathaniel said boldly. "Our banners shall protect us from the balls of the Germans."

"Would that it were so," Frost said soberly. He dismounted with difficulty, rummaged in his saddlebag for the sponge, and began rubbing Bwindi vigorously. Bwindi whinnied from the pleasure of the brush strokes and curved her neck rearward to nuzzle Frost.

Nathaniel Dance returned quickly with the two banners, which indicated that Darius and Ishmael were in the offing, and promptly affixed them to ramrods dedicated to the husbandry of the cannons. "Please proceed, Ensign Dance," Frost said quietly. "We have only a short distance to go before we shall be in the Germans' front yard." Frost swung wearily into Bwindi's saddle. How many hours had it been since he slept? Doubtless Glover's men had been at their stations longer, so he could not compare his situation with them. Indeed, Glover's men were moving mountains, though posterity in all probability would little note their sacrifices.

Frost patted Bwindi's neck, noting with satisfaction that Nathaniel Dance had been circulating among *Audacity*'s marines, checking that each man's flintlock had been reloaded and fresh priming powder lay in every pan before the locks were rewrapped in canvas or deerskin.

"What charges bear your cannons, Ensign Dance?" Frost inquired.

"Canister, both tubes, Capt'n Frost," Nathaniel answered quickly. Then: "Marines, at the quick-step, forward!" Nathaniel said in a clear voice without any trace of a quaver. "Matrosses, mind yere linstocks, be ready to bring yere cannons forward and unlimber on the moment." Nathaniel ran to the head of his marines and stepped out confidently. Geoffrey Frost felt a bittersweet pang as he acknowledged that the youth whose life he had spared on *Jaguar*'s main deck just eight months earlier was quickly and readily evolving into a commander. If he could but remain alive through all this tumult of war between cousins, Frost had no doubt that

Nathaniel Dance would tread his own quarterdeck before his age had doubled.

Audacity's marines, their rifles shouldered, were making brisk time, so brisk that Nathaniel fairly skipped in order to remain in front of them. Frost heard the ring of axe on wood as the marines negotiated a curve in the road, and there was Trenton town, half-hidden under a wreath of wood smoke, stagnant now that the night's wind had abated away to light airs. A stone boat and two oxen stood patiently in a field twenty yards to the left of the road, and a wood cutter, his axe arrested and suspended high above a billet of wood at the unexpected appearance of armed men, gawked at them in disbelief.

"Ho! Mister wood cutter!" Nathaniel Dance called out authoritatively, "Be there any Brunswickers about?"

The wood cutter let his axe fall to the ground and pointed mutely toward the nearest house, no more than fifty yards away. As the wood cutter pointed, two soldiers in blue coats, brass plates surmounted by red pompons on their caps, stepped out of the house onto the stoop. One man was scratching himself prodigiously, and the other was yawning mightily. Both activities terminated abruptly as the soldiers incredulously caught sight of the advancing marines.

"Heraus! Der Feind!" one soldier shouted, darting back inside the house, followed a moment later by his companion.

"Marines! At the double march—advance! Matrosses! Cannons forward! Deploy for firing!" Nathaniel drew and bravely waved his shortened cutlass. The house erupted soldiers, some dressed in blue tunics, a few with their black leggings buttoned over their boots, but the majority clad in breeches and shirts only, though to a man they all held muskets.

"Front rank—kneel! Present yere pieces! Cock yere pieces! Mass fire at the soldiers on the porch." The Ferguson rifles fired immediately as soon as Nathaniel's last order was given, but not in one simultaneous volley, as would have been the case had the ex-*Jaguars* been trained as British infantry. But at Caleb Mansfield's urging, and with assistance from all of his woods-cruisers, the *Audacity* marines had been trained as marksmen. The light sleet beat down the powder smoke, though the distinctive smell of sulfur tainted the air.

"Front rank—fall back and reload! Second rank—kneel! Present yere pieces! Cock yere pieces! Independent fire!"

Only four soldiers out of a dozen were still standing on or near the stoop, their faces ashen. Then those four men were down, sprawling democratically atop their fallen companions. "Matrosses! Cannons forward! Wheel! Unlimber!" A musket thrust out a window in the front of the house banged and Frost heard something buzz past his ear like an angry wasp, but he heard it only briefly.

"Matrosses! Lay yere tubes directly on the windows," Nathaniel shouted. "Fire as ye bear!"

Frost sat impassively, his Ferguson rifle balanced across the saddle, though Bwindi flinched mildly, arching her neck and prancing slightly, at the cannons' heavy snarl, while George Three sneezed, rattling the spikes on his leather collar, then stood stoically beside the molly-mule. Frost divided his attention between the shattered front of the house and Nathaniel Dance, noting with approval that Nathaniel had already assured himself every marine had reloaded his rifle. "Form column of fours, front ranks, double march! Matrosses! Reload and limber up!"

Tobin Tuttle had slipped off his horse and stood with his rifle resting across the saddle, sighting coolly along the rifle's barrel, hammer cocked. After a moment he uncocked his rifle and swung into the saddle in one fluid motion. From the north, soldiers of Greene's corps were running toward them, hoarsely screaming. "Reckon we kin let 'em comes after finish pokin' thet snake, Capt'n. Ain't nobody in thet house wantin' to cause us no trouble."

"Repeat your sentiments to Ensign Dance, Tobin," Frost said. "Ensign Dance commands our marines."

"Aye, thet he do, by gar," Tobin Tuttle said, his face creasing in a bemused smile.

But Nathaniel had already taken in the situation, and as

soon as the last harness attachment fell into place, he was urging the matrosses and their cannons forward as fast as ever they could.

Caleb Mansfield trotted ahead of Frost and leaned over to shout as he drew abreast of Nathaniel. "Place up ahead whar ye kin look straight down two streets, Mister Dance."

"A signal place for cannons," Nathaniel replied tersely. "We make for it directly."

Frost had kept his eyes in constant quest, acutely alert as he always was in the midst of battle, fearful, a cautious fear that restrained impetuosity, and aware that Washington's lose-all-or-take-all gambit had achieved a complete tactical surprise. He ignored the fact that his clothes were thoroughly soaked and partially frozen and whistled Bwindi forward, reveling in the flexing of the molly-mule's muscles beneath his legs, aware that many soldiers from Greene's corps were spilling off the road. A reinforced squad went hallooing away toward the partially demolished house that had quartered German mercenaries, the rest stumbling, pushing through the snowy fields to the east ever as fast as they could to flank the German forces in Trenton town.

From the corner of his right eye Frost saw the rotund, very excited Henry Knox, Colonel of Artillery, pelting toward the same destination Nathaniel Dance had fixed upon. Knox had somehow dropped his horse's reins and was holding desperately to the horse's mane with his left hand while valiantly waving on his matrosses and their cannons jolting over the frozen road with his right.

Knox saw Frost and shouted in a hoarse though not frightened voice: "Frost, I say, Frost, can you head this beast for me? I fear to overshoot my mark."

Frost nudged Bwindi into a run and easily caught up the dangling reins. The horse obligingly slowed to a walk. "As you remarked earlier, Colonel, 'twas but a slight distance to the ground," Frost observed dryly.

"True, true!" Knox spluttered. "'Twas not the falling off I minded, but the getting back on, or as you seagoing chaps would opine, back aboard, I dare say. And catching up this froward animal, who now exhibits a most obstinate, most unwelcome moodiness, would have taxed a saint." Knox gratefully took the reins Frost handed him. "We have come upon the enemy handily, Frost. Please to tell your man to position his cannons to command the length of that street to the left . . . I believe it is called Queen Street . . . while I shall have Captain Forrest set up his six cannons to deny movement on this thoroughfare to the right."

"Exactly so," Frost said, though he had no intention of repeating the order to Nathaniel, because Nathaniel was making unerringly for the head of the street and was even now preparing to wheel the muzzles of the two 12-pounders to point southward.

There were numerous targets of opportunity as scarlet-clad soldiers of the Lossberg regiment erupted from houses on either side of Queen Street. Most of the soldiers milled about in confusion, awaiting some competent non-commissioned officer to give them the comfort of orders, any orders. Nathaniel did not give the Germans time or opportunity to form ranks. He wheeled both 12-pounders wheel hub to wheel hub and began pouring an enthusiastic, wilting sheet of canister shot down both sides of Queen Street. The marines had thrown out a semicircular perimeter to defend the matrosses plying their deadly trade and were independently engaging targets. Yes, they were targets, Frost consoled himself, as he saw two Lossbergs stagger backwards, then collapse into the snow, both men clutching at the agony suddenly sprouting in their bellies as they fell. Targets. Not living men such as himself, not men with muscle and skin framed over solid bone, who lived, laughed, cried, ate, drank, and slept in the same wise he and all who were dear to him lived, laughed, cried, ate, drank, and slept. Though the German mercenaries who fell, kicking, onto the snow, were apt to begin an eternal sleep. Throughout the constant concussion of cannons, Frost knew himself to be, for the moment, an onlooker only, not a participant.

Caleb Mansfield maneuvered his large gray gelding close

enough to Frost's Bwindi to be heard above the concussion of artillery, Nathaniel's and Knox's, though with great difficulty, and shouted directly into the ear. "No need to keep 'n eye on the boy," Caleb shouted. "He's got his mates protectin' 'im much as they kin, though nothin' be certain 'n' this life. 'N' I've got Jack Dawes 'n' Homer Clark keepin' a close eye on Darius 'n' Hannibal. Ishmael's got his own minder 'n Row Gaffney, since he massaged 'n' manipulated out o' Row's jaw two gone-off teeth without pain, 'n' Beelzebub 'n' all his devils ain't got no chance 'n the universe o' gettin' near Ishmael so long as Row lives. General Greene tells me we's got th' road to Princeton plugged, but he's almighty affrighted the Brunswickers will break out south'ard, so he's askin' us to cut 'em off at th' bridge spannin' some creek."

Frost turned toward Ming Tsun, who registered his vigorous assent. "I hold these youths dear beyond reckoning, Caleb, Hymsinger and his healing arts equally. But we have dallied here. It's time we had work of substance. Who joins us to the south?"

Caleb Mansfield flashed his lupine grin. "Yere friend Glover, if'n ye had any doubt. Thet little banty be 'n th' thick o' it, wherever th' thick be. Glover's headin' Sullivan's corps over th' river side."

"You have exhausted breath, Caleb," Frost said, "better used in getting us along to the juncture with John Glover's soldiers, who grow webs between their toes."

Frost, Ming Tsun, Caleb and a half dozen of his woodscruisers turned eastward and rode through the pell-mell clusters of Continental soldiers surging southward. They reached the edge of the open fields, fallow and snow-covered, then turned south themselves, the treeline marking a creek's bank some four or five hundred yards further south, just visible through the light fog and flurry of snow. To their right, Germans wearing the black tunics of Knyphausen's regiment were withdrawing southward along Queen Street in a fighting retreat. Two hundred yards further along, and Frost could make out the low stone bridge spanning the creek. The bridge swarmed with black-garbed Germans, and Frost saw two cannons being trundled over the bridge, and their muzzles swung northward.

Then a contingent of Continental troops burst over a rail fence some hundred yards to the west of the bridge, halted, and poured a ragged volley into the Germans massed on and around the bridge. Then, halloing madly, the Continental troops, led by two officers flourishing swords above their heads, charged with bayonets fixed. The Germans resisted for some moments, then fell back across the bridge as more Continental soldiers burst over the rail fence. Frost was now close enough to recognize the uniforms of Glover's Regiment. Willing hands among the Continental troops wheeled the two cannons and enthusiastically fired them at the retreating Germans, dealing out more death and confusion to the German mercenaries. Frost and his band reached the bridge a minute before the first men of Glover's Regiment rushed up. Behind them were knots of Germans in the blue tunics of Rall's Regiment and the bright Lossberg scarlet.

Frost called out to the two American officers, one with a wound to his arm that was bleeding copiously. "You may wish to staunch your men's eagerness to pursue the Germans they have so thoroughly affrighted. There are more flushed from cover and covetous of crossing this creek."

"Exactly so!" the younger of the two officers, the one with the bloody wound, said after glancing over his shoulder. "I trust Colonel Glover's men will soon reinforce us enough to hold this bridge."

Frost led his men across the bridge and toward a slight rise to the east, where he could command a view of the southern part of Trenton and the roads converging on the bridge. He tried to fumble out his small telescope, but his fingers were too clumsy to undo the button of the pocket. The two cannons had been pushed aside since the retreating Germans had borne away the ammunition and the two American officers were forming their soldiers into a line on the west side of the bridge. Glover's men, as they ran up, formed on the east side.

Caleb jumped off his horse, wrapped the reins hurriedly around a birch sapling, and ran, Gideon cradled in his arms, followed by his woods-cruisers, toward the bridge. "Got t' give 'em fellas a hand," he muttered as he ran past Frost, "like as not, most o' 'em's muskets won't give fire."

Caleb's assumption was correct; no more than half a dozen muskets were able to rise above their frequent wettings during the crossing and march and discharge when flints struck frizzens. But all of the long rifles of Caleb's woods-cruisers cracked, and nine or ten Germans went down, but the welter of Germans focused upon escape across the creek threw themselves fiercely against the bridge's defenders in a savage exchange of bayonet thrusts. Frost had dismounted, whipped off the oiled strip of deerskin and, toiling on legs that were stumps of ice, was making his way toward the fray. When he was ten yards from the bridge a trio of soldiers dressed in the menacing black of the Knyphausen Regiment, broke through the thin line of Continental troops, and one German who knew how to ply his bayonet was hotly pressing the young officer with the wounded arm. His wounded arm hampered the officer's defense, and his sword was relentlessly beat down.

The Knyphausener was less than a second away from thrusting his bayonet into the officer's belly when Frost shot him. Frost had just time to draw his brass-backed cutlass from its carriage before the other two Knyphauseners, muskets tipped with wicked bayonets, were upon him. He feinted to his right, causing one German soldier to hesitate with his bayonet's thrust. Frost ducked under bayonet, marveling at his ability to move so quickly given that the cold and damp had totally drawn all feeling from his body. He could not feel the grip of his cutlass or gauge how tightly he clasped it. But he clasped the cutlass tightly enough to hack the blade across the soldier's knuckles, severing fingers, and as the musket dropped, stepped inside the soldier's guard and speared the cutlass point into the man's throat. The third Knyphausener threw aside his musket and ran as fast as he could, vigorously pursued by George Three, southward on the Borden-town road. Frost watched the man a hundred yards before calling George Three to return.

Then the Germans were being hotly engaged in their rear, and they began dropping their muskets, raising their arms in surrender. The defeated Germans were brusquely pushed aside and John Glover, with hand extended, led a battery of artillery across the bridge. "Captain Frost! Salutations! Faith, you have done a capital job of holding this, the only causeway across Assunpink Creek." Glover wrung Frost's hand. "Good God, man! You should have retained your woolen gloves so generously given, your hand is colder than the heart of England's King." He smiled at the two Continental officers. "I see that you have already made the acquaintance of Captain William Washington and Lieutenant James Monroe of our advance party. Is that a wound you bear, Lieutenant Monroe? You should have it dressed presently. Captain Frost has a capital surgeon's mate attending our forces."

"If you are seeking a place to employ your cannons," Frost interrupted, "there is a slight eminence to the right and behind that commands an excellent view of the approaches to this bridge."

"Capital! Capital!" Glover fairly purred. "General Greene's troops have pressed the Rall and Lossberg Regiments into the orchards east of Trenton, and General St. Clair's brigade is chivying the Knyphausen Regiment just a ways the other side of this creek. Captain Sargent, your cannons into position on the hill Captain Frost describes as quickly as you can unlimber! We have hot work ahead of us." The force of black and white mariners recruited from Marblehead and other ports, hardened and disciplined by the sea trade, swept by Frost, revealing Caleb Mansfield and Ming Tsun.

"Waal, I collect Colonel Glover 'n' his matrosses got things in hand this side o' Trenton town, 'nough fer us t' find a place t' warm," Caleb said, sliding Gideon's ramrod into its thimbles. He reached down to retrieve the Ferguson Rifle Frost had let fall when he drew his cutlass. Caleb's eyes fell on a German soldier marching dejectedly past, thrust the rifles into

Ming Tsun's hands, and with an oath fell upon the man, hammering the man to the icy ground with his fists. Caleb knelt on the man's belly, seized the collar of the man's tunic and swore at him in staccato German, shaking him violently all the while in a white-hot fury.

"Caleb!" a taken-aback Frost ordered sharply. "The man has surrendered. He has given no offense. We do not treat prisoners so! Bear off!"

The terrified prisoner had made no effort to resist Caleb's blows, receiving them passively, one of which bloodied his lips. Then he spoke a few words in a low voice. Caleb abruptly released the prisoner's lapels, rose and pulled the German to his feet. He pointed to the ragged group of surrendered soldiers, all gawking, spat several sharp, bitter words, and the prisoner shuffled away, though with head turned back over his shoulder to see if Caleb pursued.

Caleb faced a frowning Geoffrey Frost. "I recognized 'im as one o' 'em Brunswickers 'n th' boats off th' sunk transport."

Frost understood Caleb's anger immediately, and his own flared. "When we succored Riedesel's Brunswickers from the *Tuscany Countess* transport, Major Heroes von Fendig gave his parole that the Brunswickers would not take up arms against the United States for the remainder of this year. He gave that parole personally—to me."

"Seems he kept his word t' ye, Capt'n Frost," Caleb answered softly. "Th' ship given fer transport . . ."

"The *Sagittarius*," Frost interrupted.

"Her name all right, waal, seems she fell in with another convoy o' Britishers 'n' was took to New York, August it was. Major von Fendig told his superiors he weren't to fight none this year. Said he had given parole 'n honor would not bear it." Caleb spat with distaste toward the cluster of German prisoners. "So his superiors ordered 'im hung as if he wus a dog with the hydrophobe. He begged th' dignity t' be shot instead, but he wus hung up. He kept his parole t' ye right enough."

XXIII

GEORGE WASHINGTON'S AIDE-DE-CAMP, ALEXANDER HAMILTON, WAS UNCHARACTERISTICALLY DESPONDENT. HIS THIN SHOULDERS WERE HUNCHED BENEATH A square of rumbowline canvas that served to keep the wind from clawing away the pieces of foolscap atop his portable secretary as he morosely regarded the lines of disarmed and dispirited Hessians taken prisoner before ten of the clock filing down to the Durham boats that John Glover's boneweary men were holding against the eastern bank of McKonkey's Ferry landing. "The six hundred Hessians of Donop's Regiment are got completely away." He made another notation on a piece of foolscap with a pencil, then beat his ungloved hands vigorously and exhaled his breath to warm them.

"Young sir, you are too far possessed of a sanguinary countenance," Geoffrey Frost, sitting on the driftwood log beside Hamilton, with an extremely tired and footsore George Three sprawled across his boots, replied, bending across to pluck the foolscap from the bottom of the papers. "Verily as you say, a number of the Germans escaped—though I warrant the ones who slipped past us on the Assunpink did not pause for breath until they were well past Borden-town. What should be noted, as you have correctly extracted, is that of over eighteen hundred mercenaries hired by George Three from the innumerable various corrupt princelings of the Germans collected around the Trenton garrison, almost nine hundred men—

unwounded and fit to bear arms—have surrendered to you. You have also received all their priceless muskets, in addition to some cannons and ammunition wagons. One hundred Hessians—or Brunswickers—or whatever—Germans were killed or wounded. Against this incredible turn of fortune you must balance four men wounded—the wound sustained by Lieutenant Monroe the most grievous, but that wound so light that Ishmael Hymsinger fairly laughed with joy as he bound it up.

"And," Frost paused, drawing his boat cloak around him more closely, "two unfortunates whose bodies had been so weakened they succumbed to the cold." The unidentified private who had been temporarily shrouded in Frost's cloak—no hand had filched the cloak, though perhaps some might have been tempted—and the body of another unidentified soldier found frozen under a light dusting of snow beside the River Road as the weary though triumphant Continental Army returned from Trenton, had been wrapped in canvas and sent over to the western shore in an earlier boat. "I believe you may in good conscience reflect more upon the victory signally won by Americans . . ." Frost looked toward the aid-station, a Durham boat drawn out of the water and turned on its side as a windbreak, where Ishmael Hymsinger and Darius Langdon were ministering to wounded Hessians, "Americans of polychromatic hues, than recriminate the victory could be more complete. Your log must reflect that John Glover's Marbleheaders got over some twenty-five hundred men, eighteen cannons, and some two hundred horses without the loss of nary a one. And they return alive all but two, and a smashing great lot of German prisoners." Insh'allah, he whispered to himself, but truly the Great Buddha had turned not his face away from American forces this day.

Hannibal Bowditch was at the water's edge, carefully marshalling the cargoes going into each Durham boat. Hannibal had become an excellent load master. The four Durham boats of which he had supervised the lading this past hour had their cargoes evenly and expertly divided. Remarkably so, taking into account the fact that any two boats, given differences in their lengths, beams, depths and quality of materials, would rarely weigh within five hundred pounds of each other, yet all four had the same freeboard. What was more, all the men he directed listened to him attentively, respectfully.

Directly Hannibal possessed all the qualities that would develop him into an outstanding sailing master and trader, Frost mused. He was already an accomplished navigator and a scholar of no poor means; it was evident he had a predilection for the sea, but could he in the fullness of time command the allegiance of men? Direct them in extremities? Would men follow him willingly? That was the enigma to be ciphered.

Nathaniel Dance, now he had developed into a leader of men, doubting not that men would follow his lead, and confidently advancing to the front. But would his abilities be better channeled toward the sea or the land? Could Frost but blend the two youths into one possessing the superior traits of each, the result would be a mariner such as had seldom visited the world. But each youth was his own man and would develop in his own fashion, according to the plan the Great Buddha envisioned. Insh'allah.

And Darius Langdon? His future was clear. Though with characteristic modesty he disavowed it, Darius bore the mark of the healer conspicuously, though he could not be unaware of it. He was as compassionate as Ishmael Hymsinger, had quickly learned Ishmael's gentle touch, and had sought out Ming Tsun on every possible occasion, quickly learning the rudiments of the sign language so that he could partake of the healer's knowledge Ming Tsun so willingly shared. Darius was fated to be a physician, though he did not yet realize it. It remained for Frost to provide the opportunity, and he would, of course. Frost looked at Darius and his heart ached, for his fey instinct told him Darius would be launched firmly on his own path before this year next concluded. Frost would miss the lad sorely.

Nathaniel's study under Frost was somewhat more obscure to Frost's vision, but Frost's mentoring would end before two years had run their courses. He would enjoy Hannibal's company for some time longer, but at some point their paths would diverge; it was foreordained. Joss. But of course he had to keep the three youths alive in order for each of them to fulfill their destinies.

Hamilton awkwardly thrust the papers into the secretary and got to his feet, stamping them briskly for warmth. "I forget myself," he said with humility. "The sacrifice of your cloak for the temporary shroud of a man who died as he marched toward the cannons was noted and cheered all who saw it." Hamilton cleared his throat: "We sought a victory, but what has obtained today is a miracle, truly. Though I must appeal directly to Saint Mark for another miracle to provision the Hessians. Alas, the stores you brought all that arduous way from Portsmouth have been consumed by our army, and I have not even good Saint Mark's five loaves and two fishes to offer the prisoners now in our care. Hello, there is your man, Mansfield. It is time we found passage for ourselves."

Frost turned, saw Caleb Mansfield and several of his *coureuse des bois*, and frowned. Caleb and five of his woodscruisers were heaving a light spring-wagon aboard a Durham boat. Cook Barnes hovered around the spring-wagon like a mother hen anxiously searching for a chick. "Belonged t' th' Brunswicker colonel named Rall," Caleb said by way of explanation. "Carried his personal vittles, 'n' my boys claim it 'cause we gave him proper burial this noon, 'n th' churchyard. Colonel Rall, don't be needin' this wagon, 'n' we do."

"Looks as if Rall's personal vittles are still loaded aboard the wagon," Frost observed mildly, surveying the bales, trunks, firkins, kids, covered tubs, sacks and jars in the wagon, all being eyed hungrily by Cook Barnes. "But I cannot conceive that the commander of a German regiment would convey a plough, much less various saws, hammers, broad axes, and barrels of nails, even a forge, such as reside atop the vittles."

"Me 'n' th' boys got a use fer all this," Caleb said, not at all defensively, but in a matter-of-fact voice. "Th' implements fer farmin' wus took from a Tory's barn a-fore it got burned by th' Trenton patriots who collected thar senses 'n time t' bring thar muskets t' our aid." Caleb rubbed at a grubby charcoal stain on his forehead. "Fact o' th' matter, we wus lucky t' winkle out what we did, 'cause th' rightly indignant done started th' fire a-fore us'ns got thar. What us'ns couldn't fetch out be ashes long betimes."

"Captain Frost, sir," Hannibal Bowditch said formally as he approached, "there be sufficient capacity for you and your molly-mule in the Durham boat that is lading directly, and the crew would take it kindly if you favor it with your presence, and for sure they would be greatly honored by the presence of Mister Ming Tsun."

"Thank you, Mister Bowditch," Frost replied in equally formal terms. "I am certain your invitation extends to such of our woods-cruizers can accommodate themselves in crannies about the barky." He glanced at the sheaf of papers Hannibal clutched in his ungloved hand and looked out dubiously over the angry, wind-whipped floodwaters of the Delaware, hurrying along their floes of ice at a reckless speed. "Does your tally indicate when Colonel Knox embarked for the Pennsylvania shore?"

"Oh yes, sir," Hannibal piped, "he and General Washington was across two hours ago. Generals Sullivan and Greene have been told off to bring across our people and the prisoners. General Washington, he has a power of thinking to do about his next move on the chess board."

"Please to convey this note to my General," Hamilton said, hastily folding several pieces of foolscap and thrusting them out to Frost.

"I can make a place for you in Captain Frost's boat, sir," Hannibal cried, "easily enough done."

"No, I am bid remain here and cross last in order to provide as complete a report as possible, and see to our prisoners," Hamilton said with a smile. "The conditions are damnable, but the private soldiers bear up admirably; so must I. Your shaman and his devoted surgeon's assistant, perforce with their necessary trade, will be my company in the last boat returning to the Pennsylvania shore this night." Hamilton was almost bowled over as George Three rushed past him and bounded onto the Durham boat with the spring-wagon aboard, just preparing to shove off. The great Newfoundland dog jumped again, onto the spring-wagon, displacing Cook Barnes; he barked happily for a moment, then settled contentedly into the foot well.

And Frost also had a power of thinking to do as the Durham boat, propelled lethargically, though with an occasional outburst of cheering, by Glover's exhausted men, ferried him to the western shore. Glover's men had to be dead on their feet, having been engaged in prodigious physical activity nonstop for well over thirty hours, with no chance to rest, much less sleep.

Frost was in need of rest himself, and he managed a few minutes of fitful sleep, his arms thrown across Bwindi's wet saddle, as he slumped against the mule's animal warmth, held to her by the press of exhausted men and equipment in the Durham boat. He awakened guiltily as the bow of the boat grounded in the mud of the Pennsylvania shore, and his first thought was of Joseph.

A seemingly indefatigable and perpetually cheerful Caleb Mansfield provided a step for Frost to swing himself wearily into Bwindi's saddle. Then he went off to supervise the hitching of a matched pair of lively looking blue-colored mules to the light spring-wagon. Ming Tsun, carrying the Ferguson rifle and his halberd across his saddle, was a comforting presence on Frost's right. Very little feeling had returned to Frost's hands, so he wrapped the reins around his forearms and chirruped Bwindi into a trot along the frozen road on the eight-mile slog separating McKonkey's Ferry from the farmhouse where George Washington had his temporary headquarters. He rode past the Continental officer attired in a beaverskin cloak who had earlier imparted his notions of the status of black men under arms, noting with satisfaction that the officer's face was smeared with blood and the grime of gunpowder. Frost saluted and took a fierce pleasure in the fact that the officer could not raise his own right arm because it was bound tightly his chest beneath the beaverskin cloak, whether from wound or frostbite Frost could not tell. "You sir," Frost shouted as he passed the somewhat crestfallen officer, "know you not that pain is but the body's way of assuring you that you live?"

Frost searched futilely for his watch, then remembered that he had loaned the timepiece to Washington. All right, he would reclaim it from Washington in the next hour plus one. A glance at the overcast sky confirmed that no sun would peer through for the remainder of the day. But at least the wind, snow, rain and sleet had abated, and the time had to be nigh on to two of the afternoon's clock. And how far from Washington's headquarters to Philadelphia, and the lazarette where a fevered Joseph lay? Or had Joseph's body already been consigned to a hastily dug, unmarked, common grave? He would soon know. He could ride through the night on the surefooted, uncomplaining molly-mule. Joseph, Mary and the Holy Infant, but grant he would find his brother alive. Frost knotted the reins awkwardly, dropped them across the saddle, and thrust his frozen hands under his armpits. He was glad indeed to have his boat cloak reclaimed, but the thought of the Continental soldier who had walked to his death, and willingly, jousted with thoughts of Joseph for his numbed memory.

Frost was vaguely aware of the clop of hooves behind him—the spring-wagon led by Caleb Mansfield, Cook Barnes perched on the seat—but he concentrated on returning feeling to his hands. The loss of feeling in his hands and feet caused him some concern, for he had been sorely bitten by the cold when brutal winds had thrown the East Indiaman on which he had been the master's mate far southward of the forties, into the latitudes of perpetual ice. His fingers and toes burned with excruciating pain as he flexed them. How had he ever managed to fire the Ferguson rifle, or employ his cutlass to advantage? Frost thought of the bliss that surely awaited if he would but throw himself off the molly-mule and curl up in a snow bank along the frozen road for a brief nap. But that insanity would mean death, he knew, so he resorted to the mantra he had repeated in his mind earlier, the snatch of song from the Mozart opera. He refused to think of the Lady Cygnet again and concentrated on the fragment of song, all the while flexing both fingers and toes as fiercely as he could, and gradually there came a warmth. The warmth was a cruel one, so cruel that he had to bite his lip to keep from crying aloud as the blood began to circulate once again in his frozen hands and feet.

Frost and Ming Tsun reached the farmhouse that was Washington's temporary quarters just at twilight, the poor twilight that the gloomy and overcast day afforded, though such a momentous day. Bwindi appeared fresh, not at all jaded, though Frost now acknowledged that he could not think of riding her all the way to Philadelphia without a rest and food. Caleb brought the lively mules pulling the spring-wagon to a stop in the frozen mud before the farmhouse and gave the reins and some brief instructions grunted to Tobin Tuttle. "See t' the wagon's unloadin' 'n' the mules' water."

Caleb joined Frost on the stoop of the farmhouse. "Guess I kin make my good byes t' th' General with ye, then other good byes as needs be said, a-fore we take th' road t' Gomorrah."

"I had not intended for you to accompany me to Philadelphia," Frost said, "but to get our people fairly begun on the return to Portsmouth. You know the route up to the Delaware Forks, and Ming Tsun and I shall catch up to you—with Joseph—well before then."

"Lot among us kin see t' thet," Caleb retorted. "'N' I put forward Nathaniel 'n' Hannibal as th' able o' th' ablest t' see our people carted early 'n' lightin' a shuck fer th' Forks. With Nathaniel 'n' Hannibal leadin' we'd be pressed hard t' o'ertake our people afore they hit the Forks."

"Captain Frost," George Washington exclaimed amidst the rectangle of light that spilled around him as the farmhouse door opened and he stepped out onto the porch. The two sentries on either side of the door came to attention with an enthusiasm no doubt occasioned by their vicarious association with the day's victory, since they had remained behind as a small headquarters guard. If they saw anything unusual in the fact that Washington was not wearing his tunic and his waistcoat was partially unbuttoned, they of course did not remark upon it. "I had left word to be summoned directly you appeared, but I had the pleasure of hearing your voice, so typical of a mariner, and came at once. May I invite you inside, sir, for some refreshment?"

"Most kind of you, General," Frost said, advancing up the stoop and withdrawing the fold of papers entrusted to him by Alexander Hamilton. "I regretfully must decline, since I must be on the road to Philadelphia as soon as I can locate Colonel Knox and ascertain the location of the lazarette where my brother is invalided."

"Why, Frost, surely," Henry Knox boomed as he joined Washington on the porch, "I have a man picked to guide you at morrow's first light. You cannot contemplate such a journey now, you and your animals are completely fagged."

Caleb coughed as delicately as he could. "Waal now, Colonel, we's got this spring-wagon, 'n' some fresh mules to fetch Joseph, 'n' granted th' loan o' such fresh mounts as ye kin spare, 'n' th' address o' th' hospital where Joseph be keepin', we reckon t' fetch th' hospital right enough."

Frost was overwhelmed. So that was why Caleb had appropriated the spring-wagon! To convey Joseph! Otherwise they would be forced to the slow pace of a boat-wagon and oxen!

"Well, if you be determined," Knox said hesitantly. He named the location of the church that had been turned into a field hospital for the innumerable casualties of typhus among the Continental Army. "But I have no horse other than the one that carried me so nobly today, and I believe it, like all the army's mounts, has been sorely used these past hours, ridden hard, though not put away wet."

"No matter," Frost said quickly. "We can roust horses from amongst our people. That will give me time enough to inquire of the woman, Salome, and her babe."

"The babe!" Washington exclaimed, "I've taken, to my great mortification, no thought at all of the poor lady in her confinement a few paces away. With permission I shall join you. It shall refresh me wondrously to gaze upon the innocence of a child after all the day's carnage and woe." He stepped inside the farmhouse and reappeared a moment later with a blanket draped hastily over his shoulders. The blanket gave him all the more the appearance of a Roman noble in Frost's eyes.

The party, led by Henry Knox, who had hastily caught up a lantern, with George Three slightly in front, rounded the corner of the farmhouse and went on to the former sheep cote, pausing before the door; then Knox knocked, somewhat timidly and self-consciously, on the wooden panel. "Madame," Knox addressed the door, "we deplore the lateness of the hour, but Captain Frost is on the wing for Philadelphia to recover his brother, and he begs the privilege to bid you and your child *adieu*."

The sounds of movement within the sheep cote followed, and a moment later the door was opened by Simon, his pocked face gentle and warm in the light of the phoebe-lamp he held. "In the Lord's name we bid thee all most welcome," Simon said quietly. "Salome requires a small moment to arrange her costume."

George Three, thankfully removed of his spiked collar, crowded past Simon and Henry Knox and was first into the small room. Salome half-reclined on a mattress formed from a pitch of dry, sweet-smelling hay cast over with a rough blanket, another blanket covered her from feet to mid-waist, and a coverlet was snuggled around her shoulders. "Why, dear George!" Salome exclaimed with delight as the great Newfoundland dog, nostrils quivering and his great saber of a tail wagging happily, drew near the swaddle held in the crook of her right arm, as with her left hand she smoothed the coverlet over her breast. Then she reached out to caress George's head and brought him near the rude bed. "Thee shall be first to see our babe!" Salome turned back a fold of the swaddle; a small red face appeared amidst the swaddle and George immediately licked the baby's face. The baby's tiny hands appeared out of the swaddle and interposed tiny fists in a futile effort to defend against the dog's tongue. The small, delicate lips parted, revealing tiny pink gums, and the baby gurgled in delight.

"No, no, dear George," Salome laughed, "the wee bairn hath already been washed well." The men crowded awkwardly into the sheep cote; so confined was the room that they stood shoulders touching. Salome smiled up at the men. "Simon and I hath chosen Ruth as her name."

"Ruth," Frost said softly as he bent to look at the child, "great-grandmother of David. Compassionate friend. Daughter-in-law of Naomi. An appropriate name."

Washington knelt on one knee to bring himself down to a level with Salome as Simon brought the phoebe-lamp closer. He reached out his hands: "Good lady, would you suffer me to hold your child for a moment?"

"Willingly, sir," Salome said, "other than Simon and the women who attended me, thee are the first to hold this Ruth."

George Washington held the bundle of swaddling cloth and baby carefully, tenderly, then handed her over to Frost, who took her awkwardly, terrified that he might drop the child. He was ill-suited to hold a babe—indeed, had held his nephew and niece only for the briefest of moments. Frost thought he saw a tear glisten in the corner of the eye of the Commander-in-Chief of the Continental Army. Rising, Washington had to keep his head bowed when he stood upright, so close was the roof of wood shingles. His hands moved to the base of his throat, and a moment later he extended a locket on a gold chain. "Madame, I pray you, accept this locket for your daughter. It contains a portrait of my wife. I offer it with the hope and firm belief that the victory our forces have just won shall bring a peace and virtue far more abiding than any spoils of war."

Salome blushed. "Thee doth me too much honor, sir, though I thank thee, and accept it gladly for this Ruth scarce a day old. Though I beg thee for a lock of thy hair to enclose within the locket against the day this Ruth shall understand the manner of her birthing."

Washington swung his head uncertainly, but Caleb was at his side, fearsome knife already unsheathed, blade gleaming dully in the dim light. "Stand ye easy, Gener'l. I reckon ye don't want any hide attached t' this hair goes into thet gimcrack. Yore's ain't th' first scalp this blade's lifted." The knife moved swiftly, and Caleb's callused and powder-grimed palm extended a small tuft of iron-gray hair to Salome. Then Caleb addressed Simon. "A spring-wagon 'n' two mules outside be yourn t' see ye on yere way t' th' Ohio Country whenever it be convenient like. Some ploughs 'n' saws 'n' things might come in useful be in t' wagon, though the Capt'n 'n' I got th' use o' th' wagon t' fetch the Capt'n's brother from Philadelphia."

Cook Barnes squeezed between Washington and Frost and placed a large brown-glazed crock on the earthen floor beside Salome. "This be honey fer th' child. Nothin' like honey to keep th' fret out of a youn'un 'n' lay the colic, specially when teeth be cuttin'."

Frost held the wonder of the girl baby a second or two longer, then gently knelt to lay the swaddle once again in Salome's arms. He was more than a little taken aback at the emotion he experienced in holding the new life. The Great Buddha grant serenity to the souls of the men dead by his hand—in Trenton town and elsewhere. "We are vastly heartened to discover you and your child in such bloom after the hardships you and Simon have endured. We pray the three of you resume your journey only after you have collected your strength." Frost clumsily regained his feet, keeping his head bowed, like Washington, to avoid the roof. The posture made Frost feel very much like he was on the cable deck of *Audacity*.

He took a pace toward the door of the sheep cote, then paused as he came abreast Simon, extending his hand in farewell. "Sir, your pardon I beg, but I am discomfited that during our travels together I have known you and the Lady Salome only by your Christian names. As we part, with scant likelihood we shall ever meet again, may I have the pleasure of knowing your surname?"

Simon took Frost's hand in both of his. "The name of those thee and thy companions succored be Flamonde," Simon said, pressing Frost's hand tightly. Frost returned the pressure, turned for a final look at the mother and her child, and was through the door.

Washington detained him briefly, handing over Jonathan's Bréquet. "Warmest thanks for the lending of your timepiece, Captain Frost. I wish you joy in finding your brother." Frost thrust the precious watch securely into a pocket of his waistcoat and spoke his own thanks hurriedly over his shoulder. He walked as rapidly as he could toward the spring-wagon, now laden only with hay, the same sweet-smelling hay upon which the woman and child lay inside the sheep cote, and blankets; Caleb Mansfield was already in the seat. The indefatigable Ming Tsun held the reins of two fresh horses, and Geoffrey Frost, struggling to conceal his weariness, thrust a boot into the left stirrup, heaved himself into the saddle, and sought out the road trending roughly southwest that would take him to Philadelphia.

HISTORICAL NOTE

In sorting through the tumultuous events attendant to the midwifery of our Revolution that extended from Concord to Yorktown, it is easy to give short shrift to George Washington's daring, desperate attack on the Hessian mercenaries hired by the British Crown and comfortably garrisoned in Trenton, New Jersey, the day following Christmas Day 1776. This brief, sharp engagement, and the rout of British troops at Princeton two days later, followed by the second Battle of Trenton, are underappreciated. But these "ten crucial days" were, by any measure, a pivotal event in the long struggle for American Independence.

These days also defined George Washington. The Continental Army that Washington directly commanded had melted away to slightly more than three thousand regular soldiers—roughly the number of Continental Army soldiers taken prisoner when Fort Washington on the Hudson fell to the British General Burgoyne and Hessian Colonel Rall. The materiél lost during the retreat from Long Island, or falling into enemy hands, was irreplaceable. The members of the New Jersey Militia, preoccupied with protecting their homes and properties from the avaricious British and Hessian forces, mustered barely a thousand men to Washington's aid. The enlistments of the majority of his few thousand regular troops would expire on the last day of 1776—six days following Washington's audacious attack. The officers and men of the Continental Army—any one of whom could have been the last person to die for the nascent Cause of American Liberty—were considerably braver than the Continental Congress, who, fearing capture if the British marched on the largest city in North America, hastily decamped from Philadelphia for Baltimore—but not before investing Washington with dictatorial powers.

Perhaps no man other than George Washington could have resisted the blandishments of absolute power. But he did, and shrewdly combining his intuition with intelligence gleaned from his operatives in New Jersey, he infused his ill-equipped, exhausted army with the will to challenge the impossible, a nighttime crossing of the Delaware in appalling weather to attack Trenton. Among the officers who believed in the American cause and willingly and uncomplainingly followed George Washington on the treacherous crossing were Aaron Burr, John Glover, Nathanael Greene, Alexander Hamilton, Henry Knox, James Madison, John Marshall, James Monroe, and John Sullivan—all destined to play significant rôles in subsequent American history. To use a phrase made popular during the rescue of the Apollo Thirteen astronauts, "failure was not an option."

Washington must have been impressed by the simplicity and directness of Frost's tactic of crossing the Connecticut River at night to fall upon the unsuspecting, unprepared rabble of Tories. He must also have been impressed by Frost's willingness to take the fight to the enemy, as evidenced by Frost's attack on the colliery fleet at Tynemouth. The information that Caleb Mansfield's woods-cruisers gleaned from the farmers and small-holders around Trenton confirmed the intelligence provided to Washington by an apparently itinerant cattle dealer, John Honeyman, who had access to the German encampment at Trenton and convinced Washington that his daring attack could be brought off. A little known facet of this remarkable man was George Washington's skill as a consummate spymaster. Honeyman's identity was revealed some time ago, but other agents "who are of particular use to us," in Washington's words, and for whom Washington sought hard money to pay for their intelligence, remain unknown to this day.

There is not a scintilla of evidence that Frost was ever reimbursed by a grateful nation for his generosity. The vast majority of Revolutionary Era veterans who petitioned for reimbursement of personal expenses incurred met the same fate as detailed in Perkelach Webster's sad little pamphlet, *Plea from a Poor Soldier; or an Essay to Demonstrate that the Soldiers and other Public Creditors Who Really and Actually Supported the Burden of the Late War Have Not Been Paid! Ought to Be Paid! Can Be and Must Be Paid!* But then, Geoffrey Frost had taken those fine words that conclude the Declaration of Independence very much to heart . . .